STONE GODS, WOODEN ELEPHANTS

T0159495

STONE GODS,
WOODEN ELEPHANTS

Bob Bergin

IMPACT PUBLICATIONS
Manassas Park, VA

Copyright © 2002 by Bob Bergin. All rights reserved. Printed in the United States of America. No part of this book may be used or reproduced in any manner whatsoever without written permission of the publisher: IMPACT PUBLICATIONS, 9104 Manassas Drive, Suite N, Manassas Park, VA 20111, USA, Tel. 703-361-7300 or Fax 703-335-9486.

Liability: *Stone Gods, Wooden Elephants* is a work of fiction. None of the characters or incidents mentioned in the book are real or based on real persons or events. Any resemblance is purely coincidental. The author and publisher shall not be liable for any presumptions to the contrary.

Library of Congress Cataloguing-in-Publication Data

Bob Bergin
    Stone gods, wooden elephants / Bob Bergin.
      p. cm.
    ISBN 1-57023-177-X
    1. Khmers – Antiquities – Fiction. 2. Archaeological thefts – Fiction. 3. Americans – Cambodia – Fiction. 4. Smugglers – Fiction. 5. Cambodia – Fiction. I. Title

PS3602.E755 S76 2001
813'.6–dc21   2001039614

Publisher: For information on Impact Publications, including current and forthcoming publications, authors, press kits, online bookstore, and submissions, visit our website: *www.impactpublications.com.*

Publicity/Rights: For information on publicity, author interviews, and subsidiary rights, contact Media Relations Department: Tel. 703-361-7300, Fax 703-335-9486, or email: *info@impactpublications.com.*

Sales/Distribution: All bookstore sales are handled through Impact's trade distributor: National Book Network, 15200 NBN Way, Blue Ridge Summit, PA 17214, Tel. 1-800-462-6420. All other sales and distribution inquiries should be directed to the publisher: Sales Department, IMPACT PUBLICA-TIONS, 9104 Manassas Drive, Suite N, Manassas Park, VA 20111-5211, Tel. 703-361-7300, Fax 703-335-9486, or email: *info@impactpublications.com.*

For Monique,
accomplice in adventure

STONE GODS, WOODEN ELEPHANTS

Prologue

The man entered and bowed low. Across the room another man sat at a desk, staring out the window. Below him, the rooftops and streets of the Tokyo neighborhood were bathed in the cool light of a winter's full moon. He remembered nights like this, when he was young. His face would grow numb from the wind as he walked home from school. When he entered the house, the air would be still and feel warm. Real warmth would come later, when he could edge near the hibachi and rub his hands together in the soft glow of the coals.

The man at the door cleared his throat. "Watanabe-san, I am sorry to interrupt your thoughts. The messenger from the South has arrived. He reports that the final phase of the special project will be initiated this evening."

Watanabe turned to face him. "Ah, Ichiro. The final phase.... " He thought for a moment. He was always good with the details, even the smallest ones.

"It was to start with a telephone call, if I remember correctly. Has the call been made?"

"This evening." Ichiro answered, and tried to steal a glance at his wrist-watch without Watanabe seeing him do it. His eyes were not good enough to see the watch face without bringing his arm closer.

"Perhaps the call is being made as we speak." It was the best Ichiro could think to say.

"Perhaps," Watanabe said, his voice low, like a growl. "Perhaps the call is being made. Perhaps the call will work. Perhaps it will not work." After a long moment he voiced what had bothered him from the start. "Perhaps this whole project is too complex."

Ichiro stood quietly, head bowed, waiting for the storm that sometimes followed the expression of such concerns. This time the storm did not come.

1

"Well," Watanabe said. There was an unusual softness in his tone. "Now, we will see. Everything rides on the success of this last phase. Our special project will succeed. Or it will not succeed." He shrugged. It was in the hands of the gods.

Ichiro knew he had been dismissed, but he did not move.

"Watanabe-san, there is one last thing...," he started to say.

"Yes?" Watanabe grunted.

"The messenger from the South. He brought a gift from your old friend."

"Oh...."

"I will have it brought in." Ichiro bowed and stepped backwards through the doorway. A moment later he came back into the room, moving quickly to the side to make way.

Two men in white coveralls shuffled slowly and carefully through the doorway, straining under the weight of the object they carried between them. Watanabe pulled himself upright in his chair and gestured. "There," he said. "Put it there, by the wall, under the light."

They set the statue down. It was not half as tall as they were, but it was heavy. Of stone, it had been carved centuries ago into a graceful male form, one leg bent slightly at the knee, a hand held at chest level, palm out. Above the serene face was a high and elaborate headdress.

Watanabe rose to his feet, better to see the statue. A smile came to his lips.

"Yes," he said. "Yes, I know it. Siva. It must be the old man's joke. But it is a beautiful piece. I must thank the old man.

After contemplating the statue for a while longer, Watanabe sat back down behind the desk. "I wonder," he said. "It looks so good. What do you think, Ichiro? Is it real?"

Ichiro looked worried now. "I don't know what to think," he said. "I never know when the old man is joking."

When nothing else was said for a time, Ichiro took a single step backwards, but stopped again when Watanabe spoke.

"Our project is in the final phase. We need another name for it, a code name. I think it is appropriate to call it, Stone...Stone God."

"Yes, Stone God," Ichiro said. "It is a good name for our project."

1

Three things occurred simultaneously when Harry Ross turned the key and pushed open the door of the Happy Dragon that windy November morning. The most notable event was the siren that suddenly screamed its outrage into the street, torn from electronic slumber by the Happy Dragon's overly sensitive intrusion alarm. The second was the not unexpected rush of leaves and other windborne debris that preceded him into the Happy Dragon whenever he was the first to open its door. The third was a voice from out of his past coming from his overly sensitive telephone recorder. Above the din of the siren, he made out the last words of the message:

"...And that's the bottom line, Harry. A lost city. Adventure. Money to be made. Just like old times again. Get your ass to Bangkok, Harry." There was a brief snatch of music, and the connection was broken.

Across the street, passersby attracted by the wailing siren began to gather in agitated little groups. They stared and pointed at the Happy Dragon. A police patrol car silently glided to a stop a few doors away from the shop. Two police officers climbed out, adjusting their gun belts as they came.

Walking down the street toward them was a young lady. Although she was bundled warmly against the brisk winds, it was easy to see that she was attractive. With a smile and a graceful wave of her hand, she stopped both officers in their tracks. To the older of the two she said, "Never mind, Officer Bailey, it is only Mr. Harry again. He must have come to the shop early. Sorry you had to come." Her accent was Asian.

Officer Bailey, normally a gruff man, was not unaffected by young ladies who smiled at him, whatever the time of day.

"Well, Miss Lotus," he said, adjusting the gun belt on his hip. "Good thing for Mr. Harry you're here. Tell him to get that alarm fixed, or to wait outside until you can get here in the mornings."

"I will tell him," the young lady said. "Thank you again, Officer Bailey." She gave him another smile and turned to walk to the Happy Dragon.

"Fine young lady," Officer Bailey said to his partner. "Too bad she's got to work for that nut."

Inside the shop, Miss Lotus found Harry standing in a pile of street trash and windblown leaves, poking at the telephone. "Morning, Mitchiko," he shouted over the siren. "Something has to be done about this telephone. It records only bits of what anybody says to it. It plays it back whenever it wants." He poked at the phone again. "I think I got it," he said.

"Get your ass to Bangkok, Harry," the telephone said. There was a screech, and then a blast of music.

"Hear that?" he asked. "Did you hear that? He's sitting in the Exorcist. I recognize the tune. Wonder what he's up to now?"

Mitchiko did not ask what the Exorcist was, or who was sitting there. The shop was suddenly silent as she turned off the alarm. That seemed to remind Harry of something.

"We have to do something about that alarm, too. It goes off if I just look at the door in the morning. What happened to that built-in time delay?"

"Oh, Harry. Maybe you should just wait for me in the morning. I never have that problem. Setting off the alarm is not good for business. And filling the store with dead leaves is not good, either."

"It's the aerodynamics of the entrance way. It's a natural funnel for every piece of trash on the street."

Mitchiko did not trouble to point out that this never happened to her. In fact, it happened to no one but Harry. She quietly swept the leaves into a pile.

The door swung open with the day's first customer. She was a large and expensively dressed middle-aged woman. Her ample cheeks were ruddy, due less to the wind than to a heavy hand with her makeup. She looked first at Harry, then at Mitchiko, then back at Harry.

"I am seeking the proprietor," she announced. "A Mr. Harry C. Ross."

"That's me," he admitted.

"Oh," she said, and proceeded to examine him more closely. He had shed his leather aviator jacket and stood before her, resplendent in an aged turtleneck sweater to which leaves from his morning adventure still clung. His trousers were baggy and faded. Without even trying that morning, he had achieved a windblown and mildly disreputable look. It was not quite what she expected of a dealer in ancient artifacts.

The woman looked over his shoulder, beyond him as if half expecting that the real Harry C. Ross would appear from the back of the shop at any moment. When that did not occur, she decided to make do with the gentleman before her, undistinguished though he might be.

"General Phillips of the Asiatic Study Society recommended Mr. Harry C. Ross most highly," she told him. "I'm particularly interested in a bronze

Buddha image, preferably Thai. Preferably of the Chieng Sen period."

"I'm pleased that the general remembered us," Harry said affably. Of course, General Phillips would. Several of his pieces, including a bronze Chieng Sen Buddha, were on display in the Happy Dragon, and on consignment. This was a "favor" that Harry sometimes did for the local old Asia hands. "The general is quite an expert on Asia and Asian art," he added.

"The general said that Mr. Ross is quite knowledgeable about art. And very reasonable about prices. He said Mr. Ross would have such a piece if anyone would."

"Please," Harry said, and walked her toward the rear of the shop where the Chieng Sen Buddha sat in peaceful repose. The woman paused once to utter an admiring comment about a collection of Burmese woodcarvings, and then again to examine two 11th-century Khmer stone torsos. "Where do you find all these things?" she asked, obviously impressed.

"In Asia," he said, stating the obvious. "The Happy Dragon imports directly from Asia, Southeast Asia, primarily. We do all our own buying and importing."

"My goodness. You travel there, do you? That can be dangerous, can't it?" The woman looked at him with new interest.

"Not really," he replied. "At least not if you know your way about. I lived there for many years." This he said with modesty. He had found that people, particularly ladies of a certain age and social status, expected the "East" to be mysterious and dangerous, even at tag end of the 20th century. Some people, and especially such ladies, also expected that someone like Harry, who might accept a large sum of their money in exchange for mysterious and ancient objects, would be modest about the danger he faced in acquiring these objects. Generally, he found it good for business to appear to possess many of the qualities of Gordon of Khartoum.

Standing now before the Chieng Sen Buddha, Harry lowered his voice in respect. In his best art dealer manner he called the woman's attention to the serenity of the Buddha's face, the fine proportion of the torso, and the magnificent patina that added to the beauty and mystery of the seated figure.

Shifting his eyes carefully to his customer, he saw these were all the right things to say. The woman leaned toward the Buddha, looking at it intently. The figure was calling to her. "This is most beautiful," she said, and continued to look at the Buddha's face with reverence.

The moment was right. He went for her jugular. "It is said," he spoke with great solemnity, "that such an ancient figure brings good fortune to the home where it is kept."

The impact of the words was visible. The desired object was now not only a thing of great beauty, but it was also an investment in the future good fortune of her family. "Yes," she said as if waking from a reverie.

"Please...." The words sounded urgent. "I must.... I do want this piece."

He took a step back. He seemed to consider her proposal for a moment. "I will miss this piece," he said, a hint of sadness in his voice. As an afterthought he added, "The price is fifteen thousand dollars."

She recognized he was giving it up. Victory was hers. "You do take checks?" she asked nervously.

"Of course," he replied. He looked vaguely around the shop. "Miss Lotus will assist you with the details."

Mitchiko had been standing by, ready to move into whatever role Harry cast for her as he devised his scenario. This particular sale had been straightforward, and she now became "Miss Lotus, assistant to the proprietor."

Despite her surname – Burns – Mitchiko was of Japanese descent. He had wanted her for the Happy Dragon from the day he first set eyes on her. She was cute, bright, a student in Southeast Asian art and – most importantly – she was willing to work on Sundays.

He saw a certain disadvantage in having a Japanese work in a shop selling Southeast Asian art, although he recognized that in this age there were few for whom the "Japanese Greater Co-Prosperity Sphere" of the Empire of the Rising Sun had any significance. In any case, this minor misgiving was easily resolved by calling Mitchiko "Miss Lotus." Harry did not think Mitchiko looked particularly Japanese and, as Americans generally expected Southeast Asian women to have nice names, like "Lotus," her Japanese ancestry was easily obscured.

Miss Lotus now stepped forward demurely, bowed, and led the woman toward the desk where the transaction would be concluded. Harry nonchalantly took his leave of the customer, and made his way to the basement.

As soon as he had turned his back on the woman, his face lit up. The sale was an excellent one, even after he paid that old warlord, General Phillips, his portion for the Buddha. In fact, as he headed down the basement stairs, his heel-clicking exuberance was tempered only by words repeating themselves in his head. The words on his telephone recorder:

"...Get your ass to Bangkok, Harry."

His trips to the basement were a regular early morning ritual. Despite this, he was always momentarily stunned when he flicked on the light switch. Down here, in the cavernous basement of the Happy Dragon was the center of his power.

The light thrown off by a few unshaded bulbs hanging from the ceiling on frayed cords revealed legions of wooden animals. There was row upon row of wooden ducks. Standing ducks, sitting ducks, ducks picking at their behinds. There were great flocks of doves in racks, in bins, in shadowy piles on the floor. There was a mishmash of rabbits and cats in all shapes and sizes. There was an army of elephants and a legion of pigs. They were grouped by size, shoulder to shoulder, standing, sitting, lying on the floor.

Color was everywhere in grand confusion: the natural colors of rabbits and cats, as well as deep reds and blues and other combinations that God had never intended an animal to wear. There were strange mutations: a golf club-swinging frog, a green and yellow cat on skis, and a chorus line of blue and white ceramic pigs in frilly pink dresses.

This was all his. He glanced over to where a sign at the bottom of the stairs proclaimed "Uncle Noah's Wonder World Imports Incorporated." He had long ago come to realize that the existence of this basement enterprise must never come to the knowledge of the regular Happy Dragon clientele.

Harry quietly surveyed his empire. In a relatively well-lighted area directly at the bottom of the wooden stairs he had just descended, was a framed portrait of "Our Founder," Uncle Noah, himself. The portrait, in fact, was a blowup of the very photograph displayed on the inside front cover of every Uncle Noah's Wonder World Imports catalogue. Uncle Noah's mop of disheveled white hair, his crooked white mustache, intense eyes, and a long-stemmed Bavarian pipe tightly clenched in his teeth gave him the look of a demented Bavarian cuckoo clockmaker. Some of Uncle Noah's customers felt that the large woodcarving knife, grasped like a dagger in his left hand, detracted from his otherwise benign expression. But no one ever said so aloud.

Harry paused now to look closely at the portrait. "You old devil," he said. "We did it, but it was my sale." He looked closer still at the portrait and could not hold back the laughter. He saw in Uncle Noah what no one else did, because he never let anyone who knew him see the portrait.

He knew why Uncle Noah's eyes were so intense, why the pipe was so tightly clenched in his teeth, why his mustache was askew. He knew that this was all caused by the difficulty of trying to suppress giggles when he saw his own likeness in the mirror moments before the photo was taken. Wonder World was a low-budget enterprise; it was less expensive to be Uncle Noah than to rent one. Once Harry made this decision, he never looked back. He could not be both the dashing, adventurous proprietor of the Happy Dragon and the unassuming non-threatening Uncle Noah from whom any gray-haired lady could safely buy wooden bunnies or the pink-skirted ceramic piggy that was Uncle Noah's bestseller.

Surveying his subterranean empire usually brought him great satisfaction. Today the voice from his telephone niggled somewhere at the back of his head. "Get your ass to Bangkok, Harry," it kept saying.

He shook his head sadly. Here he had all this. A well-established shop that sold beautiful pieces of art and brought him a certain recognition. Although few knew it, he also had Uncle Noah and Wonder World, an enterprise that brought him something even more important than recognition: money. Could he give all this up for the uncertainty of some swashbuckling adventure with Aloysius P. Grant? For it was Aloysius P. Grant whom he recognized as the nagging voice in the back of his head.

Harry sighed heavily and started slowly up the steps. When he reached the top, he paused for a moment. Then, his mind made up, he shouted to Mitchiko.

"Miss Lotus, I'm on my way to Bangkok. You're in charge. Don't screw it up."

2

The flight to Bangkok was long but uneventful. On its final leg now, Harry stared out into the cold blackness beyond the window. Thirty thousand feet below, where he could catch an occasional dot of light, was Vietnam. Poor, tragic Vietnam, he thought, but only for a moment. That kind of thinking brought guilt pangs. The war was bad, no question, but it had been an exciting time for him. It had turned his early infatuation with Asia into a drawn-out affair where love was tempered by bouts of profound incomprehension. Vietnam was the apex of that incomprehension.

It had been 20 years since anything that had mattered to him in Vietnam had happened. It had been another world, another life. On those rare occasions when he talked about Vietnam at all, he could speak easily about all the bad things as "fun" and about some of the really terrible things as "interesting." When he first caught himself doing that, he broke into a cold sweat. That kind of perspective was a punishment for growing old.

He laid his head back against the seat, closing his eyes. All of his 20 years in Asia seemed to flicker by. Some of the scenes were bright with light and color. More often the light was so poor that all that could be seen was a gray fog with indistinct forms moving in the background. Despite all of that, all the turmoil, all the unpleasant things that had happened to him and to others, it was only in Asia where he felt himself completely at ease.

"Ladies and gentlemen, please fasten your seat belts. We are beginning our descent into Bangkok."

The voice on the aircraft PA system was smooth and only vaguely Asian. It ended his reverie and brought him back to the present. Here in the great silver bird sat Harry C. Ross, retail merchant, purveyor of Asian antiquities and art. Adventurer and treasure hunter. Surreptitious wholesaler of imaginative Asian bric-a-brac. Where had the ideals of his youth fled? He shook his head, but in a back corner of his brain, a voice kept repeating, "Get your ass to Bangkok, Harry." Unlike the voice on the PA system, this one was not smooth or anything but American. Or at least mostly American. It was overlaid with the mixed inflections of many differ-ent places. Harry shook his head as if to make the voice stop, but on his face was a small smile of anticipation.

*   *   *   *   *

"Where you go, Boss?" the taxi driver just outside the terminal shouted at him. For reasons Harry never understood, any flight he made into Bang-kok from anywhere in the world always arrived after midnight. There were no exceptions. That was the way it was. The terminal itself was well lit. It had been rebuilt in the last few years and was up-to-date. The same could not be said for the taxi drivers. The same ones had milled around the ter-minal for years and were getting long in the tooth.

"Maybe you want to see sex show, Boss? You see show, then I take you to hotel. What hotel you go?"

"How much to Patpong Road?" Harry asked.

The taxi driver looked astonished. "Patpong! Now?" He stopped in his tracks. "Patpong all closed now, Boss. Police make everybody close twenty-three hundred hours." He pointed at his watch. "That means 11 o'clock, Boss." Helpfully he added, "Maybe you want drink? Maybe nice girl? I know good place."

It was a ritual as old as Bangkok. "One hundred baht to Patpong," Harry said simply.

"Oh, Boss. Patpong is too far. This year Bangkok is very expensive. I cannot feed my children. You give me one hundred fifty baht."

"One hundred ten," Harry said.

"Okay. One hundred twenty. We go." Without further ceremony the driver picked up Harry's bag and led him to a taxi parked nearby.

The drive into the city had changed over the 20-odd years since Harry had first come to Bangkok. Twenty years ago this well-lit superhighway had been a rough two-lane blacktop strip that ran alongside a "klong" or canal. There had been rice paddies, and water buffalo to be seen working in the fields or wallowing in the klong. Now there was little room for water buffalo between the 20-story office buildings and the sprawling industrial areas that had grown from the paddies. All along the highway and into the city there was new construction. Much of it seemed to have started in the six months since Harry last drove this way.

The taxi entered the city and passed newly rising condos and office buildings, while he watched for familiar scenes, not always with success. Finally the taxi pulled to a curb as the driver said, "Okay, this is Patpong."

Patpong, the street of pleasure – at least for some. Patpong Road and the area around it teemed with nightclubs, bars, several massage parlors, and a growing number of restaurants. In recent years Patpong had been overrun by vendors of locally made French designer clothing, knock-off Rolex watches, and the peculiar kind of souvenirs that seem to attract people when they have been away from home too long. The stalls where these items were sold were deserted and covered with tarps. Most of the neon signs above the bars that lined the street had been turned off.

Harry paid off the driver, took his bag, and started down Patpong. Despite the late hour, the street was far from empty. No street in Bangkok ever is, regardless of the time of day. Before he reached the small alley he was aiming for, he turned down a number of business and personal proposals. These involved wristwatches, young ladies and other young persons of indeterminate sex, T-shirts, a small fortune in semi-precious stones, and a Ferrari Testa Rosa. The Ferrari seller claimed it had been consigned to him only because its owner had suffered a severe reverse on the Bangkok Stock Exchange that day.

When Harry got to his corner he could see that the neon sign he was looking for was still lit. Halfway down the alley he was able to read the bold red letters: "Exorcist Bar & Nightclub."

Thai businessmen had a penchant for naming their business establishments after things that caught the public imagination. A business name was thus often the result of a popular film, but not always. There was, for example, a Hitler Shirt Shop and a John Paul II bookstore. There were two Gemini 7 restaurants and one Apollo 9 grocer. There was a Lassie Club, a Bambi Bar, and a Jaws II Nightclub. Many of these establishments did not outlast the fads that begat them. The Exorcist Bar & Nightclub was a hit from the beginning and had endured. Good prices and imaginative management gave it a loyal following among Bangkok's expatriate community and drew in a fair amount of tourists as well.

Harry opened the door under the sign and was struck by a blast of music that almost knocked him back into the street. It was black as night inside, except for a thin beam of light that illuminated two dancers gyrating on top of the bar, more or less in time with the music.

He paused just inside the door and watched the dancers with interest – not because their well-turned bodies were bare below their necks, but because he could not immediately identify what they wore on their heads. The Exorcist dance corps had often worn masks in the past, but these were different. They were mostly hair, rather shaggy, and covered the entire head of the young ladies who wore them. The one on the left was a were-wolf apparently, although the hair on her head was spiky and tinted green. The one on the right was harder to make out. She was either a very poorly done vampire or some local demon he was not familiar with.

"Please. This way, sir." The small voice came from a Frankenstein-headed but otherwise comely young body that wore both ends of a bikini. He looked closely at the torso, but did not recognize the lady. He followed her to a booth facing the bar and gave her his order for a drink.

His eyes were becoming accustomed to the darkness. There was not much of a crowd in the Exorcist tonight; not the one face he expected, and no regulars at all. The clientele seemed to be all tourists with a particular interest in monsters. Or so it seemed from the intensity with which they followed the movements of the Werewolf and the Vampire, now holding hands and swaying side by side on top of the bar.

On the wall just behind the dancers he noticed a sign that read: "Come Friday to Happy Hour; Barf Bonanza! Free To Everyone! Great Prizes!" He looked away, then looked back. The sign still said "Barf Bonanza!" He shrugged unconsciously. Must point that out to management, he thought.

The comely Frankenstein reappeared with Harry's Scotch and water. She wiggled gently into the booth next to him. "Good girl, Frankie," he said as he took his drink. "You new here?"

Giggles came from under the mask. "You are funny. My name is not Frankie. My name is Toi. I work here five months," she said and held out the fingers of one hand to show how many.

"Toi, I'm sure you are a very pretty girl underneath it all," he said. He took a deep swallow of his drink, and then asked, "Do you know Aloysius?"

The Frankenstein face pushed right up to him. From behind the mask she seamed to be trying to take a good look at him.

"Why you want to know?" she asked. Without waiting for an answer she added, "Nobody that name come here." Then, with considerably less grace than her entry, Frankenstein bumped her bottom to the edge of the booth and all but ran back into the darkness.

Well, he thought, Aloysius always did have a peculiar effect on some people. He was not here tonight, although Harry fully expected to see him when he stepped in the door. Aloysius did not spend all his evenings at the Exorcist, but in recent years he had started to come here frequently in the early evenings. He claimed the noise and the movements of the dancers – whom he never watched – helped him think.

Everyone in the Exorcist knew Aloysius. The girls doted on him when he needed attention, which was often enough, but they left him by himself when he wanted to be alone with his thoughts.

When Aloysius sat in the Exorcist and thought, his thoughts were not reveries of the past like those of most people sitting alone in a bar. What Aloysius thought about were schemes. Schemes he was planning, schemes he was perfecting, schemes he was already carrying out. When Aloysius was in the middle of a particularly great scheme, he needed two things. First was solitude, until he could fit the individual components together. Then, as soon as everything fit, he needed an audience – not any audience, but the specific audience that would best appreciate a particular scheme. The Exorcist provided Aloysius the solitude he required in the early stages. As for the audience, since the telephone call across the Pacific, Harry knew he was it. The game was afoot.

But where was Aloysius? Without his audience Aloysius would not budge. The call had been three nights ago. Aloysius would have expected Harry to walk through the Exorcist door in 24 hours, and he would have sat in his booth every night after that until Harry appeared. Well, Harry thought, maybe he was making too much of not seeing Aloysius as soon as he walked in, but Frankenstein's reaction bothered him. Any lady of the Exorcist would be proud to say she knew Aloysius.

There was one other face Harry had hoped to see before the growing feeling of jet lag overwhelmed him completely, and he saw her now. She was coming toward him out of the darkness: Exorcist Management.

"Porntip," he said as he rose to greet her. "You are as beautiful as ever."

"Harry, it is good to see you. I thought it was you. One of the girls said somebody was asking for Aloysius. I knew you would come."

As she sat down next to him, he took a good look at her. The last six months had wrought no changes that he could perceive. For a woman who was at least as old as he was, she looked very good. She always dressed well, and maybe the poor light helped. At most she looked to be in her mid-thirties. A few years older than that if you wanted to push it.

It must have been 20 years ago that Harry had first met her in Saigon. In those days she ran a bar on Tu Do Street, and her name was Madelene. She was married to a Frenchman then – or that was what everyone believed. When she came to Bangkok in the mid-seventies, her Frenchman was not with her. Soon after her arrival she married a respectable Thai businessman – or that was what everyone believed. Then she started a series of businesses. The first was a bakery specializing in French breads, then came a small French restaurant, and then the Exorcist Bar & Nightclub.

Harry had never met either of her husbands, and was never convinced that she ever really had one. He never asked. There was one thing that he did know something about: her language skills. Her French and her English were very good. Her Thai, like her Vietnamese, was rudimentary. Her Japanese was excellent. Before she was Porntip and before she was Madelene, she was Toshiko. It was a name few knew, and fewer still dared call her. Where she got the name was a mystery to her friends who knew it, and a mystery to herself, she claimed. Harry used her Japanese name when the two of them were alone together, although it sometimes confused him. In his mind she was always Toshiko or Tosh.

Tosh seemed to be looking at him fondly, he thought. The jet lag was starting to get to him as the adrenalin rush of his arrival in Bangkok wore down. Maybe it was not fondness he saw in her look.

"Harry," she finally said. "I don't know where to begin. I told my girls to say nothing to anyone, and now I am afraid to tell even you. Poor Harry." She reached out and put her hand over his. "You came all this way. Aloysius knew you would come. Now he will not see you."

"For God's sake, Tosh, what's going on?"

Tosh looked over her shoulder to assure herself no one was nearby. "Last week," she started, quietly, "Aloysius came almost every night. Something was on his mind. He did not want to talk with the girls. He drank a lot by himself. Three nights ago he came right after we opened."

Harry interrupted. "That was the night he telephoned me?"

"Yes, he telephoned you that night, from here. He called early, so that he would reach you in the States in the morning. Later he told me that he did not talk with you, but you would come on the first flight."

Tosh paused to beckon to the young Frankenstein hovering uneasily in the corner and ordered a fresh drink for Harry. Then she sat quietly until the drink arrived. With it came a glass of green liquid. He did not ask what it was. He knew that if he did, Tosh would say it was absinthe. She took a sip and then continued.

"It was quiet here that night, like tonight. When Aloysious decided to leave, I walked with him to the door. And so I saw it. There were three men, young men, tough men who looked like they came from the North. They were waiting outside. They pushed him into his car and took him away."

"Then what happened?"

"I don't know. But the next day they found his car in the big canal, the klong by the big Muslim mosque." While he waited expectantly, she took another sip of the green liquid. "They have not found him yet," she finally said with a catch in her throat.

Harry knew the stretch of canal that ran by the old mosque. The water there was black and deep. Under the surface it was heavy with muck and vegetation that could hide a body for a long time.

"Listen, Tosh." It was his turn to try to comfort her. "Maybe it's not so bad. You know, old Aloysious drove his car into a klong before."

He had to smile when he thought of it. That car had been an old big-finned Cadillac convertible that Aloysious had found God-knew-where. He drove it around Bangkok for years, always as near to its maximum speed as he could get on Bangkok's crowded streets. One night, something in its steering finally snapped – at least that was what Aloysious said afterwards – and Aloysious and the Cadillac went ass over teakettle into a klong. That klong was not a deep one. The effect on the Cadillac was terminal, but Aloysious suffered no more than a bad stomachache for a week afterwards.

Tosh must have been thinking the same thing. She hid a giggle behind her hand. "Aloysious," she said, savoring the name. "What a great man. He was always doing something funny with his cars." She took a sip of the absinthe before meeting his eyes again.

"Harry," she began. "This time I think it is a little more serious. The police think he was in big trouble. Before he came here last week he had not been in Bangkok for months. People said he was up North. The people I saw were from the North."

"Tosh, everyone knows Aloysious. Some people love him. A lot of people hate him. But I can't think of anyone who would seriously want to hurt him."

"The police think maybe he became involved with drugs." She stared down at her drink. "I'm sorry, Harry."

That was the final straw. Between the Scotch, the jet lag, and what Tosh had just said, the blood in his veins seemed to turn slowly to lead. He was incapable of raising the glass to his mouth. His head seemed to be too heavy to turn away from her. His lips were paralyzed and no words would come. He realized now that it was quiet. The music and the dancing must have stopped some time ago. He knew the tourists must be gone, but he did not bother to look. The lights in the ceiling were starting to come on.

"Oh shit, Tosh," he was finally able to say. "It's been a long day."

"Come, Harry," she said and took his arm. "You must get some sleep. We can talk more tomorrow."

She led him back out the way he had come in. Between one side of the Exorcist and a neighboring office building ran a narrow walkway. Tosh led him down the walkway and around the back of the Exorcist. There she unlocked a small door. When he was inside she locked it behind her and went up the steps. At the top she unlocked another door, turned on a light, and let him in.

"Aladdin's cave," he said.

"No one comes up here. It is my storeroom. It is not fancy, but there is a bed where you can sleep, a TV, and a refrigerator. Tomorrow you will feel better."

He looked around. There were rows of cardboard cartons and wooden crates stacked from floor to ceiling. Cigarettes, liquor, cans of beans, vegetables, meat, toilet paper. An entire row of crates stretching across the room contained only toilet paper.

"Tosh," he said, "this is Saigon 1968. I haven't seen anything like this since the big days of the black market in Vietnam. There's no black market in Bangkok. You can get all this stuff in the supermarket right up the street. What are you doing with all this?"

"You never know, Harry. You never know."

She helped him get settled. There was fresh juice in the refrigerator. She promised him a croissant and coffee from her bakery in the morning. He was accustomed to being treated well in Bangkok. Maybe it was the jet lag that made him feel a bit overwhelmed and grateful.

"Tosh, I owe you one," he said. As partial payment he added, "There's a mistake on your sign behind the bar. It says 'Barf Bonanza'. Get it? Barf. Barf Bonanza. Don't you mean 'Bar'?"

Tosh did not react the way he expected. "Harry, how long you stay Bangkok?" The question was the rhetorical Bangkok catch-all for those who failed to see the obvious. She went on to tell him, as if he were slightly backward, "On Friday we have a Barf Bonanza. Yes, a Barf Bonanza. You remember how the girl in the film puked? Threw up? That was a well-known scene. On Friday everyone can try to drink a lot of beer fast. The one who barfs best gets the big prize."

"I think I better go to bed now, Tosh," he said, wearily. He lay back on the cot and was asleep before Tosh reached the door.

3

M orning comes quickly in Bangkok. It comes really quickly if your body is running on a clock 12 time zones away. Harry bolted out of a sound sleep at five o'clock in the morning, Bangkok time. He had no desire to get out from under the brown army blanket that covered him and, without much success, tried hard to get back to sleep. Each time he reached the edge of consciousness and was about to drift off, he would suddenly find himself plunging head-long into a fetid pool of evil-looking black water. Just as his face was about to strike the muck, he would jolt awake to find himself staring at the store-room ceiling where someone had scrawled "Why you look up here Char-lie?"

Finally, Tosh arrived with the promised croissant and a steaming pot of coffee. By then it was almost seven o'clock. She laid out breakfast over the top of a crate of giant-sized orange juice cans.

As they drank their coffee and nibbled at the bread, they talked com-fortably about what concerns people most on any given day in Bangkok – the worsening traffic and the stock market. Aloysious kept intruding into his thoughts, but when he started to talk about it, Tosh said, "Later, Harry. You will have time to look around today. I will ask more questions. Tonight we can talk."

By 7:30 he was on his way. It was the height of the rush hour as he started walking down Silom Road in the direction of the river. Silom is one of the major thoroughfares in Central Bangkok and one of the most heavi-ly traveled streets during the morning rush hour. Cars and buses moved slowly in both directions on the divided roadway and regularly stopped for long minutes, waiting for some distant stoplight to turn green again.

Despite the fumes that rose from the traffic, he enjoyed the walk down Silom. The day was still new enough to feel fresh and almost cool. The sidewalk was full of life. Bankers and businessmen, secretaries and clerks, all were walking briskly to where they were going to begin their day. Others stood along the sidewalk waiting for buses. When a bus approached, all leaned forward as if impatient to get aboard and underway. Many shops along the street were already open, while in front of others, shopkeepers sluiced down the sidewalk with buckets of water. Here and there food stalls were in full swing as customers disappeared in steam clouds rising from pots of dumplings and rice.

When he reached New Road, Harry turned right. Properly named "Charoen Krung," although few call it that, New Road, paradoxically, is one of Bangkok's oldest streets. In this area it parallels the river. Getting across New Road at any time of day is an adventure. Crossing it in the height of rush hour requires movements akin to a well-conducted military maneuver. Harry walked along until he found a small group of Thai men and women standing impatiently along the curb. He stood quietly off to one side as others approached, and the group grew larger and more impatient. When the critical mass was suddenly reached, the group stepped as one into the street. Traffic came to a screeching halt while this wall of determined pedestrians, with Harry safely at its core, made it to the other side.

He veered off on a shortcut. He turned down a small side road, walked into one end of a parking garage and out the other, crossed a driveway, and reached the main entrance of the Oriental Hotel.

The Oriental has long been judged by those who know such things to be the best hotel in the world. The Oriental is also quite expensive, which did not make it appealing to Harry. What did appeal to him were one of two areas of the original 19th century hotel that had been incorporated into the building as it stood today, and its veranda. It was to the veranda that he headed.

The veranda of the Oriental overlooks the Chao Phya River. For the price of a continental breakfast one could sit comfortably and watch life on the river go by or, do what Harry planned to do, peruse the morning newspaper under some of the most pleasant circumstances that could be found in Bangkok.

He sat quietly for a while and just watched the river. Directly in front of him a tug pulled a long line of barges. They were so heavy with rice that the river washed over their decks. Long white ferry boats, overflowing with passengers, busily crossed and re-crossed the river, touching the riverbank only to discharge one load of passengers and take one the next. Smaller boats ran along the shore, darting in to pick up passengers from the riverbank, then speeding off downriver. Farther on, a small coastal steamer slowly made its way upriver against the current.

Reluctantly, he turned to his newspaper. On an ordinary day, he could easily spend an hour going through the *Bangkok Courier*, fascinated by the diversity of its coverage of local events. Today he scanned its pages quickly, looking for police reports. A small box on page five caught his eye:

Police Continue Investigation Into Tourist Deaths. Bangkok, Nov 16. A police spokesman told the press today that investigations continue into the deaths of three tourists that occurred early this week in different parts of the country. On Monday an elderly European man was found dead in his first-class Bangkok hotel room. On the same day an Indian man was discovered hanging from his bathroom doorknob at a rented bungalow in the Pattaya seaside resort. On Tuesday, a still unidentified Western man was found alongside a road in rural Northeast Thailand. Foul play is not believed to be a factor in any of these cases, but police are continuing their investigations. The police spokesman also reported that there have been no new developments in the possible drug-related case involving a foreigner whose automobile was found submerged in the Phetburi Klong. The investigation into this case also continues.

There it was. Everything and nothing. Despite his growing grief for Aloysious, Harry could not help but be distracted by thoughts of the Indian gentleman found hanging from his doorknob. It was a strange and cruel world that he found most days reading the *Bangkok Courier*.

He may have felt grief, but he was hungry, too. He took full advantage of the continental breakfast and called for another Danish and more coffee. Aloysious would not have given up any food on his account, and he might as well start on a full stomach. Harry knew from experience that he had about five good hours of running at full steam. Then jet lag would set in and he would feel like a limp washrag. He would do what he always did when he first arrived in Bangkok, stay on his feet and drag himself to midnight before throwing himself into an exhausted sleep. In a day or so his body would adjust.

He sighed and told himself it was time to get started if he was going to find out what happened to Aloysious. That was all he wanted, just to find out. He had no illusions about making anything right if what happened to Aloysious was not right. Finding out what happened would be difficult enough, if it proved possible at all. People did sometimes drop out of sight with no trace. Sometimes they died untimely deaths for no good reason. That was the way of things.

He was acquainted with many people in Bangkok who knew Aloysious. Most of them would not even be aware that anything had happened. A few would know that something had happened, but not what it was. Some of these people would say that Aloysious was fated to come to a bad end. Under the circumstances, they would suggest, it was best not to ask questions or to dwell on it. He also knew there were one or two people who were tuned into the things that went on. They might have some idea of what Aloysious had gotten himself into. He decided that his next order of business would be to visit one of these people.

The shop of Jean Lee, which bore only its owner's name, was located in a marble-fronted corner of one of Silom Road's most prestigious buildings. Small gold-framed windows displayed things that were quite old, exquisitely beautiful, and very expensive. To Harry, the shop was one of the most beautiful places in Bangkok. While the shop was located among the offices of Bangkok's captains of finance and industry, Jean Lee's clientele were mostly European collectors and dealers, and a few Americans of wealth and pretense.

Jean Lee was with a client when Harry entered the shop. Jean Lee, who never missed anything, spotted him the instant he entered the shop and greeted him with a small nod. Harry poked around the shop, but mainly watched Jean Lee handle his customer.

The product of a Chinese father and a French mother, Jean Lee carried a quick mind and enormous energy in a small wiry body. His dark complexion was complemented by the blousy white silk shirts he always wore over tight black trousers. His dark wavy hair was long in the back in a way that almost suggested a pigtail. The impression he left was of an aging matador who, having left the ring, was now as intense about Chinese porcelains as he had been about the great bulls he had faced in his past. Jean Lee had interesting looks, an appealing personality, and good manners. Years after he had first met him, it struck Harry that Jean Lee was probably the most elegant person he knew.

By the time Jean Lee completed his sale, Harry was admiring an 11th-century Khmer stone Buddha. "Do you like it, Harry? It's a nice piece, isn't it? I found three like it in an attic in Chinatown. They must have been taken out of Angkor Wat a hundred years ago. Perhaps you need one for your shop."

"I can't afford your prices, Jean," Harry said.

"For you, Harry, I'll make it a good price. I need to sell these pieces quickly before the authorities discover I have them. With peace having broken out in the region, the Thai government is starting to return Khmer pieces to the Cambodians. Nothing is safe anymore. A dealer's lot is becoming difficult."

Jean Lee then took Harry's hand in both of his.

"It is a terrible thing, Harry. I saw Aloysious just last week. He heard that I have the Khmer pieces. He came to see them. He looked at them, but he had something else on his mind. We talked only of these pieces, so I don't know what was bothering him."

"How did you hear about it?"

"Two days ago, a man who is a senior police official told me they found Aloysious's car in the klong. He said they were still looking for Aloysious.

That was all he knew."

"Will he tell you if he learns more?"

"He is a friend. I think he will."

"What do you think happened, Jean?"

"With Aloysious, who can say? He was... Aloysious is not an ordinary man. We are indifferent to most people we meet as we go through life. With Aloysious it was hard to be indifferent. He was always involved with something. He had strong opinions about everything. Many people loved him. Some hated him. It could have been any one of a number of things."

"Drugs?" Harry asked.

"No, not drugs. Not Aloysious."

"I'm glad you think so. That's my feeling, too," Harry said. "No, I can't believe it would be drugs. But what happened? He wanted me to come to Bangkok. One thing he said got my attention. He mentioned a lost city. A lost city. Does that mean anything to you, Jean?"

Jean shrugged like a Frenchman. "It means nothing to me, except that it sounds like vintage Aloysious. He trusted you probably more than anyone, Harry. What he said to you may be something that he did not want to share with anyone else."

"But a lost city, Jean?"

"Angkor Wat was a lost city once."

Harry shook his head. "You're no help, Jean Lee."

"I'm sorry, Harry. In a day or two we may know more. Perhaps for now you need to take your mind off Aloysious. Come, see my new treasures. I have some Chinese bronzes you haven't seen. Some good porcelains." Jean Lee led him around the shop, pointing out the highlights of his recent acquisitions. The new pieces were great, Harry was sure, but somehow he could not work up much interest in art. Maybe the jet lag was coming back early. He needed to snap himself back to reality. As Jean Lee expounded before a rare and expensive Chinese oxblood vase, Harry interrupted.

"Uncle Noah sends his greetings."

Jean Lee's monologue on the vase's impressive lineage stopped abruptly.

"Oh, he does, eh?" He turned to look around the shop. "Oh, Peter," he said to a very Chinese-looking young man, "please look after things. I'm going upstairs with Mr. Harry."

Jean Lee's upstairs was as big and as elegant as his downstairs. Even more so if that were possible. Every Bangkok antiques dealer of any worth had a back room or an upstairs room. This was where the real treasures were kept, safe from the prying eyes of Fine Arts Department officials who were charged with preserving Thailand's cultural heritage. Only the initiates were allowed in these rooms, usually foreign collectors or dealers who had earned the confidence of a dealer over a period of years. Like the secret caches of other dealers, Jean Lee's secret collection contained priceless relics of Thailand's past, rare Buddhas, elaborately carved stone and wood panels, colorful pots and vases, and dainty ceramic figures.

"Just the old relics, Harry. There are some new additions. We'll look at them later."

Jean Lee walked through the room to the far end. He unlocked the door there with a key from his pocket. "Peter's a good boy," he said, "but I don't even let him in here yet." He let Harry precede him into the room and locked the door behind them.

The room had the appearance of a small workshop. Along the wall was a long worktable that contained what was obviously work in progress. Behind the table were rows of shelves where drawings and completed work could be stored.

"As you can see, Harry, I have several new projects underway. Before you return home I hope to have some prototypes ready to show you. How are the pigs working out?"

"The pigs are great, Jean Lee. For reasons I have never understood, pigs appeal to people. Put the pig in a pink dress and it becomes irresistible. I've never understood that."

Jean Lee looked ecstatic. He made a fist of his right hand, thrust it in the air, and shook it vigorously. "I knew it," he said, "I knew the pig was a winner. How many have you sold, Harry?"

"Almost all of them. How do you explain...."

"Don't look for explanations, Harry. Let Uncle Noah handle it. I learned the secret a long time ago. There's no accounting for taste. Let Uncle Noah handle it, and you can keep your illusions. Come on, we have to start work on the next bestseller. What do you think, frogs or bunnies?"

"The Indonesians are doing frogs. They've been doing frogs for years. Frogs with umbrellas, frogs playing golf. Everybody is doing bunnies. I think elephants are the big unexplored ground."

"Well, good, Harry. You have been giving it some thought. Elephants it can be. Come on, we can get started now.

Hours later, after exhausting the things one can do with wooden elephants and ceramic elephants, Harry took his leave of Jean Lee and his workshop. He was feeling the jet lag, but in many ways he felt better than he had since arriving in Bangkok. Working with Jean Lee helped restore his perspective. But as he walked back toward New Road he was suddenly overwhelmed by a sense of loss. At first he thought it was for Aloysious, but then he realized it was not just Aloysious. It was for himself. For the loss of what Aloysious had promised. A lost city. Who else was there who could bring him to a lost city?

The next stage, he thought as he waited to cross New Road again, was to get mawkishly sentimental. How many times had he walked along here and seen Aloysious poking along on the other side of the street? The old antique shops located in this area were an irresistible lure to Aloysious. In the past, he had often spotted Aloysious on the other side, but then had

been prevented from joining him by not being able to cross the street because of the insane traffic.

Aloysious had always been easy to spot in a Bangkok crowd. He was
big, and tall enough to stand out in most places. It was his walk that was
most distinctive, an over-articulated lope that made his legs appear to be
out of control even at the slowest speeds. Harry had never seen anything
quite like it.

Even as he had these thoughts he saw something very familiar across
the street. A tourist, obviously, complete with camera and funny hat. As
tall as Aloysious, but with a full beard. For a moment Harry was sure...and
then the man was hidden from view by a long line of passing buses.

For just a moment he thought he had seen Aloysious. But he did have
Aloysious on his mind, and his mind was sinking rapidly into a jet lag
haze. He was only being offered what he wanted to see. That made him
feel sadder still, and his sense of loss came back even stronger.

4

At six o'clock the next morning Harry stared intently at "Why you look up here Charlie?" on the ceiling above him and did not ask himself why. He knew. It was because his head hurt, his bowels crawled, and he was starting to recall pieces of the previous night. He was sure he had made it to midnight before he gave himself up completely to the blackness of sleep. He seemed to remember Tosh shaking him at different times of the evening to keep him awake where they sat in a corner of the Exorcist and talked while he accompanied their discussion with numerous scotch and sodas.

He had reached the Exorcist late that afternoon feeling bad, really bad. He felt he had wasted the day. He had done nothing but play silly Uncle Noah games with Jean Lee.

At the Exorcist, Tosh had almost nothing new to tell him. She had heard a rumor that some of the policemen working on the Aloysious case now believed that Aloysious's car was unoccupied when it went into the klong, and that Aloysious had been taken up North by his abductors. This news made Harry feel slightly better until Tosh added, "The consensus of my police sources is that – dead or alive – prospects for Aloysious are not good."

As he drank more Scotch to drown his sorrow, Harry became even more despondent. He was sorry for Aloysious and he was sorry for himself. Now neither of them would get to see the lost city. Most of all Harry dearly wanted to sleep. He had told Tosh to keep him up until midnight, and she had shaken him awake whenever he thought he could sneak in a few minutes of sleep. Once when she woke him, he thought he caught himself sobbing. But when he leaned over to where he could see his face reflected in a mirror, he saw himself looking quite composed, if somewhat stone-faced. The liquor and the jet lag and his sense of loss had now turned him into a stone, he thought.

25

The last thing he remembered about the whole evening had started when some of the ladies of the Exorcist dance corps decided to cheer him by dancing the *Ramwong*. Normally Harry liked the *Ramwong*. It is a traditional dance, in which the participants move in a circle as they gracefully sway their bodies and move their arms in time to the beat of gongs and wailing flutes.

The dance came at a point in the evening when Tosh was distracted and Harry, taking advantage of her inattention, had slumped over the table, getting a quick nap. The ladies of the Exorcist quietly surrounded him. They were in full dance costume. As on recent evenings, this meant they wore a creature mask covering their heads, and perfume.

Harry was unaware of the ladies dancing around him. At first. He was jolted awake by the Pong! of a particularly loud gong. He looked up. The eerie sounds of a squealing flute joined in. He saw a reindeer with huge breasts sway by the end of his nose. Then the huge black and white face of Shamu, the killer whale, peered into his face. Gracefully, the whale pranced backwards away from him, and he realized Shamu had even bigger breasts than the reindeer.

Cymbals clashed. Frankenstein swayed into focus, then paused while Harry's eyes fixed on a thin – and not unattractive – appendix scar. Somewhere deep in a corner of his brain a voice said the scar should not be there.

Eyes still on the scar, Harry rose to his feet. He became part of the *Ramwong* circle, although he did not know it. Unsteady on his feet, he swayed, and his arms swung in all directions as he fought for balance. The ladies of the Exorcist cheered. The pace of the dance quickened. He twisted around, looking for the scar. Slowly, he started to slump to the floor, still twisting as he went. His eyes were wide, as breasts, rumps, and bizarre heads whirled by.

That was all that he remembered, except, that from behind the curtain that seemed to have fallen over his eyes came Tosh's voice: "It's midnight, Harry. You made it!"

The ladies of the Exorcist cheered wildly.

* * * * *

Harry was staring at the ceiling when Tosh appeared. She looked great, as if she had been up for hours. She was laying out his breakfast on his bedside orange juice crate when he decided to sit up. Too late, he realized that he was wearing nothing under his blanket.

Trying to cover his nakedness, he asked, "How did I get to bed last night?"

"The girls took care of it. I told them they could have their way with you. If they could get you up here." Tosh smiled as she helped him adjust the sheet around his waist. "I hope it was not too exhausting. I think the girls had a good time. Especially the one you call Frankie. She looked worn out when she came down this morning. But happy."

"Oh," was the only thing he could think of saying.

* * * * *

Harry started his day back along New Road. He walked from antique shop to antique shop, concentrating on the old establishments that Aloysious favored. These were mostly owned by Chinese whose families had settled in Bangkok three or four generations ago. The shops were not as prosperous looking as the newer ones along the street that catered solely to tourists. These tourist shops had a more "cutting edge" look. They offered their versions of "antiques" as well as handicrafts, and made much more of a deliberate effort to market their wares. Signs on their doors claimed fluency in all the major and some of the minor languages of the world. Other signs guaranteed the best prices in Asia, and assured passers-by that inside the air was cool and free cola was available to those who paused to examine the merchandise.

The Chinese shops, by contrast, usually had only a single sign that proclaimed the name of the shop. Most often this was the name of its owner. A dusty window contained a few samples of the wares offered. Inside, the shops were unadorned and dark, sometimes containing real treasures of antiquity, but generally not.

Harry peered into the windows of these shops. He would enter if he saw a clerk he recognized or a shop owner he knew. With each handshake his patter was the same.

"How are you doing? You got some great stuff since I was here last. Today I'm just looking. Oh, that one is really nice. I'll be back to buy things later. How's business? Well, I guess it's bad everywhere now. Oh, by the way, has Aloysious been around? When did you see him last? Did you hear anything about some trouble he was in? What did you think it was all about? Don't want to speculate, huh? Well, I can understand that. Yeah, everybody said he was going to get into real trouble one day. Well, I'll be seeing you."

Harry learned little – about Aloysious, anyway. No one even admitted to having seen him in the last two or three months. Some had heard of the incident, but not one was willing to speculate on what had occurred.

What he did learn a lot about was the current state of the antiques business. He had learned long ago that any Bangkok antique dealer would say business was bad even as he was unloading the worst of his losers for a scandalous profit to a wealthy Japanese tourist with exceptionally bad taste. The biggest optimist among these dealers was blind to silver linings when sales actually did drop off. Despite this, Harry was still surprised when dealer after dealer, and even the lowliest of sales clerks, complained of business being bad. The reason given was always the same. It was best summed up by Mrs. Pornchai of Pornchai Supreme Antiques.

"It was you Americans first," she told Harry. "Then the Germans and the Japanese. Millions of them, Harry. You saw it. Many millions of them. And they all had to buy something. Most of it was shit. But there were many beautiful things, too. Some I am really sorry I gave away. We sold so much. And now...there is nothing left to sell."

Mrs. Pornchai was right, of course. He had watched the flow of antiques out of Thailand since he had first come here. And it had been going on before that for decades. In the early years it had probably been a dribble, nothing compared to the surge that had accompanied the hundreds of thousands of Americans whom the Vietnam War had brought to Southeast Asia in the late sixties and early seventies. The Americans were followed by wave upon wave of European tourists, who sought out Thailand's unspoiled beaches, its golden temples, and its low prices.

The Japanese were also coming to Thailand then. First in small groups, but then in ever increasing numbers as their personal wealth grew and they discovered the all-inclusive tours that combined excellent and inexpensive dental work by day with equally inexpensive and exquisitely talented sex by night. With all these visitors the Thai economy flourished, as did the Bangkok antique dealers – while there were still beautiful things to sell.

The growing scarcity of antiques had first been noted by those dealers who dealt only in the finest of Thai artifacts. As their own collections grew smaller, their sources in the countryside also were claiming to have fewer and fewer good things to replace things that were sold. Some of these dealers turned to Burmese objects that had been smuggled into Thailand for centuries over smuggler trails. A few others, who still had family ties in China, started to import antiques and art objects from there.

According to everyone Harry talked to along New Road, it was now evident to all that there were almost no Thai antiques of any kind left to sell. At the same time the stream of Burmese antiques had slowed to a dribble, and the high-quality items still reaching Thailand were few and very expensive. Cambodian or Khmer items – on the rare occasions that they did appear on the Thai market – were generally of poor quality and quickly seized by the Thai authorities. The whole antiques business in Bangkok was as grim as Harry had ever seen it. As Mrs. Pornchai said, "It's so bad, even a good counterfeit antique you can't find anymore, Harry."

Still trying to digest all of this, he was again surprised when at his next stop, the antique shop of Fu Lai Wang, he was greeted with big smiles, both by Wang and by Wang's teenage daughter. Wang's shop was one of the smallest and least pretentious along New Road. Even at the best of times Wang's collection was a mixture of old and new things, and quality ranged from mediocre to poor. From time to time Wang came up with a good piece. On those rare occasions in the past, Wang had always called Aloysious first, which was how Harry had first come to know Wang.

"Ah, Mr. Harry," Wang greeted him with a deep bow. "I knew you would come soon. Please sit. My daughter will bring tea."

"I'm all tea'd out, Wang." Harry nodded a greeting to Wang's daughter and waved her back to her seat as she started to rise to get the tea. "Business must be good. You have the only happy face I have seen all morning."

"Business is okay," Wang shrugged, still smiling. "It is just that we are pleased to see you. I just said to my daughter, 'I hope Mr. Harry comes soon'."

"I'm going to disappoint you, Wang. I'm not planning to buy much this trip."

"That is okay," Wang said. "But I have something you want."

Harry quickly turned to look around the shop, almost as a reaction. He doubted there was much he wanted among the dust-covered wooden animals, Buddhas, and classical dancers that all seemed so painfully new as they stood in their little clusters around the shop.

"Not here, Mr. Harry. You must go back to my other room. My daughter will take you there."

As the girl rose to her feet, Harry noted that she seemed taller than the last time he had seen her and was filling out her tight black trousers in the most interesting ways. "Please," she said, and with her hand indicated the way he should walk.

"After you," he said. He followed and watched her gracefully rounded hips move under the thin cloth of her trousers. He felt only a little bit like a dirty old man.

The girl led him out the back door of the shop and into a small sun-drenched courtyard. On the far side stood a large structure built of dull black wood that seemed to pull all the sun and heat of the courtyard into itself. There was a Chinese look to the building, but it was built Thai-style on huge teak posts that held its main floor a dozen feet above the ground. The space beneath was only partially enclosed and served as a storage area for Wang's least valuable artifacts and household wares.

As Harry followed the girl toward the building, two unkempt-looking white hens scattered out of the way. A small black and red rooster held his ground, but rocked back and forth nervously as if daring Harry to cross some imaginary line, while hoping he would not. When the girl reached the building, she stepped aside and gestured for him to continue up a narrow stairway immediately inside the building.

When he reached the floor above, he found it not as hot or dark as he expected. He was in a single large room with wide windows on each of the side walls. The windows were open; the air was still.

The wall at the far end of the room was in shadow, but Harry could see a double row of Buddha images. The first row of Buddhas was against the wall. These were all standing images, of stone, bronze, and wood. In front of that was a second row of Buddhas, seated in traditional positions of blessing, teaching, or meditating.

Between Harry and the Buddhas were rows of disciples and monks. There were also stone and wooden heads, and fragments of what must have been massive Buddha torsos. There was a smell of incense that probably came from a personal shrine Wang had in some corner of the room. Perhaps the entire room was Wang's personal shrine.

He fixed on one particular image, a really magnificent stone Buddha. It was 11th-century Khmer and totally intact, having not only its head but also its hands and feet. A piece like this – if it was real – would never be found outside a museum or a well-guarded private collection. He stepped toward it when a movement at the back of the room caught his eye. In the shadows against the far wall, one of the Buddhas began to stir. Harry's mind was suspended in uncertainty. Then the figure spoke.

"Harry, I taught you better than that. You should be able to recognize even a good reproduction from that distance. Even with your aging eyes."

Harry focused on the figure. Big as he had always been, wearing loose black Chinese trousers and a once white T-shirt with a charging red elephant emblazoned across its front, sat Aloysious P. Grant. His broad face wore his smug look, but there was also an air of expectancy as he awaited Harry's reaction.

It is time to be cool, Harry said to himself. Speaking slowly to hide his excitement, he said, "It doesn't look like your dip in the canal disagreed with you at all. But you could have changed your shirt."

Aloysious was rising to his feet. "Hey, I was close to not getting out, buddy. I swallowed a lot of muck. I was sick for a week."

"It only happened four days ago."

"Whatever," Aloysious said. He turned to the Khmer stone carving. It was as tall as he was, and he put his hand irreverently on its shoulder.

"Look at this, Harry. Look close. It looks like a real one, doesn't it?" Aloysious dropped his hand and took a step back. He squinted at the statue. "If it wasn't in such good condition, I could almost believe it was real."

"I hope you didn't bring me all the way to Bangkok to show me a particularly nice reproduction stone carving."

"Harry, this is only an hors d'oeuvre. Come. Sit. We have a lot to talk about." With that, Aloysious led Harry back to where he had been sitting. There was a low Thai-style teak table and cushions to sit on. Aloysious gestured for Harry to sit.

Aloysious settled down across from him. "Harry," he started, "I am really glad to see you." The stress was on 'really.' "I'm sorry my problem kept me from meeting you at the airport." Whatever the problem was, Aloysious dismissed it as if it were a flat tire on the way to the airport.

The smile on Harry's face felt a little tight. "What exactly is going on?" he asked.

"Oh, a misunderstanding."

"A misunderstanding? Somebody dumped you and your car in a canal. The police are looking all over for you...."

"People get emotional, Harry. It was no big thing."

Harry knew Aloysious well enough to recognize that it would be futile to discuss the "misunderstanding" any further, at least at this point. As if in confirmation, Aloysious pressed on to other things.

"Look, Harry, the point is you're here. We have a lot to do in the next couple of days. If you're ready, we can be on our way tonight."

"Tonight?" Harry repeated. "Where are we going?"

"Up North."

"Where up North?"

"To a place I want to show you."

"Where?" Harry asked, still patient. "What's the name of this place?"

"It's a city, Harry. I don't know its name. It doesn't have a name. Not now. The name was forgotten a thousand years ago."

Harry felt his patience slipping away. "Aloysious, why are you putting me on? I came all the way from the States. I thought there was a reason for me to come here."

"Harry, Harry. I'm not putting you on." Aloysious leaned in toward him, his eyes glowing. "I want to take you to see a city. A city no one has seen for a thousand years. You want a name for the place? We can make up a name. Call it what the hell you want."

"You're saying that you found a city? A city that you just happened to find? A lost city?"

"That's what I'm trying to tell you, Charlie. A lost city, pal. Or at least it was lost – until I found it."

5

Harry waited for the punch line. Aloysious leaned in closer and spoke slowly, in a quiet voice, as if to assure that Harry would miss nothing of what he said. "It was about four months ago. I was up in the hills, north of Chiang Rai. I was way off the roads in a hilly area. You know how dense the forest is up there. One afternoon, I was deep in the bush and I tripped over some stones. Not rocks. Not just stones that happened to be there, but stones that had been cut and made to fit together like a wall. Or a step. I poked around a little. I found another group of stones. And then another one. They all fit together. It was a staircase going up the hill."

Aloysious watched Harry's face for a reaction as he continued. "I couldn't do much that first day, but I went back. Those steps led all the way up to the top of the hill. And up there, spread all over the top, was the rest of it, Harry. Buildings, big stone buildings. You couldn't see them all at once. There are a lot of trees, moss, all kinds of vegetation. It's all overgrown. From what I could see, it's pretty much intact. It's like a city up there. There's more on the slope of the hill, too. Maybe they had their temple complex on the side of the hill. The buildings are amazing; they're big, and decorated with beautiful work all carved into the stone. The place looks completely intact. It is really something to see.

Harry heard him out without interrupting. When Aloysious finished speaking, he remained silent for a long minute. Then he leaned in toward Aloysious.

"Aloysious, listen to me. This is the latter part of the 20th century. In fact, we are butting our heads against the beginning of the 21st century. How – in this age of airplanes, helicopters, and satellites, when every square foot of this planet has been mapped a dozen times over, when tourists routinely camp out in places that are both wild and remote – how can there still be a lost city that no one has ever found? And then, one day, you stumble across it.

"I don't know." Aloysious shook his head. He looked genuinely puz-

33

zled. "I've thought of that, too. I know it sounds crazy. All that I can say is that the area is away from everything. It's remote. It's heavily overgrown. Maybe you just can't see it from above. I know I had to fall over it before I could see it."

"You are serious about this?"

"I am absolutely serious about this, Harry. I am as serious about this as I have ever been about anything. I would not put you on about something like this. We have both been through a lot of crap in our time, but this is different. This is real. I guarantee it."

"Fantastic!" Harry felt a sense of elation. There were lost cities! Harry jumped up and clapped Aloysious on the back. "Goddamn, Aloysious, you'll be famous, like Schulman, or whatever his name was."

"Who?" Aloysious looked startled.

"The guy who discovered Troy. You'll be famous, Aloysious. Absolutely famous. Who else have you told about this?"

"Nobody. I don't want anyone to know about this."

"Why not? Somebody has to know sometime. And you're the one who's going to have to tell them. If you don't, somebody else will."

"Now, hang on there, Harry. Who's going to tell somebody if I don't?"

"If you found it, somebody else can find it. You found it first. You should get the credit for it."

"I don't want any credit. For now, I don't want anybody to know about it."

"That's crazy. Why not?"

"I have to show you."

"Show me?"

"You have to see it. Once you get up there you'll understand." Aloysious's eyes shifted from Harry's face to a point over Harry's shoulder. He was looking out the window, somewhere into space.

"It's absolutely beautiful, Harry. The place is absolutely beautiful. The buildings look like no one has been in them in a thousand years. Like one day they walked away from it and nobody ever came back. You know, Harry, it's Khmer. The style of the architecture is Khmer. Some of it looks like Angkor Wat. On a much smaller scale, but the look of the buildings and the carvings is just like Angkor."

"Khmer? That's impossible! Come on, Aloysious, the Cambodians never got that far north. They never built temple complexes in North Thailand."

"They did," Aloysious said simply and with conviction. "I saw it and I touched it. And you will see it and touch it." As he said this he shook his finger in Harry's face, then relaxed and leaned his back against the wall. "I have thought about it a lot. I don't think that what they built on that hill up north was just a temple complex. It was more like an outpost. Maybe the farthest outpost on the edge of the Khmer empire. Think of it, Harry, a thousand years ago the Khmer reached the pinnacle of their civilization around Angkor Wat. Way up north, where they built this place – the place I found – there was nothing then. There couldn't have been any kind of civilization up there, even by 11th-century standards. What the Khmer would have found there were barbarians, and probably very few of them. They must have known of the Chinese to the north. And I think that was the main reason the city got built up on that hill. I think it was an outpost of the Khmer empire built to trade with the North. Maybe it was Angkor Wat's eyes and ears into China."

Harry must have looked at least a little skeptical. Aloysious held up his hand. "There is a lot to learn about the place. I don't know all the answers. In fact, I'm not sure I know any of the answers. But you'll understand what I'm talking about when you get up there and get a look at it."

Aloysious looked at his watch. "If we move, we can still get underway tonight. I should say – if *you* move, Harry. You're going to have to do most of what needs to be done. I can't fly up north. I guess the police are still looking for me. I would never get through the airport. You'll have to get a car. Jean Lee has all kinds of cars. He'll probably be glad to let you use one."

"Look, if this thing – this problem where the canal swallowed your car.... If that was a simple misunderstanding, can't you let the cops know you are alive and well? It would certainly simplify matters. Make it a lot easier for us to get around."

"No, absolutely not!"

"All right, all right. Just thought I'd check. I'll go see Jean Lee. He'll be glad to know you're okay."

"Christ, don't tell him. Don't tell anyone."

"Why not? What about Tosh?"

"Especially not Tosh. Don't tell her anything."

"Great. She'll think I fell in the Klong too." Harry shook his head. "Okay, Aloysious, I'll go along with that. But you are not making this easy. Why don't you pack us a picnic basket while I see if I can sweet-talk Jean Lee out of one of his many cars?"

Harry found Jean Lee not only most generous with his cars, but also ready to accept his story without any question. He told Jean Lee that he had a lead to Aloysious in the North that could require visiting a number of places outside the city of Chiang Mai. It would facilitate matters if he had a car. Jean Lee saw the point of that, nodded, and handed over the keys to a shiny BMW 735i. It was a magnificent machine, completely black inside and out. The windows were tinted a dark bronze that kept anyone from seeing inside the car. Harry slipped behind the wheel to familiarize himself with the switches. When he turned to tell Jean Lee not to worry, that he would take care of the car, Jean Lee said only, "Don't worry about the car. Just find Aloysious."

Harry spent the next two hours in a parking garage in a Bangkok shopping center. It had already been dark for an hour when he started out for New Road a little after 7:00 o'clock. Aloysious had said not to try to pick him up until about 7:30 that evening. By then the evening rush hour would have almost exhausted itself, and the roads out of Bangkok would be more drivable.

At 7:30 sharp, Harry pulled into a small alley off New Road 50 meters down from Hu Lai Wang's antique shop. He stopped and turned off the lights. There was a sudden blur of movement off to the side. The passenger door was pulled open and Aloysious piled inside, in one continuous smooth move, despite having his arms locked around a small overnight bag and a much larger wicker basket. He flung the bag into the back seat, but clung to the basket.

"To the North, James, to the North." Aloysious looked around and whooped. "Wow," he said. "This is one fancy vehicle. I didn't know you and Jean Lee were so close." With one hand still on the basket, Aloysious used the other to start pushing all buttons within reach. The sunroof opened, his seat moved back and forth, and the stereo flashed lights as it turned itself on and off.

"Jean Lee wouldn't have given it to me if it hadn't been for you. Says he's going to bill the car to you once I find you. Or bill your estate if I don't."

"Ha ha. Let him bill my estate. If he gets anything, we'll split it."

Aloysious still had the wicker basket balanced on his knees. "What the hell's that?" Harry asked. "Why don't you throw it in the back?"

"It's our picnic basket. You said to bring one." Aloysious opened it and started poking around inside. "Let's see, we got hot and sour pork tongue. Got some calf innards with bean sprouts and fish brain. Got some nice oyster dumplings. What will you have, sir?"

"Doesn't sound very exciting. I think I'll pass."

"Good. More for me. How about a beer?"

"I'm driving – if you haven't noticed."

"Too bad. I'll drink yours and mine, too."

In moments Aloysious had a couple of beer cans open and a bowl of American-style potato chips perched precariously on the dashboard. All Harry could make out in the wicker basket were beer cans. As he started driving slowly down New Road, Harry turned down the dash lights. In the dim red-tinted glow that remained, Aloysious looked content and completely at home, as if he had been lounging in that black leather seat for hours. He managed to get the car's stereo system to do what he wanted, and one of Jean Lee's classical disks now played softly in the background. Aloysious took a deep drink from one beer can, set it into the car's beverage holder, and took a sip from the second can.

"This is the way to go," he said. "A nice car, a good driver – you are a good driver, aren't you, Harry? And a fine meal at hand." With these last words he scooped up a fistful of potato chips and crammed them into his mouth. He raised his beer can in a toast at Harry.

Harry could not help grinning. He knew that Aloysious meant what he said, at least when it came to the part about the beer. Aloysious liked beer. He drank prodigious quantities of it, and never with any apparent effect on his physical coordination or mental agility. It was true that in the last few years Aloysious's girth had increased slowly but steadily. Half an inch a year, and maybe less than that. When this phenomenon was once pointed out to him, Aloysious attributed it to age, simple age, and nothing more.

On the superhighway leading out of Bangkok, Harry started to settle into the rhythm of driving. Here it was easy. Visibility was good, and the four-lane divided highway made it easy to pass the overloaded trucks and buses that strained their way north. Beyond the superhighway, on the main road heading north, driving would be difficult and dangerous. There the road narrowed to two undivided lanes, and drivers of faster vehicles easily became impatient behind the slower moving cargo carriers. When one lunged into the oncoming lane to get around a slow vehicle, a second would often join in, and two cars or maybe two buses in tandem would try to race around a vehicle in the same lane. An oncoming driver would suddenly be confronted by three sets of headlights where there should only have been one, and coming right at him. Bus crashes with high fatality rates were not uncommon.

Harry glanced at the clock on the dash. Normally it was a ten-hour drive to the North. With this sleek black machine he was sure his time would be well below that. He glanced over at Aloysious. "Well, if we don't get run over by any buses, we should get into Chiang Mai at about 4 A.M. I don't suppose you have a place where we'll hunker down and get some rest for our weary bodies?"

"Your weary body, Harry. I'm going to get some sleep right here. Somebody has to be well rested when we get there. Once we get just outside the city, I'll show you which way to go. This fine machine is too conspicuous to navigate around the boondocks. If I can make a quick connection in Chiang Mai, we can stash the car and head for the hills in something more appropriate – like an oxcart. You a qualified oxcart driver, Harry?"

Harry did not bother to answer, and they drove on in a comfortable silence. Aloysious finally broke it.

"Did you wonder why I called you? Why I got you involved in this?"

"Figured you needed a good driver," Harry answered.

"No, really."

"Then it must be my winning way."

"Harry," Aloysious said admonishingly, "you're not being serious. I called you for one reason. This is big stuff. Lost cities. Khmer temples. Here we are, charging up to the North in a BMW. This is the big time,

Harry, and I had to choose carefully. I chose you, because you are the only man I know who can sit there watching the road, and not make a move on my potato chips. I mean, that is heroic. That is the quality I see in you, Harry."

Harry twisted the steering wheel quickly to the right and then back hard to the left. Aloysious said, "Oh, shit," as the beer sloshed over his leg. "Jean Lee is not going to like this thing smelling like the inside of a beer keg. Although that may not be a bad thing. Hey, Harry, do you remember the day we tried to drive up the coast from Danang? We spilled a lot of beer that day."

You spilled the beer. I held on to mine," Harry answered. Aloysious's words had brought him a quick flashback of an incident he had not thought of in years. He saw the rice paddies again spinning around him as their jeep left the road and started to roll over. The jeep's left front end had been blown away by a mine.

When the jeep stopped rolling, their Vietnamese driver lay silent, pinned under the wreckage. Aloysious emerged crawling from the tall grass alongside the road. He was sopping wet, drenched by a deluge of locally made "33" beer when his two cases of litre bottles disintegrated in the crash. Harry was on his feet, casually holding on to the bottle of beer he had opened just as the jeep went over. He was not aware then of the bottle in his hand, or that he drank from it as they walked around the wreckage. But it made a big impression on Aloysious.

"That was something else," Aloysious said, remembering. "You held on to your beer through a land mine explosion and a crash. That was cool. I always held that up as an outstanding example of cool to the young troops. Of course, the young troops figured anybody that cool has to be first-class bat shit. Maybe they weren't so far wrong."

Aloysious watched Harry out of the corner of his eye. When it looked like Harry had nothing to say about it, Aloysious settled back. "Those were the good old days," he said. "Like you, I'm old and wretched now. I'm going to turn on some of Jean Lee's nice music and go to sleep. Try not to hit any bumps. I'll see you in the morning."

"Good night, Aloysious," Harry said and turned the dash lights off. It was easier to see what was happening outside. The traffic was light, and he felt alert and alive. The jet lag that had troubled him yesterday had not made an appearance, and he did not expect it to. Yesterday he was bored and middle-aged. Today he was an adventurer. Mature, perhaps, or better yet, experienced. But an adventurer still. There were lost cities, by God. Maybe there always would be while there were men like Aloysious P. Grant.

Not Aloysious P. Grant, Harry corrected himself. Aloysious. Always Aloysious and only Aloysious. No one ever called him anything else. No one ever called him just 'Grant', even in the military where that was the common practice. Certainly no one ever dared call him Al, not to his face. The 'P' was for Patrick as far as Harry knew, but no one even thought of calling him Pat. Or, God forbid, A. Patrick Grant. Or Mister Grant. Aloysious was Aloysious. On some men the name would have seemed silly. On Aloysious it seemed to fit and set him apart from everybody else – at least everybody else whom Harry had ever met.

Aloysious, who was reasonably fluent in French and had a good command of written French, had once written for a magazine in Paris. When Vietnam ended and Harry went off to knock around Asia, Aloysious headed to Europe. Years later, Aloysious reappeared in Bangkok. He had made a name for himself in European circles as an expert on Indochina. He dabbled in art and got involved in business deals. Somewhere along the line he became a collector. Some people began to look on him as a connoisseur of the art of ancient Southeast Asia. Harry had known Aloysious too long not to recognize his limitations – in art and in other things. But in many ways, Aloysious had been the inspiration for Harry's plunge into the art business with the Happy Dragon.

"But who the hell would have thought it would come to this?" Harry said it to himself, but perhaps a little too loudly. Next to him, Aloysious P. Grant mumbled something in his sleep. It was one word, and it sounded like "Siva."

6

The pop of a beer can top signaled Aloysious's return to consciousness. The almost complete silence in the BMW's cabin, and the fact that Aloysious had positioned the can directly behind Harry's ear before he pulled the tab caused the car to swerve satisfyingly as Harry was jolted out of his reverie.

"Christ!" Harry half shouted. "Don't do that."

"Morning," Aloysious said. "I was just checking your hearing. You still hear good." After peering through the dark glass of the BMW's windows into the blackness outside, Aloysious fumbled around and finally found the button that lowered the window. The wind that whipped through the cabin was a lot colder than either expected.

"Get that window back up," Harry yelled. "Potato chips are blowing all over the back of the car."

"I can't see where we are. Where the hell are we? Don't drive so fast." Aloysious hung his head out the window. There was nothing that could be seen in the headlights except the black ribbon of road and dense vegetation on either side.

"I think we're about 40 minutes out of Chiang Mai," Harry shouted.

After another half minute Aloysious pulled his head back inside and closed the window. "I know where we are," he said. "In another ten minutes we'll turn off. I'll tell you when to turn."

They drove on in silence. There was nothing to be seen outside. Nothing on the road and nothing off to the side. They could have been in an airplane at 40,000 feet. Harry turned up the dash lights and glanced at his watch. It was a bit after 3 A.M. He looked quickly at Aloysious, who seemed to be staring out beyond the range of the headlights. How could he know where they were? Just bluffing, Harry thought.

"Slow down," Aloysious said quietly, almost whispering. "About another hundred meters, turn right. You'll see a small lane in the bushes. Just before you start to turn into the lane, turn off all your lights."

"Turn off my lights? I can't see anything out there now."

"I'll tell you when. Now! Cut your lights! Turn! Turn!"

Just before the lights went out, Harry caught a glimpse of the lane and what looked like a grove of small trees on either side. He pulled the wheel hard to the right. Whether they went through the trees or over them he did not want to know. The thuds, bumps, and screeches that accompanied their passage were bad enough. The vision of Jean Lee getting his first glimpse of his beautiful black car after this trip brought acid pouring into Harry's stomach.

"Damn! You are going to have to be quieter than that, Harry. Watch the log!"

Harry brought the car to a stop. He saw nothing.

"Shhh. Let's sit here for a minute. See if we disturbed anybody." Aloysious was actually whispering.

It was still an hour or more before the first light of dawn, but, sitting there, Harry started to make out shapes. Not that it helped much – the shapes were all trees and bushes. He had no idea where they were. Presumably Aloysious did.

After they sat in silence for several minutes, Aloysious spoke. Very quietly and very deliberately he said, "When I tell you, I want you to start the engine very quietly. No lights. No sound. We want to drive about a hundred meters straight ahead. Can you see the road?" When Harry indicated with an affirmative grunt that he could, Aloysious continued.

"After about a hundred meters, the road starts downhill, just slightly. When you get there, cut off the engine and we can drift the rest of the way, maybe another 200 meters down. I'll tell you when to stop. I'll get out of the car. I want you to stay in it – and be ready to pull out fast. Any questions?"

"Sure... but I know you won't answer them."

"You're learning, Harry. Synchronize your watch if it will make you feel better. If you need to pee, it's too bad but you'll have to wait until we're out of here."

When Harry started to say that peeing now sounded like a good idea, Aloysious raised his hand and shook his head. "Radio silence," he said. Then he looked out the back and off to both sides. "Okay. Here we go. Start your engine."

The car started quickly and quietly. Harry got it moving very slowly down the road. His eyes now were more attuned to what was outside, and he had little difficulty following the dirt lane that was somehow not as black as the brush and the trees that grew along its sides. Aloysious nudged his elbow, whispering, "Lower all windows. Switch off the overhead light so it won't flash on when I open the door." Harry did as he was told.

"Cut the engine."

Harry did. The car continued to roll forward. "Shit," he said, realizing that the power steering was also off now, and that it suddenly took effort to turn the wheel.

"Steady as she goes, Captain," Aloysious advised.

It was eerie now, moving through the darkness. Through the open windows he could hear only the slightest rustling of the tires on the lane as they rolled slowly down what must have been a very modest incline.

"Stop."

Harry used the hand brake to bring the car to a stop to avoid turning on the brake lights. They sat in silence. "Looks pretty good," Aloysious whispered. Harry felt silly about whispering and did not answer. "Here I go," Aloysious said and slowly opened the door. There was a tiny screech of metal, and Harry could only think, Oh, God, we bent the doors going through the trees. From out of the blackness came Aloysious's whispered words: "Be ready. Stay prepared."

Harry sat for what seemed like an hour. It was probably more like ten minutes. Nothing was happening. The indistinct black shapes outside remained indistinct as he continued to stare at them, but started to look more and more ominous. Something had been bothering him since they stopped here, and it suddenly struck him what it was. There were no sounds. No dogs barking. There were always dogs somewhere. Where there were people, where there was a village, there were always dogs – and they were always barking. A thought flashed by him: Aloysious can charm the dogs. But as soon as he thought that, he knew he was wrong.

The first bark was tentative, a high-pitched interrogative yelp with no conviction behind it. There was silence again for a brief moment, and then a barrage of responding barks from what must have been at least 50 dogs in earshot of the first. There was no real enthusiasm in any of the barks and they soon died out.

Silence returned, and it was complete. Harry felt more confident now, and was just starting to congratulate himself and Aloysious when it happened. It was hard to hear. From somewhere, not very far away, came a dull thud. This was followed by a second thud, then a third. Then came the tinkle of breaking glass. There was a pause. It was a moment of absolute silence as though the world waited for what would come next. It came. Aloysious in his deepest and loudest voice, singing, "When the moon hits your eye like a big pizza pie - that's amore...."

How much more of the song Aloysious knew, Harry was not to find out. Aloysious's voice was overpowered by the fury of a hundred dogs screaming outrage at this disturbance of their sleep and the peace of their village. Human voices joined in, calling to one another. Lights flashed on. Several were very close to the car. Harry suddenly realized that some of the indistinct forms he had been staring at were not trees, but small village houses. Above the din, Harry heard a female voice shouting, "Aloysious, Aloysious."

Lights went on not five feet from Harry's face. It was a bedroom, a woman's bedroom. Harry watched in fascination as the woman pulled a shawl around her shoulders and peered out the window. She was looking directly at him, but not seeing him in the darkness.

"Turn your headlights on. Turn your headlights on." It was Aloysious, and not very far off. Harry flicked on the headlights and the woman in the window screamed as she dropped out of sight below the windowsill.

The dogs barked louder and more furiously. Harry flashed the high beams. The light picked up Aloysious running hard, hand-in-hand with a young woman who seemed to be wearing a kind of nightshirt. A dozen very angry dogs were in hot pursuit, and behind them Harry caught a glimpse of two-legged pursuers carrying what he hoped were only sticks.

"Get her started, Harry." Aloysious yelled as he ran. "Let's get the hell out of here." As Aloysious reached the car, he stopped dead, made an exaggerated bow and opened the rear door for the young woman.

"Harry," he said, conversationally, "I would like you to meet Ting."

Ting flashed him a beautiful smile as she slid into the backseat. "I am so pleased to meet you, Khun Harry. Aloysious told me so much about you."

Harry tried to return the smile, but he was getting very preoccupied trying to help Aloysious through the door. The boldest of the dog pack had a mouthful of Aloysious's trouser leg and defied Aloysious's best efforts to shake him off. Aloysious leaned back on the car seat and put all his strength into a final kick. Harry could hear the trouser leg tear.

"Spin her around and let's get out of here," Aloysious shouted. Harry did just that. He pressed the pedal to the floor and spun the steering wheel. The car responded beautifully. Spinning on its own axis, it struck the screaming woman's house only lightly before Harry straightened it out and aimed it back the way they came.

Behind them, the running figures were too far for the sticks and rocks they threw to reach the car. Somehow in the confusion, the bold yellow cur that still held the best part of Aloysious's trouser leg in his teeth had landed on the hood of the car. It stared belligerently through the windshield at Harry and Aloysious. As Harry picked up speed, the look on the dog's face turned from fury to concern, and then to surprise as his running feet moved faster and faster to keep his balance. Then he was gone.

By the time they reached the main road, Aloysious had two beers open. This time Harry took one. Aloysious leaned over the back of his seat.

"I don't have any Coke, Ting. Mr. Harry said I could only bring beer."

"It's okay, Aloysious. I don't need anything. I am just happy you came to see me. And brought Mr. Harry, too." Harry could see her smiling in the mirror. She was young and pretty, and sat with her legs pulled up on the seat, covered demurely by her nightshirt.

Outside, it was starting to get light. Aloysious had found a Bach disk and, except for the beer smell, the world inside Jean Lee's BMW was civilized again. When it seemed the girl must have dozed off, Harry said in his best conversational tone, "What the hell was all that about?"

"What was all what about?"

"The attack on the village we just participated in."

"Oh, that. It's Ting's father...her stepfather, really. He doesn't like me to come around when he's there. I knew he would be there tonight."

"Having witnessed how you make your visits, I can understand the man's feelings."

"Shit, if the window hadn't broken we could have been in and out and no one would have known."

"You don't think they would have noticed the singing?"

"That was a diversion, Harry. Nobody up here expects to hear somebody singing an American classic. It was the surprise factor I was aiming for."

Harry gave up. "You surprised them all right. Okay, so what now? We'll be in Chiang Mai soon. Do we attack the city? What about Ting? Are we kidnapping her?"

"Harry, you worry too much," Aloysious said. In a reassuring tone he added, "There is absolutely nothing to worry about. I have a plan." He glanced at his wristwatch. "In fact, we are following that plan now, and we are right on schedule. Ting has a girlfriend who lives at the edge of town. We'll trade this heap for some less conspicuous transport. Maybe get some rest. How you holding up?"

The question surprised Harry. He had had a long day and had driven all night. Despite that he felt great.

"Don't worry about me, Aloysious. A young guy like me is still vital. An old guy like you probably needs his sleep. You can rack out when we get there. I'll stand watch. Just like the old days.

7

Half an hour later Harry was not feeling quite so great. "Oh, God," he mumbled in despair as he walked around the BMW. Its sleek black surface was no longer pristine as it had been only ten hours earlier. There were deep scratches along both sides of the car. The paint on the hood bore a hundred tiny, almost invisible scratches where the bold yellow dog had scrambled frantically for a foothold before disappearing into the night.

"Oh geez," he said, and his hand went up to support his forehead when he saw the dent in the rear fender where it had grazed the house. How was he going to explain this to Jean Lee?

He looked over his shoulder to where Aloysious stood in the doorway of the house. They had pulled into the compound only minutes earlier. The house was a long three-story concrete rectangle. Like many houses in Thailand, it was almost hidden behind a tall cement block wall that surrounded the property on all four sides. According to Aloysious, it belonged to the parents of one of Ting's friends.

It was apparent that Aloysious was known here. When they arrived, Harry stopped the car in front of the steel gate that barred the way into the compound. He hooted. An eye peered at them through a narrow slit, but nothing happened. Then Aloysious leaned out the window and shouted, "Hey, man, it's me," and the gate opened without further hesitation.

"Hey, Harry," Aloysious called, "come here. I want you to meet somebody." By the time Harry was halfway to the house, Aloysious was already walking toward him, with a Thai man and woman in tow. Both were smiling broadly, as if meeting Harry would indeed be pleasant. Following behind were Ting and a second and equally lovely young Thai woman.

"Harry, this is Khun Sompong and his wife Khun Noi." Turning to Sompong and Noi, Aloysious began speaking in Thai, going through a formal introduction. Aloysious's accent sounded strange, and his Thai was not great, but Harry could understand him. Harry responded to the introduction in Thai, which pleased Sompong and Noi greatly. They welcomed Harry to their home, and complimented him on the fluency of his Thai. Then Sompong took Harry by the arm and started to lead him to the house. He continued to speak in Thai.

"I have known Aloysious for many years and anyone who is his friend is always welcome in my house." Sompong pronounced Aloysious's name in the Thai way, Alo-witchet, where the final "s" in a Thai word becomes a "t." Sompong started to say how great a friend Alo-witchet was, when Aloysious came alongside and interrupted.

"Sompong," he said, "slow down. I still have to introduce Harry to a very important person. Harry, this is Ting's very good friend, Tong."

Harry could not believe it. It was hard not to grin out the side of his mouth. "Tong?" He said, looking Aloysious right in the eye. "Ting's friend, Tong?"

"Yes," Aloysious replied, "a young lady as lovely as her name. A name, Harry, that you may recall means 'gold'."

"Of course," Harry said, and now he felt bad. He turned to the young lady who was already bowing, her hands held together before her face in the graceful, traditional "wai." Harry greeted her in his most formal and polite Thai to make up for any boorishness she may have detected in his manner. Tong responded in English, which Harry knew was considerably better than his Thai.

"Khun Harry, my parents and I are very pleased to have you here. Khun Aloysious has told us very much about you. I think he is most fortunate to have you for a friend. We do not have much time now. My parents and Ting and I have to be on our way. Tonight we will have dinner together before you and Khun Aloysious must leave again."

Sompong at this point was backing an aged but shiny white Mercedes from the garage that appeared to take up half of the front part of the ground floor of the house. Noi was already seated beside her husband. Ting waved a quick farewell and got into the car behind her father, while Tong climbed in the other side.

"Ting and Tong," Harry said. "What a remarkable combination. What lovely girls."

"Come on, Harry. We got work to do." Aloysious got behind the wheel of Jean Lee's BMW and slowly drove it through the door of the garage. Inside, the car almost dropped from view. The garage was deep and could easily have held three vehicles parked end to end. The young Thai who was gate guard or gardener was already tugging on a huge folded canvas.

"Give him a hand, Harry," Aloysious shouted from inside the car. "Be with you as soon as I get my beer together."

The canvas was heavy and hard to manage. When Aloysious joined them, he took one side of the canvas and dragged it up over the top of the car. "We have to get this heap out of sight," he said. "A lot of people walk in and out of Sompong's compound. They don't need to see what's back here."

Harry winced as the stiff canvas slid over the surface of Jean Lee's BMW. In the end, he thought, what did a few more scratches matter? Aloysious stepped back to admire their work, and walked completely around the car. "Well," he said, "it looks good. Nobody will know if it's a BMW or a pickup truck."

The gate guard laughed. "Pickup," he said, pointing at the BMW, "pickup." He stuck his thumb in the air, approving the concealment.

"How about him?" Harry asked, gesturing toward the guard with his chin.

"No problem," Aloysious replied. "He's an old family retainer. At least as trustworthy as you. Grab some beer. It's time for bed. Sompong has given us the whole top floor. There's ice up there, and more beer if we need it."

They walked through the ground floor of the house and up to the third floor by a staircase at the back of the building. On the third floor they found two large rooms, a sitting room at the front, and a large bedroom with an attached bath at the rear.

While Harry looked around the room, Aloysious concentrated on the refrigerator. "You can shower first," he said to Harry. "I have to make sure we have enough beer."

"Where did everybody go?"

"To town, to pick up our transport for tonight. You better get some sleep. We have a long drive ahead of us. I want to get started right after dark tonight. How are you feeling?"

"Fine right now, but I do need sleep," Harry said, and then felt like he had made the understatement of the year. "Wow," he added, rubbing the back of his neck. "I am starting to feel it now. I guess I better rack out if I'm going to run that ox cart tonight."

"You'll have it easy tonight. Ting-Tong can handle some of the driving."

"Ting and Tong? We're taking the girls? I thought this was a serious expedition."

"We are taking them all the way. And it is serious." Aloysious stopped stacking beer cans in the refrigerator. He poked around, found a cold can of beer, and tossed it to Harry. "Here. Have a drink. You'll sleep better."

Harry snagged the beer can just before it passed over his shoulder. Aloysious had an open beer in his hand and sat down on the edge of the bed facing Harry. Harry sensed the time was right to get at least a couple of answers from Aloysious.

"Tell me about the girls," he said. "Ting and Tong." He tipped the can back and took a long drink. "You know, I find it hard to believe the girls had those names before you came along."

"Well, they did. Ting-Tong. A matched pair. They're also my business partners."

"Business partners! I compliment your taste in partners." Harry raised his beer can. "What kind of business do you guys do?"

"We have a company."

"What kind of company?"

"A tour company. It's called 'Pachyderm Tours'. Our motto is: 'Walk the Way of the Elephant'."

Harry could not help it. He started to laugh and spilled beer on the bed.

"What the hell's so funny?"

"I'm sorry. I guess I'm tired. I knew there was something familiar about that strange walk you have. Now I know how you walk. Some of your tourists are going to have a hell of a time trying to walk like an elephant."

"That's not what it means, Harry." Aloysious saw nothing funny about this. "We do a lot of walking tours. Into tribal areas. It means you walk where the elephant walks."

"Aloysious, I'm sorry. I know what you mean. Tell me about the business. Where do Ting and Tong come in?"

"Well, I've always considered this very personal, Harry. I knew Ting's father. He was a Royal Thai Army officer when I was still writing for the French magazines. He got to be a good friend. During one of those mini border hassles...what was it, 15, 20 years ago? He stepped on a mine. Ting was just a kid. Her father had nothing to leave her. Her mother had nothing. I helped take care of the two of them for a while. Ting made it through school. By the time she was ready for college, her mother remarried. The new husband wouldn't give anything to Ting. He wanted her to work. I paid for her university studies."

Aloysious took a long pull from the beer can before continuing. "Ting studied business management. When she graduated, I decided to use her talent and a little money I had saved to start a business. Pachyderm Tours was born. Ting is the manager. Tong is chief tour guide. Ting-Tong were kids together. They went all the way through the university together. I am the chief stockholder and occasional tour guide. We take tourists on walking tours into the mountains. It's a low-budget operation. We have a Landrover, an old minibus, and a one-room office in Chiang Mai."

"I'm impressed, Aloysious. I never looked on you as a philanthropist."

"I'm not. I'm looking out for myself. Look at you. You're all set up. You have a business, buying and selling art. I have to start looking out for myself. I'm getting old, Harry. You're getting old, too. I know you don't see so good anymore. And I don't think you hear too good, either. And look how your chin's starting to sag."

"I think that's because I'm falling asleep," Harry said, and leaned further back on the bed. "I'll see you tonight." His last words were mumbled. The last thing he heard as he drifted off into sleep was Aloysious saying,

"We both got to make some money for our old age."

Several hours later, when Harry opened his eyes again, it was dark. Someone had thrown a light blanket over him and removed the beer can he had fallen asleep with. When he turned on the light, he found on the small table next to the bed a pile of fresh clothing, camouflage fatigues and forest green underwear.

"Hey, sleeping beauty. Time to rise. Dinner in 15 minutes." Aloysious, dressed in camouflage, was in the door for only a moment and then he was gone. Harry started out of bed. He seemed to creak when he moved, and felt like he needed another 24 hours of sleep.

When he got downstairs, he found the food was already on the way to the table. Sompong sat at its head and waved Harry next to him and across from Aloysious. Ting and Tong shuttled dishes to the table before taking their places. Noi appeared last with a steaming bowl of rice and took her chair at the end of the table opposite Sompong.

The food was good, and so was the talk. Sompong had been an NCO under Ting's father. He and Aloysious had known each other for years and had a lot of war stories to share. Ting and Tong proved to be everything he expected. They were not only lovely, but bright, well informed, and articulate. If Pachyderm Tours was not successful, it would not be for any lack of business acumen or common sense. Behind those sparkling dark eyes were minds that were quick and determined.

No one was eager for dinner to be over, and even Noi sipped at a glass of cognac at the end. Aloysious finally announced that it was time to go. "Okay, girls. Get yourselves ready. We mount up in ten minutes. Harry, you better go pee now."

The girls helped Noi clear the table. Sompong and Aloysious stepped outside. Harry went upstairs to get his things. When he went out into the compound a few minutes later, he found Sompong and Aloysious standing by a Landrover painted in camouflage. On its door, between the words "Pachyderm Tours" was the charging bull elephant he had first seen emblazoned across the front of Aloysious's T-shirt the night before. It struck him then that it was only yesterday that he was in Bangkok. That seemed like weeks ago.

"Like it?" Aloysious asked.

"I do." Harry hesitated, but then added, "The elephant – it's African."

Aloysious shrugged. "We already had that design. It was cheaper than new art work."

Ting and Tong appeared, both in camouflage suits. "Everything is stowed on board, Mr. Harry," Ting said. "We are ready to go."

Tong walked over to the driver's door. "I will drive the first hour," she said. "Mr. Harry, you and Aloysious can get in back. There is beer on ice."

Aloysious had two beers open before they pulled clear of the compound. He flipped one to Harry and said, "Welcome to the Pachyderm

Tours expedition to the lost city, Mr. Harry. Your tour guides are here to serve you. We promise you a thrilling time." Then Aloysious cupped his hands in front of his mouth. He shouted, almost directly in Harry's ear, "Pachyderm Tours. Walk the way of the elephant. Pachyderm Tours. A class act."

Up front the girls giggled.

8

Aloysious got to his feet slowly, arms stretched out at his sides as if hanging on to invisible wires to keep his balance. His body swayed to one side, then to the other. With no warning he was abruptly jerked forward. Fifty feet back, Harry watched. He was certain that in the next instant Aloysious would be tipped from his perch to bounce on the trail just once before plunging to the rocky creek bed hundreds of feet below.

Aloysious found a rhythm where Harry could see none. He was fully upright now. His body rolled and swayed in harmony with the gait of the walking elephant. The ornate teak chair he stood on was strapped to the back of the beast. It pitched and bobbed like a small boat in a heavy sea. Aloysious raised his arms high and threw back his head. His victory cry was vintage Tarzan. Birds scattered as it echoed across the hills. There was a brief return to silence and peace. Then it was shattered again by the announcement Aloysious shouted over the head of the elephant: "Pachyderm Tours walks the way of the elephant. By appointment only!"

Harry could hear the answering giggles of Ting and Tong who were perched on the third elephant somewhere just behind him.

"Hey, Harry!" Aloysious had turned around completely on the chair to face him. "Like that touch? 'By appointment only!' Wouldn't that make a great TV commercial?"

Clinging to the chair on the bouncing back of the great gray beast he rode, Harry continued to watch with fascination. No one could stand on a "howdah," the chair that served as a saddle atop an elephant – not on a trail as rough as this. Finally, when nothing dramatic happened, he shouted back, "It would be more impressive if you fell off for a finale."

Aloysious responded to this taunt by jumping up and down on the chair. It was his imitation of a tribal dance. It almost undid him. The elephant, patience totally exhausted, stopped dead in its tracks. Aloysious saved himself from rolling over the unhappy beast's head only by sitting down quickly. It was more a crash than a sit, and Harry winced at the thud Aloysious made when he hit the chair.

Aloysious grasped the side of the chair and held tight. This was fortuitous. The elephant decided to rock from side to side, usually an effective maneuver, intended to shake Aloysious, chair and all, off his back. Over the snorts that accompanied the elephant's efforts, Aloysious's voice could be heard.

"Oh, shit! Where's the driver of this rig?"

There were giggles from Ting and Tong. Then what looked like an undersized ten-year old ran around Harry's elephant toward the scene of impending disaster. Soon after leaving the Karen village, the mahouts had dismounted and ambled along behind. The hustling youth, a Karen teenager who had probably grown up with the elephant, brandished a long switch cut from a tree. A few well-placed hits on the elephant's ear, some well-chosen Karen threats, and order was quickly restored.

Looking sheepish, Aloysious dismounted with more speed than grace. He walked away from the offended elephant and back toward Harry.

"The man says I have to ride up there with you now, Harry. Make room."

Harry grabbed one of Aloysious's outstretched arms and pulled. Another Karen mahout pushed from behind. Finally aboard and seated alongside Harry, Aloysious tried to explain.

"It's this heat. You never know when an elephant will go completely batshit. I should have better sense than to name Pachyderm Tours after such an unpredictable animal."

Harry was half listening. From where he sat he could see nothing but hills. Hills in front, hills behind. Nothing but more hills. "How far do we have to go on these springless wonders?" he asked.

"Not too far as the crow flies. Maybe three or four hours as the elephant walks."

"Wonderful," Harry said. The pain in his butt instantly grew worse. His fingers burned, rubbed raw from hanging onto the chair. It was going to be a long day.

The day had started well enough. The night ride in the Land Rover had been far more pleasant and comfortable than he appreciated until now. He and Aloysious had spent most of the evening in the back of the Rover with the beer. Ting and Tong alternated driving and tour-hostess chores. Like all Thais, they started a journey well prepared for any famine they might encounter en route. Fried chicken, pork ribs, highly spiced creatures from the sea. There were Thai sweets made of coconut and rice that many Westerners found too sweet. Harry loved them.

They drove and ate their way through the night. Ting and Tong told tourist stories and giggled. It was a moving feast. Toward morning, Aloysious took the wheel. It was time, he said, for serious work to begin.

It was still dark when Aloysious turned the Rover off on a faint trail that grew even fainter as it led deeper into the bush. When the trail seemed about to disappear completely, they emerged into a clearing on the edge of a village. Aloysious turned off the headlights and said to hunker down and wait for first light.

"Karen people," Tong whispered to Harry, identifying the village as belonging to one of the six major tribal groups scattered over this part of Northern Thailand. Their dwellings were small and simple, more huts than houses that crouched low among the gray morning mists.

Dawn arrived almost imperceptibly. With the first faint light came movement in the village. Harry watched in disbelief as a mound of jungle – bigger than the house next to it – started to move and roll back and forth. He held his breath. Then Aloysious said, "Look at the elephant over there. Finally getting up. Lazy bugger." Harry relaxed again.

Minutes later, it seemed, the village was full of life. Aloysious decided it was time to leave the Land Rover and walk to the village headman's house. The villagers who noticed them seemed wholly unconcerned by their presence. Some greeted Aloysious by name. By the time they reached their destination, they had an escort. A dozen Karen children followed behind, quietly at first. By the end of the walk they were chanting, "A-lo-wi-chit, A-lo-wi-chit, A-lo-wi-chit."

At first Aloysious pretended not to hear. The chants grew louder and more insistent. Finally he stopped. In dismay, he threw his hands in the air. Slowly, dramatically, he turned around. He looked down at the children grouped before him, and shook his head slowly. Then, in English, he addressed them. "Okay, gang. You win. First I see the Chief. Then we have the market."

The response was immediate. A loud prolonged cheer rose from the little people, then they were gone, running in all directions.

The meeting with the Chief was friendly but formal and brief. Aloysious asked for three elephants and three mahouts. For Harry's benefit, Aloysious explained that he was fully capable of driving his own elephant. But he knew the Chief would not release an elephant without a driver.

At this the Chief smiled, raised his hand with his thumb pointing up, and said, "Alo-wichit. Number one elephant driver."

From the Chief's house they walked back to the center of the village. Harry could see the children starting to gather around mats they had laid out on the ground. Their excitement was easy to see, even from a distance.

"Market time," Aloysious explained. "All the kids want to be salesmen. They don't get a lot of practice. Not many customers come this way. Pachyderm Tours gets treated pretty good up here, so we try to help out."

Aloysious knelt down on one of the mats. "Let's see what you got there, kid," he said. The children started to lay their wares before him. The merchandise was not very exciting. There was not much of it, but each kid had something. Most of it was colorful bits of embroidery and small pieces of jewelry made of a tarnished white metal that definitely was not silver.

Aloysious examined every piece carefully, occasionally praising the workmanship. Sometimes he asked for information about a piece. Then he made his selection. Somehow each child had at least one piece under consideration. Aloysious started to bargain. This was a good-natured process, particularly as Aloysious often conceded that a piece was worth more than he first thought it was. At the end, each child had achieved a sale. And Aloysious accumulated a small pile of handicrafts.

Ting knelt down next to Aloysious and started to put the items in a bag. "I will put these in the office," she told him, "with all the rest." She had a small frown on her face.

Aloysious looked up at Harry and shrugged. "It's a tax write-off."

When they started their trek on the elephants, it had seemed like fun. Like earlier-day astronauts, they mounted by climbing a wooden tower and dropping down on to the "howdah" or chair on the elephant's back. Once mounted, they moved regally down the main village road, their teak chairs higher than the roof of the tallest house. At that moment it seemed a swell way to travel.

An hour later it seemed less swell. The chairs creaked and heaved with each ponderous footstep the elephants took on a trail that grew rougher and rougher. Just hanging on to the chair was a challenge. By the second hour Ting and Tong's giggling stopped. By then, the elephants seemed tired and were moving slower. Everyone was tired – everyone except Aloysious. He was bored.

*   *   *   *   *

Three lifetimes after Aloysious joined Harry in his chair, Harry felt their elephant's pace quicken. Aloysious was quiet for once, sitting with his eyes closed. He had also felt the pace pick up, and said a single word: "River."

With this Harry started to revive. The river. The end of the elephant trail. The ordeal would be over and he would survive another of life's little tests.

The elephant started to move even faster. After hours of ambling along in slow motion, it seemed like freeway speed. Harry was enjoying the breeze caused by their passage when they reached a curve in the trail. Just ahead was the bank of the river. They were approaching it at elephant top speed.

Aloysious sensed it, his eyes wide open now. He saw the river and with no further ado started climbing over the back of the chair. "Bail out," he said to Harry, "bail out!," and slid down the elephant's rump.

Harry suddenly understood what was happening. But it was already too late. He got no further than to say "Oh shit!" when the elephant hit the water.

Later Harry would say it had felt good, but he was scared witless when it happened. Not that the elephant got into very deep water, and the warm spray from the elephant's trunk that caught Harry in the face was kind of funny. It was the part where the elephant got on his knees and started to roll over on his back in the mud of the river bottom that made Harry move.

He moved like he had not moved in years. Even then he was almost completely submerged when he finally kicked free of the chair that perversely was now holding him. One moment the elephant's bulk looked over him, in the next he was half standing, half swimming, but still holding tightly to a splintered piece of the chair. The rest of the chair floated in a hundred pieces around him.

Aloysious stood on the bank pointing and laughing. Harry could not hear, but he could see Ting and Tong giggling. A dozen meters away the elephant raised up from his bath just slightly, and looked Harry straight in the eye. Harry knew the elephant was laughing, too.

Later, when he was almost dried out, Harry noticed something that added to his chagrin. He was sitting on the riverbank, drawing circles in the sand for lack of anything more productive to do. Behind him, Aloysious, Ting, and Tong were repacking the loads in their backpacks. As he looked down at the sand, it struck Harry all at once.

"Aloysious, you bastard."

"Que, Senor?" Aloysious looked up with great puzzlement on his face.

"Que nothing. Come here and look at this."

Aloysious ambled over. "What ees bothereeng you, my fren?" Aloysious had terrible Spanish. Harry knew he used his Spanish voice only when there was something to cover up.

"What's this?" Harry asked, pointing straight down.

"Eet is dirt, Senor."

"Not dirt. This. The thing that stretches from here to where you're standing, and goes this way and that way along the bank of the river."

"Oh, you mean the road?"

"Yes, Aloysious, the road."

"Eef you know what eet is, why you ask me?"

"I know what it is. I want to know why it's here. I want to know why we just rode elephants over half of Northern Thailand when there's a road here. We could have driven here in the Land Rover."

"Well, Harry," Aloysious switched to his schoolmaster's voice.

"Certainly we could have driven here, if you really want to be like everyone else. I felt that you probably wanted to know what this part of Northern Thailand is really like. Pachyderm Tours wanted you to enjoy your trip here, and you did, didn't you, Harry? Come on, admit it."

"I sure as hell do not look on what we endured these last few hours as enjoyable. I'll be sore for days, and that damned elephant near killed me."

"Hey, listen. I am sorry if you didn't have a good time, Harry. We did. Look at Ting and Tong over there. A couple of kids, joking, laughing, and having a lot of fun. Tong was just saying that watching you ride that elephant into the river was one of the high points of her young life."

What could he say? Harry sighed instead. "Now that I have seen Pachyderm Tours in operation, I may have to consider other arrangements in the future." He added, "May the rest of this tour be a little less strenuous."

Aloysious clapped him on the shoulder. "From here it's a breeze. A little boat ride, a little walk. Don't worry. It will all be worth it."

Moments later the next stage of the trip started with a roar. A long-tail boat sped down the middle of the river. A great plume of white water rose high in the air behind to attest to its high speed.

With no warning, the boat turned abruptly toward the bank where Harry stood. It roared in straight with no decrease in speed until he started to get concerned for his safety.

At the last possible moment the engine was cut, and the boat slowed to drift silently just offshore. Some 20 feet long and four wide, it was a long-tail boat because of the ten-foot-long propeller shaft that trailed behind the rebuilt Japanese auto engine that powered it. The boat's single occupant stood up and stared silently at Harry. Then the boatman's eyes shifted over Harry's shoulder, and he broke into a smile.

"Alo-wichit. Alo-wichit," the boatman shouted. He pointed at his wristwatch. "I come at exact time. You give me big bonus."

"I give you big kick in ass," Aloysious shouted back.

Harry pulled the boat to the bank while Aloysious and the boatman shook hands and engaged briefly in a greeting rite of mock kickboxing. Aloysious introduced the boatman as "Wit, an important cog in the Pachyderm Tour wheel."

"I am big wheel," Wit added. When he learned that Harry spoke Thai, Wit laughed and said he hoped that Harry could also drive a long-tail boat. According to "Alo-wichit," Harry was the designated driver. Arrangements for this rendezvous had been prearranged by Ting and Tong.

"What are you going to do?" Harry asked Wit.

"I will wait here for two days until you bring the boat of Alo-wichit back here."

Harry picked up the nuance of the Thai phrasing. "Khun Wit," he asked, "why do you call it the boat of Alo-wichit?"

"Because the boat belongs to Alo-wichit. He won it from me playing cards. I like to play cards with Alo-wichit when we travel on the river. Last time he won the boat. The engine is still mine. We will play for the engine next time. Now I will show you how to drive the boat. When you are in the boat, the first lesson is watch the left knee of Alo-wichit. When it moves up and down very quickly, it means his cards are not good."

Wit checked Harry out very quickly. Harry 's boat-handling skills were a little rusty, but handling the long-tail boat was not unlike handling a noisy, oversized outboard. It just took a little more muscle. Ten minutes later Pachyderm Tours was on board and headed for the middle of the river. Wit waved forlornly from the shore.

Settled at the helm, Harry felt in control for the first time in days. It made him feel expansive. "Navigator," he said to Aloysious, "give me a course."

Aloysious pointed upriver. "Go that away, Gridley. Damn the torpedoes, but don't make waves."

The first few kilometers were relaxing. It was much cooler out here than on the riverbank. An occasional spray of water over the bow was refreshing when it brushed their faces. The river was wide where they started, and the banks on either side were flat and almost featureless.

As they moved farther upriver, the banks started to close in and the water grew shallow. In time Harry had to stand up so that he could see to steer a zigzag course around sandbars and other obstructions that emerged from the surface or lurked just below. Ting and Tong were in their best form, passing out food, and ice-cold beer that they had kept somehow in one of the backpacks. Aloysious was content. He sat cross-legged on a mat in the bow of the boat, playing solitaire with Wit's cards and working on two open cans of beer.

The scenery along the banks changed gradually as they moved upstream. The vegetation became more dense. Where at first occasional bare karst hills jutted out of the landscape like solitary tombstones, the hills now started to come more frequently, and stood higher than the ones that preceded them. Then the hills became bigger and more substantial, almost like small mountains that were more tolerant of the foliage crowding their flanks. Farther on, the hills seemed to crowd together, and only the stone faces of the highest ones were visible above a heavy green blanket of trees.

When he had an open stretch of river and could safely take his eyes away from it, Harry would watch the hills and try to imagine what it was like in the dark shadows under the trees. Once, Aloysious caught him at it.

"It's different up here, isn't it? Different from back there. The brush is thicker here. There are more trees, because there's nobody to burn them out or cut them down. Nobody's been here for a long time. Not for many years. In some places maybe not for centuries, maybe never. It's the look of the wild, the look of nature where man has not yet brought his multitudes. Enjoy it, Harry. There's not much of it left."

The river was getting really shallow now, and twice Ting and Tong volunteered to get out into the river and push the boat off a sandbar where it had wedged itself. On both occasions Aloysious graciously slid toward the rear of the boat to let the bow ride free and to make the work easier for Ting and Tong. It was still fun, but it was becoming evident to Harry that the boat ride would not last much longer. Aloysious was also showing signs of being more alert to what was passing on the banks.

As they approached the shadow of a particularly large and dark hill that had dominated their view of the countryside for miles, Aloysious raised his hand.

"Head for the shore, Captain. Aim for that sandy area in the lee of the mountain. Run her hard aground. We're going to have to pull her ashore and hide her."

Once ashore, Harry and Aloysious threw shrubs and small tree limbs over the boat where they had pushed it between some huge rocks. On the small beach above them Ting and Tong prepared dinner. When they finished covering the boat Aloysious surveyed the scene.

"We camp here tonight. Tomorrow we start early. We're close to the city, but it's still a walk."

Harry looked up at the mountain. "Where are we?"

"Where are we? Nowhere. Look back," Aloysious said and pointed back down the river from where they had come. He turned around to face the hill. "No one comes up here. Ever. There is no reason to. There is nothing up here. Nothing anyone wants. Nothing of value that anyone knows about. This area never was a road for some army on its way to burn down some other guy's city. This is not a natural route to anywhere."

Aloysious pointed up at the mountain.

"Up on that hill, that mountain, there is something so splendid, something so grand, that it will make you gasp when you see it. Why it was built here I don't know. Maybe because it was in a place where no one would ever bother it. Maybe at some brief moment in history this place was somewhere. And maybe now everybody has forgotten why. One day – maybe – it will be someplace again. For now, Harry, we are in the middle of nowhere. For a while we have to keep it that way. I know you have questions. Tomorrow you'll have some answers."

They walked toward the small fire where Ting and Tong were preparing dinner. Aloysious stopped and looked toward the hill.

"There's no way to get up that mountain from this side. Anybody approaching from the river could spend days and never get near it. It's a tangle of thick brush that leads to nothing but rock face that can't be climbed – even if you had a reason to. That's probably why no one has been up there for years."

Harry waited. Finally he asked, "And...? What's the rest? How did you find a way in?"

"By luck. I found it by sheer luck. But...something called to me, Harry. I swear to God, something in there called to me."

It was growing dark. "Come on, let's eat," Aloysious said. "Tomorrow we get up before the sun."

9

L et's hit it! Let's roll! Mount up! Mount up!" Aloysious's voice was a roar that on any other day would have made Harry bury his head under his pillow or in the riverbank sand on which he had spent the night. This morning it was music, and he was awake instantly and ready to move. It was still dark as he helped Ting and Tong break camp. In his eagerness to get on the trail he was not particularly neat as he stuffed things in the backpacks.

"Harry, you must be careful how you put things in the pack, or we will not have room for everything," Ting said.

"Harry, you must not put wet things in with our clothes." Tong said.

"I'm sorry, ladies. But you can blame Aloysious for getting us up so early. I can't see what I'm doing."

"It is because you are so excited. You cannot wait to see Aloysious's surprise on the hill," Tong said.

"It will be a surprise all right if we ever get there at all," Harry answered. He felt embarrassed that his excitement was so apparent, even in the dark.

When everything was packed, the packs were cached among the trees that stood away from the river. Aloysious surveyed the scene. He used a branch to sweep sand over the place where their little fire had been. Finally he stepped back and looked over the area again. He was satisfied. "Good. No sign of human habitation."

"I didn't think anybody would ever be up here to care," Harry said.

"Just to be safe," Aloysious answered. "Just to be safe."

They started walking along the riverbank, back in the direction they had come. They went single file at first. Then the way got wider, and they were able to stroll side by side for a while. Just when Harry was starting to think that it would be a piece of cake, Aloysious raised his hand and brought the party to a halt.

"The fun begins," Aloysious announced. "It is time, ladies and gentlemen, for Pachyderm Tours to enter bush country. In there," he went on solemnly, "we are all equal. Except the jungle, and the jungle is neutral. That's what I read in a book."

For a long minute Ting, Tong, and Harry, stared at the bush, jungle, or whatever it was. They did indeed feel very equal in not relishing the prospect of stepping into it.

"Come on," Aloysious said. "It only looks rough. Follow me!"

It did look rough, and it was. Once they stepped off the riverbank sand, they were immediately swallowed up in plants, and Harry could see no way through. Aloysious had led them into a thicket of bushes and tangled vines. They had to fight for each step of the way, although Aloysious was quick to find and exploit the smallest chinks as they beat their way through the green wall.

Once through the thicket, they dropped down to a dry streambed that had sunken deep below its banks and was almost completely roofed over by a canopy of foliage. In the shadows of this leafy tunnel it was cool, and there was room enough to walk almost upright. The streambed itself was packed down hard and devoid of growth but for occasional clumps of tall grass that grew here and there.

The going was not particularly difficult and they made good time. Harry usually prided himself on his nearly infallible sense of direction, but walking along the meandering streambed with little sign of the sky was disorienting. After a time he had no idea if they were heading north or south, or if the trail was leading them up or down. It was like flying an aircraft in the fog where you could not trust your senses. Here it was worse. There were no instruments to trust.

By mid-morning it was evident from long stretches of silence that Ting and Tong were getting tired. The group had covered a lot of ground since daybreak, and Harry's shoulders ached from having to walk crouched over almost constantly now as the foliage over the streambed reached further down toward them. If Aloysious was also starting to feel the strain, he gave no sign of it. But, finally, he did call a halt. Everyone dropped down where they had stopped. Ting and Tong broke out a bag of Japanese rice crackers from a small daypack Ting carried, and one can of beer.

"You must share this," Ting said. "I think we must save the rest for later."

Surprisingly, Aloysious gestured to Harry to take the first drink. This was unprecedented in Harry's experience, and an opportunity not to be missed. He tossed down his share in a couple of thirsty gulps. The beer was still cool. He was tempted, but he passed the half-full can to Aloysious.

"How much farther?" he asked.

"Not far. We'll be there soon."

The break finished too soon. They continued to follow the streambed for a while. It started to get more overgrown and the grass that grew sparsely out of the streambed before was replaced by nasty-looking shrubs with thorns that clutched at their clothes and sometimes snared a piece of skin. Their progress slowed further, and words like "shit" and "damn" as well as more gentle feminine squeals punctuated the air. Harry was starting to look on this journey as penance for all the sins of his past life, when Aloysious said the words Harry didn't think he would live long enough to hear. "Okay. Here's where we get off."

Inside the tunnel of the streambed, this particular place looked like any other. There was nothing to distinguish it. There was nothing to be seen outside. Either Aloysious depended on another sense or had a landmark invisible to anyone else. He bent some shrubbery back from the streambank above them and held it so they could pass. Ting went first, and then Tong. Harry went next.

They emerged from the streambed into a small open area that was littered with big black rocks. Over them loomed the dark bulk of the mountain. They must have walked around one side of the mountain and were now looking up at its backside, the side not visible from the river.

From what Harry could see, the slopes were as steep and as treacherous here as they were on the other side. The approaches to the mountain looked no more inviting than did those seen from the river.

They walked toward the mountain, and the slope was gentle enough. It ran up through old gnarled trees that stood like old men guarding the mountain's flanks. The slope grew steeper. Harry could see that the line they were taking would end at the bottom of a sheer rock face at least a hundred feet high. As they got closer, Aloysious stopped. "Up there," he said. "See the cave?"

Harry followed Aloysious's pointing finger. "That's where the spirits are," Aloysious continued. "If anybody gets this far, the idea of what lives up there will discourage him from going farther."

The mouth of the cave looked just like that – a great open mouth. A few small bushes that grew along its edge looked like spinach stuck in its teeth. It was hard to make out, but it appeared that white things scattered at the entrance could be bones, large animal bones.

"The white things. Are they what I think they are?" Harry asked.

"I don't know. But there must be some kind of animal living up there."

Harry felt a little shiver go down his back. "What kind of animal could get up there?"

"I don't know. No kind of animal I want to meet."

Aloysious looked back to where Ting and Tong stood close together, studying the cave. "Anyway," he added, "we're not going up there." He turned to the right and started to walk along the face of the cliff.

They followed him to where a crack in the rock spouted a heavy growth of weeds. As Aloysious approached it, he grabbed the trunk of a shrub that looked like an overmuscled arm sticking out of the crack. He used it to haul himself up and then just dropped away out of sight. His voice came from somewhere behind the weeds.

"Come on up. Grab hold of that little tree like I did, and hop over. Don't break anything."

Ting and Tong giggled a little nervously, so Harry went first. He grabbed hold of the tree and pulled himself up. As he tried to get a purchase on the lip of the rock he suddenly half fell through a wall. The overgrown crack in the rock face was an opening to another cave. "Tunnel" might have been a better description. The light was dim where he was, but 40 or 50 feet away, he could see daylight streaming through another large opening.

"Holland Tunnel," Aloysious said as he helped Harry back to his feet, "pay your 20-cent toll on the New Jersey side."

"Wow, it's been a long time since you've been there."

"You mean it doesn't go to Jersey anymore?"

"Oh, never mind."

While Aloysious helped the girls through, Harry walked to what in his mind was now the Jersey side. Outside was a small saucer-shaped valley. It contained a sea of grass that was encircled by rock face on three sides. The fourth side sloped gently upwards. Trees grew here and there, but the valley had a look of innocence about it, as if no one had ever walked across it. The silence had a heaviness that he associated with empty cathedrals at dusk. At first he heard no sound at all except for some muted scrabbling from Aloysious in the cave behind. Then there was a call of a distant bird, just once, and nothing else.

Harry couldn't resist walking on the grass. It was tall, about knee high, but soft and springy underfoot. He walked on, looking up the slope of the hill where the vegetation was heavier, when he caught something with the toe of his boot. His ankle seemed to just give up and he went sprawling. It was like hitting a big dry sponge. It made him think of soldier games he had played when he was a kid. Then you could throw yourself down in a field and not feel any pain. Just like it was now. It was comfortable where he lay. He rolled over on his back and closed his eyes against the sun, content in the sweet-smelling grass, until a shadow passed over him.

"Hey, guy." Aloysious prodded him gently with his foot. "I see you didn't waste time finding the city."

"Are we finally there, Aloysious?" he said without opening his eyes. "Or do we have to walk another thousand miles through the brambles?"

"You have arrived, my boy. Just look. Just look around you."

Harry sat up and looked directly at Aloysious instead. "Before I look anywhere else, I want you to know that every once in a while I get this feeling that you're putting me on. I will look now, Aloysious. If I don't see a lost city, I will kill you."

Then he looked, as Aloysious said, "Would I do that to you?"

"Yes. Now...what am I looking at?"

"By your foot. Do you see it?"

"I see a rock."

"It's not just a rock. Look again. Push some of that grass aside."

Harry rearranged some of the grass he had flattened as he fell. Then it struck him all at once. "Goddamn," he said. It was like those optical illusions made of rows of stacked blocks. You stare and see nothing but rows of blocks. Then you blink your eye and the blocks have all rearranged themselves to form the pattern you were supposed to see but couldn't.

It was a rock, but it was a rock that had been cut and shaped and made to fit its neighbor. And its neighbor had also been cut and shaped by someone's hand. Harry could feel the excitement welling up inside him. Then a big smile took over his face, and he knew he would wear it for the rest of the day.

Aloysious was on his hands and knees, talking quietly to Ting and Tong, who had joined them down on the grass.

"This is one of the steps that lead up the hill. Down here where the slope is gradual, the steps are spaced far apart. The formal stairway starts 50 meters up the slope. The steps there are proper steps. There are Nagas that run up each side."

Ting and Tong moved in for a close examination of the step. There was no giggling now. Harry was already moving on, his eyes sweeping the features of the landscape ahead, looking for the Nagas. The Nagas were the giant multi-headed serpents whose bodies often served as balustrades, undulating down a hillside on either side of a stairway that led to the sacred precincts above. Their heads, with hoods spread wide, reared high above the entrance to the stairway, guarding access to the top.

"Harry. Over here." Aloysious's voice was uncharacteristically soft, almost solemn. "The Nagas are over here. In the trees."

The hill was steeper where Aloysious took him, and the vegetation was very dense. At the point where the hill began its quick rise stood two prominent mounds, almost uniform in size and shape. For a minute Harry was not sure what he was looking at. Then, above the leaves and twisted vines he saw the stone heads of a great serpent high above him, looking out over the valley.

"The other one is there," Aloysious said, pointing at the second mound. "It's hard to see from here, but I checked. There is a lot of vegetation covering them, but both seem to be intact. Come on, let's go up the steps. They're pretty well covered in silt and brush, but you can see how they move up the hill."

The four of them started up, walking carefully up the ancient staircase as though the steps could somehow be damaged under the blanket of silt the centuries had laid over them. On either side, standing as high as Aloysious's chest in most places, were the rounded mounds that moved like waves toward the top of the hill – the bodies of great stone serpents.

A hundred meters up the hill they reached the first stage, a flat, heavily overgrown area that they would have to cross to reach the bottom of the second flight of steps.

"Want to rest a while?" Aloysious asked. Harry shook his head. Ting and Tong followed suit.

"Then come over here." Aloysious led the way toward what Harry first thought was a large rock standing in the shadows of several large trees. A little closer, and Harry realized he was looking at a building constructed of precisely shaped stone blocks. The building was a single story, and not large. Its entrance faced up the hill. In each wall were two windows with complex floral patterns carved into the stone frames. Four knurled stone rods that looked as though they had been turned on a lathe were set vertically in each window, like bars.

"What do you think?" Aloysious asked after Harry completed a walk around the structure.

"Incredible. Beautiful. Fantastic. And in almost perfect shape."

"Not almost, Harry. It is perfect. Maybe not all of the buildings are this good, but most are in pretty good shape. The wind and the rain over hundreds of years had some effect. The carvings on some of the stone are not as sharp as they were a thousand years ago. I guess the remarkable thing is that there are any carvings at all."

"What do you think this building was?"

"I don't know. It's the only stone building down at this level, and it was probably a shrine. There are a couple of brick buildings over there, but on this level most of the buildings were probably wood. They rotted away centuries ago. Over there is a pool. A big one, probably a reservoir. Other than that, there's not much here. It's up above where it gets interesting."

They walked over to where Harry could make out the arched stone gateway that opened to the second stairway that led farther up the hill. On either side of the gateway was a Singh, a mythological guardian lion that still stood watch.

The lines of their bodies were softened by the moss that grew over them, but there was no hiding the tension in their stance, crouched forward ready to spring at the throat of an unwanted intruder.

Shifting his eyes to the gateway, Harry could see intricate forms worked into the stone – demons, Nagas, and other fantastic beasts that added to the force guarding the entrance to the precincts above.

"Past the gate it's all sacred ground," Aloysious said. "The next level is relatively small. A half dozen small shrines and some pools. A way station to prepare yourself to enter the temple complex above."

They walked through the gateway and up the steps. The shrines may have been small ones, but their presence, once detected among the trees and vines, was overpowering. The jungle growth was very heavy at this level, and none of the shrines stood out immediately, or were even visible at first. As the group approached, the shrines seemed to be in darker and more forbidding areas of the jungle that surrounded them. When they drew closer, their fantastic stone forms materialized, first as hulking mounds of vegetation – until the eye caught an exposed corner or a panel of the stone structure where bas-relief armies marched and were joined in fierce battle.

Here or there a doorway could be seen. The doorways were the most intricately formed parts of these structures, with arches that rose high above, like elaborate fans, and lintels carved with a riot of gods and demons and kings.

"Harry, look at this."

Harry walked over to where Aloysious stood at the base of one of the shrines that towered 30 or 40 feet over him. Aloysious had pulled some foliage from a wall panel where a dozen "apsara" or celestial maidens danced as they had for a thousand years. Harry looked closely at the beautiful stone maidens with their enigmatic smiles. Angkor Wat supposedly was decorated with more than 17,000 of these dancers, and he doubted that any could be lovelier than these.

"Aren't they beautiful?" Aloysious asked. "We could probably chop that whole panel right out of there. Jean Lee would give his right testicle for it."

Harry shook his head sadly.

Aloysious was already moving on. "Let's go. We have a lot to do before it gets dark. Let's make it to the top."

The top of the mountain was not far. Up a staircase grander than those that came before, and through a gateway that stood taller, larger, and more beautiful than those below.

Standing at the top, Harry realized that the area was much larger than he had expected. The jungle had not reached here, and the vegetation was not as thick as it had been below. There were obviously a number of buildings here that were larger and more elaborate than those below. He could not see the entire complex. It was enclosed and partially hidden by what he recognized as a wall, although it appeared as a long rounded mound on which shrubs and trees seemed to flourish.

From where he stood, he could see the towers of buildings inside the walls. The towers were clear of vegetation, but were protected from being viewed from above by huge trees that seemed to grow everywhere. The trees were higher than the towers and – it seemed to Harry – covered the entire top of the hill under their joined canopies.

Led by Aloysious, the group made their way slowly down the grand entranceway to the main gate in the wall. A line of Singhs, or lions, on either side guarded the way. The entrance, another elaborately carved stone gateway, rose high above them. The most prominent of the figures cut into the stone was Siva, the Destroyer, who paradoxically was the protector of this sacred precinct that had defied time. The sunlight that reached here was filtered through the layers of the leaves that sheltered the compound. The denseness of the vegetation made even the air seem green.

In the center of the compound was the temple itself, five tall, rounded towers set on a single base that was itself raised 20 feet or more above the ground. There was a tower in each corner and a fifth that rose from the center, larger and higher than the others. The towers were linked one to the other by long open galleries. This group of five towers and galleries was enclosed by an outer perimeter of four long galleries set in a square.

It took Harry a while to comprehend what he was looking at. There were other buildings within the compound, but they were so subordinate to the main temple that he did not really notice them. From where he stood, the temple looked almost like a huge and elaborate wedding cake made of layer upon decorated layer of finely cut stone. The size of the temple and its beauty were overwhelming. Not an imperfection was evident. It seemed that at any moment the sound of a gong would signal the entrance of the dancers and a procession of worshipers. But there was only silence, and their eyes caught no movement save the rustling of leaves overhead. None of them, not even Aloysious, had found a word to say since they had entered the temple precinct.

As the group moved closer to the temple, they saw the shallow pools that surrounded it, or perhaps these were the remnants of a moat. Once these pools would have reflected the glory of the towers in the clear waters. Now they were full of muck. There was a familiarity about all of this that took Harry some time to recognize. It finally struck him.

"Good Christ," he said, "it's a mini Angkor Wat."

"Yup," Aloysious replied. "It's a lot like it. This one is a lot smaller, but I think the work is better. This one is in better shape, and there are no land mines."

Harry could feel the big smile that would not leave his face. He turned to look at the others. Ting was smiling too. When she caught him looking at her, she just shook her head. Next to her, Tong, with a big smile on her face, threw her hands in the air. It was beyond any words they had. Aloysious was grinning broadly, too.

"You unbeliever!" he said to Harry. "Here's your lost city, just like I promised you."

Before Harry could say anything, Aloysious spoke again. "Harry, why don't you and Ting-Tong go ahead and look around. We have an hour or so before dark. I'm going over to the library and have a beer." Aloysious picked up one of the packs and started toward a small building that stood near a corner of the temple compound.

Harry spent the next hour walking around the temple and looking at the bas-relief scenes carved on the walls. There was everything from moments of daily village life to scenes of battles that had raged a thousand years ago – and from myths that lived thousands of years before that. As he circled the walls, Harry marveled at their condition. Discoloration and wear had been caused by the elements, but there was no sign of the massive damage that had been caused at Angkor and elsewhere by the roots of trees and by other vegetation as the jungle moved in. There was no damage caused by war. Apparently no war had ever reached here.

When darkness came, Harry made his way to the small building Aloysious had called the library. Ting and Tong were camped out in front of the steps leading up to the building, and with the magic of their backpacks had a meal already prepared. Aloysious was sitting on the steps, looking like a settler in some frontier town surveying his land holdings.

"Nice of you to come by, neighbor," he said. "Things are a little quiet around town tonight."

"Looks like it's been quiet around here for a long time," Harry said as he took a seat next to Aloysious on the steps. "The condition of this place is fantastic. It's been 20 years since I've seen Angkor Wat. Fabulous as Angkor is, it's a shambles compared to this. The only place that even remotely compares to this is Khao Phra Wihan, at least before the Khmer Rouge got up on that hill."

"I remember Khao Phra Wihan," Aloysious said. "It must be 20 years ago we went up there." They talked for a while about Khao Phra Wihan, a Khmer temple located on the Thai-Cambodian border. It had been built high on an escarpment overlooking the Cambodian plains. Its position had spared it from many of the depredations of man and jungle suffered by temples built on lower and more accessible ground. Aloysious summed up both their feelings. "Khao Phra Wihan was beautiful when we saw it. A lot of it was intact as I remember. The K.R. got up there a couple of years later and dug in. There was some heavy fighting at some point. God knows what it looks like now. There were probably a lot of places that looked good after a thousand years. And then man got near them."

"What's next for this place?" Harry asked. "You're the man here now."

"I told you I had a scheme. It's too late to get into that now. We'll talk about it in the morning. There's something I have to show you."

"I can't wait," Harry said, and meant it.

10

arry. Come with me. Ting-Tong, you guys stay here." Aloysious started across the inner courtyard where they had spent the night. They had all been awake for an hour or more. It had been a pleasant night on the mountain – cool, with no sign of mosquitoes. Despite that, Harry had slept for no more than an hour or two. He simply could not bring himself to spend time in this place doing something so unproductive as sleep. The moon had been bright, and he had spent most of the night exploring. Ting and Tong had also roamed around for much of the night, almost as excited as he was. Only Aloysious had slept the night through.

Harry followed Aloysious across the rear of the courtyard, then through the outer gallery. He kept his eyes constantly moving, scanning over the towers and the galleries, seeing something new with each step.

Behind the temple and some distance away from it was a deep and ornate pool that had probably been used for ritual bathing. Harry had looked it over the night before, and it was here that Aloysious led him. The pool was a large square, and on one side of it stone steps led down to where leaves and other debris floated on the black water.

"Follow me," Aloysious said. He started down the steps. Near the bottom, a narrow ledge ran around the inside of the pool, a foot or two above the surface of the water. When Aloysious reached the ledge, he carefully stepped out on it. Then he turned around and found Harry still standing at the top. "Come on," he said. "Let's get rolling."

"I'm not swimming in that crap," Harry mumbled, but he started down the steps.

Aloysious ignored him. He was busy with something. He had moved further along the ledge, and had his back to Harry now. Harry could not see clearly what Aloysious was doing, but it looked like he was tugging at a stone in the wall. Harry stepped out on the ledge and, standing sideways, carefully made his way toward Aloysious. When he reached him, Aloysious turned to ask, "Can you get in there?"

Harry now could see an opening in the wall. It was waist high, and there was enough light to see that it went back for about ten feet. It was big enough; there would be no problem crawling into it.

"I can, but I don't think I want to."

"Then I'll go first," Aloysious said. Without further ado he crawled into the hole. "Okay," his voice came back hollowly from inside. "Now you come on in here."

On his hands and knees Harry crawled into the hole, saying, "I'm not even going to ask what this is all about."

Perversely, Aloysious gave him an answer. "Water is what it's all about. When the pool is full of water, this passage is underwater. This whole area is flooded. Now, look up there." Harry looked up. About five feet above him was another opening.

Aloysious went on. "The water never reaches as high as that hole up there – I think. Anyway, if it does, it doesn't really matter. It would just run off the back side." Aloysious started to raise himself up. "Now, I'm going to climb up there. I want you to follow after I get through." There were outcroppings of rock on the wall, and Aloysious used these as steps and handholds. After much scrabbling and kicking of feet he disappeared through the opening.

Harry waited for a moment, then started up. It was not as easy as he thought it would be. Inches from the top, he started to lose his grip. He would have slid back down if Aloysious had not appeared just then and grabbed the back of his shirt. As he was half pulled through the opening, it struck Harry that crawling through holes was starting to be a familiar exercise.

Instead of the darkness he had expected, there was bright light. As he crouched in what was like an opening in a wall, he could see Aloysious just below him, a powerful battery-powered lantern in his hand.

"When you're ready," Aloysious said, "come down here." Harry did not waste any more time scrambling down to where Aloysious stood.

They were standing on a platform, or a ledge, near the ceiling of what seemed to be a vast cavern. Aloysious beamed the light a few feet in front of them where steps were cut into the stone, leading down into the blackness. The bottom seemed far below. As Aloysious swung the light around, the cavern filled with moving shadows.

Harry could barely make out the floor of the chamber, but it seemed there were things standing on the floor, or growing out of it. "What is all that down there?" he asked. The darkness answered back.

"There...there...there."

"What's it look like?" Aloysious said, and swung the lamp back and forth in wide arcs. With every swing, hundreds of shadows leaped back and forth, expanding into huge forms that raced up the sides of the cavern, then collapsed suddenly and slid back down to the floor.

Harry tried to follow the beam of light as it passed over the things on the floor. It was hard to make out the real forms among the dancing shadows. Then all of a sudden he knew what he was looking at.

"Good God! I don't believe it."

"Come on," Aloysious said. "Let's go down. Watch your step."

They started down. Near the bottom Harry could see more clearly, but he still did not believe what he saw. When they stepped down on the floor of the cavern and stood among them, Harry knew he had to believe it.

The floor of the cavern was crowded with rows of figures. There were statues of gods. There were bronzes and woodcarvings of demons and dancers. There were elephants and kneeling monks. There were Buddhas of every shape and size, sitting and standing, all serenely gazing into eternity.

Harry walked among the figures and could not keep himself from running his hand over them as he passed. It was if to reassure himself that they were real. Many of the statues were life-size. Some were bigger than life, much bigger. Other pieces were smaller. Stone seemed to be the material of choice, but there were also bronzes and beautiful pieces carved of wood. And here and there Harry could see the soft glow of blackened old silver.

"What do you think?" Aloysious asked.

"I don't know what to think," Harry said. "It's so fantastic. I have never seen so many...."

"Antiques." Aloysious jumped in to finish the sentence for him. "They're all antiques, Harry. And most are museum quality." He swung the lantern around. "And this is only room one. Come on back here."

Harry followed Aloysious into an adjoining chamber. Like the first, this one was crowded with figures. But here there were also other objects. Great vessels and pots stood in clusters – ceramic vases and fired clay pots.

"Room three and room four are back here," Aloysious said. "And then over this way...." Harry was walking around in wide-eyed wonder and never heard.

The sheer magnitude of what he was looking at was numbing. Harry moved in a daze. One moment he felt compelled to count the pieces he saw. The next he was completely lost in the beauty of an individual piece. Aloysious let him wander. He followed behind, letting the light fall where Harry could see. After a long while, Harry stopped. It took him a moment to realize that Aloysious was right behind.

"There must be thousands of pieces in these rooms," he said to Aloysious. "It's hard to comprehend. The quality of everything I've seen is outstanding. There is so much history here. There are pieces from the Angkor Wat period. There are pre-Angkor pieces. I've seen dozens of old Thai bronzes from all the different periods.

"Chinese pieces too," Aloysious offered.

Harry had his hand to his forehead. "It's beyond imagination," he said.

"The city above. Now all this down here. What is it all? What the hell do we have here?"

"I don't know that I have the answer, Harry. At least I don't know anything for sure. I'm no archeologist. I have poked around down here a bit, and I've had time to think about it. What I have is a theory. Do you want to hear it?"

"Yeah. Of course I want to hear it."

"Okay. The Khmer. The ancient Cambodians. The guys who built the city up on top made a lot of the pieces down here too. Some of the statues were intended to decorate the city. There were probably other shrines on the side of the mountain and in other places in the area. Some of the pieces were made for that. Maybe some pieces – the smaller ones – were made for trade. But the old guys who made the city didn't make everything we see here. A lot of pieces don't seem to come from here. I've poked around in these caves. The stuff is different ages. It comes from different places. It looks as if it was collected over a long period of time. Who knows why. Some strange circumstance of history brought this all together. Now history has brought it to us."

They walked through the caverns. Aloysious pointed at the walls and went on. "There were caves in this mountain to start with. Then the builders of the city got down here to cut the stone they needed for the buildings up above. By the time they finished cutting rock, the mountain was practically hollow. Then one of them figured out that the caverns could be useful. They could be used to store things. Or to hide. Maybe the caves had some kind of defense purpose, too. I've found places where caves are filled in. And there are other openings to the outside. Like here."

They had entered an area bathed in natural light. There was a large opening in the far wall of this chamber. Through it Harry could see blue sky outside.

"Take a look down there," Aloysious said, looking out over the side. Harry joined him at the edge of what obviously was the cave's open mouth to the outside. Far below he could see the river.

"We're right over the beach where we slept two nights ago," Aloysious said. "We're maybe 200 meters above the river here. You can't see this opening from down there. This may be one of the ways they brought some of the stuff in here. It's also a way we can get stuff out."

Even without the help of the clear sky above him now, Harry was starting to see the light. He chuckled. "Son of a bitch," he said. "Now I think I see what you want to do."

Aloysious's face lit up with excitement. "Do you know? Do you think you have it figured out?"

"You want to haul this stuff out of here. And then you want to sell it."

"That's almost it, Harry. Almost, but not quite. I can't haul this stuff out of here by myself. You have to help me."

"That's why you didn't want anybody to know about this place."

"Of course not. Once we finish our work here, we can let the public have it."

"But Aloysious," Harry went on, "you'll never get this stuff out of here. You would need an army to do it."

"I don't think so...."

"Then how the hell are you going to do it?"

"Not just me, Harry. You have to stop thinking that. It's you and me. The two of us, together. We can do it. I've got a scheme."

"If you have a scheme to do that, it's pure bat shit. Absolutely pure bat shit."

"Maybe, but I think we can do it. Come on, let's get out in the sun and talk. It's cold in here."

They got back outside with less difficulty than they had getting in. They walked away from the pool toward the riverside of the mountain. They stood as close to the edge as they could. The air was clear and they could see for miles. After looking out over the countryside for a while, Aloysious spoke. "Harry, I think it's possible. It won't be easy, but it's worth a shot."

Harry turned to face him directly. "Stop me if I'm wrong. You propose to move stone carvings and bronzes. Things that are as big as you are, and bigger. You want to move these huge, heavy things out of the caves and off the mountain, right? Then you want to take them down the river and across the hills to Bangkok. Now, once you get them to Bangkok, I guess you'll want to sell them. And this is the hilarious part – you want to do all of this without anybody knowing you're doing it. And – to make it just a little more difficult – you want to do all this while, all over the countryside, the police are looking for you. Is that what you're talking about doing?"

"Well, yeah. That's it," Aloysious agreed. "Sort of, but not exactly. For one thing, none of this stuff can be sold in Bangkok. We'll have to move it to Europe. Or someplace else. If any of this surfaced in Thailand, we'd be grabbed by the Thai police pretty quick."

"Oh, wonderful. Okay, so we smuggle all this stuff to Europe. Why not? Compared to the other problems, that should be easy." Harry's voice took on a more serious tone. "You're completely crazy, Aloysious. You'll never get any of this stuff out of here."

"Why not? Why can't we do it? Why can't we try? Look at it this way, Harry. All that stuff down there. When you look at it, you see beautiful stone and bronze antiques. When I look at it, I see my retirement fund. Maybe you don't need it, but I do. I have to try it. If we could sell only a little of what's down there, we will make ourselves a fortune."

"Aloysious, you're not talking about working a gold mine that you just happened to stumble across. You're talking about plundering a major ar- cheological find. You're talking national treasure. Sell some of that and you go to jail."

"Harry, goddammit. It's easy for you to talk. You have that fancy antique shop of yours. You're set for life. Well, I'm not. I have to worry about my retirement. Like everybody else, I'm getting older. I have to try it. It's all I've got."

Aloysious sat down on a rock. He took a stick and started drawing circles in the dirt. "Look, Harry. I've thought about this a lot. I know it's not going to be easy. That's why I called you. Between us we can work it out. We start with a winch. With a winch we move the stuff out of the caves and down to the beach. Down there we have Wit's boat. With that we move the stuff down river. We have Ting-Tong and the Land Rover. They can run the stuff down to Bangkok. I know it would take a lot of trips. I know it would take a lot of work, but we can do it."

Harry said nothing at first. He thought about it. There had to be something more here. "Where exactly do I fit in?" he asked.

"You've always been smart about some things. First, I'll need you to help with the muscle work. But that's not your main job. Your main job is marketing. You have to figure out how we can sell all this stuff. Don't ask me how. I don't know where to start. Maybe you can talk to that fancy friend of yours, Jean Lee. He has contacts in Europe. Hell, you know the American market as well as anybody. I know some Japanese guys. All we have to do is get this stuff out of the country."

"All we have to do.... Jesus, Aloysious! Do you know how difficult it would be to get any of that stuff out of the country?"

"Sure I know. That's why I called you. You work it out. You find the way."

"God, there's no discouraging you," Harry said and laughed. From the edge of the cliff where they were standing, he turned around to face the city. He could see a lot of it from here. He let his eyes roam over the towers and the tops of the buildings. When he had his fill, he turned back to Aloysious.

"You know, Alo-wichit, I never thought I would be one of the first to see a real live lost city. And I sure as hell never thought that I would be invited to plunder a lost city. To market a treasure trove buried under a lost city. That really is unique. And for that I owe you something, I guess."

Aloysious looked at him uncertainly. "You'll do it?"

"You haven't let me say no, yet."

"Yeah, but will you do it, Harry?"

Harry hesitated. Finally, with a sigh, he said, "Yeah, I'll do it. Or at least I'll try."

"Son of a bitch. I knew you would." Aloysious bent over and pulled two cans of beer from behind the rock he was sitting on. He got to his feet, then jumped up and down in a kind of victory dance as he popped the tops of the cans. Harry was sprayed in a shower of warm beer.

"I knew it. Goddammit, I knew it, Harry," he shouted. "I knew you couldn't resist an old ruin. I knew you couldn't resist the world's greatest scheme." Aloysious stopped shouting long enough to suck some beer from his can. When he put the can down, looked at Harry and said, "You haven't changed, Harry, in all these years. You're still a sucker for a scheme. In this case, though," he added more seriously, "it's a damn good scheme."

"Okay," Aloysious said, as soon as they finished the beer. He was all business now. "Here's the plan. We leave here today. You go back to Bangkok to start the ball rolling. Go see Jean Lee first. See if he's with us. See what he can do for us. You and I should stay in close touch. Take Tong with you. She'll stay in contact with Ting and me. The two of us will stay in Chiang Mai at Ting's parents' place. Once you finish things in Bangkok, you come back up here and we'll start moving stuff downriver."

Harry listened and said nothing until Aloysious finished. "You have been thinking about this," he said.

"Yeah, I have, Harry. For a long time. And I know we're going to do it. And when we've done it, we'll all be very rich."

11

Jean Lee lived on the top of a condo apartment tower, high above Silom Road. Situated in the center of Bangkok's booming financial district, it was probably one of the most expensive properties in Thailand – or all of Southeast Asia for that matter. Security was excellent. Harry had to get past a doorman, a reception desk manned by two uniformed security officers, and finally a uniformed officer who controlled access to the elevators. Each asked to know his business, and each snapped into a military brace when he said the magic words, "Floor 25." Jean Lee must have put them on alert. They were friendly enough, but the guard by the elevator insisted on joining Harry for the ride to the top. Then the guard waited with him in the hallway until Jean Lee's door opened.

It was Jean Lee himself who appeared at the door to receive Harry, although he had a staff of two or three. "Harry, please come in. It's good to see you back. Let's go to my den where we can talk."

Harry followed Jean Lee through the living room where windows two stories high looked out on the lights of Bangkok's business and entertainment district 25 floors below. From that height and with the city's sounds held back by the windows, Bangkok looked serene.

As they settled in the den, Jean Lee poured two cognacs. Handing one to Harry, he asked, "Tell me, Harry, about your quest. Was it a success?"

"It was."

"And, Aloysious...?"

"He's well. As he always is."

Jean Lee set his glass on the table and looked up at Harry with a small smile. "Harry, why do you keep me in suspense? Come, tell me the story. I'm sure it's a completely improbable Aloysious tale."

"Okay, Jean Lee. You asked for it." Harry stared up at the ceiling and began, "You're going to find this hard to believe...."

He went on to tell Jean Lee the whole improbable tale of a lost city and the incredible trove of antique treasure cached beneath it. At least he told as much of it as seemed appropriate. He left out certain parts, but did include Ting and Tong, or Ting-Tong as he, too, was starting to refer to them. He hoped the way he presented the story gave him some credibility and at least the appearance of objectivity. As he went on with his account, he knew that in places his enthusiasm must be showing through.

Jean Lee sat back and listened attentively, with little change in the expression on his face. When Harry finished, Jean Lee hesitated for just a moment before he said, "An absolutely fascinating story, Harry. You must forgive me for saying so, but it does sound a bit far-fetched. Even for Aloysious."

Harry reached down for the flight bag that he had carried with him and had propped against his chair. He took two small figures from the bag and handed them to Jean Lee.

"I think these will speak for me."

Jean picked up the figures, one in each hand, and started to examine them closely. One was an exquisitely shaped female figure cut from stone. One of her hips, covered by folds of a sarong, was thrust out provocatively. Her breasts were uncovered. They were full and beautifully formed. The smile on her face was as inviting as it had been when it was first put on her lips many centuries ago. The second piece was a fragment of a bronze Buddha, just the head and upper torso. The face was striking. It was a young man's face, smooth and serene, untouched by time. It reflected such dignity and wisdom that it could only have been formed with the great skill of a master stonecutter.

"Well...," Jean Lee said. "Your story may sound far-fetched...but your credentials for it are impeccable. He held the female figure out directly before his eyes. "I have never before seen a small Khmer piece that is more perfect. Tenth century, I would say, and there is no question that it is real." He glanced at the Buddha on the table before him. "That, too, is exquisite. But it's Thai, and a much later period."

Referring to the Thai piece, Harry told Jean Lee of Aloysious's theory that the caverns under the city were used to store art objects that had been collected over a long period of time.

"Remarkable." Jean Lee said when Harry finished. "The first collectors of ancient Khmer and Thai antiquities. They were our predecessors, Harry, yours and mine. But tell me, where does this story of yours lead?"

"At this moment," Harry said, "it leads right to you. You know Aloysious. He has a scheme, a plan, and you fit into the plan, like I do. This will not come as a surprise to you, but the plan is to sell the lot. Or as much as can be sold before the authorities get wise. You would be part of the marketing organization."

Jean Lee folded his hands under his chin and leaned back in his chair. "Yes, go on," he said.

"Okay. The plan is to sell as much as we can – as quickly as we can. We would do this simultaneously in Europe, America, and Japan. That's the big picture, as Aloysious conceives it. The details are for you and me to work out. You have a large European clientele, and you know the antiques market in Europe. My focus will be America. That's where I know the market and have connections. Aloysious says he will handle Japan. He claims that he has contacts in Tokyo that will let him exploit the Japanese market. We'll see."

"Japan." Jean Lee smiled. "So, Aloysious wants to take on the Japanese. Japan could be a bottomless pit for high-quality pieces like these – if the pieces are made expensive enough and wrapped in mystery. And perhaps given the glamorous title of 'contraband'. If done right, the whole packet could be sold in Japan."

Harry grinned, but he shook his head in disagreement. "I wish you were right. It would make things easy. But you haven't seen how much stock we have. There's too much, even for the Japanese."

Jean Lee raised his eyebrows. "It's that big, is it? Good God. Well, then there's no question, the marketing effort would have to be worldwide. Let me think out loud for a minute, Harry. The logistics of implementing such a scheme would be enormous. As you pointed out, it would have to be done quickly. There would be a need for extreme secrecy. If word of large sales of Khmer antiquities got out prematurely, the whole scheme would become impossible and even dangerous."

Jean Lee's hand came up, two fingers extended. "News of a major find of Southeast Asian antiquities would bring problems on two fronts. First, if collectors abroad came to believe that a major find of antiquities had occurred, prices for all such pieces would plummet. That happened a few years ago when Chinese ceramics from newly discovered tombs flooded the market. Second, on this end, the Thai authorities would take a dim view of such sales. They would take steps to locate the source of these antiquities and dry it up. I do not particularly want to be dried up, Harry."

Harry took a sip of the cognac. He stared into the glass for a moment, then said, "There are problems. I can't say that I have answers for all of them. Some problems can be handled as they occur. Others we can anticipate and prepare for. I can't guarantee that you won't get dried up, Jean Lee, but I think that we can handle things in a way that would make it highly unlikely."

"Reassure me, Harry," Jean Lee said.

"Well, for example, the Thai authorities would certainly move quickly if they thought a new source of antiquities was located on their soil. It's a question of national treasure. So we start with the Khmer pieces. These would normally be found in Cambodia. And, if the source of these antiquities cannot be confirmed to be in Thailand, it's not a matter for the Thai authorities. No one will learn of the location of the source from us. We must make sure of that. Only a small number of people will know that we are even involved in anything like this. Each of them will have a personal stake in seeing that nothing does leak out.

Jean Lee offered to pour more cognac into Harry's glass. Harry waved him off and continued. "Once we approach our buyers, it's a completely different ball game. To contain that problem from the start, we approach collectors and dealers very selectively. We talk only to the real players, the big-money men who already have holdings of Khmer pieces. As you point-ed out, no major dealer or collector in his right mind would disclose the possibility of a new find. It would devalue his own collection. I think we can move a lot of pieces quietly that way. At least at the start. The situa-tion changes again if our goods start to flood the market in a very conspic-uous way. Over time there may be no avoiding that.

"And then we get grabbed, Harry?"

"No, I don't think so. For argument's sake, say that word of a major find does get out. Our damage control is simple. Word will go out that the location of the new find is in an area of northwestern Cambodia controlled by the Khmer Rouge. Not even the most avid collector of Khmer antiqui-ties is likely to do much poking about on Khmer Rouge turf. If the find is across the border, the Thai authorities have no reason to get involved."

"And how exactly do we arrange to get everyone looking into Cambodia for our treasure trove?" Jean Lee asked.

"The mechanics are simple enough. The major market for Khmer an-tiques is Bangkok. If rumors of a new Khmer find did get out, collectors, dealers, and anyone else interested in the trade will turn to Bangkok to find out what's going on. It doesn't matter if they're in Paris, New York, or Tokyo. They will look here. And who will tell them what's going on? You and I, Jean Lee. We'll tell them. Not directly, of course. Our friends in the trade here will do it for us. I drop a word here, you drop a word there. The rumor starts and we crank the mill. For lack of other definitive rumors, our rumor becomes the word from Bangkok trade circles. And the word from Bangkok becomes truth in London, Tokyo, or New York."

Jean Lee chuckled. "I think you are absolutely right. Bangkok loves a good rumor. There is a distinct lack of originality among the current lot. With judicious use of a good story for our friends in the trade, I think you and I could get everyone looking south to Cambodia, while Aloysious la-bors on at the site in North Thailand. But let's hope that it never comes to that."

Jean Lee went on. "You have obviously thought a lot of this through, Harry. There is one major problem that may not be so easily solved. How do we get all these magnificent objets d'art out of Thailand to the coun-tries where the buyers are? One doesn't carry large bronzes and stone carv-ings through Customs in a briefcase."

"I wish you hadn't asked that," Harry sighed and shook his head.

"That's the big question. Aloysious thought you might be able to help us in that area. And I certainly hope you can."

"Sorry, old man. I don't see how I can help with that. Clever I may be, but I see no easy way to do it. In fact, I see no way to do it at all. You are talking huge quantities, Harry. Big numbers of things that will include large heavy objects not easy to disguise or conceal. A three-ton stone Buddha is not as easy to smuggle across a border as a three-karat diamond or even three kilos of heroin. There was a time when any competent Bangkok antiques dealer, myself included, could ship any antique out of this country with impunity, and guarantee its safe delivery anywhere in the world. Those days are over. The Thai take the protection of national treasure very seriously, and the officials involved are quite competent. Once or twice a year I might test the system and get away with it. With the quantity you're talking about, you will need a whole infrastructure just to move it: trucks, boats, people. I just don't see how it can be done."

Harry sighed. "You're a great disappointment to me, Jean Lee. I thought a man of your stature in the world antiques trade would have vast smuggling networks." He shrugged. "I do agree with you. I've spent a lot of time thinking about all this, and I don't see any way to move a couple of hundred tons of stone and bronze across the world without anyone knowing it. Sometimes I think the whole idea is crazy, just like every other scheme Aloysious has ever come up with. But that's the beauty of it. It becomes a challenge. It can't be done, so we will have to find the way to do it. Are you with us, Jean Lee?"

"Of course I am. I'm pleased you asked. The antiques trade is a bore this time of year. I am prepared to help you in any way I can. Here, in Europe, or anywhere else. I do not see how I can help you move the goods out of here. I can certainly help sell them to the Europeans. I'm ready any time. I'm ready now. What's the next move?"

"I don't know. I think the next move is going to be up to Aloysious. When I left him, he had something on his mind about moving the things. Either he hadn't thought it out completely, or it's something he is reluctant to try. He wanted to see if you could help first."

"Again, I'm sorry that I can't offer any help in that area. I know just enough about how difficult that sort of thing is, even on small scale, that I can't be very optimistic. We can work on it, Harry, and I'm sure we'll come up with something. Perhaps we can enlist the aid of Uncle Noah. I can see you are eager to get off. But, first, a cognac for the road."

Jean Lee poured a good measure of the premium cognac into Harry's glass balloon and an equal share into his own. He raised his glass to Harry.

"A toast, Harry. To treasure hunters everywhere. And to Aloysious – who brought us the biggest treasure of all. May we sell all that we do not covet for our own collections. May we grow fat on the proceeds. May we all live well and happily forever after."

"I'll drink to that," Harry said. "All of it." He took a deep swallow. Somehow Jean Lee's cognac was always smoother and richer than any cognac he had ever had anywhere else. Maybe it was the ambiance, the sense of well being that Jean Lee brought with his cognac.

"Harry, you look pleased."

"Your cognac puts a smile on my face. It's always better than I remember. You know, Jean Lee," Harry said, looking around the room, "you already do live very well."

Jean Lee's study was all leather and rich wood. Most of his personal antique collection was in the living area outside and in two of the large rooms on the second floor of the flat. In this room were only a few odds and ends, a pair of bronze figures, a jade seal that now served as an oversize paperweight, and several Sung dynasty monochrome bowls that stood in the bookcase and were used as letter boxes. These few pieces were probably worth more than Harry's and Uncle Noah's net worth combined. It was a humbling thought.

"I always thought you were beyond money, Jean Lee. Motivated by your love of art. Your toast seemed to have at least a reassuring trace of greed."

Jean Lee shrugged. "I'm one of the lucky ones. I do love art, and I have the means to enjoy it. My father had a lot of money and he did well by me. My business was successful from the start. Not because I was wise, but because I was in the right business at the right time. I bought at good prices when the Vietnam War – and later the Khmer Rouge takeover in Cambodia – dumped a lot of quality antiques on the market. I didn't have to work hard at it. A few European collectors came to me because I had good things. Word got around. The money came easily. When money comes easily, it's easy to spend. I learned to live well, Harry, and I thoroughly enjoy it."

He poured more cognac in Harry's glass. "I make money," he continued. "I spend it, and I enjoy what I spend it on. If that's greed, I have it. There is greed in all of us. It's one of the basics, like sex or cognac. But enough profundity. Where are you off to tonight, Harry?"

"First I've got to go back to the Sweet-T Hotel." Jean Lee raised an eyebrow, and Harry explained. "One of Aloysious's young ladies accompanied me back to Bangkok and is ensconced there. She's keeping in touch with the north and Aloysious. I'm expecting him to call about midnight. He'll want a report of our meeting. After that I'm off to bed."

Harry realized that the evening was now at the point that he had been dreading for days. He mustered his courage. "Oh. One other thing," he started casually. "The BMW. The doorman has the keys. There were a few problems. Not with the car itself," he added quickly. "It drove fine. It was the paint. There are some problems with the paint. And the doors stick a bit. The back fender...."

"No problem." Jean Lee dismissed it all with a wave of his hand. "I know what driving with Aloysious is like, although I only ever did that once. I had a smaller BMW then. You wouldn't believe what it looked like when we finished."

* * * * *

The Sweet-T Hotel was located on a "Soi" or side street off Sukhmwit Road, the major thoroughfare that runs east out of Bangkok. The Sweet-T was one of the few small Vietnam-era hotels that survived the war. It was built in the mid-sixties to house the very first wave of American troops who paid their Rest and Recreation visits to Bangkok. Unlike a hundred other small hotels built in Bangkok in the years that followed, the Sweet-T continued on after the war to become, first, a love hotel for male Japanese tourists. These particular visitors spent the daylight hours of their Bangkok holidays getting quality dental work done at bargain prices at a nearby clinic, and their evenings engrossed in other pleasures at the Sweet-T. Later the Sweet-T served European backpackers and middle-aged French couples who were either frugal or adventurous, or both. For a year or two in the early eighties, the Sweet-T was abandoned to a completely Thai clientele, petty criminals for the most part, who used the hotel as a place to gamble, to keep their girl friends, or to just hide from their wives. When the Sweet-T was mentioned in a popular German budget tour book by an author who had not visited Bangkok in years, the Sweet-T again was favored by young Europeans, and the Thai petty criminals moved on. Through it all, the Sweet-T had a devoted clientele of American visitors who had first stayed there on R&R from Vietnam, and continued to come back because they were never charged more than 20 US dollars a day.

Harry had first come to the Sweet-T on R&R and had many fond memories of that era. Now he looked on the hotel as a small piece of contemporary Thai history. He stayed there whenever he felt a need for a port in a storm, particularly when the storm was caused by an angry female who knew other places she could reach him. Sometimes he stayed there because a particularly good or particularly bad buying trip had all but exhausted his finances. It was to the Sweet-T that he brought Tong, feeling that she would be secure and at least moderately comfortable.

Harry did feel a twinge of guilt for not putting Tong in one of Bangkok's luxurious international-class hotels. This was her first visit to the capital, after all, but he reasoned he could always do that on some other occasion. He had not booked a room for himself at the Sweet-T, but he knew he could get one if he needed it. He wasn't sure he wanted to stay at the Sweet-T, and part of this had to do with his feelings about Tong.

On their long drive from the North, and away from Ting, Tong's personality started to bloom. She was bright, with a good sense of humor and common sense. She also had good teeth, a firm young body, and a pretty face. He was taken with her youth and inexperience. She was an upcountry girl, quite unlike Bangkok girls, or at least unlike the Bangkok girls Harry knew. Bangkok girls were anything but inexperienced, and could handle any situation better than he could. Harry was starting to feel a little protective about Tong. At the same time, he felt himself attracted to her in a way one should not be attracted to a business partner. Maybe he was just being a bit foolish about it all, but it was better at this stage of Aloysious's scheme not to add to an already complex scenario.

Tong let him into her room, and went right back to the telephone. She said something to the other end and then covered the mouthpiece with her hand.

"I am speaking to Ting. Aloysious is waiting for you."

Harry took the receiver and sat on the edge of the bed. As he waited, he glanced quite casually at Tong, who smiled brightly back at him. In a T-shirt and tight jeans, she looked even better than he remembered. Must be the cognac, he thought. There was crackling in his ear, and Aloysious's voice came through loud and clear.

"Did you see your rich friend? Is he with us?

"All the way."

"Can he move the goods?"

"Not overseas he can't. He doesn't think it's going to be easy."

"Shit. I know it's not going to be easy."

There was a long silence. Then, Aloysious's voice again. "Life is never easy. We'll have to go to Plan Two. Listen, I don't want to spell everything out. Go see Sato. He can help."

"Who?" asked Harry.

"Sato. Sato. Go see Tosh. Don't tell her anything. Ask her to put you in touch with Sato."

"Sato? You want to tell me more?"

"No."

"All right. I'll go see Tosh tomorrow."

"Go see her tonight. See Sato tomorrow. We've got to get rolling."

"As you wish, Sire."

There was only a click from the other end. "Well," Harry said putting down the receiver and turning back to Tong, "looks like I have to go out again."

Tong frowned. "But it is so late. I will go, too."

"I don't think tonight is a good idea, Tong. I have to talk business with someone at the Exorcist. It's a nightclub."

"But Harry," Tong said, her frown deepening, "you promised. Aloysious said you would show me Bangkok. You promised me you would."

"Not tonight, Tong. It's too late. I have business to take care of."

Tong looked absolutely betrayed. Her expression was suddenly so sad that Harry was not sure whether he should try to make her feel better or merely feel manipulated.

"How about tomorrow, Tong? We'll go to dinner. We'll make a night of it."

"But it is so boring here," she said with pain in her voice. "I waited here for you so long...." There was a long sad sigh. "But it is okay, Harry. If you cannot take me tonight, I understand. I will stay here. I will try to sleep."

It was too much to bear. "Okay," Harry said, "you can come. But don't say I didn't warn you. Let's go."

12

From a block away Harry could tell it was an exciting night at the Exorcist. He and Tong could hear shouts over the snatches of music reaching them, punctuated by an occasional enthusiastic scream. They paused at the door to read a hand-lettered sign: "2 Nite BEESTS NITE. Nite of BULL."

"What does it mean?" Tong asked.

Harry shrugged. "I'm not certain, but I think..." He was drowned out by a chorus of male voices.

"Ole!"

"...It's a bullfight," he completed his sentence.

Once inside it took them a moment to get oriented. The music as usual was overly loud. He had to concentrate to identify the *March of the Toreadores*, which was being played at least a few RPM too fast.

There was another "Ole!" Under the tightly focused spotlight he caught a flash of red and a glimpse of a gleaming female rump.

"Ole!"

Harry started to make out what was happening. One member of the Exorcist dance corps, bent at the waist, was pursuing a red cloth. Her complete attire was a full head animal mask, a faded pink American bison with long red horns and sad eyes. The red cloth, which he identified as a not inexpensive Thai silk scarf, was held in one hand by another member of the Exorcist dance corps. In her other hand she held a long wooden sword. The scarf was not very large, but it was all she had. She used it alternatively to protect her modesty and to lure the "bull" into movement. The "Ole's!" spurred on both bull and matador.

"Ole!" The bull reared up at the end of her run to jiggle her ample breasts. "Ole!" The bull dropped down into position like a football quarterback, rump high in the air.

"Ole!"

The bull charged low at the matador who was demurely covering herself.

"Ole!"

The cape whirled through the air and caught on the end of a bright red horn.

"Ole!" The matador stood capeless, in uncovered glory before the cheering throng.

"Ole!"

The matador was not finished. A quick movement of her wrist brought a "thwack" as her "sword" caught the fleeing bull's rump. A piercing scream was drowned out by a rousing:

"Ole!"

Tong watched, wide-eyed. Harry felt just a small twinge of guilt as he tried to explain. "It's a popular show. Based on the Carmen original, I think. It received very favorable reviews. The costumes in particular got high marks." Tong looked up at him. It seemed to take her a moment to realize he was talking to her.

"It is a Spanish dance?" she asked.

"Sort of."

He was relieved to be interrupted by a hostess wearing the grinning black and white head of a Guernsey cow. They let the happy Guernsey lead them through the darkness to a booth. Tong slid in first and Harry edged in next to her. Tong could not take her eyes from the stage. He was almost sorry that he had given in and brought her here. She had probably seen more of this side of life in the last three minutes than she would in a lifetime upcountry. And yet, he reflected, she was older than many of the girls who worked here. And, it served her right for insisting on coming here. Her horizons would be broadened by the experience, and she would probably survive.

Within minutes, word of his arrival reached Tosh, as he knew it would. Tosh appeared out of the darkness, stylishly dressed in a designer version of a matador suit, complete with a red mini cape and a fringed wide-brimmed red hat. She snapped into the pose of a victorious matador, her right hand raised high in salute.

"Ole, Harry," she said. Noticing Tong, she greeted her in Thai, joining her hands together before her face in a *wai*. Still speaking Thai, she asked if she could join them for a moment.

Tong had been well briefed on her role. In the taxi enroute to the Exorcist, Harry had told her to play the "casual new girlfriend," an upcountry girl who did not know Aloysious or anything about him. "Don't overplay it," he had warned her. "Tosh will see right through that." He need not have worried. Without even trying, Tong was doing an excellent job of looking like an overwhelmed upcountry kid.

Tosh sat directly across from Harry. She leaned close so that he could hear her over the din. She switched to English. "Harry," she asked, "where have you been? It has been days. I was afraid you fell in a klong, too."

"I'm sorry, Tosh. It all happened very quickly. I took a quick trip up North. I thought there was a chance I might find something."

"It seems you did," Tosh replied, glancing at Tong with a little smile. "She's very pretty, very young. Did you find anything else new?"

Harry shook his head. "Nothing, not a thing. What's been happening here? What are your police friends saying?"

"There is nothing new here. No one is saying anything. You know Bangkok, Harry. No one has time for anything for very long. Two, three days and they forget. Next week no one will remember Aloysious. It's very sad in a way."

"It is sad. But don't write him off yet. You know Aloysious. I would not be surprised if he walked in that door right now."

Tosh twisted around to look toward the door as if she expected Aloysious to walk through it at that moment. Catching herself, she turned back to Harry and sighed. He felt a little badly about lying to her, but Aloysious must have his reasons for not wanting her to know. At the very least, he could try to reassure her. He took her hand and looked into her sad eyes.

"Don't give up yet, Tosh. There are still things that we can do before we have to give up on him. In fact, there is something you can help me with. There is a man named Sato...."

Tosh jerked her hand away from him and sat straight up. "Sato?" she said, "Sato? You mean Sato-san?"

Then Tosh did the only real Japanese thing Harry had ever seen her do. She sucked her breath nervously through her teeth. It set him completely aback. She was never intimidated by anyone, but just his mention of Sato's name had the most remarkable effect. He was speechless.

"My God, Harry," Tosh finally said after staring at him for a long minute. "Sato-san. The Samurai of the River Kwai. Tell me, Harry, why do you want to talk to him?"

He was still not sure what to say. "Ah, somebody mentioned his name," he mumbled. "Said he knew all kinds of stuff. It's a Japanese name, so I thought maybe you could put me in touch." Out of genuine curiosity he added, "What was that poetic thing you said. About the River Kwai?"

"Sato-san. He was the Samurai of the River Kwai. It was what they called him. He was a high officer of the Imperial Japanese Army during the World War. He fought the British in Singapore. And in Burma. He was very brave. And famous. Maybe you would say, 'infamous'."

"But what's he doing now? Is he in Bangkok?" Harry asked.

"Yes, now he is in Bangkok. When the war was lost he did not return to Japan. He came to Thailand. He is a businessman now. He is very, very rich. Very important. All the top people in the government here know him. Many important people from Japan visit him. Sato-san is a real V.I.P.,

Harry."

"Where do I find him?"

Tosh thought for a moment. "If you really want to see him, you must go to the Black Tower. Do you know it? It is on New Phetburi Road. All the taxi drivers know where."

"What do I do?" Harry asked. "Just walk in on him?"

"It is not so easy, Harry. I will call a friend. My friend will tell Sato-san you want to meet him. You must go tomorrow and wait. If Sato-san wants to see you, you must be there."

She reached over to take his hand. "Harry," she said, "it is good to see you again. I hope you know what you are doing. I must go now. Be careful, and come back soon. Bring your friend, too," she added nodding toward Tong. "She is very pretty."

In the next moment Tosh had disappeared into the darker reaches of the Exorcist. Harry started to feel a little peculiar. But, before letting himself reflect further on Tosh's strange reaction, he looked to see how Tong was doing. She hadn't moved. She sat transfixed, her eyes glued to the stage, where a couple of regular go-go dancers had replaced the Spanish duo. He was afraid she had gone into shock, and was pleasantly surprised to see her hand drumming on the table in time with the music.

"Enjoying yourself?" he asked.

"Oh, Harry," she said, "you missed the end of the Beast show. It was very artistic."

"Did the matador kill the bull?"

"Oh, no, Harry! They made love. Right on the stage!"

"Oh," he said, very casually. "That's nice." Farewell, innocence, he thought.

* * * * *

Early the next morning Harry, wearing a necktie and long-sleeve shirt, hailed a cab and asked for the Black Tower. The cabdriver looked him over, and then offered him a fare so low that he was sure he had been misunderstood. He got in anyway, and settled back for what could be a long ride in the traffic.

The night before had ended with him sleeping, alone, upstairs at the Exorcist, after he had taken Tong back to the Sweet-T Hotel. She had been so taken with the stage show at the Exorcist, that he could not stop her from talking about it. He was not sure that she actually enjoyed it, but to her impressionable mind it was something new and rather curious. Something to be turned over and looked at from different angles. She made no moral judgments and seemed not to have reached any conclusions about what she had seen. She probably would not until she had more of a "database" to work with. At least that was what he thought.

Tong was also full of questions. Where did the girls learn to dance? Who taught them? Did they enjoy it? What were they paid? Who designed the costumes? Did the foreigners pay much to see them? He gave her answers, but not all of them were right. He felt like an older brother.

Harry recognized the Black Tower when he saw it. The building loomed high above the traffic on New Phetburi Road, and over all of its close neighbors. Black tile had been used to surface the exterior of the building. Where there was no tile there were huge windows coated with a dark sun-reflecting material that made the windows look like shining sheets of black steel. Were it not mid-morning and were the sun not so bright, the Black Tower would have had a decidedly sinister appearance. To Harry, nothing under a tropical sun could ever look sinister.

The cabdriver said not a word during the drive. For Bangkok, that was unusual. When Harry paid the fare, the driver lowered his eyes and mumbled something in chant-like Thai that sounded like "Remember me to Sato-san."

The lobby was black marble and gleaming brass. Guards in tight black uniforms sat at a reception desk and stood by the elevators. Surveillance cameras in the ceiling slowly swept back and forth. As Harry approached the desk, he decided to be direct.

"I'm here to see Sato-san," he said in English. "He's expecting me. Mr. Harry."

There was no surprise or hesitation in the guard's response. He simply said, "Elevator Two," and jerked his chin in the elevator's general direction across the lobby. That was fast work, Harry thought. Tosh must have some effective friends.

Harry boarded Elevator Two. There was no operator and no control panel. The door slid shut and he almost panicked. His reflections looked desperately out at him from the highly polished brass panels that covered all four sides. He looked up at the ceiling and saw himself looking down.

The door opened silently before a desk where a highly competent looking young lady in a black suit smiled at him.

"Mr. Harry, please take a seat. We will keep you not too long."

In less than a minute, a door on the far side of the room opened. A well-proportioned man in a dark suit entered. He was the taller, modern version of the cosmopolitan Japanese gentlemen Harry had known during his days in Tokyo many years ago. The man looked purposeful, like a Samurai should, Harry thought. But he was much too young to be the Samurai of the River Kwai. When he reached Harry, the man he started to think of as the Samurai extended his hand.

"Mr. Harry," he said. "Welcome to Black Lion Enterprises. We will try not to make you wait too long. Mr. Sato is very busy today. He will be happy to see you in a few minutes."

The Samurai's eyes swept over Harry like the surveillance cameras in the lobby, pausing only briefly where his pockets bulged. When the Samurai looked over Harry's shoulder, Harry twisted his head and saw that his reflected back was being scanned by the Samurai in a mirror on the wall behind him. It was the first time he had been frisked without having a hand laid on him.

The Samurai looked toward the receptionist and she nodded. "Come, Mr. Harry," the Samurai said. He led the way across the room where they boarded another elevator. This time the interior was dark wood. There were no mirrors, not even on the ceiling.

They exited the elevator on what was obviously the top floor. A large area of Bangkok was spread out before them. The Samurai gestured downward with his hand and said, "A beautiful sight." Harry agreed. Then he looked down. What he saw was the "Rembrandt Massage Parlour," the Black Tower's nearest neighbor. The Samurai might even have a sense of humor, he thought.

They entered a large corner office. A long highly polished table was set back near a window that formed one wall of the room. Closer to the door was an informal seating area, and that was where the Samurai led him.

Only after he was seated did Harry realize there were two other men in the room. They stood against the dark paneled wood wall on the far side and almost blended into it. They wore dark suits like the Samurai, but were much younger and much thicker in their bodies. They looked very Japanese and not very cosmopolitan.

Side by side on the same couch, Harry made several attempts to draw the Samurai into conversation, first about Black Lion Enterprises, then golfing, then about the weather. The Samurai would admit only that Bangkok was "too hot." Harry gave up and stared at the clouds moving past the far window.

An almost imperceptible "beep" came from across the room. The Samurai straightened in his seat; the two young men across the room snapped to attention. Harry was impressed, although nothing else happened for another few minutes. Then two middle-aged Japanese entered the room. One held the door, and both bowed while a third Japanese walked through the doorway. All three walked directly to where Harry and the Samurai sat and bowed low to them. They sat down in the chairs, and then all sat silently and avoided looking at one another.

The door opened again. Two men, older, well dressed, but harassed-looking, came through the door and quickly stepped to one side. Behind them came a short stocky old man. He was so short that he seemed only half the size of the others. What hair he still had on his head was cropped down to his skin. He had the face of a benign schoolmaster, and looked around the room with a small smile. Everybody was on their feet now, but Harry. All were bowing low. Belatedly Harry rose and inclined his head, keeping his eyes on the old man. There was no question in his mind. This must be him, Sato-san himself, the Samurai of the River Kwai.

The old man stopped where he was and mumbled something in Japanese. Everyone froze. The two men who had entered just before him looked particularly uncomfortable, as if they had just been asked to perform ritual suicide. The old man laughed. He started walking toward the group where Harry sat, but then stopped again and looked down. He reached down and tried to zip up the front of his trousers, tugging with no success. One of the burly young men knelt before him and zipped him up. The old man spoke again. This time everyone laughed. The old man gestured toward Harry, and the Samurai spoke up.

"Mr. Sato made a joke. He said he cannot take a shit without the Bangkok stock market falling 100 points. Because everyone knows this, he asks, why cannot Black Lion profit from his bowel movements?"

Harry laughed for what he hoped was an appropriate amount of time. The old man watched him with the hooded eyes of a cobra. Harry felt like a bird with a broken wing being looked over by a snake as a possible snack. The old man walked to where Harry stood. He bowed low and said in Japanese that was slow and distinct enough for Harry to understand that he was honored by this meeting.

Harry knew the drill. He said the appropriate words that he still remembered, and he bowed in turn. The old man invited Harry to sit and took a chair directly across from him.

The old man began asking questions in rapid Japanese. Or, rather, he spoke Japanese directly at Harry, while from over Harry's shoulder came an almost simultaneous English translation from the Samurai. The Samurai did not translate Harry's response back into Japanese. Sato obviously understood English well.

"Mr. Sato would like to know the nature of the business you are engaged in, Mr. Harry."

Harry said he was an American-based dealer in antiques and art objects from Asia.

"Mr. Sato would like to know what brings you to Thailand." Harry replied that he came regularly to Thailand to buy art objects to sell in America.

"Mr. Sato would like to know what Black Lion Enterprises can do for Mr. Harry."

Harry knew this question was coming. He had rehearsed a variety of possible answers that ranged from the very direct "I would like you to smuggle 100 tons of antiques out of Thailand" to the more obtuse "It is a matter of some delicacy." It was decision time, time for the right answer, the one that best fit the circumstances. Nine pairs of Japanese eyes were fixed on him.

"It is a matter of some delicacy," Harry said.

Sato's eyes wavered and left Harry for the first time. They swept the floor, returned to Harry, then moved over him to some abstract point over Harry's forehead. Sato tensed his brow, leaned toward the Samurai and grunted a Japanese word. The Samurai answered him in Japanese at some length. Sato looked back at Harry. He grinned and his eyes were almost buried in wrinkles. "De-rek-a-see," Sato said.

"Mr. Sato would like to know who referred you to him and Black Lion Enterprises?" Again, a careful answer was called for.

"It was ah...well, Mr. Sato – that is, Black Lion Enterprises – is known throughout the world. I...ah, am dealing with a most difficult undertaking. Many friends suggested that I ah...."

"Mr. Sato would like to know which friends."

"Well, one is a gentleman named Aloysious...."

The old man slapped his knee. "Alo-wichit!" he said. Without taking his eyes off Harry, he leaned toward the Samurai and said something else in rapid Japanese.

The Samurai turned to Harry. "Mr. Sato would like to move to another room where he can offer you some tea."

The torture chamber, Harry thought.

They moved to a smaller room, but only three of them were to enter. Harry was invited to go in first. Sato paused at the door and said something to the Samurai. The Samurai looked less than pleased, and shook his head once. The old man spoke again, and one of the two burly young men entered the room. Sato entered and closed the door behind him

The room was tiny compared to the one they had just left, and looked very Japanese. There were no chairs, only a low table in the center of the room, with pillows on bamboo mats. There were scroll paintings on the walls, and paper screens divided off small sections of the room. In the background was the faint sound of a samisen.

With their shoes off, Harry and Sato sat across the table from each other. The young man moved to a corner of the room where he sat cross-legged on the floor, watching them.

Sato smiled and began to speak. It was English, although Harry did not immediately recognize it. Sato could not have had much English practice over the years.

"Mr. Harry. I am very pleased to meet friend of Mr. Alo-wichit. English is difficult language for me to speak. You understand some Japanese. Do you speak also Thai?"

"I do, sir."

"Then we must go on in Thai." Sato switched to Thai easily. He had an obvious command of this language and spoke it with only the slightest of accents.

"I am sorry if this has all been a bother for you," Sato went on in Thai. "When one gets old, many things become a bother. It seems I can no longer go anywhere alone. They say I am too important to Black Lion. When

I was young I had no fear. I had strength and cunning. Now they act as if I lost everything when I lost my youth. I still have no fear. I am not so strong now, but I have even more cunning than when I was young."

A woman in a kimono entered and started serving tea. Sato indicated that the young man in the corner be given tea as well. He nodded toward the young man and said to Harry, "That one is all right. He is honest and simple. Like my troops. I can understand him. It is the other young ones, the modern ones that I find hard to deal with. We speak the same Japanese language, but we no longer understand one another."

They drank tea as Sato went on talking, no longer about his own countrymen, but about Thailand's booming economy and the changes the boom was bringing. "But there are some things that never change, Mr. Harry," he said and nodded at the tea lady. She left the room and came back a moment later carrying a tray with a bottle of cognac and two water glasses.

"Tea is necessary, but so is cognac. That is what the old Chinese traders here taught me many years ago." Sato poured out a large measure for Harry and then for himself. "Come. Drink. It is never too early in the day." Harry did as he was told. When he set the glass down, Sato said, "Now tell me. How can I help you?"

"I want to move some things. Art works."

"Ah," Sato said. "Art works. I never became involved with art. It does not pay very well to trade in individual things. But I think I understand. If Alo-wichit is involved, I am sure these art works are things that the Thai government would not like to see leave the country. Is the quantity large?"

"The quantity is very large. As are many of the items."

Sate nodded. "And where are these items to be sent?"

"To Europe. To America. To Japan"

"I like people who can think on a global scale. Good. I do not see a problem. It will require ocean-going ships. And smaller vessels that can go into isolated beaches. Cargo can be loaded there and transferred to the ships. None of this is a problem. Black Lion has sea-going ships. I also have a fleet of Thai fishing boats that can go anywhere."

"And this can be done quietly?"

"It can be done without a sound."

"And the cost?"

"The cost will depend on the profit. The profit will depend on the quality of your goods. I will take 50 percent of the profit. Before you say that is too high, you must know, as Alo-wichit does, that I will be a full partner. I will take full responsibility for getting the goods out of the country and for getting them into any other country you wish. There will be no problem. Whatever occurs, whatever gets in the way, I will take care of it. You will have no concerns."

"You make it sound easy. But...50 percent for transporting goods is a very high freight charge."

"It is easy if you have worked here for 50 years. You are concerned about the expense. As a freight charge, 50 percent is expensive. I am more than a freight forwarder. My services are complete. They cover all contingencies. As such they are not expensive. Think about it, Mr. Harry. There is no need to make a decision this moment. Now, let us have some pickles and more cognac. It is almost lunchtime. You must be my guest."

Harry stayed for lunch. It was pickles and noodles and soup. And cognac that they drank out of glasses like water. He found himself liking the old man, who had a quick and clear mind and was exceptionally knowledgeable about the local political and economic scene. He seemed to know the background to everything that ever happened in Thailand.

They talked a little more about business. Things became clearer as they drank, and Harry agreed that 50 percent for Sato's services was really not excessive. He would talk to Alo-wichit about it.

Harry also remembered the winch. They needed something to get big stone statues down the mountain to the beach – something light and strong, something that would let one man lift tons. Sato shrugged and said that was no problem. Black Lion handled a product just like that. Harry would have it in Chiang Mai in three days.

By the time lunch ended, Harry was surprised he could stand up at all, even with Sato supporting him. They stepped into the hallway where Sato's entourage awaited him, and Sato took his leave.

"Ha-Lee," Sato said, still speaking in Thai, but giving Harry's name a Japanese pronunciation, "please remember me to Alo-wichit. Tell him Sato and Black Lion stand ready. I will see you in Chiang Mai, Ha-Lee."

13

The days that followed Harry's return to Chiang Mai went quickly. Aloysious, Ting, and Tong went back up to the mountain to carry in equipment and supplies. Harry stayed on in Chiang Mai for another two days waiting for Sato's winch. He took advantage of the free time to visit the handicraft villages just outside the city to select new pieces for Uncle Noah's Wonderful World.

On both mornings Harry visited the Pachyderm Tours office. The office was manned by a pleasant old Thai gentleman who answered the telephone when both Ting and Tong were out. The second morning he went there, three boxes were waiting. They were marked "Mr. Harry. Pachyderm Tours."

"A most unusual shipment," the Thai gentleman assured Harry. "Delivered by a Japanese man in a dark suit and necktie, who said it was 'necessary' that Mr. Harry get this immediately. The Japanese himself was brought to the office in a black Mercedes."

Tong arrived back in Chiang Mai with the Land Rover late that same afternoon. Her instructions from Aloysious were to drive Harry and the winch up to the mountain as soon as possible, and to bring a lot of beer. It was the first time they had been alone together since returning from Bangkok, and Tong seemed genuinely pleased to see him.

They could not leave until the early morning hours, so they had time for a nice dinner together. Harry chose a French restaurant at one of Chiang Mai's more expensive hotels, where he knew the food was good and they would be inconspicuous. It was also his way of making up for Tong's bad experience at the Exorcist. Not that he admitted that to her. The Exorcist episode was an area of their brief relationship that he thought best to leave alone.

"Oh, Harry," Tong said as she dug into a large seafood cocktail, "I told Ting about the Exorcist. She is very excited to see it. She told Aloysious he must take her there. Aloysious said you are 'bat shit'. What does 'bat shit' mean, Harry?"

"It means something like 'highly regarded', I think, when Aloysious uses it," he replied. Then, to change the subject, he added, "What have you guys been doing up on the hill?"

"Ting and I went up on the mountain three times. Up and down. We had to carry things. Lanterns. Food. Beer. We must arrange everything. Like in a house. Aloysious said we will have to work there a long time. Ting had to drive the boat. Aloysious does not want Wit to know where we go."

Tong smiled sweetly at Harry while she wiped a spot of red sauce from her lip. "But Ting does not drive the boat as good as you, Harry," she added. He felt a little shiver go up his spine.

"I've had a lot of practice," he muttered. "In boats, I mean. What has Aloysious been doing all this time?"

"Aloysious goes in the cave very often. He said to Ting that he will touch nothing until you come. He said you must decide what will be moved."

When dinner was over, they drove back to the Pachyderm Tours office, where Harry loaded the winch and other items he had bought over the last two days for the mountain. He told Tong to get some sleep in the back room while he loaded. When he finished he got a few hours of sleep himself, curled up on the back seat of the Land Rover. When it was time to go, he was a little stiff, but otherwise felt refreshed and ready.

The drive North was uneventful. As they neared the river, Tong directed him down a trail that ran along the bank to where Wit had established a small camp. Ting was to meet them there with the boat at midday.

Wit crawled out of a little reed hut when he heard the Land Rover approach. He scratched the back of his head as he watched them come closer. He was looking a little unhappy, but he brightened when he saw Harry.

"Hey! Mr. Harry!" he shouted in English before switching to Thai. "I am happy to see you. Now the ladies will not have to drive the boat. Ting is a good driver, but she does not look for the rocks. She will break the bottom. I have won two card games from Alo-wichit. One more and the boat will be mine again."

"What have you been doing here, Wit?" Harry asked.

"I sit and I wait. Alo-wichit says I must stay here now. I must guard the Land Rover and tell those who come that the Big Elephant Company is making new trails for the tourist. If someone from Bangkok comes this way, if a foreigner comes, I must shout loudly, 'Walk like the Big Elephant'"

Wit crouched down and waddled like a duck. He stood up, shrugged and said, "Alo-wichit says it is advertising. I don't know. Advertising on the TV is always pretty girls. When the tourists see me, they will laugh."

Harry tried not to laugh. "Actually, that's pretty good, Wit. I think you have your responsibilities well in hand."

"But no one ever comes here."

"Well, you're prepared if they ever do."

Harry had heard the sound of the motor in the background. Now he could see the boat turning toward the shore. A figure at the stern that had to be Ting was waving. Tong waved back. Wit shook his head. "She will hit the bank again."

She did, but it was only a light bump that seemed to damage neither the boat nor herself. "Harry. Hello!" Ting shouted, holding the rocking boat with one hand and brushing back her hair with the other. "Aloysious said you must hurry. There is a lot of work to do."

They all pitched in to load the boat. In 15 minutes Wit pushed them off into the current. Ting insisted that Harry drive, and Wit gravely agreed.

* * * * *

They pulled the boat up on the little beach under the mountain and covered it with brush. They cached most of their supplies behind the tree line. They divided up some food, a couple of cans of beer, and the components of Sato's portable winch that had to be carried up the mountain. The winch was compact and not heavy, but it would require a second trip to get the cable to the top.

Ting led the way through the brush and into the old streambed. Harry was unaccustomed to the pack on his back, but somehow the journey was not as bad as he remembered. Maybe the weather was cooler. Maybe it was the fact that Ting was leading, and broke up the walk with more frequent stops.

At their second break, Tong pulled a thermos of hot coffee from her backpack. She said she knew that Aloysious always liked to drink beer, but Harry sometimes liked coffee. Harry was touched by the gesture. Even if he did have to urinate three times before the next break.

When they finally emerged from the trail and started up the hill toward the temple, they found Aloysious lounging on a step in the shadow of one of the Nagas.

"Lord," he said, "I had just about given up hope. Tong, I hope you told Harry to buy a lot of beer. We're all out up here. Maybe you can give me one now.

Ting answered, "Tong and Harry brought a lot of beer. But we left it by the river. We brought the winch instead."

"Oh, shit," Aloysious moaned. "What can I say. We need the winch. You girls run it up to the top. Then run back down to the river to get the rest. Come on, Harry, show you what we did."

A little tent camp greeted Harry in the courtyard of the temple. Four small camouflage tents were set in a small square around what Harry assumed were the cooking facilities.

"There's a tent for you. A tent for me. And a tent for the ladies. The fourth tent is for our supplies. We'll probably need a couple more as we bring more stuff in. Maybe a separate one for the beer cooler."

Aloysious poked around the entrance of one tent and pulled out the pair of beers that Ting and Tong had brought up the hill and hidden away from him for later. "You're teaching those girls bad habits, Harry. I knew they must have brought some beer up. Ting never forgets. Of course, that was before she heard about the Exorcist." He glowered meaningfully at Harry, then pitched him a beer. He went on.

"I spent a lot of time looking at what we have in the caves. Tomorrow, the girls and I will get the rest of our equipment organized. Your main job is to go down in the caves and decide how to start. Set up priorities. That kind of thing. I've picked out a bunch of small stuff for starts. Pieces we can use as samples with our foreign buyers. I picked out some real nice small Khmer pieces, and some small Thai things too. I thought it would help if I started to put some of it together."

"Okay, sounds good to me," Harry said. "I brought the camera and a lot of film. I want to get pictures of all the big pieces I think are the most sale-able. Jean Lee can take a set of pictures to Europe. I'll take a set to the States. Our buyers can order the big pieces from the pictures."

"Good. Once we get that sorted out, you and Ting can stay down on the beach during the day. Tong and I will winch the stuff down to you. When you guys have a boatload, you can run it down to Wit. Wit will stash it away until we're ready to haul it back to Chiang Mai by Land Rover. Where does Sato want it picked up?"

I'm not sure, yet." Harry answered. He was not completely sure of all that happened at his lunch with Sato after the second glass of cognac. He had a faint recollection of Sato saying, "We will meet in Chiang Mai, Ha-Lee." And, when Harry asked, "Where?," Sato had replied, "Anywhere. I will find you Harry. Wherever you are." That must have been very funny at the time, because he laughed, and Sato laughed. They both had laughed together and Harry started choking on a pickle. Sato pounded on his back and that made everything even funnier.

Aloysious broke into his reverie. "Well, you find out where the old man wants the stuff. Once we get it off the hill, it's gotta move quick."

"Why don't we get started now?" Harry asked.

"Why not. Let's do it." Aloysious started to his feet.

And they started what Harry later came to think of as the plunder of the Khmer mountain.

* * * * *

Harry spent most of the next 36 hours in the caves. He did a lot of looking around just to familiarize himself. When he felt that he had some grasp of the vast number of artifacts in the cave, he started to push pieces around, to get at those that he thought should be the first to go. He examined the small pieces that Aloysious had chosen as their "samples." Most were excellent choices, but there were a few where he thought he could do better. He quietly exchanged those for others he found in the caves.

Ting and Tong were also busy. They made another two trips to the beach for more supplies. When they brought the cable up, they carried all the winch components into the cave and assembled them. Aloysious supervised. The winch was a rickety looking affair, with long crank handles and gears everywhere. It looked like it wouldn't hold much of anything, but Ting pronounced it "state of art, capable of holding many tons." She added that they would not need the men to crank things up and down. The assembly instructions she read from stated, "The winch can turn easy for a child."

The winch was placed in the mouth of the cave overlooking their beach. To the end of the cable Aloysious attached a large wicker basket that had been hauled up in several pieces and put back together by Tong.

"In school I study business," Ting said. "Tong studied basket-weaving. Now we see basket-weaving is more important than business." Ting and Tong giggled over the joke, but Harry thought they were probably right.

"We need a volunteer to sit in the basket," Aloysious said.

"I volunteer, Aloysious," Ting said.

"I volunteer, Aloysious, too," Tong said.

"Why don't we use one of the less valuable stone carvings?" Aloysious said. "It will be a true test of our winch capabilities."

They found a crude carving that Aloysious did not like and that Harry did not think much of either. It was big, and they had to wrestle it into the basket. Then they pushed the basket over the side and watched the carving free-fall into the trees far below. Harry and Aloysious looked at each other.

"The basket tipped," Aloysious said, stating the obvious. "We'll have to center the load better."

After that first try, it worked well. The first load was successfully cranked to the bottom. Aloysious dispatched Ting and Tong to walk back down to the beach to unload the basket and then load it with supplies that remained in the cache. For the rest of that day Harry took pictures while Aloysious cranked artifacts down to the beach and cranked supplies back up into the cave.

The next day Harry went down the hill with Tong. They worked the bottom end of the winch, taking the stone carvings out of the basket and piling them on the beach near the boat. At mid-afternoon, Harry called a halt to the winching. He sent a note up to Aloysious. "Take a break. It's time for us to load the boat. See you tomorrow at eight."

Aloysious's note came back with a last load: "Okay, but don't think I won't know if you're just screwing around. Tell Wit I want a report on advertising campaign."

They re-floated the boat and loaded it, carefully. The boat took more of the stone pieces than Harry thought it would. When the waterline dipped into the river as far as Harry thought it should, he called a halt to the loading.

"Okay, Tong, that's it. Let's clean up the beach and we can be on our way." Tong looked happy but tired. She had been working hard and had made more trips up and down the hill than he wanted to think about. A few minutes after they pushed off from shore, she was curled up on a mat in the center of the boat, sound asleep.

* * * * *

Wit was on the bank, watching them come in. "Don't hit the rock, Mr. Harry. Don't hit the bank."

Wit looked tired too. "I am sorry to yell, Mr. Harry. I have nothing to do but worry about my boat. I need work to do."

Harry gave him work. The two of them unloaded the stone carvings from the boat and carried them inland to a place Wit had prepared. There they could remain hidden until they were ready to be moved to Chiang Mai.

Wit worked quickly and said very little. When they finished and were walking back toward the river, Wit chuckled. "Alo-wichit said I must prepare a place to store artifacts that he will get from the tribal people upriver. I do not know these tribal people, but they must be very clever." As Harry looked at him, Wit shook his head.

"They carve the stone to look like old Khmer gods," Wit laughed.

Darkness came almost before they were ready for it. Wit prepared a simple but very tasty meal from supplies that had been left with him. He invited Tong to use his hut, but Tong preferred to sleep in the back of the Land Rover. Harry also declined Wit's offer. He preferred the Land Rover's front seat. It would be cramped, but it was less likely to be shared by crawling things.

The next two days went in a similar fashion. They unloaded the basket on the winch. They loaded the boat. They unloaded the boat. With the final load of the second day came a note from Aloysious. "Last load today. Bring boat for us in morning. Will be on beach at 10 AM. Time to make a run to Chiang Mai. You're buying dinner."

"I'll be more than happy to buy," Harry said to himself. To Tong he said, "Day off, tomorrow. We'll go back to civilization for a while."

All Tong said was, "I need a bath." Her camouflage suit was stained with sweat. Her long hair was tangled, and strands stuck to her forehead and face. "All I want is a bath, Harry," she said and waved away a fly.

14

It was mid-afternoon of the following day before they were able to leave Wit's camp on the riverbank and head south to Chiang Mai. The Land Rover was loaded with stone carvings until it sagged on its springs. The artifacts left behind in Wit's care were in several large bush-covered piles in the weeds behind his camp. Wit was reassured that he would not be left alone for long. The all promised him that the first one of them to return would bring him many cans of his long-time favorites, Spam and spaghetti in meat sauce.

They were in high spirits when they finally got underway. Ting and Tong, catching up after being separated for a couple of days, chattered away happily up front. In back, Aloysious cracked open a beer in the first 30 meters and passed it to Harry. He took one for himself and they both sat back to relax. The two of them had probably worked harder than they had in years.

"Never thought a world-class scheme would be so goddamn tiring," Aloysious said.

"Thank God for the winch. Can you imagine carrying that stuff down the hill?"

"No way, Jose. Thank God for old Sato. Reminds me. You have to set up the transfer for this stuff as soon as you get to Chiang Mai. Tell old Sato we got a lot more stuff on the way."

"What do you mean, when I get to Chiang Mai?" Harry asked. "Aren't you coming with us?"

"I don't know. Hang on." Aloysious leaned forward and yelled in Ting's ear. "Hey, Ting. Where will we be at dinnertime tonight?"

Ting looked at her wristwatch. "Maybe near Chiang Rai."

Aloysious sat back again. "We'll have dinner in Chiang Rai. I know a good place. It's expensive, but you're the one who's buying, Harry. I have a friend just outside Chiang Rai city. I'll stay there. You and Ting-Tong go on to Chiang Mai tonight. You can pick me up on the way back in two days. How's that?"

Harry shrugged. "Sounds good."

It had already been dark for an hour when they reached Chiang Rai. Located about 200 kilometers north of Chiang Mai, Chiang Rai is a compact little city that retains a certain provincial charm. To Harry, who had loved Bangkok in the sixties and enjoyed Chiang Mai in the seventies – and then watched both cities start to disappear under a haze of automotive smog – Chiang Rai was the last frontier.

They drove down what Harry regarded as the main street of Chiang Rai and pulled around the back of one of the newer hotels. The parking lot there was well lit and had guards at the exit. The Land Rover and its cargo would be reasonably safe while they had dinner.

Aloysious gave Harry directions to the restaurant, a short walk away. "You and Tong go on," he said. "Ting and I will stop in the hotel. I want to call my friend to make sure I'm expected. We'll be right behind you."

The restaurant was on the corner of a quiet street. It occupied the entire bottom floor of a small three-story building and was open to the street on the two sides that faced the corner. It was obviously a good place. The smells coming from it were enticing, and most of the round wood tables were taken. Harry and Tong took a table that had just been cleared and sat down.

True to his word, Aloysious was there within minutes. Harry had already ordered the coldest beers in the house. Aloysious talked Ting and Tong into joining them in a toast with the first cold beer that any of them had had in almost a week.

As they were ordering, Harry noticed two men enter the restaurant and take the table next to theirs. The two newcomers were unlike the rest of the restaurant's clientele in that they were not middle class, middle-aged Thai. They were young, tough-looking men. Harry might not have given them another thought, except for the way they looked at him – and at Aloysious. Harry was directly across from them and could look them over without being obvious about it.

The two were in their late twenties, short, but well muscled. They could have been a couple of Army NCOs out on the town, except their hair was too long and their clothes a bit unusual. They wore camouflage fatigue trousers under loosely hanging Thai peasant shirts, and boots, highly polished items that more likely were made in Italy than in the tannery around the corner. One of them had a suggestion of a goatee. Harry was looking at him when the man crossed his legs. The goatee had a fat sock, and Harry caught just a glimpse of metal and pearly white.

"I think they are tribal people." Tong said quietly at Harry's shoulder. She missed nothing and had caught him eyeing the two newcomers.

Aloysious had his back to the two men. Harry leaned toward him. "The two guys that just came in. They gave us a hard look. One has a gun in his boot. A pearl-handled thing, for crissakes."

"I got a glimpse as they went by. I don't think I know them. Keep your eye on them. It's probably nothing, but I don't like the look of them."

Harry kept his eye on the two. They glanced at the menu and ordered drinks. Then their main interest seemed to be staring at Harry. Their drink order came quickly, a bottle of the local whiskey, a bottle of club soda, and two tall glasses. Goatee filled his glass with whiskey and immediately tossed down half of it. Harry almost gagged. He turned away for just a moment. When he turned back, Goatee was up and standing next to Aloysious.

"Alo-wichit-san," Goatee said, and went on in Thai, "I did not recognize you immediately. But I saw the pretty Thai girl with a foreigner, and I thought it must be Alo-wichit-san."

Aloysious turned his head to look at the man, but said nothing.

"Yes, thank you, Alo-wichit-san, I will join you," Goatee said. He reached back for a chair and pulled it to him. He stood for a moment, a little unsteady on his feet, then sat down. There was just enough room for him to wedge himself at the table between Ting and Aloysious. Aloysious watched but remained quiet.

"Perhaps you will invite my friend and me to join you and your pretty girls for dinner, Alo-wichit-san," Goatee said.

Aloysious still said nothing, but Harry ran out of patience. He had to say it. In Thai, as polite as he could possibly make it, he asked, "Are you, sir, by any chance of Japanese nationality?"

Goatee swung away from Aloysious to face him. He regarded the question seriously. With a small bow toward Harry he said, "No, sir, I am not."

"Then what the fuck is this Alo-wichit-san shit?" Harry asked.

Goatee was taken completely aback by this unaccountable shift from politeness to profanity. The whiskey he had dumped into himself was also taking hold. He looked at Harry with big glazed fish eyes, trying hard to comprehend what was going on.

This very moment was picked by the waitress to arrive with the first course, a steaming hot bowl of Tom Yam Kung, a spicy shrimp soup. Right behind her, a second waitress brought a huge bowl of rice that trailed clouds of steam. Goatee's friend – whom Harry had started thinking of as "Pinkey" for the odd color of his shirt – took advantage of this distraction to pull his chair over and sit between Tong and Harry.

"Wonderful," Aloysious said to him. "I am so happy you could join us here tonight." Then he turned to Harry. "I think these turkeys followed me from the hotel. I spotted that one in the lobby when I was making a call. Keep cool. Let's see what they want."

Goatee looked like what he wanted most was to topple out of his chair. He swayed back forth, looking like he wanted to say something. Finally with great difficulty he started to speak in English.

"No.... I not Japan. Alo-wichit is Japan man. I see him in Bangkok. Now

I shoot him."

The announcement completed, Goatee reached under the table. Ting, sitting next to him, said in a very conversational tone, "Oh, perhaps you would like some Tom Yam Kung...," and dumped the steaming pot of soup in his lap.

There was a moment of shocked silence. Goatee stared down at his lap where the hot soup was pooling around his delicate regions. The front of his trousers was buried under a smoking mound of pink and white shrimp. The numbness he had achieved with whiskey – and the thickness of his trousers – spared him from the heat. For about one and a half seconds. Then it hit him all at once.

"Yoooooooooow!" Goatee screamed in anguish.

Harry watched the rest unfold in slow motion.

Goatee shot upright, hands beating at his lap, yowling. Aloysious back-handed Goatee's face. Goatee careened backwards across the room.

Ting was on her feet, screaming "*Kamoey! Kamoey!*" Thief! Thief!

Pinkey sat and stared – until Tong caught him square in the face with the large rice bowl. His head disappeared in the bowl. Then the bowl slid slowly off his face, turned over once in mid-air, and shattered on the floor. The rice burning his face animated Pinkey. He was up and running for the street. Harry got in a quick poke at his ribs.

Harry glanced at Tong. She looked astonished, pointing at Pinkey as he went by. "The rice, Harry. Look, it sticks to his face. We ordered plain rice, not sticky rice. The restaurant made a mistake."

Most of the patrons were already on their feet. Several just standing up got bowled over like ten pins as Goatee tumbled into them. One good citizen tripped Pinkey as he went by. Pinkey sprawled on his face on the sidewalk.

Aloysious, still sitting, yawned and took a sip of beer. "I think we better call it a night," he said to no one in particular. "Come, young lady," he tugged Ting's sleeve. "Time to go." Ting yelled, "*Kamoey!*" one last time and reached for her purse. Harry grabbed Tong's arm and pulled her along.

No one moved to stop them as they left the restaurant. Just outside two pedicabs were parked along the sidewalk, the drivers perched on their bicycle seats, smoking.

"Exactly what we need," Aloysious said. "Quick, Harry, mount up. Time to make our escape." Aloysious piled into the two-wheeled basket behind the driver and pulled Ting after him.

Harry hesitated. Inside the restaurant, several customers, looking none-to-happy about having their dinner demolished, started walking his way. Harry hesitated no longer. He threw himself under the folding top of the pedicab's seat and pulled Tong in with him. She came down on top of him. "Top speed, diver." he yelled. "Follow that cab with the broken springs." Aloysious's pedicab was already rounding the corner.

In moments they also rounded the corner and were riding along in darkness. There were no street lamps. Now and again they would ride through a pool of light that spilled into the street from an open shop. It was like moving through a dream. The driver's legs pumped up and down like pistons. The only sound was the whisper of the rubber tires on the road and the groans of the cab's bicycle frame as it twisted under their weight.

Tong was squeezed tight against him. The narrow seat was small for one. For two it was an intimate experience. Harry did not mind at all. His arm was thrown over Tong's shoulder and he felt her warmth. He moved his hand gently down her bare arm. The skin was soft and smooth. It was almost romantic: a brawl, a quick escape, a pretty girl at his side. He squeezed Tong's arm gently. "You know, Harry," she said, "they never make such a mistake."

"What?"

"The restaurant. I ate there before. They never make such a mistake. We ordered plain rice, steamed. They brought sticky rice. Like people eat in Northeast Thailand." She shook her head. "It is hard to get good service."

Something came rushing out of the darkness of the lane on their right. Harry felt a rush of wind as it missed them by inches.

"Race! Race!" Aloysious yelled. He hung out of his pedicab. It veered to that side and almost tipped over. Aloysious had waited in the alley and ambushed them as they went by.

Harry could feel their cab begin to move faster as their driver took up the challenge. "One hundred baht to the first man to reach the Clock Tower!" he shouted.

They careened down the street with Harry's man gaining on Aloysious. It was going to be close. They pulled out of an alley and onto a wide and well-lit street. The Clock Tower loomed over the intersection, a hundred meters away. Harry could see they were pulling ahead. Aloysious yelled, "Faster! Goddamn it, faster!" For once it looked like Aloysious would lose.

After they dismounted, Harry and Aloysious took a short cut to the hotel. They walked down a back alley, slowly. Ting and Tong walked behind. Behind the girls came the two pedicabs, slowest of all.

"Everybody hates a winner," Aloysious said. "You know that, don't you?"

"You learn to live with it."

They walked in silence for a while. Harry asked, "What was all that about?"

"Que?"

"The brawl."

"Maybe eet ees because dey do not like dee food."

"You knew that guy, didn't you?"

"I do not know wheech hombre you speak of, Senor."

"You know bloody well which one."

"Hey, Senor. Look what I have." Aloysious opened his hand to show Harry a snub-nosed pearl-handled pistol. "Ees a pistola," he said.

"How did you get that? You better get rid of it."

"He drop eet when I hit him in the snoot."

"Come on, Aloysious. Bullshit aside, what was all that Japanese stuff about? Why did he say Alo-wichit-san is Japan man?"

"I theenk he ees just talk funny."

"Maybe. But to me they looked like a couple of hired toughs. They screwed up tonight. If they don't get fired for it, we'll probably see them again."

Aloysious shrugged. "Don't worry about it, Harry." His Spanish voice was gone. "I got it all under control."

"I hope you do."

15

In Chiang Mai the next day, Harry slept until noon and felt absolutely no guilt about it. Ting and Tong had dropped him at his hotel on the bank of the Ping River in the early morning hours. It had been a long drive from Chiang Rai. The two girls continued to Tong's parents' house, where they would stash the Land Rover and its load of antiquities. Aloysious, left behind in Chiang Rai, was expecting them to pick him up in two days. By that time Harry's business in Chiang Mai would have to be completed.

Harry's only real business was his appointment with Sato-san. Or at least that was what he thought the game plan was. He had no idea how the meeting would come about, but he would work something out. The local telephone directory had no listing for a Black Lion office in Chiang Mai. There was a number under the Bangkok Black Lion listing for "All Up-country Locations." Time enough to do something later, he thought, and took his time over a leisurely breakfast as he caught up on world news in a week-old copy of the *International Herald Tribune*.

Mid-afternoon came and went and he had accomplished nothing. He attempted to call Bangkok a number of times, but got only busy signals. When he finally did get through, he was told by the Black Lion operator that there was no Black Lion office in Chiang Mai. He asked to be put through to Sato.

The operator said, "I am sorry. Mr. Sato is not available."

Well, so much for that, Harry thought. From what he could recall through the haze of his lunch with Sato, the old man did say he would contact him. Of course, Sato had no idea where Harry would stay or even when he would arrive in Chiang Mai. Ah, well. There was nothing else to do. He might as well take a stroll around the city and see what was going on.

He walked over toward the Night Bazaar. Most shops here opened about 8 P.M. or later and stayed open until after midnight. A few of the shops were kept open all day. On the sidewalks, vendors were already setting up stalls and getting ready for the evening surge of tourist shoppers.

As he walked through the area, Harry had the feeling he was being watched. He found opportunities to stop and position himself where he could casually glance back the way he had come. No one seemed even remotely interested in him. He was starting to think it was a touch of residual paranoia, an after-effect of the previous evening's dinner brawl, when he got a glimpse of someone looking at him. Just a quick glimpse of dark glasses under a crew cut. Farther along the street, there he was again. No face. The man must have pulled back just as Harry looked his way.

Harry turned into the Night Bazaar itself. A large open concrete and steel warehouse-like structure, it had individual shops and stalls crowded together on two floors and a gallery that ran around the walls above. This time of day there was almost no activity inside. There were few people to be seen, and only a stall here and there was open. If anyone was interested in him, Harry thought he might be able to spot the man here – or elude whomever it was by exiting into the alley via the stairs at the back of the market.

He climbed the stairs to the gallery and walked along one side. He leaned on the iron railing and for a time watched what little activity there was below. A few foreigners wandered among the shuttered stalls, hoping perhaps to find one open. There were a few small groups of Thais standing about, probably workers with little to do until the night's activities started.

Seeing nothing out of the ordinary, he decided it was time to move on, and headed for the rear stairs that would put him in the alley – just in case.

At the bottom of the stairs, he stopped. The smart thing, he thought, would be to stick his head out and have a good look up and down the alley before stepping into it. He stood on the last step for another two seconds. Then he stuck his head out to the right.

"Ha-Lee San." The husky voice came from the left, behind him.

Harry whirled around. His heart stopped an hour ago. His face was up against the dark glasses. The crew cut head towered over him. No smile. Only a serious looking round face set on a stocky body in a dark suit. A Sato bodyguard.

"Christ," Harry said. "You scared the bejesus out of me."

"*Gomenasai*," the guard said as he bowed, pardon me. Then, extending his arm, "*Hai, Dozo.*" As if by magic, a black Mercedes with black-tinted windows appeared at the end of his arm. The guard held the back door for Harry, then joined the driver up front.

Not another word was spoken on the drive that took them out the west gate of the old city wall, through the suburbs, and up into the hills. They drove into a heavily wooded area Harry did not know, where there were very few houses. Soon there were no houses that could be seen from the road.

Occasionally, they passed roads leading off to one side or the other.

Sometimes they passed paved driveways. At one of these, the Mercedes turned in. Two hundred meters farther on they met a steel gate that was opened for them by a helmeted guard in black coveralls.

Past the gate, the grounds had a well-kept look. The driveway wound through the trees for another hundred meters. Fruit trees seemed predominant, and the underbrush looked more ornamental than serious. They passed two men raking among the trees.

The house appeared when they rounded the last curve. It was built in traditional northern Thai style, and looked old. Entirely of teak, it had three separate steeply peaked roofs, and stood high above the ground on huge teak pillars. The Mercedes parked 50 meters away. The guard jumped out of the front and opened the door for Harry. He extended his arm toward the house and again said, "*Dozo*." If you please.

As Harry walked toward the house he could see that it was situated on the edge of a pond or small lake. The front of the house extended out over the water. He walked under the house, among the huge pillars that supported it, to look at the water. Flashes of silver came from a small disturbed area of the otherwise placid lake. Looking just beyond the overhang of the house above him, he could see massive carp push up through the surface of the lake and then slowly roll over on their backs to sink back down again.

When he reached the top of the teak staircase, he could see the source of the carps' agitation, the small bandy-legged figure of Sato. Dressed in loose, black cotton peasant pajamas, he leaned out over the rail at the front of the house. "Come, Ha-Lee," Sato said without turning. "It is dinner time."

When Harry reached him, the old man gave him a loaf of soft bread. "Feed them, Ha-Lee. You will be their friend." Harry joined Sato in flinging pieces of bread to the carp. He watched the silver fish use their bodies like Sumo wrestlers, moving competitors aside with their weight to get at the morsels of bread.

"Why should I want friends like that?"

"Carp are for long life, Ha-Lee. Why take a chance?"

When the carp were fed, Sato led Harry to the main part of the house. This was in a separate structure, the largest of three such structures built on the platform that rested on teak poles 15 feet above the ground. Each of the three structures was like a separate and self-contained little house. The first was the sleeping area with a large bath. The second was for dining. Cooking was done below the house in an area where the heat and the smells would not bother anyone.

"Quite a place, Sato-san," Harry said as they walked.

"I come here when I can. Here I live like a Thai peasant."

Not many Thai peasants ever lived like this, Harry thought, but he did not say it.

"It is a very old house," Sato said. "It stood in this place for many years. When I found it, it needed much work. I did little to change it. Over there," he said, pointing to the third structure, "I have an air-conditioned office. The rest is as it was."

When Sato finished showing him the house, they went out on the platform – or porch as Harry thought of it – to look over the lake.

"There is much land here. Many fruit trees. Later we will have to walk through the orchards. It is very pleasant in the evening."

Off to one side was another structure, also a Thai house, but not as grand as this.

"What is that?" Harry asked.

"Tonight it is yours. It is the guesthouse. It is very pleasant. Tonight we will have dinner. We will walk through the orchard. In the morning my boys can take you back."

Harry was about to object. Then he thought, what the hell, and said simply, "Thank you."

Sato asked, "Your business, Ha-Lee. Is it completed?"

"We have a first shipment. Small items. A relatively small quantity. We will want some of it sent to Europe. Some to America. We will need it sent as soon as possible."

"If it is a small shipment, we can do it quickly. Here it is better to pick it up by boat. Later, we can transfer it to aircraft to deliver it quickly."

"Where do you want us to deliver the shipment, Sato-san?"

"We can pick it up wherever it is convenient. Somewhere in Chiang Mai will be best. It will be done quietly."

"If I give you an address...."

"It is all I need."

"And the delivery?"

"The same. Just an address. It will be delivered by hand."

"Whether it is New York or Paris?"

"Yes."

"Sato-san, you are an easy man to do business with."

Sato bowed. "Whatever we can do for our friends. But now, Ha-Lee, perhaps you would like to rest before dinner. Come, I will show you to your house."

The guesthouse was also raised above the ground on teak posts, and Sato led the way up the steps. At the top, Sato stopped and made a little bow. "I will leave you here. You are in good hands. Her name is Little Mouse."

Harry returned the bow as Sato started down the steps. He turned to find a young lady in the doorway. She was slim and light skinned. Her features were very fine, and her hair hung down over her shoulders. She wore a short kimono that came to just below her knees. In Thai she said, "Please this way, Khun Harry. The bath is ready."

He walked into the dark and cool room. It had a large bed covered in a white sheet and two small antique Thai cabinets. Through an open door at the far end he could see a large wooden tub on a white tile floor. He followed Little Mouse into the bathroom. An open window was almost completely filled with the leaves of a tree that grew alongside the house. There was just enough space in the window to let a light breeze through.

"I will take your clothes," Little Mouse said.

"Is that so?" Harry replied, but he took off his shirt and put it in her waiting arm. She continued to wait. He gave her his trousers. He felt silly standing there in his socks and underwear, so he gave her those too.

Little Mouse led him to a low tile bench built into the tile floor. She held his arm as if concerned that he might slip on the tile. She left the room with his clothes, but came back in moments. She took off her robe. Harry pretended indifference, but doubted that he was being very successful at it. At least he tried not to stare.

She was wearing a small white bikini. She moved behind him and started sluicing water over him and scrubbing his back with a brush. When the rest of him was also scrubbed to her satisfaction, she gestured for him to get into the tub. She hovered over him until he was seated, then wiped the beads of sweat that formed on his brow.

The water was unbelievably hot, but his skin quickly came to tolerate it, and then it became soothing. Little Mouse stepped out of the room. It was cool and quiet, except for the rustling of leaves in the window. Harry closed his eyes and soaked. After a while the heat of the water reached the point of maximum comfort, just before it got too hot. At that precise moment Little Mouse returned, holding a glass of cool water with just a touch of lime.

He stood while she toweled him dry. He watched her body move. She was slim, but all muscle under smooth unblemished skin. There was nothing angular about her. She was round in all the right places, and very firm. He was very tempted to touch her to see if she was soft where she should be, but he did not. He was not certain what Black Lion protocol was, and he was prepared to wait to find out.

"Come, Khun Harry," she said, and led him into the bedroom. He lay down on the sheet and she began to massage him. He could feel the strength in her hands. It was a good, satisfying feeling. It was also quite erotic, he thought, just before he fell asleep.

He headed for dinner dressed like Sato's idea of a peasant in black pajamas and rubber sandals. Sato waited near the bottom of the stairs. There was still light, and he suggested they walk for a while. They followed a stone path through the trees. There were dozens of lychee trees, and dozens more of lamyai, the sweet luscious fruit Chiang Mai is famous for. There were trees of more exotic varieties, and a whole area devoted to orchids. Harry noted other buildings on the grounds that looked almost like barracks, but built low to blend into the sylvan background.

Sato was quite proud of all of this, particularly when he showed Harry an especially esoteric species of orchid. Harry asked him, "Are you the one who does all this?"

"I have no time for this, nor the patience. Others must labor so I can enjoy it."

Dinner was a leisurely affair of Japanese dishes, most of which Harry recognized and all of which he enjoyed. Their conversation was easy and roamed over things past and present, mostly in Northern Thailand but relating to other parts of the country as well.

At the end of dinner they talked business, but only briefly. An agreement was reached on where to unload the Land Rover's ancient cargo. Sato suggested a small warehouse on the edge of Chiang Mai that belonged to Black Lion. The Land Rover could easily be driven in and unloaded without coming to anyone's attention. Only one man would be there and he was personally loyal to Sato.

They also made arrangements for Harry to pass Sato the addresses in the U.S. and Europe where the goods would ultimately be delivered to him and to Jean Lee. Sato gave Harry a telephone number through which he could be reached 24 hours a day.

"But don't worry, Ha-Lee," he added, "I will always find you."

With dinner over they went out on the "porch" where they sat and looked out over the lake while sipping cognac. Harry was feeling a pleasant glow induced by the food and the cognac.

"Tell me, Sato-san. Did they really call you that: the Samurai of the River Kwai?"

"Yes. I was an officer of the Imperial Japanese Army. I was a fierce warrior. So were we all. That was many years ago."

"And, after the war. You never went home?"

"My duty was here."

"But the fighting was over. The war ended."

"My duty was still here."

Harry sipped his cognac in silence, listening to the night sounds. After a while he said, "I've never wanted to leave Asia. Not permanently. I feel like Asia is a part of me. At the same time I know that I can never be part of Asia."

"This is not your world, Ha-Lee. This is not a place for those from the West. You all tried to make it your world. The French, the British, the Americans. You all tried to create a role for yourself here. In the end, you were all driven out."

"As were the Japanese," Harry pointed out.

Sato disagreed. "The Japanese were not driven out. Not by the Asian people. We were driven out by the superior military force of the Americans and British."

"The people here want the Japanese no more than they want the French, the British, or the Americans."

"Ha-Lee. I first came to Southeast Asia 50 years ago. It was not to fight the Thais or the Burmese or the Malaysians. It was to fight their colonial masters. We had no quarrel with our fellow Asians. We came to liberate them. The fought alongside us like brothers."

"Some did. Others fought you. The people of Southeast Asia did not want to replace Western colonialism with Japanese colonialism."

"We did not come as colonialists. We came as liberators. We came as leaders. We came to show the rest of Asia the road to prosperity."

"The Greater East Asia Co-prosperity Sphere."

"Yes. Co-prosperity. It is as true today. Japan has achieved prosperity. It can lead the rest of Asia to prosperity."

"Maybe the Thais and the others here want to find their own road to prosperity. There are many who do not want Japan to seek a role beyond its homeland. Not everyone sees a role for Japan in Southeast Asia."

"But that is our role, Ha-Lee. Japan will be the dominant power in East Asia. East Asia is our world. This is our right. What is the American word for it? I will say it in English. Manifest destiny. There. It is not so difficult to say. It is Japan's manifest destiny to rule in this part of the world. As it is America's manifest destiny to be the dominant power in the West."

Sato went on. "50 years ago, we lost a war. But were we defeated here? Look at our achievements. Thailand and the other countries in the region have prospered. The people live well. Better than they ever did. Why did they prosper? Because of Japan. Because Japan built factories here. Because Japan poured money and skilled people into the region to manage the factories and make the economies grow. Yes, Ha-Lee. Japan benefits from this. So do the Thai. So do the Malaysians and all the others. You see. My fight was not in vain."

Harry listened and said nothing. Sato said what most Japanese would deny. But the economic success of the Japanese in Southeast Asia could not be denied. Nor could the fact that Japanese success drove the economic boom that Southeast Asia now experienced.

"You listen to the ramblings of an old soldier, Ha-Lee. But you are not surprised. You do not criticize. This is not your world. But you understand it."

"Sometimes I think I understand it. Other times I know I don't."

"To recognize one's own ignorance is the beginning of wisdom."

Without any preamble, Harry asked, "Is Alo-wichit close to the Japanese?"

Sato was silent for a moment, then, "Why do you ask?"

"Last night in Chiang Rai, a man said something like he thought Alo-wichit was close to the Japanese. Then he wanted to shoot him."

"I have known Alo-wichit for some years. I can see why someone might want to shoot him."

"But is he close to the Japanese?"

Sato seemed to ponder this for a while. Then he leaned toward Harry and touched his sleeve. "No closer than you are, Ha-Lee san."

Harry laughed. "You are a devil, old man."

"Only an old man. And a tired one. It gets late. I will do you a favor and not offer you more cognac. Little Mouse must wonder when you will return."

"I told her I needed nothing more."

"A man always needs something more. She waits for you, Ha-Lee."

Harry got back to the guesthouse to find Little Mouse standing at the top of the steps. Without a word she led him into the house. She helped him out of his black pajamas.

"It is warm tonight," Little Mouse said. "You will not need that. Come, I will massage your back and help you relax."

That certainly seemed like a good idea. Harry laid on the bed and rolled over. He could feel Little Mouse kneel on the bed beside him. She started kneading his shoulders, then moved down his back. Despite the food and drink he was not sleepy as before. He was very conscious of the girl's touch and fragrance as she leaned over him, her hair gently brushing his back as her hands worked.

He turned to look at her. Her kimono was gone and there was no bikini to cover even the smallest part of her. He had to know. He rolled over and ran his hand lightly over her skin. She was soft where she should be, but he could also feel the strength of the muscles in her back and in her thighs. Her hands continued to do their work, but seemed more gentle now. He reached for her again, and felt no resistance as he drew her toward him.

16

Harry, why do you smile so much today? "Harry looked up from the papaya that he had been attacking with a big smile on his face. "Gee, Tong. I guess it's because this is one great papaya." "You were smiling before the papaya came," Tong said. She took a slow sip of her coffee. "You were already smiling when I got here."

Harry put down his spoon. Tong watched him very closely. It was very hard to keep anything from a Thai woman once she got to know you. Harry wiped his mouth carefully with his napkin. There it was again – a vivid flashback of Little Mouse and her deft little hands. He smiled into his napkin. When he looked back up he wore the most serious expression he could get on his face.

"Actually, I'm very pleased this morning. I accomplished a great deal last night." He smiled just briefly, then went on.

"The Japanese, Mr. Sato, brought me back here to the hotel just before you arrived. Everything is ready for our first shipment. We will deliver it tonight. Then we can go back up North."

"Maybe you will not go back up North. I heard from Aloysious last night. At 10 o'clock he will call the Pachyderm Tours office. He wants to talk with you there."

Harry looked across the veranda to the clock on the far wall. It was just a little after 8 A.M.

"Almost two hours. We don't have to rush through breakfast. How about some more coffee?"

"I must worry if you go with Japanese men. They are always chasing women. Very bad." Tong shook her head.

"Mr. Sato is old. I don't thing he has much interest in women anymore."

"Old men are the worst."

"Harry swallowed a mouthful of his four-egg omelet. "How do you know all this?"

"I watch. I see. Mostly I read the letters in the Thai newspaper to Miss

Bupha. She gives advice to people with such problems. It is educational."

"I'll bet it is. What does Miss Bupha have to say about old men?"

"Miss Bupha says 'Old fire burns low. Low fire burns very hot.'"

"Well, that sounds about right," Harry laughed. "How does Miss Bupha know all this?"

"She has been disappointed in love many times. She has experience. Sometimes I think she is not always right."

"Why do you say that?"

"Because you are already old, Harry. Your fire burns low. But I do not see it burn hot."

Harry started to cough. A fragment of toast got caught up his nose. He coughed and choked, and finally sneezed.

"You almost made me choke," he said. She poured more coffee into his cup. "I'm not that old, Tong."

"Maybe it is only old Japanese men who burn hot. I will have to write to Miss Bupha."

At 10 o'clock they were in the Pachyderm Tours office. An hour later Aloysious finally called. Harry told him that the transfer of the Land Rover load of artifacts to Sato's people would be made that evening and that arrangements for delivery in Europe and America were in place.

"Sounds good, Harry," Aloysious said when he had finished. It was as much of a pat on the back as anyone ever got from Aloysious.

"When can they deliver the stuff overseas?" Aloysious asked.

"In a couple of days if we need it. It's a small load. It can go by air."

"In that case, you get your ass back to the States as soon as you can. And start marketing. Your rich friend should get on his way to Europe. While you guys are enjoying yourselves, I'll keep hauling stuff out. By the time you get back, we'll have a big load ready to go. Can you be back in two weeks?"

"Ten days is about what I need. How about you? You can't move the big stuff by yourself."

"I got Ting-Tong. Don't worry. I'll save the tough work for you. Just get moving and make money."

As he hung up he looked at Tong. She was sitting on the other side of the desk and looked at him with her big brown eyes. "Does that mean you must go back to America?" she asked.

"For a couple of weeks, maybe."

"I will have to find an old Japanese."

"You won't have time. Aloysious will have you working in the caves. Right now we better call the airport and get me a seat on the Bangkok shuttle first thing in the morning. I should call Jean Lee and let him know I'm coming."

At dusk they headed for Sato's warehouse. It was located in a small industrial park a bit off the beaten path. The warehouse itself was unmarked, but well fenced. As the Land Rover reached the gate, a man in black coveralls stepped up and unlocked the gate.

"Good evening, Mr. Harry," he said in good English. He was Thai and young, wore spectacles, and had a paperback sticking out of his back pocket. He led the way to the building and rolled up the door. He stepped aside and waved the Land Rover inside.

They stayed in the warehouse much longer than Harry intended. He needed to separate the load into two piles. While they were still in the cavern, Harry had chosen pieces for his first shipment and for Jean Lee. When the load was transferred from the boat to Wit's camp and later loaded into the Land Rover, too many hands were involved. Everything was mixed together again. Although all of these pieces were relatively small and easy enough to lift, there were so many of them that even with Tong's help it got tiring. The guard seemed more interested in his paperback than art treasures and stayed outside to watch the gate.

It was late when Tong drove him back to his hotel. She could not stay. She was expected for a dinner at home where her parents were entertaining a small busload of relatives. He told her he was disappointed that they could not spend the evening together, but he really wasn't. He was just tired. The memory of Little Mouse was not as strong now, but it had not faded completely. Just before he fell into a deep dreamless sleep, he felt her fingers move slowly down his chest and across his stomach. "No more," he muttered, but no thought of stopping her fingers entered his mind.

At the airport departure gate the next morning, Tong shook Harry's hand as the business partner she had become. About to turn away, she suddenly pushed in close and pressed her face against his. "Come back soon," she said. Then she turned and walked away. He put his finger to his cheek where he felt the moisture of a single tear.

On his arrival in Bangkok, he went directly to Jean Lee's apartment. Lunch was laid out on the large balcony off the living room. An umbrella kept the sun off the table and a gentle breeze kept the balcony cool. The sounds of traffic below were muted and far away.

"I was afraid you have been living on canned things – or worse," Jean Lee said. "I had my cook do some traditional French dishes. You probably haven't had much of that in the caverns."

They sat down at a beautifully set table. The dishes were ivory china with a design of large pastel flowers, an art deco look that was not a reproduction. The silver was heavy, old, and ornate. There were more pieces than Harry knew what to do with. He did recognize the two pieces that signaled snails were on the way. He could already taste the garlic. A manservant came in and started serving lunch.

"From what you said on the telephone, I assume everything went well," Jean Lee said.

"Everything went fine. Better than I expected. I leave for the States in two days. I hope you're ready to travel."

"I'm prepared to go. Anytime. I would prefer to leave at the end of the week. How much time are you giving yourself to do everything?"

"I'll need about ten days at most. This is an expensive line of merchandise. I have only a few regular clients who can deal at that price level. I can handle them quickly. Then there are another ten or so people around the country that I want to contact. Most of my business can be handled by phone and courier. There are a few clients I will have to talk to directly."

"What about delivery?"

"I transferred the goods to our Japanese 'shipping agent' last night. Tonight, the shipment will be put on a boat, probably a small fishing vessel. Tomorrow or the next day it will be transferred to a seagoing vessel. Two days after that it will be on an aircraft. The following day you could take delivery in Paris. Or Frankfurt or London if you prefer. That should make it about a week from today."

"Splendid," Jean Lee said. "Delivery in Paris will be fine. I stay there with a very good friend. Remind me to give you an address before you leave here today. Earlier you mentioned photos of the big pieces...."

"Oh, yes," Harry said, pulling a large manila envelope from his flight bag. "Here you are. I had these done on an automatic Japanese minute-print machine that asks no questions. These are the big pieces still in the cave. There's a set for you."

He dug into his bag again. "And here are photos of the pieces you will find in your shipment when it reaches Paris. Take a look. They're some of the finer small pieces I could find in the mass of stuff in the cavern. I would say market value of any one of these pieces ranges from about 100,000 US dollars to maybe a million. That's my judgment. I defer to you on what the European market will bear. You will probably run a higher range of prices in Europe than I will in the States."

Jean lee looked at the photographs at some length. He finally laid them aside and shook his head.

"Absolutely remarkable! I am astounded at what you have here. These pieces are absolutely beautiful." Jean Lee chuckled. "I was about to say these things were rare. They were rare – until Aloysious found his city. To get back to your earlier statement about market value. You are right. There are pieces here that will fetch up to a million. Easily. And that's after the bargaining is done. Now, tell me, how will we handle 'orders' on the big pieces?"

"You show a photo and quote a price. If they like what they see and agree on a price, we can guarantee delivery within 90 days. Terms are 30 percent up front, 70 percent on delivery. Cash is preferred. Checks will do. Funds go into one of several convenient bank accounts in Europe."

"Bank accounts in Europe! You have been busy, Harry."

"Courtesy of our Japanese friend."

"Our Japanese friend." Jean Lee winced, theatrically. "He plays a very big role in all this. Are you comfortable with him?"

Harry thought about it. "I'm comfortable with him. I like the man and I have no reason not to trust him. Besides, I see no alternatives."

"Speaking as a businessman, Harry, it strikes me that the Japanese gentleman controls the shipment of goods. Before it's all over, he may control the money. Let's hope we all stay friends."

"There is a weakness there," Harry admitted. "I just don't see any other way to do it, given the time we have. You might consider setting up an account in Switzerland, or Liechtenstein, or wherever, while you're over there. As insurance. We can start dumping in some of the money you collect on this trip. It's not that easy for me in the States. Everyone back there is very conscious of money laundering. I can't dump hundreds of thousands of dollars into any of my accounts without lights flashing. Again, my Japanese friend came to the rescue. He has business accounts through which I can pass millions without being conspicuous."

Jean Lee shrugged. "So long as you are comfortable with it."

Harry gave what he hoped was a reassuring smile. "I am," he said, but then added, "There is something that bothers me. There is just too much Japanese in all of this."

Jean Lee continued to look at him intently, but said nothing.

"I don't know how to explain it," Harry continued. "It's a feeling I have. Part of it is that I can't believe our luck. It's all been very easy. Almost too easy. And a lot of that is due to our Japanese friend. Maybe I'm just afraid our luck will run out.

"The other thing," he went on, "is Aloysious. He doesn't share a lot of what he knows or what he does. He's involved in something that he's not talking about. I know he is. On top of all that, somebody is really pissed off at him. I still don't know what happened to him before I arrived. Then a couple of nights ago, a tribal gentleman up in Chiang Rai wanted to shoot him. The weird thing is, he wanted to shoot Aloysious because he was somehow tied in with the Japanese."

After pouring that all out, Harry fell silent. When it seemed that he had nothing more to add, Jean Lee asked, "Are we in league with the Japanese? Or are we not?"

"Well...we are," Harry said. "But we're not. Not in a way that some guy up in the Thai hills would even know about it. Or want to blow one of us away. Besides, I'm the one who's been in touch with Sato. Not Aloysious."

Jean Lee shrugged. "What can I say? We make do with what we have. Cheer up. Think of the money we will find at the end of this rainbow."

"I'm thinking of it, Jean Lee," Harry said. "But, remember: before the rainbow, comes the storm."

17

The fax was waiting for Harry when he went to breakfast in the Sweet-T Coffee Shop the next morning. He looked it over twice before he recognized where it came from. It was signed, "Miss Lotus, the Director, The Happy Dragon Gallery. "Lotus, or Mitchiko as he preferred to think of her on such occasions, really had taken charge. The letterhead on the fax was new. It incorporated his trademark dragon, but the lettering spelling out the name was new and rather elegant looking, as was the word Gallery. He had never viewed the Happy Dragon as a "gallery." The word had a suggestion of pretentiousness that Harry thought his efforts to sell old Asian things did not deserve. And Mitchiko had taken on a new title. She was now "Miss Lotus, the Director."

He studied the letterhead for a minute. Then he said the words to himself: "The Happy Dragon Gallery." He liked the sound of it. What the hell, he thought. Why not? A touch of class.

He had sent Mitchiko a short fax from Chiang Mai, asking her for a list of items he could buy for the Happy Dragon before leaving Bangkok. This was the response.

"Dear Mr. Harry," the fax began. "Business very good. Need new stock quick as listed below. Note Baby Jesus for Uncle Noah. This item Very Important. Christmas here very soon. Everything O.K. Made a few changes. Regards, Miss Lotus, the Director." There followed a list of items such as (1) Buddha, antique, small standing, three; (2) Buddha, antique, small sitting, two; (3) Elephants, old/new, all position, all size, many. And so on for another two dozen items.

At the bottom was a handwritten note: "Very Important. (Underlined three times.) Christmas coming. Uncle Noah needs Baby Jesus set w/Animals, Angels, Field worker, 300 set. Also Ornament for Christmas tree, assorted wood, cloth 1,000 piece. Miss Lotus, Dir." Oh, God, he had overlooked the proximity of the Christmas retail season. That was something he had not done very often in recent years. If nothing else, Uncle

Noah would not let him forget it. It was a busy time of year for Harry and the Happy Dragon, but it was an especially active time for Uncle Noah's Wonder World Imports Incorporated. It goes to show you, he thought, what finding a lost city and tens of millions of dollars worth of artifacts will do to a man's memory.

He ate his toast and studied the list. Time was short, but maybe it wasn't too bad. At least he had had the foresight to buy some of the more obvious things during his free moments in Chiang Mai. What he had bought there was already on the way to Bangkok where it would be consolidated by his shipping agent and sent on to the Happy Dragon. There was very little on the list that he could not buy quickly in Bangkok.

One item bothered him. Baby Jesus sets. This was a little out of his line. Baby Jesus sets were not exactly an indigenous folk craft item in Buddhist Thailand. Where could he begin to look?

He got up from his breakfast and walked to the telephone just outside the coffee shop. He dialed Jean Lee's number. A young male voice answered. "Give me Jean Lee quick," Harry said. "This is urgent."Jean Lee came on the line. "Jean Lee. Harry here. I need a bunch of Baby Jesus sets."

"Harry? You all right?"

"Of course I'm all right. I need Baby Jesus sets. For Uncle Noah."

"You mean crèches, Harry."

"Whatever. Where can I get a couple hundred? Christmas is on the way and Uncle Noah has a big order. You know Uncle Noah's motto: 'Uncle Noah never disappoints'.'"

"I believe Uncle Noah is saved. My research and development section has produced an excellent crèche. I never thought it was your kind of thing. I will have to check our inventory, but it's just possible that we may be able to fill your order."

"Okay, but it has to be right. Your set includes animals and field workers?"

"Yes, the usual. Geese, ducks, water buffalo, at least one elephant. I'm not sure what kind of workers they are. One or two may be in from the field. One looks like a cab driver."

"Cab driver?"

"Well, pedicab."

"Oh. I guess that's okay. Don't want anything too contemporary. All right, try to get me 300 sets if you can. We'll have to send them air. I'll be in touch."

He went back to the coffee shop to finish his breakfast. In a way it was good to be back dealing with a mundane but familiar reality. The last couple of weeks had been a bit unreal, to say the least. He looked at the fax again. His eyes caught on "Made a few changes." Harry wondered. The rest of that day and the next were taken up with Harry rushing around Bangkok trying to find some of the items on Lotus's list, and others that he thought might sell well at Christmas. Gradually, he realized, he was starting to slide back into his Stateside frame of mind. From Daring Adventurer, Treasure Hunter, Discoverer of Lost Cities, he was already sliding back to his more banal identity as a merchant, a retailer of Oriental curiosities.

"Shit," Harry said, rather loudly.

The antiques dealer Fu Lai Wang, with whom he had been bargaining for a small antique lacquer bowl when he had these thoughts, was taken aback by such a crudity from Harry.

"Well. If you feel that way, Harry," Fu Lai Wang said a bit crossly, "I will reduce the price. But only by 1,000 baht. I have children to feed."

Pulled away from his own thoughts by these words, Harry looked at Fu Lai Wang quizzically. The old man's eyes were on the lacquer bowl. It was Fu Lai Wang's teenage daughter, standing behind her father, who snapped Harry back to reality. She gave him a big wink, and her face lit up brightly with a smile.

He did a double take. "Whatever, Wang," he said, then looked again beyond Wang to the daughter. Her face had returned to a wooden mask of inscrutability. It was as if the wink and smile had never happened. The cold winds of home seemed far away again.

The flight back was unending. To Harry it seemed he had been confined within this plastic-lined metal cylinder all his life. He slipped in and out of consciousness, awaking each time to find yet another movie on the small screen five seats away, still another meal being served.

He closed his eyes again to shut it all off. He was visited by great stone snakes that reared over him. The sound of a flute filled his ears. A Khmer dancer appeared, bare-breasted and smooth-skinned. Her hands danced like serpents before her face. Harry's eyes followed down along the curve of her stomach. She moved closer, almost close enough to touch.

"Harry. Harry." His eyes were pulled back to the dancer's face. Her hands continued to move with a life of their own, hiding her features. His eyes dropped back to her stomach. The music stopped. "Harry, why do you smile so much?" The hands before Tong's face had stopped dancing. One was now shaking him gently.

"Chicken or beef, sir? Would you like some wine with your meal?"

Harry watched the remains of his dinner congeal, and mused how like life that was. You get old and used up, and then you start to congeal. But not Harry. Not for now. Seeing the lost city, walking through buildings that no one had entered in centuries had stirred the juices of his life. And there was more to come.

There was one aspect to his future that he had not given any real thought to. That was the money. There would be a lot of it when all this was over. He would have enough to do as he pleased. To buy an apartment like Jean Lee's high above Bangkok, and live elegantly. He laughed out loud at that, and then looked around self-consciously. His seatmates, plugged into their headsets, never noticed. Live elegantly. That was not really his style. He would congeal very quickly. No. There would be other things to do with money, real money. He didn't know what, but he knew he would find something to do with the money when it came. Something amusing, or at least interesting. Find another lost city. In fact, it didn't really matter if he found another lost city. It was the looking for it that counted. That was a way to keep life from congealing.

The flight eventually ended as it had to, but not before putting Harry into Washington's Dulles Airport hours behind schedule. It was dark, cold, and windy when he arrived, and his ambition extended only as far as the nearest hotel, where he spent a long dreamless night. The next morning he took a cab directly to the Happy Dragon.

He stood before the window of the Happy Dragon – or The Happy Dragon Gallery, as the sign overhead now read. The window looked good. It looked rich. Classy. Each piece was displayed in a way that best brought out its individual character and emphasized its best points. He had always disliked doing things in the window. It didn't seem proper somehow. If Mitchiko could do this well, he would have to let her do more of it – all of it if she wanted.

"Oh, Harry," Mitchiko said as he stepped in the door. She looked disappointed somehow. He followed her eyes down to his shoes that were buried in a mound of leaves. "We had no problems with debris from outside while you were gone." She said this as she approached him with a broom in hand, and he was not absolutely certain what the broom was going to be used for.

While Mitchiko swept the leaves back outside, he looked around. The shop looked as good as the window. Nothing was very different. It was just that everything was displayed to its best advantage.

"I have to hand it to you, Mitchiko. You really have the place looking great."

"Thank you, Harry. It is all the doing of Miss Annabelle."

"Annabelle?"

"Our new employee. She is from Hong Kong, I think. At least she was employed by a design studio there. She has exquisite taste. She has advised me on how to make things more attractive. She designed the new logo. She suggested we call ourselves a Gallery. She has many ideas."

Harry looked around the shop. "Where is this paragon of good taste? I can't wait to meet her."

"Actually, Miss Annabelle is an employee of Uncle Noah. Things were very busy, Harry. Uncle Noah received many Christmas orders. There were many things to send out."

"You let her in the basement!"

Mitchiko ignored the edge in Harry's voice. "Miss Annabelle lives there now."

"Lives there? Lives in the basement?"

Mitchiko ignored the incredulity in Harry's voice. "Well, she has no passport," she said. "We thought it best that she not spend too much time up here. She does the window dressing in the evening."

"No passport?"

"It doesn't really matter. She said she would never have been given a visa to enter America anyway."

"She's some kind of illegal immigrant? We'll all go to jail."

"Oh, Harry. You worry too much. It's only some kinda political thing."

"Oh, yes. Of course," he said. "I see," although he really did not see at all. "Just keep her out of sight for now. We'll sort it all out later."

"You will have to wear your things," Mitchiko said, making small gestures with her fingers under her nose. "She really believes she works for Uncle Noah. She has admired his picture in the catalogue. She thinks Uncle Noah is very handsome."

"Oh, wonderful," Harry said. "I can't wait to dress up and meet her. But I will. Right now we have some work to do. I want to go back in the office and draft some letters. I'll need the 'A' list and the 'B' list."

"They are in the file, Harry. If you need me, please call me."

In the little office at the back of the shop, he pulled two folders from the cabinet, settled into a chair, and laid the folders out on the desk before him. The "A" list and the "B" list. These were two of the Happy Dragon's biggest assets.

The "A" list was an even half-dozen names. The criteria for the "A" list was having a great deal of money and a demonstrated willingness to part with some of it at the Happy Dragon. The "B" list, with the same criteria, included some 30-odd names. The difference between the "A" list and the "B" list was simply taste. The six individuals on the "A" list had it. The 30-odd on the "B" list did not. At least not what was generally accepted as "taste." Not "taste" as an "art dealer" might perceive it.

Each of the six "A" list persons was a collector steeped in the knowledge of a particular field. At a glance each could place a piece in its historical context. With the same glance each could judge the authenticity of the piece, and hold it forever after with the strongest conviction. Each of these individuals understood his particular field intimately, and measured everything by the standard set by the penultimate piece of that era. Because of that, none of these people was easily separated from any money for a piece they considered inferior, which was virtually everything that came on the market in the last two or three hundred years. Dealing with serious collectors was difficult.

The "B" list was a happier group. Some were quite serious collectors. Others were dabblers. Not one had anything like the knowledge of the "A" list. The "B" list made up for it with enthusiasm. All had in common an ability to react to a thing itself. Some loved Asia and the things that came from there. Others didn't care. It did not matter if an object was Asian or Albanian. The object had to have a proper form, a pleasing look. The appeal was in the thing itself, not the tradition it came from or the history it was burdened with. The "B" list was much quicker to hand over money for an object perceived as beautiful – or only "interesting."

Harry went down the names. He knew the "A" list by heart. Even before he looked, he knew there were only two possibilities. One, a middle-aged professor of Southeast Asian art, who had considerable family wealth. The other, an old man who had made an immense fortune doing business in Asia after the Second World War. Both were collectors of Asian art with highly developed tastes.

The "B" list was more difficult. Interests were more eclectic. There were only a handful with purely Asian tastes. He wrote those names down. There were others. Some with interest in statuary. Some with interest in forms. Of the latter there were five with particular interest in the female form, three with specific interest in the male form. He noted these. A handful were interested in the primitive. He rejected these. There were three, each interested only in paintings or wooden architectural pieces. He rejected these as well. There was one whose primary interest was birdbaths. He puzzled over this one for a time, and then added it to his list.

Twenty-three "B" list names made Harry's short list. Not because he detected a good possibility of interest in what he would offer, but because "B" list interests were so unpredictable. What the hell, we'll send them all a letter, he concluded. Curiosity will bring most of them here for a look. Once they're here – zap! A percentage would be intrigued, fall in love with a particular piece, and buy.

By late afternoon he had drafted the two letters. One for the two "A" list clients; another for the "B" list. Each said essentially: Dear valued client. It has been our good fortune to be chosen as agent for an estate disposing of a major collection of Southeast Asian art. We invite you, valued client, to this once-in-a-lifetime opportunity to acquire a major art work from this region. These magnificent pieces will be on display at the Happy Dragon Gallery on the following dates, etc., etc. Yours Most Sincerely, Harry C. Ross.

At closing time Mitchiko found Harry C. Ross slumped over his desk, sound asleep. She threw a blanket over him, and advised Miss Annabelle in Uncle Noah's Wonder World Imports Incorporated below, not to worry herself about the window that evening, and that it was best to stay out of sight.

18

When Mitchiko arrived the next morning she found Harry already hard at work on the telephone. On the desk in front of him he had a jug of coffee and a little black notebook. He had rarely used the phone numbers in the notebook. These did not belong to clients as such, but to contacts Harry had made over the years. All of them had money. All had some interest in Asian art, although neither Asia nor art was their main interest. Most were "investors." All were bargain hunters.

He had already spoken with a high-ranking official in the World Bank, a Wall Street bond salesman, a Texas oilman, an exotic car dealer in Miami, and a mutual fund manager in the Midwest. In each case his pitch was the same as that he used with the senior European UN diplomat he was speaking with now.

"I represent a client liquidating a major collection of the highest quality Southeast Asian stone and bronze pieces. None of these pieces has ever been available on the American market. We are looking for quick sales. Consequently our prices are exceptionally good. My client is a very private individual. He desires no publicity from the sale. If you have an interest in seeing what we're offering, I will send you photographs."

The pitch invariably generated questions – and then interest that Harry could feel grow as he continued to speak and his listener picked up the scent of a bargain. As Harry spoke, it became obvious to them that a major collection was being dumped. And being dumped in a way that would avoid the taxman. This was an opportunity not to be missed. He was not surprised when all but two of those he called requested the photos. In the voices of the two who did not ask for photos, he was sure he heard regret, probably because they were over-invested in other areas.

By early afternoon, with all his calls made, he was quite pleased with himself. Things were moving along better than he could have hoped. There were real prospects out there. He had already ordered another two dozen copies of prints and would have Mitchiko start sending these out as soon as they were ready. Mitchiko buzzed him from up front.

"Someone on the phone for you, Harry. He will not give his name." Mitchiko giggled. "I think it is Karlo."

Harry sat up. Karlo! God, he hoped it was Karlo. Karlo was the first one he had called this morning. He had left a message on his machine. He picked up the phone. "Ross here."

"Ah, Ross. 'K' here." A languid voice. It was Karlo. "I received your message. I'm very, very busy. However, I will be passing through your area in three days. If we can meet as before...."

"The hotel near Dulles?" Harry asked.

There was a stony silence on Karlo's end.

"All right," Harry conceded.

"As before." It came as a command from Karlo's end. "In three days."

"In three days," Harry repeated. There was nothing but a click on the line as Karlo hung up.

Damn fool, Harry thought. He has to do it like a covert operative. Ah, well, he sighed. Damn fool Karlo might be, but he was a damn fool who was Harry's best prospect for a really big sale. Karlo was in a class by himself. Mitchiko buzzed back.

"Was it Karlo?" she asked.

"It was Karlo."

"A strange man," she said.

"I plan to see that strange man on Friday morning. Don't you let me forget."

"You will not forget, Harry. Guarantee it." Mitchiko was giggling as she clicked off.

It was the middle of the next afternoon when the event occurred that he had been waiting for. He was nodding off in the warmth of his office when Mitchiko buzzed.

"Mr. Ross, I have a gentleman here. He says he is delivering a shipment for you."

"Miss Lotus, I'll be right there." This had to be it. The shipment of artifacts from Thailand, courtesy of Sato.

A young Japanese in a business suit was standing at attention next to Mitchiko. He bowed as Harry approached.

"Sato-san sends Mr. Harry best regards. Sato-san hopes our service meets all expectations."

"Where's the stuff?" Harry asked.

"We deliver now," the young man said. Then he brought a compact radio up to his lips and said something in Japanese. Almost instantly two men in dark coveralls came through the door, each carrying a box. After stacking the boxes where they were told, the two went out and got more. Before long there was a neat pile of boxes on the floor.

The business suit snapped to attention again. "Our instructions: To remove boxes from shipping container before we deliver to Mr. Harry. We must not make mess for Mr. Harry."

"Mr. Harry appreciates the nice thought," Harry said.

"If nothing else, sir...." The young man left with a final bow to Harry.

Harry carried the boxes back to the office. Once they were all opened and he was satisfied that the shipment was complete, he called Mitchiko.

"Well, Miss Lotus, what do you think of that?"

"Oh, such beautiful pieces, Harry. And so many. Where shall we put them all?"

"The ones over there are for the shop. I'll help you put them out. Somewhere near the back. I don't want any of these pieces put in the window. The rest will stay here. Some on the desk. Some on the floor. Maybe you can get some into the bookcase."

"It is a shame no one will see these."

"I don't want anybody to see these except the "A" list and "B" list. And only if they ask. Some of this will be my traveling exhibit for people like Karlo."

Mitchiko got busy. Before long, a dozen of the smaller Khmer pieces were displayed with good effect at the rear of the shop. Because they were small pieces, they were not conspicuous. The eyes of the average browser would pass over them without hesitation. Few of the Happy Dragon regulars would recognize what the pieces represented in either monetary or historical terms. It was not that they could not recognize a great piece. It was simply that they would not credit what they saw. The Happy Dragon had never had a collection of pieces like this. Even world class "galleries" rarely did.

By Thursday, several "B" list clients telephoned in response to Harry's letter, as did the "A" list Southeast Asian art professor. Harry made separate appointments for them to visit the Happy Dragon.

On Friday morning Harry showed up at the Happy Dragon early. Mitchiko knew the drill and was there when he arrived. Together they carefully packed into metal cases the 15 pieces that he had selected for Karlo. When the packing was done to his and Mitchiko's satisfaction, he loaded the cases into a beat-up Volvo station wagon that served him on such occasions.

"Okay, Miss Lotus. Don't expect me until late in the afternoon."

"I hope you have a good day with Karlo. Sell a lot, Harry."

Harry wore a big smile as he slid into the Volvo for the long ride out to Dulles Airport. The place that Karlo invariably chose for their meetings was a hotel a short way from Dulles. It was one of a growing number of hotels that in recent years had sprung out of the farmland which decades earlier had spawned Dulles Airport. There was nothing to distinguish this hotel from any other. It was gray and remote, and anonymous. And that was why Karlo liked it.

Karlo was not his real name. The young man who later would become Karlo had started his working life in a well-endowed museum as a bean counter. He had studied art for his mother and accounting for his father. He became an accountant with a good eye. His eye for art was so exceptional – it was said – that with a glance he could date any Chinese piece to within ten years of its creation, and then say precisely what the piece would fetch at the next major auction. His eye for Southeast Asian art was not quite that good, but it was good.

Because of his eye, Karlo was moved early on by his museum from accounting to acquisitions. Soon he was in charge of acquisitions. On the side he became a consultant and a highly paid buyer for several major private collectors.

Karlo's real name, Harry remembered, was something like Wilber. When Karlo left his ledgers, he left behind his name, his conservative hairstyle, and his wardrobe of three-piece suits. At the time he felt his name should be European-sounding, and became Mr. Andre. The name Karlo came later. He used it to deal "anonymously" with acquisitions that required the utmost discretion.

From the beginning Karlo understood that art could be a highly dangerous business. As his reputation as Mr. Andre grew, so did his fear that Mr. Andre would lose his good name. There was indeed reason for this. Mr. Andre sought out art anywhere it might be found at a bargain. It was not unusual to find him poking through flea markets in Paris, or tribal villages outside Chiang Mai. Mr. Andre traveled everywhere, dealt with everyone. With each trip his fear grew that in buying magnificent art at the lowest possible price, fate would sooner or later put in his hands stolen, counterfeit, or otherwise embarrassing goods. Not that Karlo would not consider buying such objects if the price was right. He just did not want to be caught at it.

And thus Wilber became Mr. Andre, and Mr. Andre became Karlo, the mysterious buyer of art. If one had access to great art and to a certain telephone number, a simple call would ultimately cause Karlo to appear.

Harry had dealt with Karlo on occasions in the past and always found the experience profitable. The secret for dealing with the Karlos of this world had been told him by an old French antiques dealer in Saigon many years ago: "Set your first price high. Come down only with a show of great reluctance. Let him see that you really covet the piece for yourself. Finally, learn to make great beads of sweat stand out on your forehead when you name the price you really want."

Harry had never been able to sweat from his forehead on command, but he could be a tremendously reluctant seller. He also knew better than to let Karlo know that he knew Karlo's identity as Mr. Andre. Or, God forbid, Wilber. That was easy enough. Harry had forgotten Karlo's real name long ago.

Harry lugged the shiny metal cases into the lobby. The place was dismal. It was done in a dozen shades of tan, and was all but deserted. He piled the cases near a potted tropical tree and waited. The only interest he drew was from an impatient looking woman seated nearby, who stared at him through bifocals for a time before getting up and walking to the desk. He looked up from his watch just in time to see Karlo go by no more than a foot away.

"Four-oh-eight," Karlo whispered.

Harry stood and watched until Karlo was gone. Then he started lugging the cases to where Karlo had gotten on the elevator.

Karlo met him at the door to room 408, his pencil-thin mustache quivering in the air. "Good Lord, Ross. How many cases are there?"

"Six. There are four more in the elevator. I have the door blocked."

"Ross, Ross. You will have everyone in the hotel wondering what we're doing. This just won't do."

"Take it easy there, Karlo. Just hold the door. I'll have everything inside in a minute."

"Oh, my God. How much more is there?"

"That's the lot. Shut the door and no one will be the wiser."

"Oh, God. Everyone downstairs will wonder what you brought up here."

"I told the guy on the desk I was a brush salesman. Told him I had to demonstrate my extensive new toilet bowl line in your room."

"Ross, sometimes I think you do things like that just to irritate me."

Harry started to unpack the pieces, slowly. Karlo took each piece as it came out of the case, then cradled it carefully in his arms to examine it. Harry remembered that Karlo rarely said much during his examinations, but this time he obviously could not contain himself.

"These are absolutely beautiful. I've never seen a collection like this. I hope your prices are reasonable. I see a lot of things I like."

Karlo watched as Harry emptied the last two cases. "My God, there's even more," Karlo said.

"I have pictures for you, too."

After examining each piece, Karlo looked at the photographs. Then he laid back on the couch as if exhausted. With his hand to his forehead he said, "Harry, this is an incredible find. Wherever did you get it all?"

"My client is an old collector. He lived in Asia 50 or 60 years ago, when prices were nothing. Now he's liquidating. Getting rid of all this – and more. But the price has to be right, or the old man won't sell."

"Won't sell? He has to sell, Harry! These pieces are meant to be enjoyed by many others."

"One other thing you should know. The old man knows that if he sells, he'll make a lot of money. He wants to do that without turning the whole thing into the world's biggest taxable event."

"Harry, Harry, I understand that. Of course, I do. You know I'm discreet. We will handle the money however you like. Switzerland, the Channel Islands, wherever you wish."

"Good. We'll discuss that later. Let's do some prices."

Karlo was on his feet, shaking his finger in the air, excitedly. "One thing you must understand, Harry. I have clients I know will be most interested in this collection. These are important clients. One is a major museum. We...ah, they will want some of this."

Karlo gestured at the figures that now stood on the tables and on the floor around the room. "And, I'm sure, they will want some of the big pieces in the photos. But there must be no problems." Karlo looked around the room and then continued. "These look like excellent pieces to me. I'm sure they are. But the museum has to be certain. They will do tests. They must do tests. I cannot afford to buy bad pieces."

Harry had never seen Karlo less than supremely confident in his abilities. He must be planning to spend a lot of the museum's money if he was so concerned.

Harry shrugged. "So, let them test."

"Good. Good. I knew I could count on you, Harry." Karlo rubbed his hands together. "Now let's get on with it. I will separate out the pieces I definitely want. Then I will show you the ones in the photographs that I want. Then we can talk prices."

As Karlo worked he paused once to look up at Harry. "You say there is even more?"

"In a month or two. If the old man decides he wants to sell it all."

Karlo shook his head silently. After a time he said, "I shall want to see it all. Tell your man that."

Harry smiled conspiratorially. "Not to worry. I'll give you first crack. If...if he wants to sell." He knew that talk like that drove Karlo up the wall.

19

The weekend was busy. Telephone calls and visits by "B" list clientele kept Harry running. As he expected, sales success with the Happy Dragon's regular clientele was modest. Three of the small pieces, the least expensive ones, went to the "B" list. The "A" list surprised him pleasantly. The professor bought a nice mid-range piece. The old businessman could not make up his mind between three pieces he liked. He said he would call back with his choice before the end of the weekend, and Harry was sure he would.

Harry still glowed over his big success with Karlo. Of the 15 pieces he had carried over to Karlo's hotel room, only two came back. For the 13 pieces he took, Karlo agreed to deposit into one of Sato's European accounts 1,650,000 dollars. Harry's mind reeled when he said the figure aloud to himself – which he did several times that weekend. His mind absolutely boggled when he thought of the figure that Karlo had agreed to pay for the 12 large pieces he "ordered" from the photographs: Six Million Dollars!

Harry was not simply smiling when he drove back from Karlo's hotel in the old Volvo. He was laughing out loud. Super salesman Harry Ross. One world-class sale of Asian antiquities equaled 7,650,000 American dollars. One for the books. Now, let's see. What was his percentage of that...?

All through the weekend he walked on air. Clients who had received photographs and telephoned back with questions were met with new confidence.

"The collection is world-class. We have museums fighting over it. Pardon me? Oh, the item in photo number 24. Let me see. Ah, yes. It's an 11th-century piece. How do I know? I know the provenance of the piece, sir. Yes, exactly. I know from whence it came. Ha, ha. Discount? No, sir, I'm afraid there can be no discount on these items. Immediate payment? Cash? Well...in those circumstances, I think we may be able to work out something where we can absorb ten percent of the price. Yes sir, not to worry. I will hold number 24 for you. We will send you instructions on payment. Thank you for calling."

The phone rang again. He let Mitchiko take it. A second later Mitchiko buzzed him. "It's for you," she said.

"Got it. Hello."

"Ross? That you?" An unmistakable Texas twang.

"Yes, Harry Ross here."

"Ross, goddammit! Buzz Dorkin here."

Harry's face split in another big smile. "Hey, Colonel. How you doing?"

"Fine, son. How you?"

"Great, Colonel. What's up?"

"Some of that artsy crowd you hang around with are saying you have a treasure trove of ill-gotten goods. I'm real disappointed you didn't call me first thing."

"Colonel, I've been calling you for days. I don't get anything but a busy signal."

"That goddamn dog has knocked the phone off the hook again. I'm going to have to give you some numbers that goddamn dog don't know. Hey, can you get your ass out here to see me? I'm a little busy right now. No way I can get over to your place in the next couple of weeks. I don't want the artsy fuckers to buy up all the nice stuff you have."

"Hey, Colonel. You just tell me when. I'll be there."

"Okay, son. Tell you what. My boy will be up there beginning of the week with the Lear. He'll be turning right around anyway. You can come back with him."

"That's great, Colonel. I'll bring you things you won't be able to live without."

"Well, son, I hope you have some real nice stuff to show me. My boy will be in touch with you. Keep 'em flying, son."

"Keep 'em flying, Colonel."

"Hot damn!" Harry said to himself. No wrong moves. Everything was working out better than he dared hope. Buzz Dorkin. Son of a bitch. He had thought he might not be able to get hold of him. Now it looked like he was going to get a free trip to Texas. Before it was over, he would tie up a deal with Dorkin worth another million. Harry stuck his head out of the office, looking around carefully. Mitchiko was up front. There was no one else in the Happy Dragon. He threw his head back.

"Wahoooo!" He yelled at the top of his lungs.

"Harrrrry! Stop that!" Mitchiko had her fingers in her ears.

"I'll buy you dinner, Miss Lotus. We'll all be rich," he shouted back at her.

"Don't yell," she said.

Harry started walking up front, when out of the corner of his eye he caught a movement behind the partially open door leading to the basement. Something big was moving there.

Instinctively Harry hunkered down into a low crouch. Mitchiko was on tiptoes trying to see what was going on. "What the hell is that?" he asked, and started moving toward the door. Whatever it was, it was big.

"Harry...," Mitchiko said.

It was big. And it was covered in batik. Harry moved closer. One eye was watching him. He picked up a small bronze figure and held it like a club. The eye watched.

"Harry...Harry! It's only Miss Annabelle."

Harry stopped in mid-crawl. "It's what?"

"Miss Annabelle. She was bringing a box up from the basement while no one was here." Mitchiko walked quickly back to where Harry was still crouched down. "Come, Mr. Harry. You can meet her. Uncle Noah can meet her some other time."

Miss Annabelle was a big lady. And she was covered in batik. At least the loose shirt she wore was batik. Her trousers looked like black silk. The shirt was big enough to be not one, but probably a matched pair of antique Indonesian sarongs that once belonged to the Happy Dragon.

Miss Annabelle bowed repeatedly as Mitchiko introduced her. She was about as tall as Harry, but maybe three times as wide. She had a big, round, happy-looking face that was framed by straight black hair chopped off even with the bottom of her ears. She examined Harry from behind a pair of round steel-rimmed glasses that looked as big as dinner plates.

"Most happy to meet you," she said. She took Harry's extended hand when he offered it, and pumped it three times, like the handle of a cistern. "Happy to meet you," she said again.

"Miss Annabelle has been very useful, Mr. Harry," Mitchiko said.

"Most happy to meet you," Miss Annabelle said.

"Miss Annabelle has not only given us good advice, but she carries the heavy boxes up and down the stairs," Mitchiko said.

"Most happy to meet you," Miss Annabelle said again.

"She has been particularly useful to Uncle Noah's work," Mitchiko added.

"Uncle Noah?" Miss Annabelle said, looking quizzically at Harry.

"Uh...," he said.

"Mister Harry," Mitchiko said.

"Most happy to meet you," Miss Annabelle said.

"Miss Lotus," he said, "I have a feeling that Miss Annabelle speaks little or no English."

"I have been teaching her, Harry."

"That's great. But how do you manage to communicate?"

"We speak a little Chinese, a little Japanese."

"Japanese! I thought you said she came from Hong Kong."

"I think maybe she had a Japanese uncle."

"Oh, Christ!" he said, "Ask her if his name is Sato." And then, "Oh, never mind. I was only joking." He walked back to the office shaking his head and mumbling to himself.

* * * * *

On Monday morning the word came. At 8 A.M. on Tuesday, Harry was to present himself at lounge three in National Airport's General Aviation terminal. He was to ask for the Dorkin Lear.

It was bright and early Tuesday when a young lady with a badge pointed out two gentlemen sitting at a low table reading the morning papers. Harry started over.

"Mr. Ross?"

The voice came from behind. Harry turned around. The man was solid looking and tanned. "Don't know if you remember me," he said. "I'm Donney Dorkin."

Harry did remember. "Sure I remember you. You're Buzz's kid. It's been a long time." They shook hands.

"You our captain today?" Harry asked.

"You bet. I've got the Lear. Dad had me fly some of his friends up here yesterday. Only two of them going back. Once we're in the air, you come up front and we'll chat some."

Harry joined the two other passengers in the aircraft's cabin and strapped himself in. It was claustrophobic after flying in 747s for so long. Only minutes later it seemed, they were pointed straight up at the sky, climbing out of National Airport. He got a glimpse of the Washington Monument before clouds filled the window. Soon after they leveled off, a young man came back into the cabin. He leaned over Harry. "Mr. Dorkin would like you to go up front, sir."

Donney Dorkin motioned for Harry to take the co-pilot's seat. "You've had some stick time, haven't you, Mr. Ross?"

"Some, but not in anything like this. Better keep her on autopilot."

Harry settled back and flicked his eyes over the panel. He recognized some of it. "How's your dad?" he asked.

"Like always. Dad is fine. Still chasing the women. Still flying his airplanes. Hard to believe sometimes that he's over 70 years old."

"How's his business?"

"Well, the oil business has had its ups and downs in the last few years. But Dad is involved in so many other things that he's always busy. He's looking for an interstate bank to buy now. Says it's a good time for it."

"I'm sure it is. You say he's still flying his airplanes?"

"Oh, my God. Is he flying! He's got a new toy now. He doesn't spend any time on the ground he doesn't have to."

Harry laughed. "Colonel Buzz Dorkin. Sounds like he's still the hottest pilot this side of Tokyo."

"He sure is. But don't you get him talking about the war again. We have a hell of a time calming him down afterwards."

"Don't worry. I won't say a word about it – if he doesn't

They sat in silence for a while. The cloud base was 20,000 feet below them and the air was clear. It seemed they could see a thousand miles in any direction. There was nothing in sight but one tiny speck that moved like an insect across the side of the windshield.

Donney raised his eyebrows. "Bogey," he said.

Harry sighted down his finger at the airliner ten miles away. He flicked his thumb down. "Got em!" he said.

"Give it to Dad. It would make his day." They both laughed at that old joke. Anybody who knew Colonel Buzz Dorkin would.

It didn't seem like very much later that Donney Dorkin pointed his finger downward. "Dorkin Field. Right there off the port wing."

"This thing fits in there?"

"The old man had the runway paved since you last saw it. Hang on."

The landing was beautiful. Harry never knew when the airplane stopped flying. He got a good look at Dorkin Field on the way in. Last time there was one hangar and a small shed. There were two hangars now and a long single-story structure that looked almost like a proper terminal. The hangars stood off by themselves. They were big, but had an old-fashioned look about them.

Donney stopped the Learjet near one of the hangars and shut down the engines. Harry unbuckled himself. He stepped down on the tarmac and waited for Donney to complete some cockpit chores. In a couple of minutes Donney joined him.

"Thought I might see your dad. He's always been around here somewhere when we landed."

"I think he probably is," Donney Dorkin said with a slow smile growing on his face. "Let's walk on over to the operations building."

They started walking over to what Harry thought of as the terminal, about a hundred feet away. They chatted as they walked, and Harry just happened to be looking at Donney when Donney's eyes suddenly shifted to something over Harry's shoulder and grew wide. Harry swiveled his head.

A silver mass hurtled down, filling the sky over him like a giant fly swatter. Harry was pushed down flat on his stomach by instinct and by the wind and the sound the thing flung back as it roared over. Donney, on the ground next to him, was on his back laughing. "There he is. There goes Dad," he yelled.

Off in the distance now, Harry could see a silver P-38 climb and turn in a soaring chandelle. Wings flashed in the sun and Harry's ears rang with the sound of this great machine that was now too far away to hear.

"Buzz Dorkin! You son of a bitch!" Harry yelled and shook his fist indignantly. Donney was still laughing. Harry felt silly. He started laughing too. "Son of a bitch," Harry said again. "I walked right into an ambush. I should have known."

20

Harry watched warily as the big airplane taxied to a halt 20 feet away. The two huge propellers ticked over slowly and then stopped. A section of the pilot's canopy swung up and back, and Buzz Dorkin stood up in the cockpit. "Hey, Ross," he shouted. "Come look at my new airplane." Harry walked over. The size of the thing was impressive. Twin booms, each with an engine on the end, flanked the shorter fuselage that housed the pilot in the center of the aircraft. The plane sat high on its tricycle landing gear, high enough to let Harry walk under a wing without bending over. The plane was all highly polished aluminum except for numbers and Army Air Corps stars painted on the side of the booms and on the wings. On the nose, in painted flowing black script was "Pretty Lady." Under the words, a small standing nude seen from the back, studying her face in the mirror held in her hand.

"How do you like her, Ross?"

"She's beautiful, Colonel. Absolutely beautiful."

"She's a P-38 Lockheed Lightning," Dorkin said, patting the fuselage. "Queen of the Pacific Skies. A real lady. The P-38 killed more Jap airplanes than anything else with wings."

Harry ran a hand along the smooth aluminum flank. "She looks awfully fast, Colonel."

"Bet your ass she's fast. She's got turbo-superchargers. She'll do 400 an hour easy. Come on up."

Harry climbed up on the wing. Dorkin stood outside the cockpit and showed Harry how to climb in behind what looked like an automobile steering wheel. The cockpit was warm. An amalgam of smells rose from the airplane: gasoline, rubber fittings, hydraulic fluids, and the worn paint on the cockpit walls. The scent of vintage airplane. Hands on the yoke, feet on the rudder pedals, and eyes watching the sky through the scratched old windshield, Harry was at 20,000 feet closing on a Zero. The big red meatballs on the Zero's wings grew bigger as he closed in.

"Wanna take her up, Harry?"

Harry laughed. "God, I'd love to, Colonel. But I'm afraid neither of us would survive the experience."

"Wish I could take you up in her, Ross. But you can see, it's cramped with just one in there."

Harry climbed out, reluctantly. "I'll let you buy me a steak instead, Colonel."

"Now, Harry, how'd you know we were having steak?"

It was always steak at the Dorkin house. The house was just a couple of miles away from Dorkin Field. Dorkin himself always cooked them over a grill on the patio. While Dorkin organized dinner, Harry poked around looking for the hard liquor. Look in the study, Dorkin had told him.

Harry had visited the house before, and he had been in the study, but he had never had an opportunity to really look at the framed photos that covered most of one wall. He ran his eyes over them now.

The first things that caught his eye were the airplanes. He focused on one in particular. A P-38 Lockheed Lightning. It could have been the one he had just climbed out of, but he knew it wasn't. The photo had been taken in 1945 on some unremembered island in the Pacific. A young Dorkin was standing up in the cockpit, smiling. He held four fingers of his right hand out to the camera. On the side of the aircraft's nose, Harry could see three small painted Japanese flags. Each represented a destroyed enemy airplane. In front of the flags preened the same "Pretty Lady" that graced Dorkin's new toy.

"Yep. That was her, Harry." Dorkin stuck his head in the study door. "That was the original 'Pretty Lady'. The booze is over in that cabinet. Bring some Scotch and whatever you want out on the patio. Finish looking at the pictures first. I can't seem to get people interested in them anymore."

"OK, Buzz," Harry said and kept on examining the photographs. They represented the service life of Colonel Buzz Dorkin, from the skinny Army Air Corps Flight Cadet marching in formation with his classmates, to the US Air Force Colonel strapped into a 21st century-looking pressure suit in front of a needle-nosed jet fighter.

Colonel "Buzz" Dorkin, born Sonny Dorkin some 70-odd years ago in a small west Texas town, had come a long way. Over the years Harry had heard a lot of the stories, some from Dorkin and some from Dorkin's drinking buddies. Tonight he was sure to hear some more.

"That photo you were looking at, Ross," Dorkin told him later as they started tearing into their steaks. "That was a great day. The one with the P-38. I got my fourth kill that day. One more and I'd be an ace."

For a while the only sound was their knives scraping the dishes under the steak. Harry knew the story. Everybody who knew Dorkin did, although Dorkin himself rarely talked about it.

"Shit." Dorkin broke the silence. "I never did get to be an ace." Dorkin stared at his steak. "Do you know why?" The question was rhetorical. "The goddamn war ended! The goddamn war ended, and I only had a crack at one more Jap. I got the son of a bitch, too!" There was a long pause while Dorkin chewed a piece of meat. He swallowed and continued.

"My C.O., my Commanding Officer, was in the air that day. He was flying on my wing. When we went for the Jap, the C.O. was right behind me, shooting all over the sky. He never hit a thing in his whole life. He never hit anything that day. But they awarded him one-quarter of that Zero, just so he would have a score when the war ended. Goddamn it. I ended the war with four and three-quarter kills. One-quarter of a Jap shy of the five I needed to be an ace."

For Dorkin, who had aspired from childhood to be an ace, it was the ultimate humiliation. It was worse even than being born "Sonny" or having a name that made it so easy for all his friends to call him "Big Dork." Harry understood this and often wondered if it was this that drove him to his great success in business.

"At least we won the goddamn war, Ross. Although sometimes I wonder who the hell won. I guess what really happened is that we stopped fighting, and the Japs never did. A remarkable people, the Japanese. Great fighters. Maybe one day we'll have to fight 'em again."

"You don't mean that, Colonel?"

"Hell, we need an enemy. Having an enemy brings out the best in America. We don't have the Soviets anymore. The Soviets defeated themselves. Where's the threat now? If it's not the Soviets, the Chinese, or the Cubans, who is it? The Japanese are the only ones who can hurt us. Not with guns, but with money. With brains, for godsakes. Only goddamn thing they don't make better than we do is airplanes. And how long is that going to last? The Japs already supply most of the electronics for our planes."

Dorkin took a big swallow of Scotch. "You must know the Japanese pretty well, Ross. You lived there with them. They're all over Southeast Asia now. We beat them to their knees, and now they're back trying to conquer the rest of Asia." Dorkin stared morosely into his drink. Suddenly he looked up.

"You don't deal with any of those Japs now, do you, Ross?" he asked.

"Oh no, sir, Colonel!" Harry replied. In a distant corner of his mind Sato smiled a sly smile.

"They're treacherous," Dorkin went on. "Don't ever trust a Jap, Ross." After a while Dorkin added, "You know, I never could understand how people so caught up in their own superiority as the Japanese are, could be so humble in the creation of their art."

"Speaking of art, Colonel...."

"Ross, you're just trying to get me away from the Japs. Well, come on, show me what you brought."

Harry lugged out one of his metal cases. "I brought along only a couple of things. These are small pieces, Colonel. I didn't think you would be too interested. What I really want to show you are some photos."

Dorkin started going through the photos, bobbing eyebrows indicating a lot of interest. Dorkin's big interest – after airplanes – was art. His tastes were eclectic, but tended toward big, dramatic things, whatever the medium. Dorkin had the money to buy big.

"You got some collection here, son. What'd you do? Rob a museum?"

Harry was tempted to tell him where the pieces really came from. Dorkin would have gotten a kick out of it. Discretion prevailed, however. "No, unfortunately. An old collector is closing out his collection."

"It's a shame to break up a collection like this. You ought to tell the man to build his own museum."

For a minute Harry feared that Dorkin would beg off buying anything out of concern for the integrity of the collection whose existence Harry alleged. He needn't have worried.

Dorkin put down the photos. "Those little things you brought along. The little dancing girls. I kind of like them. They're cute. I'll take all three. They'll make good Christmas presents. Now, what are the terms on these big jobs here? What the hell are they? Some kind of gods? Buddhas?"

Harry explained photo by photo. By the time he was through, Dorkin selected four big pieces. But he wasn't through yet. After studying the pictures for a while longer, he finally said, "Why don't you pick out two more for me, Harry? They're all so nice, I can't make up my mind." Harry selected two that he thought were the best of what remained, and started to tell Dorkin why he thought so.

"Oh, hell, Ross. If you pick them, I know they're good. Just send a bill to my office in Dallas. Now, come on. Enough of this artsy stuff. Let's talk airplanes."

And talk airplanes they did, until the early morning hours. At the crack of dawn, Harry was up and ready. Donney would fly him to Dallas, where he could get a commercial ride back to the Washington area.

As Harry was getting ready to board the Learjet, Buzz Dorkin pulled him aside to where he could be heard over the whine of an engine.

"What I was saying last night, Ross, about the Japanese. It's not just that I'm pissed off about not getting my five. I really think the Jap is not to be trusted. Even now. So you watch your ass when you get back in Asia." He slapped Harry on the back. "Keep 'em flying, Ross."

"Keep 'em flyin', Colonel."

As the Lear roared into the sky, Harry could see Dorkin standing near the silver P-38, his arm high, his thumb up.

21

Ladies and gentlemen, please fasten your seat belts. We are beginning our descent into Bangkok." The announcement caught Harry daydreaming about the Ferrari Testa Rosa he was going to buy as soon as he got his percentage of the sales. He was still astounded by the amount of money he had caused to flow. His sales, when he included the big-dollar Dorkin and Karlo deals, were in excess of 11 million dollars. Not that he personally had anything to show for it. Not yet. But Sato's bank account should be bulging.

Harry's more immediate reward to himself was a business class ticket for his flight back to Bangkok, something he would normally regard an extravagant waste of money. Having done it, he enjoyed it. It bought him space on the 747's sparsely populated upper deck where he stretched out and daydreamed about an affluent future in between bouts of fitful sleep.

With Miss Lotus, or Mitchiko – that was the way he thought of her now that he was 12,000 miles away from that part of his life again – in control of the Happy Dragon's day-to-day affairs, breaking away had not been difficult. When his business with Buzz Dorkin was concluded, there was little left to be done. He had a brief pre-departure talk with Miss Lotus, told her she was doing an excellent job, raised her salary by a generous 25 percent, and left open the possibility of a sizable year-end bonus. In a very un-Japanese way, Miss Lotus had clapped her hands, kissed his cheek, and said how sweet he was to adopt the best of Japanese management practice. This show of gratitude had caught Harry completely off guard, and he had blushed as he mumbled, "*Domo arigato*."

"Where you go, boss?" the taxi driver outside the Bangkok air terminal asked. He looked a little closer at Harry. "Oh, it's you, boss. How are you? We go Patpong now?"

Harry squinted past him, into the darkness beyond. He detected a small movement near a gleaming black Mercedes that was all but invisible in the darkness. He had been half expecting a reception committee.

"Ah...not tonight. Thank you," Harry told the taxi driver and walked to where a stocky figure near the Mercedes held up a hand to get Harry's attention. The man opened the rear door as Harry approached.

"Welcome, Ha-Lee san," the stocky man said, and bowed. Up front, the driver turned as Harry climbed in the back. For just an instant something flickered across the man's somber face. It could have been a smile, Harry thought, and he felt almost among friends.

The Mercedes turned off the superhighway and into one of Bangkok's older residential areas. It was a section of town Harry did not know well. The streets were narrow here and all he could see from the back of the car were high walls and steel gates. Under the street lights, splintered shards of broken bottles glinted from where they were cemented into the tops of high walls. The Mercedes aimed at a gate that swung open as the car approached. It came to a stop under a portico at the side of a big house. From what Harry could see of it, the house was an oversized copy of something Frank Lloyd Wright might have done on a bad day. He stepped out of the car and followed the bodyguard.

They walked down a stone path through a lush tropical garden. In daylight it probably looked tame. In the darkness it was a tangle of giant leaves and dark, ragged forms that reached out at them as they walked by. The air was hot and heavy with moisture, but Harry shivered. They came into a clearing lit by stone lanterns and walked across the brushed sand to a small Japanese house at the center. Only an occasional rock glowed like old silver under the lanterns. Here the scene was friendly, and Harry relaxed. The guard stopped. He looked at Harry and pointed to where a soft light came through an open doorway.

Just inside the door, Harry saw that the light came from an inner room. He could see Sato bent over a small table. He was wearing a brown silk kimono with a pattern of delicate flowers etched in black. Harry thought the old man was asleep. It was a scene out of an old Japanese print.

"Ha-Lee. Welcome," Sato said as he turned his head and started to rise. "Please sit, Ha-Lee," he invited. "We will drink tea and talk. I hope your journey was not tiring."

"Not too tiring, Sato-san. It was a successful trip. Success is invigorating."

Harry seated himself at the table, Japanese style. He cast a glance around the room. "This is a fine house," he said. "Neither the wood nor the workmanship is Thai." Looking toward the ceiling, he added, "I would say the house was built a hundred years ago, on the Kanto plain, not far from Tokyo."

"You are indeed an expert, Ha-Lee. This house was my first extravagance. I had it brought from Tokyo and rebuilt here. It was the first time I spent money on myself easily. That was many years ago."

"And now you live here like an old Japanese lord," Harry said.

"I live here like an old Japanese poet. In the big ugly house up front I live like a Japanese lord. A modern one."

"I did not know you were also a poet, Sato-san."

"In my aspirations I am a poet. And perhaps only there. One day I will read you my poetry. It is difficult to translate. On days like today I come here to read words others have written. And to experience nature."

Sato seemed to be listening to something far off. "Listen, Ha-Lee. Do you hear it?"

Harry listened. "I hear nothing." There was silence that was absolute. He did not think it could be so quiet in the middle of one of the noisiest cities on earth. Then he heard it. "A cricket," he said. Sato smiled.

"Your prisoner?" Harry asked.

"In a cage that is a work of art."

"Is there a lesson in that, old man?" Harry asked.

"Only that humble things can be valued highly. But you have had much experience with that. Especially in recent days."

"Yes," Harry admitted. "We have made money. A lot of it. Have your bankers advised you?"

"I have seen the accounts. You did well, Ha-Lee. Now I need to know only what still needs to be done. What I can do to help you further."

"For the moment, nothing. I will go North tomorrow or the day after. Once I meet with Aloysious, I will see where things stand. He has had enough time to move more items into the city."

"I hope Alo-wichit does not have problems," Sato said with a sound of concern in his voice that made Harry smile.

"You look worried," Harry said, looking closely at Sato's face. But Sato looked as he always did. Harry added, "Don't worry, Sato-san, everything is going well. Very well."

"Too well, perhaps?" Sato asked with a quizzical smile. "When things work too well, I do get worried, Ha-Lee. It causes fate to step in. In Thailand, it causes evil spirits to become spiteful."

Harry laughed. "You are just trying to worry me, old man. You don't want me too relaxed. Is that it? Is that the Japanese way?"

"No, Ha-Lee, I do not want you to worry. You are doing very well. I know of no problems. The only real problem may be that we are too philosophical. Sitting in the quiet of this house does that to me. Come, let us go to the ugly house. You must have rest. I have things to show you." A vision of a girl in a short white kimono flashed past Harry's eyes. "Sure, Sato," he said. "Let's go."

The interior of the main house looked better than Harry expected, but not much. The rooms were big. They looked vaguely Japanese, but were filled with mostly European furniture. An occasional woodcarving on a wall or a bronze Buddha in a corner provided a Thai highlight.

Sato led Harry into a large windowless room that glowed with a dozen flickering screens. Several showed the ongoing action on Wall Street, others brought news from Europe, still others scrolled columns of numbers or neat rolls of Japanese script. Two young men watched the screens intently and occasionally flipped a switch to edit or record something of interest.

Sato took Harry to one monitor and softly said something to one of the young men. The screen flickered for a second, then showed a row of figures and dates. "Your account, Harry," Sato said. From the amounts on the screen Harry could identify deposits he had made directly to Sato's account. Others were bank transfers from Karlo and other clients.

After studying the list for a while, Harry said, "I made other sales that don't show here."

"I thought so," Sato grunted. Harry looked at him, shook his head, and laughed.

"I guess I can't get anything past you. How's my friend in Europe doing?" Harry asked.

"He is behind you in sales."

Another series of dates and numbers came up on the screen. "See there" Sato said. "He has not done as well as you. The last few days have been better. Perhaps he is a slow starter."

"Perhaps the Europeans are not as quick to settle their debts," Harry said. Or perhaps, he thought, Jean Lee has opened a private account for us.

Sato turned toward the door. "Come, Ha-Lee. Enough of this. There is cognac to be drunk. And then sleep."

They walked into an adjoining room that in scale and décor was more inviting. They sat in soft leather chairs while a white-coated servant served cognac from a silver tray.

Harry looked at his watch. "Almost 3 A.M., Sato-san. You have all this staff running around. You must have a 24-hour a day operation here."

"It is necessary. Black Lion does business in many countries. I like to know what is happening. But these days it is not often that I need to act. In the old days it was different. Then I was alone. I did everything. Now, Black Lion has many modern Japanese managers. These young ones are efficient. They make few mistakes."

A smile worked its way slowly across Sato's face. Then he chuckled quietly, almost to himself, and said, "But when the modern Japanese managers do make a mistake, Ha-Lee...It is a disaster!"

"But you are still the boss, old man."

"Yes, I am 'boss'," Sato said the word in English. Then he turned his eyes to watch the golden brandy that he swirled around the sides of the big glass.

22

Harry took an early flight out of Bangkok the next morning and was in Chiang Mai an hour later. He went to his usual hotel on the Ping River, checked in, and telephoned Pachyderm Tours. He had not thought much about Tong since he had last seen her, but he was disappointed when another voice answered. She knew he was due to return.

"Pachyderm Tours." It was the precise voice of the pleasant old Thai gentleman who handled phone calls when neither Ting nor Tong was in the office.

"Good morning...ah." Harry had forgotten the man's name. "This is Harry. I'd like to speak with Ting or Tong."

"Ah, Mr. Harry. How are you? The young ladies are not here. Miss Tong asked that you call here at about four this afternoon."

There was no other choice. Harry hung around the hotel for the rest of the day. At four o'clock precisely, he dialed the Pachyderm Tours number.

"Ah, Mr. Harry. You are very prompt. Miss Tong said she will see you tomorrow. At one o'clock in the afternoon. At the Clock Tower in Chiang Rai."

"In Chiang Rai? But I'm in Chiang Mai."

"I'm sorry, Mr. Harry. That is what she said. Miss Tong asked that you stand on the northeast corner at the Clock Tower Square."

"Thank you," Harry said. What else could he say?

He hung up and said, "Son of a bitch." He immediately dialed Thai Airways. There was a seat on the 11 o'clock flight to Chiang Rai the next day and he grabbed it. With that done he felt better. At least he could fly to Chiang Rai. The alternative was a six-hour drive in a bus with an air conditioner that belched hot air into the cabin as it dragged itself over the mountains.

The next day, at four minutes to one, Harry pulled his suitcase from the old Toyota that had brought him from the Chiang Rai airport. The flight had arrived late. Against his better judgment, he offered the taxi driver an extra 100 baht if he could get him to the Clock Tower before the clock struck one. The ride into town was as enthusiastic as he had feared. They reached the Clock Tower a full five minutes before one. Unfortunately, the Toyota was moving with such speed that when the driver stood on the aged brakes, there were sparks, a cloud of dirty gray smoke, and an anguished metallic scream. There was an almost imperceptible decrease in speed. They overshot the Clock Tower by almost a full block.

Harry turned down the driver's offer to back the Toyota to the Clock Tower and started humping his suitcase back to the square. The sun was directly overhead. That did not seem right, but he used it to choose the northeast corner of the square. The clock struck one just as he reached the corner. Across the street, he got a glimpse of a camouflaged Land Rover with a red elephant on the door coming around the opposite corner.

"Oh, Lord," he muttered. So much for his great sense of direction. He started back across the street, his suitcase a millstone. Two and a half minutes later Tong pulled alongside in the Land Rover.

"Harry! It is so good to see you. But you are late." Tong looked at her watch. "Almost three minutes."

Harry shoved his bag in back and climbed up front with Tong. "You look great," he said, and meant it. Her face glowed, lit by her welcoming smile. She was wearing jeans and a tight camouflage shirt that revealed more curves than he remembered. He leaned toward her, instinctively. It was a kiss that never happened. A car behind honked its horn, and Tong pulled the Land Rover away from the curb. Harry recovered and asked, "How are Ting and Aloysious?"

"Ting is fine. Aloysious...." Tong shrugged. "I don't know." She was intent on her driving, and he could not see the expression on her face.

"What do you mean?" he asked. "What's wrong with Aloysious?"

"Nothing. Maybe. I have not seen him for many days. Ting and I have been staying with my parents in Chiang Mai. Aloysious is with Wit."

"You drove here from Chiang Mai? I just came from Chiang Mai. Why didn't you pick me up there?"

"Aloysious said I must not. He said we must never meet in Chiang Mai. He said Ting and I must not go into Chiang Mai alone. Ever. Even to the Pachyderm Tours office."

"Why? What's going on?" Harry asked.

"I don't know. Aloysious is worried." After she wheeled around a turn she asked, "Do you remember the men from the restaurant in Chiang Rai?" She tried to suppress a giggle. "Remember the waitress made a mistake and brought sticky rice? Well, I think Aloysious saw those men on the river."

"That doesn't sound too good. But I'm surprised that Aloysious would get upset by those two." He thought about it for a minute and added, "Did you say that Aloysious is staying with Wit?"

"Yes. At Wit's camp on the river. That's where I am taking you."

"Well," he said, and shrugged, "I guess I'll see him soon enough. Did you guys get any work done on the mountain while I was gone?"

"We worked on the mountain for two days after you left. Then Aloysious and Ting and I came back on the boat to bring some of the statues to Wit's camp. That's when something happened on the river."

"What do you mean? What happened?" he asked.

"I don't know. Aloysious saw something on the shore. Maybe those two men, but I'm not sure. Aloysious would not tell us anything. He acted strange when we got to Wit's camp."

"Aloysious always acts strange. How did he act strange this time?"

"He asked Wit about other boats on the river. And if Wit saw two men, one with a small beard. Wit said he did see other boats, but not a man with a small beard." Tong turned to look at Harry and asked, "If the beard was small, how could Wit see it?"

Harry could not argue with the logic of this. Instead he asked, "And then what happened?"

"We stayed at Wit's camp that night," Tong went on. "In the morning Aloysious said that Wit must hide the boat, and that Ting and I had to go back to Chiang Mai. He wanted us to stay with my parents until you came back. He said Ting and I must not go into Chiang Mai city. Or even go out of the house unless we are with my father."

"And he said you should pick me up?"

"Aloysious said only one of us should meet you in Chiang Rai. I thought it should be me."

"I'm glad it was you, Tong," Harry said. Her gesture touched his heart. He reached over and gently patted her knee.

"Ting drove when we came down from Chiang Rai. It was my turn to drive and pick you up."

"Oh," Harry said, and with an elaborate gesture withdrew his hand from her knee. She did not notice his hand at all.

Harry settled back to think about what she had told him. It did sound as if Aloysious was disturbed about something. It was not like Aloysious to shut down their whole operation just because of a couple of unpleasant characters. There had to be more to it than Tong knew. In another couple of hours they would be at the camp and he could ask Aloysious directly. That did not mean that he would learn any more.

For a while Harry just sat and watched her handle the Land Rover with smooth, easy movements. Her mind was on her driving. She looked relaxed; very young, but competent. She was an attractive female by anyone's standards. For the moment he was content just watching her. After a while he felt himself sinking into the seat. "Tong," he said, "wake me when we get to the camp."

He need not have worried. The track along the river was rough and he was jolted awake long before they neared the camp. They drove alongside the river for quite a while. He looked for landmarks, but saw nothing he recognized. He was still watching for the first sign of something familiar when the Land Rover rolled to a halt.

"What's the matter?" he asked.

"Nothing. You must get out here."

"Here? This is miles from anywhere."

"No, it is not far to the camp. You must walk along the river for maybe a kilometer. Aloysious said we must not bring the Land Rover near the camp. He said I must drop you at least one kilometer away."

"And this is just one kilometer?" Harry looked down at his dusty street shoes. "Okay, but before you drive off, I need to get some things out of my suitcase. You can take the suitcase back with you."

Harry pulled some clothing from his suitcase and stuffed them into a small pack he found at the back of the Land Rover. He dragged a camouflage shirt and a pair of trousers out of the bag. "Okay," he said, "avert your eyes. I have to get out of my street clothes." Tong stared at the river while he changed.

"Well, Tong," he said when he was finished, "I don't know when I'll see you, but I hope it's soon.

"I hope so, Harry. I hope everything is all right with Aloysious. I will wait for you with Ting at my father's house."

Harry pulled her to him, and brushed her forehead with a glancing kiss as she pulled back. She looked up at him very seriously. "Oh Harry, I almost forgot." She ran to the side of the Land Rover and opened the rear door. She pulled out another backpack. This one was much bigger than the one Harry had. It was obviously full, and heavy. She handed it to him.

"It's spaghetti for Wit," she said. He could feel the cans through the cloth.

"And beer for Aloysious," he noted.

"A few cans. Aloysious sends Wit for beer."

"How far am I supposed to carry this?"

"Only around the bend."

When he reached the bend, he stopped to look back and waved at Tong, a half kilometer away. She waved back, then got into the Land Rover and drove off. His shoulders were starting to ache from the two packs he had slung haphazardly over his back. If Tong was right, and he hoped she was, he had only another 500 meters or so to go. He could do that walking backwards while juggling pineapples.

Unfortunately, Tong was not right. Harry walked another 500 meters and then walked several times 500 meters. The packs got heavier with each step. He adjusted his load several times, but the straps cut into his shoulders until he thought he would yell. He felt faint, and started to think that he wasn't going to make it. He might, he thought in desperation, if he took the packs off. He could come back for them later. He slipped the straps of the larger pack over his right shoulder. It hit the ground with a plop.

"I hope that wasn't the beer." Aloysious's voice came from behind some thick brush. "Don't just let it lie there. Bring it over here."

"If you insist," Harry said indifferently. The indifference was no act. He simply had no energy to do anything but drag himself and the packs over to where Aloysious sat. He was propped comfortably up against a tree and shielded from the track by the tall grass that grew at the edge of the trail. Harry dropped down alongside him.

"You look tired," Aloysious said.

"Jet lag," Harry replied, "Just jet lag."

Aloysious started pawing through the heavier of the two bags. "Christ," he said, examining a can, "there's more spaghetti for Wit than there is beer for us." Digging deeper, Aloysious finally came up with two beers and handed one to Harry. Harry opened it quickly, and took a deep drink. When he felt better, he turned to look at Aloysious.

"You need a shave," he told him.

"And a shower. And some fresh clothes," Aloysious said and took a pull at his beer. "Guess you heard we've been roughing it."

"Yeah. What the hell is going on?"

"We'll talk about it later," Aloysious said slowly and got to his feet. "Come on, let's go find Wit and have him start dinner. I want to hear how much money you made for us."

They walked over to the lean-to where Wit could watch the river without being seen. Aloysious lobbed a can of spaghetti like a hand grenade through the thatch side of the small structure. Wit's head popped up. He looked startled. When he saw Harry he smiled.

"Hey, Mr. Harry. Welcome back. I am so happy to see you." He examined the can that had just missed him. "You bring Spam, too?"

"Get dinner ready, and put an extra plate on for Harry," Aloysious interrupted. "Come on, Harry, have another beer and tell me about your financial adventures."

They sat under a tree on the bank, and Harry gave Aloysious a rundown of all that had happened and what he had sold. Aloysious wanted to know, item by item, to whom each piece went, and how much it brought. Aloysious had a big smile on his face throughout the recitation. He slapped his thigh from time to time, or yelled, "Hot damn!"

When Harry finished, Aloysious clapped him on the back. "This is really something," he said. "If I do say so myself. I planned it right. I picked the right guy for the right job. You did a hell of a piece of work there, Harry. I can't believe you sold all that stuff so quick. And got orders for more. All those big pieces! That is really something. Toss me another one of those beers. I want to drink one to you – and to my good judgment."

Harry tossed a beer. "Speaking of orders for the big pieces," he said, I understand nothing much has happened here since I left."

Aloysious frowned. "We had a problem. I put everything on hold. I think I have it fixed. We should know tomorrow."

Harry took a big swallow of beer and looked Aloysious in the eye. "Just what the hell did happen?" he asked.

Aloysious stared at the river silently for a long time before finally starting to talk. "You remember the two we ran into in the restaurant in Chiang Rai? The drunk with the goatee and his little fart friend?"

Harry nodded.

"I saw them out on the river," Aloysious continued. "I mean, I was out on the river. They were up on a little hill looking down on us. Ting-Tong and I were coming back here with a load of art. I don't know if those two assholes were out looking for us. I think they just happened to be up on that hill when we went by. Maybe they were just reconnoitering. Ting and Tong never saw them. I never let on that anything was happening."

At that point Aloysious stood up and in Thai shouted at Wit, "Hey, uncle. How soon will dinner be ready?"

"Ten minutes," came a muffled response.

"So," Harry said, "two ugly little farts up on a hill, and you drive by in a boat. That doesn't sound too terrible. Did you blow them a kiss?"

"No...but they did." Aloysious shook his head slowly and looked away from Harry to stare at the river. He looked older than Harry remembered. It took a while before Aloysious started again.

"As soon as they spotted us, I could see the small fart level a rifle at us. The one with the goatee did the spotting. The little fart fired the thing. You couldn't hear the gun go off over the noise of our engine. We were so close to them that I could see the gun buck, and then watch the little fart bring it back down again and squint down the barrel at us.

"It was a terrible goddamn thing, Harry. I sat there with the two girls who never heard the gun and didn't see what was happening. They were smiling and didn't have the slightest goddamn idea that death was whizzing by. I saw the rounds splashing around us. I could have reached out and touched those bullets. They were that close. It all happened so fast. I never moved from where I was sitting in the middle of the boat dealing myself a hand of cards. I never moved an inch."

Aloysious bent forward and brought his fist down hard on the ground. "Damn!" he said. "That's what bothers the shit out of me, Harry. I just sat there. A goddamn frog on a log while the bullets zinged by the girls. I just goddamn sat there with my mouth hanging open. Jesus, I must be getting old."

"What could you do?" Harry asked sympathetically. "It sounds like it was all over before you could move. And that's probably what saved you. You were moving fast and were out of range before they could get a bead on you. What more could you have done?"

Aloysious took another pull at his beer. "They still could have hit one of the girls, Harry. Yeah, we were moving fast, goddamn it, but I saw at least six rounds splash near us before we were out of range. It was just luck, Harry. Sheer goddamn blind luck that Ting-Tong didn't get hit." Aloysious shook his head.

"I mean shit, Harry," he went on, earnestly. "If it was me I could accept it. If you had been there and you had been hit....Well, shit, I would figure you knew what it was all about. And I could accept that."

"Well, thanks," Harry interjected.

Aloysious leaned toward him and patted him on the knee. "Now come on. You know what I mean. Don't get sensitive." He leaned back against the tree. "They're girls, Harry. Jesus, they're just kids. For them it's all a big adventure. All fun and nobody gets hurt. If something happened to them because of me, I couldn't accept it. You and I have been through a lot of shit, Harry, but this is different."

"Okay, but now it's over. Or at least the part with the girls is. What happened afterwards?"

"Nothing. We got back here all right. I sent the girls away. Meanwhile, those two guys are still out there waiting. Somewhere between here and the mountain."

"How do you know that?"

"I just know it. Wit and I have been watching the river. Wit doesn't always understand what he sees. But he doesn't miss anything that happens on the river. Not only are those two guys still up there, but they have three friends up there with them now."

"Why are they waiting up there?" Harry asked. "Why don't they come down here after you?"

"Because I don't think they know where we are. I don't think they know about this place. But they do know that sooner or later I'll go up there."

"I get a feeling," Harry said after a while, "that there's something here you're not telling me."

Aloysious shook his head. "Harry, you asked me what the problem is, and I just told you. That's all of it. And I told you that the problem is just about fixed."

"How's it fixed?" Harry asked.

"You'll see tomorrow. In the morning. Come on, let's go eat now."

23

D awn came up, not like a clap of thunder, but like the fluid fizz of an elephant fart. Harry shook his head, remembering something about an elephant. He must have been dreaming when a sound awakened him. It came from somewhere outside the cramped straw hootch he shared with Aloysious. In the dim light that filtered into the hootch he could see Aloysious with his head buried in a crumpled up old blanket, still fast asleep. Harry crawled to the entrance and pushed aside two banana tree leaves that served as the hootch door. He stuck his head out into the cool morning air. He blinked his eyes once to clear them, then froze in place.

An elephant is a huge creature when you are on his level, eyeball to eyeball. An elephant is immense when you are on your hands and knees, like Harry was, and the beast is standing over you – maybe not even sure you are there. If anything bothered Harry more at that moment than the elephant looming over him, it was the three or more elephants right behind it.

As Harry crouched there, in a kind of suspended animation, the thought struck him that elephants never seem to just stand still. They constantly shift their weight – all the many tons of it – from one foot to another, and then back again. And that was what these elephants were doing, especially the one that loomed directly over Harry.

Very casually, but in careful slow motion, he backed into the hootch the way he had come, until the banana leaf door closed over him. He continued crawling backwards, slowly and carefully. If he was in the middle of an elephant herd, he did not want to make any sound or movement that might be misinterpreted and precipitate a stampede. Once alongside Aloysious, he reached over and put his hand lightly on the blanket about where it covered Aloysious's head. Then, with the least amount of sound and motion possible, he said, "Aloysious. Wake up. We have a problem."

Aloysious rolled over and into him, knocking Harry off balance. "What? What's happening?"

"Quiet," Harry said as loudly as he dared. "We're goddamn surrounded by elephants."

Aloysious rubbed at his eyes. "Elephants?" he mumbled.

"A whole goddamn herd. And they look fidgety as hell."

"Elephants!" Aloysious said again, more loudly this time. In confirmation, an elephant very close to them vented some of its feelings with a blast of air from its trunk. The straw hootch trembled. "Son of a bitch," Aloysious said.

"They're out there. They're fidgety. Don't piss them off." Harry realized too late that he had all but shouted this at Aloysious.

Aloysious simultaneously tried to exit the hootch and get to his feet. Most of him went through the straw roof of the hootch. Harry was momentarily buried in sticks and straw as the rest of the hootch collapsed around him. Outside there was a ponderous shuffling, and then Aloysious's voice. "All right, guys. Back off. Back off there, goddamn it!"

By the time Harry extricated himself from the wreckage of their hootch, Aloysious seemed to have everything under control.

Aloysious stood some distance off, addressing a group composed of Wit, six or seven elephants, and an equal number of tough-looking young men. He was waving his arms in the air, dramatically, and the entire group, including the elephants, gave him their complete attention. As Harry came up, picking straw out of his ear, Aloysious was just finishing.

"...And that, too, goddamn it. Why in the hell you need elephants, I can't understand. All elephants do is eat a lot. And shit. And that's how we will all spend our time. Cleaning up elephant shit, when we're not feeding them. Goddamn it! I told all of you before that an elephant is no bargain. How could you guys do this to me?" Aloysious finished his harangue by throwing his arms to the sky in despair. An elephant trumpeted. Another defecated noisily. "See," Aloysious added. "See what I told you."

The toughest looking of the young men leaned toward Wit and said something that Harry could not understand. Aloysious did not catch it either. "What he say?" he asked Wit.

In Thai Wit said, "He said, 'What did the big foreigner say?'"

"What?" Aloysious asked, incredulous.

"He said he didn't understand what you were talking about," Wit replied. "He doesn't speak English, or much Thai, either."

"Oh, for God's sake," Aloysious said, threw up his hands again, and turned away. He looked at Harry. "They got me so pissed off I gave them a speech in the wrong language. How can you win?" Aloysious turned back to Wit. "Make them some coffee or something," he said.

"Aloysious," Harry said. "Do you know these guys? What's going on?"

"Yeah, I know these guys. They're the solution."

"The solution?"

"Yeah, the solution. Remember, last night, we talked about the problem. This is the solution. This is how we fix the problem."

Harry must still have looked a little dense. "Look," Aloysious went on, "these are Karen. Their tribe has been fighting for independence from the Burmese government for the last 30 years. These guys are usually over on the Burma side of the border where the action is. They come up this way for R&R. I put out the word to some of my Karen friends that I needed to borrow some shock troops. Look at them. Don't they look like a tough bunch of cookies? They're going to blast a hole for us right up through those two troublesome farts and their friends."

"We're going to go to war?" Harry's question was rhetorical.

"Damn right we're going to war." Aloysious looked over to where Wit was acting like a mess sergeant, pouring coffee into a collection of recycled bottles and cans that now served as cups for the new troops. "But I told them no goddamn elephants. Elephants eat too much. And it makes us look bad. This is modern warfare. Hey, Wit! Ask them if they brought their artillery."

Wit said a phrase in the Karen language, and one of the young men walked over to the elephants. He came back carrying a beat-up M-16 and what looked like a deer rifle.

"He said each man has a gun," Wit translated from Karen into Thai, "but most of the guns are different. And they will need ammunition."

"Oh, wonderful!" Aloysious said to Wit. "Tell them there's a sporting goods store right around the bend. I'll run over there after breakfast. We'll buy everybody a bullet." To Harry he said, "This could be more trouble than what it's worth."

"Do you really want to start a war up here?" Harry asked. "I know we're sort of off the beaten path, but if any serious shooting starts, it won't be long before the area is overrun by Thai troops. And then what? How will we get back up to the mountain then?"

"We'll worry about that later," Aloysious replied. "Let's have coffee with the troops and talk tactics."

They all sat in a circle around the small campfire that Wit had built and sipped their coffee. Harry's coffee tasted terrible. A little like spaghetti sauce. He counted ten heads around the fire, including himself and Aloysious. That made eleven if you counted Wit, who was rushing around in the background like a temperamental chef.

Wit's scurrying to and fro finally caught Aloysious's attention. In his most official tone, he said, "Wit, get your ass over here. You are the designated interpreter. Together with Harry, here. So there is no misunderstanding, I will say my piece in English. Harry will repeat it to you in Thai. You will repeat it to the troops in Karen. To answer, they will respond in the reverse order." He turned to Harry. How does that sound? It should keep the language confusion to a minimum." Harry said nothing.

"Okay, Wit? Harry, are you ready?" Very slowly and distinctly, Aloysious went on. "First. Ask if they are ready to set out against the enemy."

Harry repeated this in Thai to Wit. Wit listened carefully, then turned to the young men and spoke at some length in the Karen language. One of the Karen, apparently the leader, responded to Wit, and then the two fell into what appeared to be a discussion of the issues.

"What the hell is going on, Harry?" Aloysious asked.

"I don't know," Harry said. "I don't speak Karen either."

Finally, Wit turned to Harry and said in Thai, "Ask the big pineapple how much everyone is going to get paid for risking their asses."

Harry turned to Aloysious. "They want to know how much they're going to get paid."

"Wit said something about pineapples," Aloysious said. "I caught something about pineapples. Where do the pineapples factor in?"

"You must have misunderstood," Harry told him bluntly. "They just want to know about money."

"Okay," Aloysious said. "They want to talk money. Tell them big bucks! Tell them they will get big bucks. In a currency of their choice. Thai baht or Burmese kyat." Then he quickly added, "On completion of the mission, of course."

"Dollars," Wit interrupted in English. "American dollars."

"Okay, okay." Aloysious shot back. "Five hundred big American dollars per man."

"Okay, okay. Five hundred big American dollars per man," Harry repeated in Wit's face. As Wit translated this for the Karen leader, Harry turned to Aloysious. "Have you got that kind of money?" he asked.

"Not now. We'll have to get an advance from Sato. Don't worry."

"One thousand dollars," Wit said. "They want one thousand dollars each man."

Aloysious caught the number. "Tell them five hundred and fifty," he said to Harry. In Thai, Harry said to Wit, "Tell them we agree to their terms." Wit repeated this in Karen, and everyone nodded.

"What happened?" Aloysious asked.

"We got a deal. A thousand a head." Before Aloysious could object, Harry added, "They want to know about tactics. You better brief them, sir." Harry saluted.

Harry's salute caused the Karen troops to rise in a mass salute to Aloysious. Wit stood up a little belatedly. His salute looked more like a nose thumbing.

"Well...right," said Aloysious, getting to his feet to return everyone's salute. "Wit, bring me a stick. A straight one."

Wit went off to find a stick while they all stood around. When Wit returned, Aloysious used the stick as a pointer to scratch lines in the ground.

"Okay," he pointed with his stick. "These wavy lines here. They are the river." He gestured for Harry and then Wit to translate. When they finished, he continued. "This X is where the enemy is. We will move upriver by boat. We will land here. We will move on both flanks to encircle them. Casualties will be kept at a minimum. Any questions?"

When all this was translated, the Karen leader asked a number of good questions related to enemy strength, precise locations, and the reliability of Aloysious's source for this information.

Aloysious listened to the translation, then turned to Harry. "Well, shit, Harry," he said. "Tell them there are maybe five or six bad guys up there. I don't know exactly where they are. We'll know when we find them. Tell them not to worry."

Harry extrapolated and gave Wit a more detailed but still vague answer. The Karen leader listened to Wit and shrugged. He looked at Harry. In English he said, "Okay."

The rest of the morning was devoted to preparing for the campaign. The Karen had agreed that the elephants would not be used in combat or even kept in the camp. One of their number, the youngest, was selected to lead the elephants back into the bush where they would be kept out of harm's way – and Aloysious's way as well.

Wit prepared the boat. There was some question whether it would hold all of them and their gear. There was no problem carrying everyone in the boat. The problem was with what exactly constituted the "gear" they were going to take with them. Aloysious had a particularly large pack that looked like it was dedicated solely to a load of beer cans. Wit had some extra cargo. He wanted to haul some wood for a campfire in case they could not find any dry wood upriver, which seemed unlikely. The Karen had a lot of things wrapped in blankets and secured to their elephants. Once removed from the elephants, this made quite a pile of what to Harry looked like trade goods. Whatever it was, the Karen believed it much too valuable to leave behind.

The riverbank looked like a bazaar, and the atmosphere was more like a Boy Scout camp-out than a military operation. In time, negotiations were carried on and compromises reached on what would go in the boat and what would stay behind. Finally, everything that was going on the boat was stowed, tied down where it needed to be, and the boat was ready for boarding. Wit stood at the helm, ready. Harry, designated First Mate, stood on the bank near the bow. He announced that boarding of the troops could now begin.

"All right, let's get rolling," Aloysious said. Then he stood back to watch the Karen start aboard, each carrying a rifle of some sort. One or two had packs. Some, like their leader, wore web belts from which dangled canteens, knives, and tin plates. In the case of the leader the collection included a holstered pistol. In a few moments they were seated and ready to go.

Aloysious boarded. He settled down on a mat near the bow. Wit signaled. Harry pushed, and the boat moved off into the river. Harry scrambled after it. When he finally got aboard with some help from the Karen troops in the bow, he was soaked to the skin.

For the next hour or so they moved upriver, but not as quickly as Harry was accustomed to going. The boat was heavy and rested low in the water, responding sluggishly to Wit's movements on the tiller.

Harry had been a little concerned that the Karen would be less than enthusiastic about being transported by boat. They were people of the hills, where water came in smaller quantities, in springs and streams that were meant to be drunk or crossed over, and not intended to be traveled on. But the Karen seemed to be enjoying the boat ride, at least at first. They seemed to like the rhythmic bumping along and the breeze that washed through their long black hair.

The first sign of trouble came from the middle of the boat. One of the Karen suddenly started to his feet and shouted something toward the bow, where his leader sat. Wit had noticed the man as he started to his feet and immediately blipped his throttle. The boat surged and the man was rolled back down. Wit shouted something in Karen, and that seemed to be the end of it. Whatever the problem had been, it was now solved. Aloysious raised his eyebrows at Harry. Harry shrugged and went back to watching the river.

A few minutes later, the same man shouted something and pointed toward the far shore. Two other Karen sitting near him looked agitated. The Karen leader, sitting next to Aloysious in the bow of the boat, looked at Harry for a moment, but then turned and said something to the Karen trooper sitting behind him. This man listened and then passed it to the man behind him. In this way, whatever the word was, it slowly made its way back to Wit. Wit and the last Karen in line chatted about whatever it was. When they finished, their conclusions were passed back up front. Harry and Aloysious watched. The word reached the Karen leader. He said nothing, but turned around and took a hard look in the direction they were going. When he turned back again and seemed to settle down, Harry relaxed. But not for long.

The Karen in the center of the boat was on his feet again and shouting. He would have gone over the side had not two of his mates grabbed him. Others joined in the shouting, and the boat rocked until it seemed that it would surely roll over. Suddenly there was absolute silence.

Wit had cut the engine. The end of its incessant roar shocked the Karen into silence. Before they could recover, Wit shouted something in Karen with all the strength of his lungs. Then he shouted in Thai, "Everybody sit! I will take the boat to the shore. We talk there. No upsetting boat!" For emphasis Wit spit into the river and in English shouted, "Son of bitch!" He started the engine. With the speed at a slow crawl, he turned the boat toward the shore.

Through all this Aloysious said nothing. Harry could see that he was steaming underneath, like a car radiator about to boil over. It was only when they had beached the boat, and everyone stood on the shore, that Aloysious vented – loudly. "Will someone! Anyone! Please tell me! What is going on?"

The Karen leader looked at Wit and Wit looked at Harry. "They cannot go on," Wit told Harry. "They cannot go farther up the river." Harry repeated this to Aloysious.

"Why, for God's sakes?" Aloysious shouted and waved his hands in the air. "Why can they go no farther? Are we mistreating them? Do we need a tea break? Is the river breeze too cool? Do we need more money?" Shaking his head, he turned to Harry. "Look, Harry, please. Find out what is troubling our Karen comrades. If we know, maybe we can fix it."

Harry turned to Wit and asked in Thai, "Do you know what's bothering our Karen friends?" Wit shook his head. "Well, then ask them," Harry said.

A discussion between Wit and the Karen leader followed. It was a long discussion again, as Wit seemed to have trouble understanding what the man was saying. Finally, he turned to Harry.

"They can go no farther. When we started, they did not know that we would go so far up the river. One of them recognized things. The man who stood up in the boat. He knew we were going too far up the river. Now they can go no farther."

"Wit," Harry said, "I still don't understand what's going on. They can go up the river, but they can go up the river only so far? Is that right?"

"Yes," Wit replied.

"And we are at that point now? We can go no farther than this?"

"Yes," Wit said.

"Okay. Now, they all know what will happen if we do not go on? We will meet the enemy. We will not shoot anyone. No one will get paid. No one will get a thousand dollars."

"Yes," Wit said again.

"Wit. I know we are not going on. You know we are not going on. But, does anyone know WHY we are not going on?"

Wit looked down at his feet and shuffled them back and forth. He looked very uncomfortable. "Come on, Wit," Harry said. "Tell me. It will be worse for everyone if I cannot explain this to Aloysious."

"It is the trees," Wit said. "The Karen cannot go farther because soon we will be where the trees are."

Harry looked toward Aloysious, who for once was being patient. Harry turned back to Wit. "The trees," he said and sighed. "Now, Wit, next to you there...is that a tree?" Wit nodded. Harry continued, "Is this a tree here? And here? There are trees everywhere, Wit. There are trees here as there are trees farther up. What the hell is the difference? Is there a difference, Wit?"

Wit nodded. "There is a difference," he said. "The Karen say that if we go farther, we will be in the land of the trees that fly."

"The trees that fly!"

"The trees that fly. They have seen it," Wit said.

"Harry," Aloysious was at his elbow. "What the hell is he saying? I can't understand much of his Thai."

Harry could not help but smile when he turned to Aloysious. "You may have a little trouble with this," he said, "but we can't go any farther because of flying trees."

To Aloysious's great credit, he took this very calmly. "Harry," he said, "I'm going to take a walk. Down along the river. You talk to these guys. When I come back, I will want to know just one thing: Are we all going upriver or not?" Then, with all the somber dignity of a defeated military commander, Aloysious disengaged himself from the group and strolled down to the river.

Wit was back in conference with the Karen. They were all agitated now, nodding their heads and pointing to where the river came from. One even hunkered down to scratch lines in the sand, like Aloysious did. Everyone looked at the sand. It might have been a map, but Harry really could not tell. It looked like lines scratched in the sand. When all the talk ended, Wit walked over to him.

"Will they go upriver, Wit?" Harry asked him.

"No. They will not change their minds. Up there are the trees that fly, and they will not go there."

"Wit, tell me about these trees."

Wit shrugged. "They are trees. Big trees. And they fly. High up, over the mountain."

"What mountain?"

"I do not know. But they say it is maybe two hours from here. The mountain. They were up there hunting. They heard a noise and over them came trees, flying through the air. Another day they saw the trees again. They walked out of that area. They will never go back. It is not wise to go back."

"When did they see this?"

Wit shouted something at the Karen leader. The man quickly shouted something back.

"Maybe six months," Wit said.

"Well, here comes Aloysious," Harry said. "He's going to be a little disappointed with all of us. Get ready for the fire storm."

24

Aloysious sighed. "Well, I never really thought that mounting a
military campaign against those little farts was such a hot idea
anyway. The way I see it, we're just going to have to employ a
little more imagination." Harry was not really listening. He and
Aloysious were sitting alone on the riverbank at Wit's camp. The Karen
were gone now. They had to wait while one of them went off to find the
elephants and brought them back. Then the Karen loaded their gear, got
on the elephants, and silently ambled off into the bush. Wit was already
building a new hootch to replace the one Aloysious destroyed in getting up
that morning.

"I think you're sitting on an elephant turd," Aloysious said pointing at
where Harry was sitting. Harry didn't bother to move. "Look! Look!"
Aloysious pointed around them. "They're everywhere, everywhere. Nothing but turds. We'll have to move camp."

"You know," Harry said, ignoring the turd crisis, "the part I didn't understand was that you didn't argue with them. You didn't seem surprised
to hear about the trees that fly. Are there such things?"

"What do you mean I didn't argue with them? What's so unusual
about that?"

"What's unusual about it? You don't miss a chance to argue. I've never
seen you accept an outrageous thing like that without taking umbrage. But
you never said anything. Except 'Fine, if that's the way you want it'. I felt
like I was the only one who found the trees that fly a little weird. Even Wit
seemed to believe them."

"What do you want me to say, Harry? They're a superstitious bunch. I
didn't see any point in trying to convince them to go into a place that's
taboo. That's spiritual stuff to them, Harry."

"Spiritual? That's never been a problem for you with Ting or Tong. Or
Wit. All they have to do is mention their grandmother's spirit and you're

laughing and pointing a finger at them."

"That's different, Harry."

"How is it different?" Harry threw up his hands. "Oh, what the hell," he said. "I'm not going to argue with you about spirits. Besides, they didn't sound like they were talking about 'spirit' trees. It sounded like they were talking about real trees. And the area they were talking about, the area where the flying trees are....It sounded like the trees over our mountain. Right over our lost city."

"Harry, I don't what they were talking about. And I don't know what you're talking about. It's done with. They're gone. What we need to do now is to figure how we're going to get back up to the city. I've got a bunch of stuff there, right out near the river. It needs to get picked up. We need to get just one load, and get it back here. Together with what Wit and I have cached in the woods behind us, we have enough to put together a shipment for Sato. Some of the pieces are the ones in the pictures. We can fill some of those orders you got."

"Wouldn't it be better to just hunker down for a while? Farts and friends are likely to get bored after a while. Maybe they'll go away."

"I don't know, Harry." Aloysious's voice was grim. "I'm getting this feeling that everything is about to come apart."

"Hey, Aloysious, take it easy. The only sign of trouble we've had is those two guys. And they don't even know about the city...or do they?"

"Look, Harry, all I know is that when I see a cloud of smoke, I usually find a hell of a fire under it. That's all I know, Harry."

On that note Aloysious got up and walked toward the back of their camp. "I'm going off to do in quiet decency what the elephants have done all over here with impunity," he said. "See you later."

Wit cooked up a reasonably good dinner, given what he had to work with. It looked like a stew, but tasted vaguely like spaghetti. The meal seemed to put Aloysious in a better mood.

"I've been thinking," Aloysious said. "Those guys up there lying for us. If they're where I think they are, they should be back a ways from the river. The riverbank there is low. It's all broken up and wet. If they want to stay dry, they have to stay up on the high ground. Up on that little hill they used before. Up there they can hear Wit's boat coming from miles away. But, if they didn't hear the boat, they wouldn't know we were coming. Maybe we could get by them."

"How are we going to get there without them hearing us coming? Are we going to row upstream? Wow! I think I'd rather take my chances being shot at."

Aloysious quietly mulled this over for a while. "You know, Harry, maybe that's not a bad idea."

"You mean getting shot at? Hey, that's really not one of my best ideas."

"What I mean is, what the hell difference does it make? What if they can hear us, but can't see us?"

"Oh, I see," Harry said with his finger on his forehead. "Sure. Of course. Stealth technology. Right. Hey, Wit, get the invisible boat paint. We're going to paint the boat. Ooops, I just thought of a problem. They won't see the boat. But they will see us."

"Harry, Harry. Don't be a wise ass. Have a little faith in what I think. Look, this is the idea. We have about another hour of daylight left today. You and I hop in the boat. We drive like hell upriver as far as we can get. When it's too dark to move, we pull over and rack out. At about 3 A.M. or whatever, we get up. We'll be on the river and blast by them while it's still dark. They won't see enough of us to shoot."

"That's about the craziest thing I ever heard. How the hell are we going to see to navigate?"

"Do you have any better ideas?"

"No, I do not." After Harry said this, he got up, rinsed off his dinner plate, and started for the hootch.

"Hey, what are you doing? Not time for bed yet," Aloysious said.

"Getting my blanket. If we're going to sleep out on the river tonight, I at least want to be warm."

Aloysious got up and threw a salute Harry's way. "I knew I could count on you, Harry." He turned to Wit. "Prepare the boat for an immediate departure, Wit. Captain Harry is going to drive. You stand by here to repel boarders." Wit walked toward the river, uncertain as to exactly what was going on.

* * * * *

The first 45 minutes or so were fine. They covered a lot of water. The light was good, the river was wide, and the boat rode high, skimming over the smooth surface. Harry kept the throttle wide open. When darkness came, it came quickly. He slowed down, but it was still possible to distinguish the river from the dark bulk of the banks. As long as the river was still reasonably wide, they could continue. But it was not much farther where the river started to narrow. The sandbanks near the shore also came frequently now. After they hit one of these and briefly grounded themselves, Harry closed the throttle to a slow crawl. Aloysious fumbled around, found a flashlight, and held it out over the bow. It was still hard to see what was out there. Finally, some clouds moved in and extinguished what natural light remained. Harry turned in toward the bank.

"We've gone as far as we can tonight," he said. "Do you have any idea where we are?"

"No, not really," Aloysious admitted. "We'll just have to get going as early as we can in the morning, and hope we get past them while it's still dark."

Harry did not say anything. He felt the boat bump the bank. He groped around in the darkness until he got hold of a small tree. To it he tied the rope he had ready in his hand. With the boat secured, there was nothing else to do. Everything was the same shade of black now, and he could not even make out Aloysious a few feet away. He could hear him moving around. A beer can popped. "Oh shit," Harry said, "don't throw it!" He reached forward in the darkness until he felt the cold can. The beer tasted good. They had one more and then settled into their blankets.

Something ringing woke Harry. It was absolutely black. The ringing stopped. "What the hell was that?" he asked. "Did you bring an alarm clock?"

"It comes with the boat. All the comforts." Aloysious turned on the flashlight. "It's three o'clock. Time for breakfast." The light went off. A beer can popped. And another.

"Don't throw it!" Harry said. After a while, when it got no lighter, he asked, "What do we do now?"

"We wait for a while. If it doesn't get lighter, we go out on the river anyway. With luck we'll pass them in the dark. They'll know we're there. So what? The main thing is to get upriver. Get up beyond them before there's enough light for them to see us."

"Okay, boss," Harry said. It was all he could think to say.

They waited, and after a while it did seem to get brighter. Looking up at the sky, Harry could just detect movement where the heavy clouds were pulling back and letting some moonlight through. There was not as much light as they had last night, but maybe there was just enough to navigate. Aloysious must have been thinking the same thing. "What do you think?" he asked.

"I think we ought to try it," Harry answered.

Harry cut the boat loose. As they drifted away from the bank, he was almost sorry that he suggested they try it. It seemed blacker here. He strained to see something of the river. After a while he started to make out the surface of the water. It was where the black seemed to have a gloss, different from the dull black of the riverbanks beyond. He started the engine and engaged the clutch slowly. As they started moving, he shouted at Aloysious, "Better turn that flashlight on. For now, anyway."

It was a hell of a strain on Harry's nerves, and probably worse for Aloysious. They brushed the banks several times, and ran aground once more. This time Aloysious had to step out on the bank and push the boat off. He mumbled under his breath while he did it. Twice Harry heard him shout, "Don't lose me out here." Aloysious sounded very uncomfortable.

It got lighter, and Harry was able to move the boat a little faster. Gradually he was able to make out the banks with no problem, and went faster still. Aloysious crawled down toward the stern. When he got near Harry, he yelled, "I recognize this area. We're not past them yet. It's another 500 meters. Go like hell!"

Harry opened the throttle as wide as it would go. The river was narrower here than downstream, and not as deep. There were more sandbars to watch for. Near the shore clusters of rocks just broke the surface. He would have to steer carefully, but he could not keep his eyes from the right bank.

Just ahead, a small hill rose above the heavy brush that covered the riverbank. It was the only real vantage point anywhere as far as Harry could see. He caught Aloysious's eye, and jerked his head toward the hill. Aloysious nodded. His lips moved. "That's it."

At first, Harry could see no sign of life on the hill. Then he saw something move. Somebody's head. Whoever it was, was keeping down out of sight. Instinctively, he pulled on the throttle, but it was already as far as it would go.

Aloysious must have seen something as well, and they both watched the hill as they drew closer. There was no sign of anything else, but Harry could see the head move as the man followed their progress on the river.

They were almost alongside the hill, and for a moment Harry thought they would get away with it. Just then he caught a movement out in front of them. "Oh, shit," he said. Intent on watching the hill, they had both missed seeing the boat pulling into their path.

Harry shouted and shoved the tiller to one side. At that instant, Aloysious turned his head just enough to suddenly see the boat in front of them. He dove for the floorboards. Whoever was piloting the other boat must have been spooked by this movement, or maybe by their impending collision. He turned his boat toward them.

In an instant the two boats flashed by each other. Their sides touched briefly and splinters flew. It was over before Harry realized what happened. He had enough sense to steer for the middle of the river and resume course upstream. He realized he had never touched the throttle and their speed had never dropped off.

Behind them the other boat was dead in the water. Then it was moving slowly and turning in their direction. In a moment it was in full speed hot pursuit.

Aloysious was on his knees in the center of the boat, staring over Harry's shoulder. He crawled back to Harry and shouted. "There are five of them in the boat. We're lighter. Maybe we can outrun them."

Harry shrugged and turned back to watch. The distance between the two boats stayed about the same. They may have had some advantage, but not much. He looked around. The river was getting even narrower. Another half hour and they would be in sight of the mountain. He looked back at the other boat. The distance between them was about the same. At this rate one thing was certain. He turned to shout at Aloysious, "We're going to lead them right to the city."

Aloysious nodded grimly. He held a finger in the air and shouted, "Wait. I have a scheme."

There was nothing else to do. Harry leaned forward to check their fuel supply. That at least seemed all right. The engine was humming along nicely as well. Wit must keep it well maintained. When he looked up again, Aloysious was at the front of the boat, looking in the direction they were headed. After a while, he crawled back to the stern. He got as close as he could to Harry's ear so nothing would be lost. "Try to let them get closer. There's a place up ahead. Maybe ten minutes. I want them close to us then."

Harry nodded and eased the throttle back, just a bit. After a minute or so there was a perceptible change in the distance between the two boats. Another two minutes and he was able to see the faces in the other boat. He looked at Aloysious. Aloysious winked and smiled.

The boat behind got bigger and the men in it were starting to look intimidating. Aloysious crawled next to Harry again. "Ahead. Maybe another minute. There are rocks on both sides. Not much room to maneuver. When you get to the rocks, get ready. When I yell, kill the engine. Then get down on the floor. Understand?"

"Cut the engine when you yell. Then I hit the floor."

Aloysious nodded.

"What the hell do you do while this is going on?" Harry shouted at him.

Aloysious smiled and rubbed the pocket on the right side of his camouflage trousers. "Watch," was all he said.

That was exactly what Harry had no desire to do. When he looked again, the other boat was uncomfortably close. He could see the men clearly now. Two of them had rifles. As he watched, both of them brought their rifles down, aiming right at him. They didn't fire, he supposed, because their platform was not very stable. Their boat was picking up some chop from Harry's wake. That and the need for their pilot to dodge around rocks and sandbars, as Harry was doing, made for a bumpy ride.

One of the men in the boat behind raised his rifle at Harry again, and then lowered it. The man laughed and waved at him. Harry felt played with. He hoped Aloysious's scheme was a good one.

Ahead, Harry could see clusters of big rocks that reached from both banks far into the river. The water was fairly shallow here, and the areas near the banks on both sides were peppered with rocks sticking through the surface and many more lying just underneath. There was ample room to navigate in the middle of the river, but not much room to clear the rocks on either side. So intent was Harry on watching the rocks that Aloysious had to yell a second time to get his attention. Harry almost cut the engine then.

"Not yet!" Aloysious shook his head sternly. "Just get ready. Get us past the rocks."

Harry stayed right in the center of the river, keeping an equal distance from the rocks on either side. In the middle of the worst concentration of rocks, Aloysious yelled, "Now! Cut the engine now!"

There was silence, but it was not complete. There was buzz in Harry's ear, and then, "Harry, goddamn it, get down." Aloysious was still sitting at the center of the boat. Their boat was still moving, drifting straight ahead, but slowing down quickly. "Get down," Aloysious said. "They're a hundred feet from us and closing fast." Harry dropped down to the floorboards. He caught a glimpse of the other boat coming up fast.

It would have taken the other pilot a few moments to even realize that Harry had cut his engine, and then a few more moments to think about what to do. In the meantime, the distance between the two boats was rapidly closing. Harry felt their own boat rocking gently. They were almost at a dead stop.

"Stay down," Aloysious said. Then suddenly he stood up and faced the oncoming boat. In his hand was a pistol, which he gripped with both hands and pointed. There was a flash of silver from the gleaming barrel, and Harry recognized the "pistola" that Aloysious had liberated in Chiang Rai from the man he was now pointing it at. The pistol seemed to jump in Aloysious's hand, then jump again and again. Blap! Blap! Blap! Sharp cracks over the growing sound of the oncoming engine.

Harry looked back to see several rifles pointed more or less in their direction. Then the rifles seemed to whirl around, as the men holding them were thrown off balance when their boat radically changed direction.

The sight of Aloysious getting closer and closer as he fired his pistol right in their faces proved too much for the boat's pilot. He shoved the tiller far away from him as he threw himself to the floor. The boat responded by heeling over in a sharp turn that put it on a heading toward the right bank at full speed. The passengers who had not voluntarily headed for the floor were thrown there by the force of the turn.

Long before the boat reached the bank, it started to strike the rocks that poked out of the river. To Harry and Aloysious, now some distance off and watching with interest, it seemed at first that the boat was skimming along the top of the rocks and might make it all the way to the bank. Then the bow hit a rock that was bigger than the others. Pieces seemed to fly from the boat, followed by one of the passengers who arced out high over the river before striking the surface not far from the bank. The boat slewed around, the stern moving faster than the bow. Two men went over the side, although in a lower and less spectacular trajectory than their colleague. The boat was still moving on the same inexorable course for the bank, but sideways now. Pieces were breaking away from it as it went. What was left – which wasn't much – struck the riverbank almost gently. There was no sound of an engine now. That had stopped earlier, when the transom shattered on a rock, and the engine tumbled out the back to drown in the shallow water.

What was left of the boat and its passengers was the rubble that marked its passage. Here and there movement in the shallow water showed that man is often harder to break than the machines he comes to depend on.

Harry and Aloysious stood in their boat and watched in awed silence. The only sound was the gentle lapping of water around their own boat. The current was not strong here, but it tugged them toward the rocks where rubble of the other boat was strewn.

Harry was the first to break the silence. Very quietly he said, "I liked your scheme. Particularly the part where the guy goes into a low earth orbit. Most impressive."

Aloysious looked down at the pearl-handled pistol in his hand. "Thank you, Captain. I'm glad I found a use for this thing. It's really too small to hurt anybody. It was big enough to scare that guy into making a U-turn. Too bad he didn't put on his brakes first."

Harry could see a man dragging himself through the shallow water near the bank. "Should we give those guys a hand?"

"Screw 'em. Let's get our engine started and get out of here. We have a lot of work to do."

Harry shrugged and started the engine.

25

By late afternoon they had the boat loaded. It had been hot, sweaty work, moving the stone and bronze statues from where they were cached under a mound of rocks and shrubs in an uninviting briar patch near the edge of the river. The mountain stood behind them. Even with his back to it, Harry could feel its presence. It hung over them like a black cloud blocking out the sun.

Harry turned to look at the mountain. It kept its secret well. There was no sign of the city, nothing that hinted at what was there. Just rock and an occasional shrub or a scraggly tree that hung on at an impossible angle. Sunlight glinted off something in a fissure in the rock high above. It was too far to the right to be their winch, which was on a ledge somewhere almost directly overhead. Maybe a beer can Aloysious threw from the top. Harry abruptly stopped scanning and fixed his eyes on one spot in disbelief. For a moment, just a moment, he thought he had seen one of the trees that fly. It was a tree, but a very stationary one, that grew far out over the rock face near the top of the mountain.

Harry walked over to look at the pieces of stone carving and cast bronze that were stacked like so many logs in the bottom of the boat. Some were like old friends that he recognized from the photos shown to Karlo and other potential buyers. That seemed so long ago now. That was another world, cooler and more orderly. There you could tell what was happening by paging through a ledger.

"You and the girls did a hell of a lot of work up here after I left," Harry said to Aloysious during one of their breaks. "Pushing those big pieces around must have been like moving houses."

"I wish we could have gotten more of it. There's still so much up there." Aloysious gazed over his shoulder at the mountain. He looked sour and pensive and had had little to say all day.

The boat was lying deeper in the water than Harry liked, but Aloysious insisted on loading three more pieces. When that was done, Aloysious stretched, yawned, and slowly surveyed the riverbank.

"Not a bad day's work," he said. "But there's a lot we're leaving behind. Let's get everything covered and neatened up. Then we can start back."

They piled stones and shrubs on what was to be left behind in the cache. Then they cleaned up any evidence that they had been there. When they both were satisfied that the riverbank showed no sign of their presence, they walked back to the boat. Harry shook his head as he regarded it.

"That's a hell of a load. The boat's too heavy. It won't handle worth a damn, and we won't have much speed." He looked at the sky. "If we wait a bit, we can be at the bad stretch at dark. We're going downriver, so we can drift past where the bad guys are."

"Fine," Aloysious replied, "but I'm not too concerned. I don't think there will be many of them there. Let me just check something." He fumbled in a stuffed cargo pocket on the side of his camouflage trouser and pulled out the pearl-handled revolver. "Well," he said with what sounded like real disappointment, "I have only one bullet left in my 'pistola'. Maybe we better sneak by them."

Just before dark Harry cast off and headed for the middle of the river. From the bank, the boat must have looked like a drifting island of garbage. For lack of anything else to do while they waited for the sun to set, Aloysious cut shrubs and branches from trees to cover the load and break up the silhouette of the boat. Covered with leaves, grass, and all the dried-out vegetation, that Aloysious could drag over to it, the boat no longer resembled anything made by man. It looked like a pile of debris. It was probably very effective, but Harry hoped no one would see them. He felt silly.

He shut down the engine and let the boat drift a while. After testing the rudder for a few minutes he said, "I can keep her on course just with the tiller. Down where they are, the water moves slower. We might wallow a bit, but I think we'll be all right."

Aloysious looked pleased enough. Sitting among the leaves, there was little of him showing besides his face. He stuck his head out from under the brush and gave Harry a thumbs up. Then he jiggled around a bit, got more of himself out of the leaves, and lobbed a can of beer at Harry. "Fortify yourself, Captain," he said, "then get this tub moving."

Harry used the engine to move them slowly as far downriver as he dared. Sound carried at night, and it was dark now. It was not the thick blackness of the night before. Tonight the sky was clear of clouds, and the stars and rising moon made it easy to see the banks on both sides of the river. The trees and hills beyond stood out like a black silhouette on a gray background. After a while Harry shut down the engine.

They drifted in a silence broken only by the periodic pop of a beer can. Harry did his best to keep them in the middle of the river, but at times they drifted close to the shore and brushed a rock or ran aground briefly, before the current swung them around and past the obstruction. Harry found it a pleasant experience, far removed from the snarling engine and spray of water that attended their passage this way just yesterday. Aloysious broke into his thoughts.

"I think they're gone." He said this in a normal tone of voice. Then, as if to reassure Harry, "We're well past the place where they crashed. We're just short of the hill where they were lying for us. There's nothing out there now. No campfire. No cooking smells. Not a sound."

"What do you expect? A neon sign?"

"Don't be smart, Harry. I know they're gone. Those guys are rowdy. If they were here, they would be cooking and drinking. We'd hear them. We'd smell them."

"Okay, Daniel Boone, but keep quiet for a while longer. We're almost there now."

They drifted, and Harry lost track of time. He felt relaxed, despite the possibility that somebody had a rifle pointed at the back of his neck. That did it. The thought of a rifle trained on him made the short hairs on the back of his neck bristle. He pulled himself a little further into the bottom of the boat.

"Harry. Harry. You asleep?"

It took Harry a moment to speak. "No, I'm just thinking."

"Let's go back. Get this thing turned around."

Harry thought he must be imagining this. "What?" he asked.

"Let's go back. Back to where they crashed."

"Go back? We'll have to use the engine. Everybody in Northern Thailand will know where we are."

"Don't worry. They're gone. Guarantee it. I want to see if there are any of them left up there."

"If there are any left! What do you think they're going to do when they hear us wallowing out here! In this heap of garbage with a rock bottom!"

"If any of them are left, it's the dead ones. I just want to see if they hauled everybody out."

"Oh for God's sake. Even if you're right, we'll be going up against the current. It will take us half the night to get there."

"What else do you have to do tonight? Come on, Harry, Crank up that engine. Let's get turned around."

Against his better judgment, Harry did it. As the engine caught and broke the peace with its unmuffled roar, every nerve in his body waited for the night to light up with the glow of tracer fire and flares exploding overhead.

But nothing happened. There was nothing. Not the smallest spark of any light. Aloysious was throwing their camouflage overboard. When most of it was gone, he crawled over their stone and bronze cargo to the bow where he knelt and peered into the night. They were getting back into the rocky area where the river narrowed.

"I'm turning on the light," Aloysious said and flicked on the flashlight.

Harry said, "Oh, shit," and tried to make himself smaller. If there was anybody out there, he and Aloysious were in the killing zone. The boat had no speed, and among these rocks it had no maneuverability. He could feel the stares of a half dozen men with small goatees squinting down the sights of their long powerful rifles. Aloysious laughed. "Son-of-a-bitch! Look at that!"

Harry's eyes followed the flashlight beam to where it fell on a half-submerged pile of metal that glistened in the beam of artificial light. The engine from the wrecked boat.

"Work your way through here, Harry," Aloysious said. "Hey, look over there. Try to steer to where I put the light." And so it went for almost an hour. To Harry it was unreal, and three lifetimes passed as he worked the boat against the pull of the current and fought the boat's clumsiness as it wallowed along under the weight of its cargo.

In the end they had found little. There was planking, and there was even almost a whole side of the boat wedged so tightly in the rocks that the current could not carry it off. From one shallow pool, Aloysious pulled an M-16, with its magazine still in place. There was a piece of cloth that could have been a shirt, but they could not be sure. But that was all. There was nothing of what Aloysious wanted to see. There were no bodies. There was no sign of injury or death.

"Shit!" Aloysious said as they were making their last pass. "Damn it! I thought we got them good. But there's nothing here. Harry, go around again."

"Aloysious, I see no reason to go around again."

"Come on, just once."

"You're like a dog, going back to sniff his own shit. Wasn't there enough for you to smell?"

"I'm just trying to be thorough, Harry."

Harry said nothing else, and pointed the boat's nose toward the center of the river. Once there, he cut the engine and let her drift again. Aloysious said nothing, and there was no other sound. Harry closed his eyes.

First light came quickly, but not quickly enough for the pains that were growing in Harry's lower back. The boat was not a comfortable place to sleep. Aloysious was on his back in the middle of the boat, arms folded behind his head.

"You awake, Harry?"

"Yeah. What's happening?"

"Nothing. We ran aground here a while back. Thought we might as well get some sleep."

They pushed off the sandbar, and Harry started the engine. They soon reached an area he recognized. They were almost home. When they neared the area where Wit's camp should be, he could see a figure standing on the bank.

"Look at that," Aloysious said, "Wit, the homing beacon. Hope it's not a service he gives every ship that passes in the night."

"He knows the sound of his engine," Harry said in Wit's defense. "Wit knows how to play the game."

Wit waded into the water as they got closer. When they got next to him, he reached over and pulled the boat in.

"Hallo, Mr. Harry. Hallo, Alo-wichit."

"What's happening, Wit?" Harry asked in Thai.

"Quiet. This morning, quiet. Yesterday, not so quiet." Wit made sure the boat was securely wedged on the bank before he continued.

"Yesterday, a long-tail boat went upriver. It was early in the morning. Two men, taking food. Later, it came back and passed here very quickly. There were three men in the boat then. Only the driver was sitting up. The other two were lying on the floor like they were sick."

Harry interrupted to ask Aloysious if he understood all of Wit's Thai and then translated when Aloysious said he had not. "What happened then, Wit?" Harry asked when he finished translating.

"Later, after about two hours, two boats went back upriver. One was the boat that passed in the morning. Each boat had three men sitting in it. Then the two boats came back. They passed here again. It was almost dark. Each had more men. Some were sitting. Some were lying down."

Harry translated this for Aloysious, then asked, "What do you think?"

"Medevac." Aloysious said. "That's why we didn't find any of them. Ask Wit how many people were sitting up when the boats came downriver for the last time."

Harry did, and Wit had to think for a moment. "One boat had three people sitting up," he said, "The other boat had five sitting up."

Aloysious understood this. "And there were three sick ones, right, Wit?" Aloysious held up three fingers. Harry translated to make sure Wit got it.

"Three sick ones," Wit confirmed.

"It's obvious what happened, Harry," Aloysious explained. "The first boat going upriver was the supply boat taking breakfast to the bad guys. They got there after we passed and found the place in a shambles. That boat came back down with the driver and two wounded. His helper stayed up there. When the driver got to where he was going, he rounded up five friends and they went back upriver in two boats. The two boats came back with the remaining three wounded, the six that went up, and the driver's helper from the first boat. A medevac. They were getting their wounded out of there, the five guys in the boat we ran aground."

Harry was still sorting out numbers. "Wit said the two boats came back with three down, and six and the driver's helper sitting up. Wit said there were eight sitting."

"That's right. The eighth man was the guy who was ashore, the one watching us from the hill. He never got in the boat and never got busted up. Hey, Wit, were any of them dead?"

Harry repeated the question for Wit. Wit replied that he could not be sure. But he did not think so. After Harry translated this for Aloysious, Wit asked him, "Did you do that, Mr. Harry? You and Alo-Wichit. Did you do that? Those people looked very sick."

"I think they had a boating accident, Wit," Harry said with a straight face. Wit had a sly grin on his face. "Hey, Mr. Harry," Wit said. "No problem."

As Aloysious walked back toward the boat he said in Thai, "Wit, did those guys get a look at you?"

"I stayed behind the brush. They never saw me."

"Good," Aloysious said, looking at Harry. "That means the odds are good that they still don't know we have a camp here. Aloysious poked at the statues in the bottom of the boat.

"Harry, I think we have to get this stuff unloaded. We'll stash it with the rest out in back. Then Wit can run you downriver to where you can get a ride into Chiang Rai. You call Ting-Tong. Tell them to bring the Land Rover up here. I want to get as much stuff out of here as we can."

"You want me to come back up here with them?"

"I think maybe it's time for you to go back to Bangkok. We'll need to coordinate with Sato. And your rich friend should be back from Europe."

"That's what I was thinking. Can't say I'm going to miss Wit's cooking."

"You'll have fancy food soon enough. Now let's get to work."

They unloaded the boat by carrying the smaller statues and dragging the bigger ones up over the riverbank and back to where they cached them in a depression among the trees. They covered them with branches. Then Aloysious insisted on dragging the turds left by the Karen elephants over to the trail that led to the cache.

Aloysious was not satisfied until a good part of the trail was covered with elephant turds.

"Nobody's going to go exploring back there now," he said. "I finally found a use for the goddamn elephants," he added with satisfaction.

Aloysious walked them back to the river. "I'll see you later," Harry said and got into the boat. Wit was already in the stern, ready to start the engine.

"Make sure Wit doesn't forget the beer," Aloysious said, and they were off.

26

The last Thai Airways flight from Chiang Rai had Harry on the ground in Bangkok just as the sun was setting. Now that he was back in the big city after a stint up North, he lost any idea he might have had about getting to bed early. Through the tail end of the evening rush hour it would take well over an hour to get into town, but the evening would still be young when he got there.

He got out of the cab at the Silom Road entrance to Patpong Road and walked down the street toward the Exorcist. It was early evening – and early evening on Patpong is like early morning anywhere else. The street was waking up. The street vendors were setting up their stalls, and the sex show touts hung out in the doorways of their clubs, sniffing at the air and wiping cobwebs out of their eyes.

Here and there along the street nightclub hostesses walked individually or two by two on their way to work. In civilian clothes, the older ones walked along quietly, looking like housewives. Their dresses were practical, their faces were serious and maybe a little sad. The young ones were not at all like their older sisters. They were thin and supple as young trees. They chatted and laughed easily as they walked. Their dresses were bright and at least a bit flamboyant. They were young and attractive, and knew they were desirable. The coming night would be a new adventure.

The nightclubs were open now. A curious tourist who stuck his head in the door might not have thought so. The air inside the bars was stale. It had not yet been stirred by the throbbing beat of rock music that would start in an hour or so and blare on for the rest of the night. The hardcore customers were already in place, usually sitting alone, bent quietly over their drinks.

Patpong was aglow with colored lights from the neon signs over a hundred doorways, so Harry was surprised when he turned the corner and found the sign over the Exorcist dark. It was not natural. Tacked on the

185

door was a small hand-lettered sign. He read it with some difficulty.

Klose 2 nite 2 9 4 prak tiss. Staf on lee.

Not much of a challenge, he thought as he translated: "Closed tonight to nine. For Practice. Staff only." He knocked anyway.

The door opened a crack. A pretty face looked out. "Hi," he said. "Tell Khun Porntip that Khun Harry is here to see her." He was pleased that he remembered Tosh's Thai name. The face disappeared and the door shut. In a moment it opened again, and two faces looked out at him. The first was the same. The second, whom he didn't recognize, said, "Okay, you come in. Watch sheep, please."

Harry thought she said "step" and was not looking for a sheep, let alone the goat he tripped over. The goat, a black and white creature, looked annoyed and headed for the door that was closing behind Harry. The goat never made it. A young lady in jeans ran up, got a good grip on the goat's tail, and dragged it back inside. The goat did not seem to mind particularly. Harry peered into the far reaches of the dimly lit club, wondering what he might see next. Surprisingly enough, it was quiet.

He turned back to the two girls who had opened the door for him. Each was wearing an ankle-length gown made of filmy material that he could see right through. He could see that the gown was the only thing they wore – or almost. For attached to their backs were things that stuck out behind their shoulders and looked like feather dusters. Harry reached around and ran his hand over one set of feathers as the girl looked up at him with a soft smile. It gave Harry the most peculiar sensation. "What's this?" he asked.

"Wings," she answered. "I am angel."

"I'll say," he said, looking at her face, and then – like Superman – looked right through her dress. "You are indeed an angel," he said, very much wanting to touch more.

"I am angel, too," the other girl said. "You know me?" she asked and pointed at her waist. Beyond the diaphanous material he could see the brown ridge of an appendix scar. Like all of them, she was young, probably much younger than she looked under the heavy makeup. Her face was pretty enough, but not one he knew. He did know the appendix scar.

"Sure, Frankie. I'd know you anywhere." He gave her a small, affectionate pat on her shoulder. The gesture pleased her. She took his hand and led him to one of the back tables he favored. After he sat down she said, "I am happy you came back. Khun Porntip is not here now. She come back maybe one hour."

Harry switched to Thai. "I'll wait for her. Bring me some Scotch, and get a drink for yourself."

"Thank you, but I cannot drink now," the girl told him. "We must all practice until nine o'clock."

"I saw the sign when I came in. What are you practicing?"

"We are practicing the Christmas...." She had trouble getting the word out. "Paa-jen," she gave it a Thai pronunciation.

Harry nodded his head in understanding. "Christmas pageant," he said. "Christmas is getting close, isn't it? And is that what the goat is for?"

"In paa-jen, he will be sheep. It is easy to find a goat, but there are not many sheeps."

"I see," he said. He looked around the Exorcist. There seemed to be nothing different from the last time he was here, except it was very quiet. There were two men at the bar, each alone with his own thoughts. There were two others at a table on the far side of the room. There was no other activity, and very few of the Exorcist's young ladies were about. "Where is the practice going on?" he asked. "Nothing much seems to be happening."

"Everyone is now in heaven." Frankie put a hand to her mouth to hide a giggle. "That is upstairs." She pointed at the ceiling. "That's what we call it now. The angels like me must come from heaven. We are fixing that now."

"Hmmm," Harry said, and thought about heaven while Frankie went to get him his Scotch. She came back with an unopened bottle of Johnny Walker Black, a pitcher of water, and an ice bucket. She made him a drink and said, "I must go now. I come back later."

"See you," he said. He sat back and started to review the events of the last few days. So engrossed was he in these thoughts that he never noticed one of the men at the bar get up and, drink in hand, walk over to his table.

"May I join you?" the man asked. It was a pleasant Thai voice with a good British accent. A young-looking man in his forties, he wore a fine white shirt and a necktie with a pattern so complex in color and design that it could only have come from an expensive European boutique. Not your average Exorcist regular, Harry thought. More the prosperous local man of business who, at this time of day, should be drinking with his colleagues at one of Bangkok's hyper-expensive, member-only watering holes.

"Have a seat," Harry said.

The man slid into the booth across from him. His drink looked like a twin of Harry's Scotch and water. That was important to know because the older Thais with real money had started with Scotch in their youth, when it was fashionable, and usually still drank it. It was a good indication that the man was what he appeared to be. On the other hand, this was Bangkok. What might happen next could be the opening chapter in a world-class scam. Harry waited for the beginning of a long story. The man got to the point much quicker than he expected.

"Mr. Harry, I am Sornchai." He held out a neat, well-kept hand to Harry. "Colonel Sornchai, Thai C.I.D., Criminal Investigation Department."

"Pleased to meet you, Colonel," Harry said as coolly as he could. "Always pleased to see you guys come by the Exorcist. Gives me confidence that the Scotch is not watered down."

Sornchai's smile showed a set of perfect teeth. "You can be sure of the Scotch here, Mr. Harry. But Scotch is really not my department." He continued to smile until Harry felt compelled to speak.

"You said something about criminals, Colonel," Harry said and casually took a swallow of Scotch.

"Criminal investigation. My part of it is theft, fraud, that kind of thing."

Harry instinctively looked toward where the cashier normally sat. There was no one there now. "Gee, I hope everything here is all right, Colonel."

"Oh, everything here is fine. It's you I was hoping to see here tonight."

"Me?" Harry asked. His hand came to his breast as he let an incredulous look slide over his face.

"Yes, Mr. Harry. I've been hoping to meet you for some time. I understand you are an art dealer. And a friend of Mr. Aloysious."

"Yes," Harry said very frankly. "I deal in art. And I did know Aloysious."

"So, I wonder if you be willing to help me with something? We could talk here, I think." Sornchai looked around the almost empty room. "I don't see any need to go to my office," he added.

"Sure, Colonel," Harry responded. What choice did he have? "I'll be happy to help. What can I do for you?"

"Just some questions. You see, my work relates to theft and fraud – where it touches on art. And antiquities. Now, I understand that you recently returned here from the States?"

"Actually, Colonel, I got here about three weeks ago. More like a month now. I come over on buying trips maybe two, three times a year."

"No, not when you first came here this time. You left here and came back five nights ago. Look, Harry. Can I call you just Harry? Please call me Sornchai. Anyway, Harry, there is something you should understand. Unlike the old days, we are now computerized. We know that you left here two weeks ago. I thought you might be back soon, and I asked to be alerted by the airport authorities when you returned. When you arrived at the airport five nights ago, I missed you because you did not take a cab from there."

Harry's attempt to say something was waved aside by Sornchai, who went on. "It doesn't matter where you went that night. That's not important. What is important is that we have a chance to talk now."

Harry poured some Scotch from his bottle into the Colonel's glass. "Colonel. Sornchai. You seem to know a lot about me already, but I'll be happy to fill in any pieces you need."

"You have been traveling up North. And you are an art expert. All I want to know is if you have heard any rumors of a big find of old Khmer and Thai art."

Modestly, Harry answered, "I do deal in art. And I do have a good feel for the market in Southeast Asian antiques. But that hardly makes me an art expert. Have I heard rumors of a big find?" He smiled. "Sornchai, when I am on a buying trip, I hear rumors of a big find every day. 'Khun Harry', one dealer says, 'look at this. A thousand years old. It was just found by an old woman in Burma.' Or, 'look at this, Khun Harry....'"

"I understand that, Harry. That is a hazard of your profession. But the rumors I hear now are more specific. They speak not of individual pieces, but of a huge cache of Angkor period and even earlier pieces that were found somewhere in Northern Thailand. These pieces are said to be in excellent condition and for sale at very high prices."

When Harry said nothing, Colonel Sornchai went on. "No one has offered you old Khmer pieces? Pieces in very good condition? Thai pieces that predate the 10th century? All in excellent condition? And all from the same source?"

Harry shrugged his shoulders. "Like I said, Sornchai, someone is always offering me something, but I have seen nothing different from what I usually see. I can't say that I've seen any kind of pieces in really excellent condition, or a lot of pieces all from the same source. The cupboard's almost bare, Sornchai. People have been taking antiques out of this area in massive quantities for decades. There's almost nothing left."

Colonel Sornchai said nothing. He looked unhappy. Harry decided he might as well go on the offensive. "Where do all these rumors start, Sornchai?" he asked.

Colonel Sornchai sighed. He made little circles on the table with his glass. "We have heard some here in Bangkok. The loudest ones are in Hong Kong."

"Hong Kong? That's it? What do you hear from Europe?" Harry asked. "From other markets in the States or Japan? Have you checked on these rumors there?"

"We've made inquiries. Hong Kong is the only place we have heard these particular rumors. Outside Thailand."

Harry took a moment to absorb this. If one of his clients in the U.S., or if one of Jean Lee's clients in Europe was talking, the rumors should lead back there. Hong Kong didn't make sense. How the hell did Hong Kong get into this? Unless Hong Kong was a red herring that Colonel Sornchai was dragging by his nose for some reason.

The Colonel also looked preoccupied. "You know, Harry," he finally said. "It's curious. In Hong Kong the rumors begin and end in the art market. In Thailand, we hear them in Bangkok, but they all seem to lead to some very bad elements up North."

"Bad elements?" Harry asked.

"Yes, bad elements. Counterfeiters. Counterfeiters of antiquities. You must know some of these elements, Harry."

Harry laughed. "You have me there, Sornchai. Some of my best friends make excellent antiques. But these are not 'bad elements'. Most of them are nice people just trying to make a living. They have a lot of skill. In most cases, their work is worth what you pay them. Even if what you get is not old. Hell, that's the antiques market, anywhere in the world. Let the buyer beware."

"I don't think you follow me, Harry. When I say very bad elements, I am not speaking of the individual artisan who occasionally makes a nice 'antique' for the tourists. I am talking about the big fish, the ones who try to control the market. Don't look surprised, Harry. Like drugs or prostitution or anything else, if there's enough money involved, the sharks move in. The bad elements I speak of, Harry, are the ones who try to organize the small artisans into groups to create 'antiques' on a large scale. If there is money enough, these situations become very bad for everyone. For your small friends, who make 'antiques'. And even for you, Harry."

Harry shook his head in disagreement. "You know, Sornchai, in all my years in this area, since I've been dealing in art and before, I have never seen anyone making 'antiques' on a large scale."

"I think you have seen it. Perhaps you did not know what you were looking at. Think of it this way. In any one village, perhaps three men are good at making 'antiques'. Right?" Harry agreed. "Now," Sornchai went on, "in ten villages there may be as many as 30 men, or more, who can make good 'antiques'. That sounds reasonable? Then, in 20 villages, 60 men. Think about it, Harry. If each man in each village makes one 'antique' a month, at least 700 'antiques' will be made every year."

Sornchai sipped at his drink and went on. "What you see, Harry, is the individual artisan who makes his 'antiques'. What you don't see – because you have never looked for it – is the element that tries to bring organization to tie all the individual effort in all the villages together."

Harry reached for his drink now and took a deep swallow. "What you're telling me, Sornchai, is pretty incredible," he said. "Does such an organization exist? If it does it can't just end there. To make it work, there has to be a way to market all the 'antiques' that are made."

"Yes, we think there is a marketing arm. That is something we are still looking for. You ask if an organization that mass-produces 'antiques' exists? Yes, on a small scale I can guarantee that it already exists. We know of two such groups. In each case a handful of villages funnel the 'antiques' they make to a small group of men that markets the 'antiques'. This group passes a small percentage of the proceeds back to the villages. But these are small efforts involving a few villages. On a large scale, ten villages, 20 villages? I don't know if that exists right now. I know that level of organization has been attempted. And for a while, at least, it was successful."

"What happened to it?"

"I don't know. It ended."

Harry shook his head again, this time as if to shake off the last remnants of his disbelief. "What can I say, Sornchai. I'm surprised something like this is going on. I wouldn't have thought the antiques business is lucrative enough for what you are talking about. You're talking about organized crime."

"In certain cases, when enough money is involved, the bad elements appear and try to take over. I suppose that's organized crime."

"Well, let me reassure you, Colonel Sornchai, this is news to me. Something I don't think I've ever seen. Or, if I have, I didn't recognize it for what it was."

Sornchai looked at Harry's face for a long moment before answering. "Yes, Harry. I think I believe you." After another moment he added, "Come, let me buy the next round, or at least find some fresh ice." Sornchai turned to look toward the bar. There was still no one to be seen there. "Let me see if I can find somebody," Sornchai said as he got up.

Harry had a lot to think about. Colonel Sornchai had shown him something new and still hard to believe: an organization that produced counterfeit antiques on a large scale. He had never seen any indication that anything like this existed. Colonel Sornchai was a professional cop – and a very intelligent one, it seemed. If he told Harry all this, it was not just to make conversation.

Okay, Harry thought, Sornchai had a reason. But where did it tie into him? God, if there was enough money, Sornchai said....

Something brushed by Harry's face. He was looking down when it went by, using his finger to stir the almost melted ice cubes in his glass. When he looked up, there was nothing to be seen. Everything seemed quiet.

He had just picked up his glass and was bringing it to his mouth when something went by him again. He certainly felt that one. There was something out there, he was sure of it. And it was big. He looked for it. What was it? A bat? If it was a bat, it was a big bat.

As usual, it was so dark in the Exorcist that he could not see anything with any great degree of clarity. He could make out Colonel Sornchai at the bar. At least Sornchai seemed to have found a bartender.

Harry sat back to relax. He stared off into the distance to relax his eyes. When it happened, it was so quick that he was left with only an impression of a pair of eyes looking deeply into his for just a brief moment. Then they were gone. Big eyes. If eyes have their own expression, these were curious and bemused. Harry sat there, paralyzed by something that looked through him and saw deeply into his soul. Seconds passed, and he was starting to think he had imagined it all. Suddenly the eyes were looking right into his again, and then they were gone.

"Well, I finally got some action." It was Colonel Sornchai, ice bucket in one hand, drinks in the other, trying to set both on the table.

"Sornchai, I just saw the damndest thing...." Harry started to say.

"Careful, Harry," Sornchai said, "don't lean forward. Here comes the goat."

Harry wasn't quick enough. He didn't see the eyes this time, but he felt it go by, brushing his face. "Goat?" was all he could manage.

"The Christmas pageant goat. They can't seem to get the trajectory right. That's where all the staff are. I was talking to the bartender."

Harry was sitting well back when the goat went by again. This time he was ready and saw it. It was looking at him, completely unconcerned, as it arced back up toward the ceiling.

"They have been working on it most of the week," Sornchai continued. "I don't know if you noticed it, but they did a good job with the harness. The goat doesn't seem to mind at all now."

"Well, it is kind of dark to make out the details," Harry said as casually as he could. "How exactly does the goat work?"

"Well, the goat is only a test, you see. In the pageant it will be the young ladies. The angels." Sornchai pointed to the far end of the Exorcist. "I don't know if you can see it up there. There is a trap door in the ceiling. The goat is pushed from there." Sornchai pointed to the center of the Exorcist ceiling. "The rope is attached there. So, when the goat is released, he swings out across the room like a big pendulum, and back up to the far ceiling. There's a trap door on that end. He could be caught there, but usually they let him swing back to the other end. It's supposed to look like he's flying. Careful, here he comes again."

Harry and Sornchai watched as the goat went by their faces once, and then once again on the return swing. Now that he knew what he was looking at, Harry could make out the black and white face easily. It looked bored, or maybe content.

"The ladies take good care of him. He seems to like it. He's not supposed to come so close to the tables. That's what they're trying to fix."

Harry nodded as if talking about the finer points of flying a goat was an everyday thing. It would be difficult to get back to art, but he wanted to try.

"Look, Sornchai. I know you must have told me about the organized antique counterfeiters for a good reason. You started out saying you were interested in rumors of a cache of Khmer art. I take it these are two different things."

"Yes, I think so, but I'm not sure. I told you about the counterfeiters so that you would understand where the rumors start. I know the rumors start with these people. What I don't know is why the rumors start with them. There are reasons why they might: to make trouble for a rival; to give credibility to their counterfeits. But there is something else here, something more complex. A piece of the puzzle that I don't have."

Sornchai leaned in toward Harry. "You are a friend of Aloysious. That's another reason I wanted to talk with you."

"Well, I was a friend of Aloysious."

"You were? Ah, you mean his disappearance, the rumors of Aloysious's death. I seem to recall that Alo-wichit has disappeared at times in the past. He always reappeared. Do you have reason to think that it will be different this time, Harry?"

"No, no, I don't. I can agree with you, Sornchai, there is always a chance that Alo-wichit will someday reappear."

"I'm glad you think so. I am sure you will be happy to see him if he does reappear. As I will be. I have so much to ask him."

"Look, Sornchai, really, is there anything else I can do for you? The art world in Thailand is my world too. I don't want to see it screwed up anymore than you do."

"You travel, you speak with many people. Keep me in mind. I would be interested if you learn anything about the things we have spoken of. You can always reach me here." He gave Harry a card. "I'm sure you understand my position, Harry. Antique art objects discovered anywhere in Thailand are the property of the Thai government. The Fine Arts Department decides if what is found is national treasure, or if it belongs to one of our neighbors, like Cambodia. Sometimes these things are released to the finder and can be sold. But that is a matter for the Fine Arts Department. My job is to assure that national treasures are not lost."

Colonel Sornchai got up from the table. "Harry, I must go now. It was a pleasure to meet you. When you go up North again, think of what I said about the bad elements there. And be careful. They are not nice people, Harry. You know the art world. It can be nasty."

Harry got up and leaned forward to extend his hand to Sornchai. As

Sornchai reached for his hand, Harry saw the smile suddenly drop from Sornchai's face.

"Harry, be careful! The goat!"

27

They were all very nice to him afterwards. Colonel Sornchai offered him a police car to take him wherever he wanted to go. Frankie rubbed Tiger Balm on the bruises on his chest and dabbed antiseptic on the scratch on his face. She offered to see him to bed. One of the regulars, whom Harry had never seen out of his seat at the bar, got up, walked over a little unsteadily, and replaced Harry's spilled drink. Somebody called a taxi to take him to the hospital.

In the end, Harry turned down all the offers, said good night to everyone, and made his way slowly and painfully out to the street. As he stepped through the door, he saw the goat, sitting like a pasha, draped over the laps of two of the Exorcist ladies.

The goat did not seem at all fazed by the experience. While he had not seen the goat coming, the goat had seen him and did the natural thing. It had lowered its head to take the full brunt of its encounter with Harry's chest on its beautifully curved horns. The impact had sent Harry over backwards as the goat arced over him. One hoofed foot had passed lightly over Harry's face, leaving a thin red line that would be deep purple in the morning. On his back, he had watched the goat pass over him again on its return swing. The goat had twisted in its harness to look down at him, full of curiosity.

From the stares he was getting as walked down Patpong Road, he knew the front of his shirt was a mess. Probably his face too. There was nothing he could do about it now. Let them think he had been in a brawl in some bar. He crossed Silom, got back in the shadows, and headed for the condo where Jean Lee lived.

When he reached the condo lobby, he was not exactly welcomed. The doorman shook his head and asked him to wait at the door while he conferred with the security desk. One of the uniformed security officers walked back with the doorman. When he saw Harry, he also shook his head slowly. He asked what Harry wanted. Harry gave him his own name,

Jean Lee's name, and the apartment number. The security officer went to telephone. He came back shortly, looking surprised. "You come with me," he said to Harry, and they rode up in the elevator together. The security officer seemed not to want to leave Harry alone in the building he was responsible for, even after Jean Lee had assured him it was all right.

"Harry!" Jean Lee said when the security officer left. "What in the name of heaven have you been doing?"

Harry let himself drop into a stiff-backed chair right inside the door. "God, I'm glad to see you, Jean Lee. I was afraid you weren't back from Europe yet."

"I got back this morning. Harry, what happened to you?"

"Nothing. Nothing serious. I got hit by a flying goat. Do you think I could have a shower? Maybe you could loan me a shirt. Once I get cleaned up a bit we can talk."

After he showered, they sat together in Jean Lee's study. His chest ached, but he felt resplendent in his borrowed clothes. He could not remember ever wearing a shirt so soft. He listened while Jean Lee talked about the success of his trip to Europe, but found it hard to concentrate on what Jean Lee was saying. He tried hard to listen again.

"...And so," Jean Lee summarized, "the French end has netted us just five million. That's five million British pounds. In U.S. dollars that's about.... Are you following me, Harry?"

"Yes... I mean no. Oh, shit, I guess what I mean is I am following you. I know what you're saying, and that we've all made a lot of money. I just seem to be having trouble focusing on the details."

"Don't worry about it, Harry. That was a nasty knock you received. You say it was a goat?"

"It was a goat, all right. A black and white one. But that's not what's bothering me. Let me tell you what happened before the goat hit me...."

"There was this guy, Sornchai," Harry said and went on to tell Jean Lee about his conversation with the Colonel. Then Harry brought him up to date on what was happening up North. "So you see, Jean Lee," he concluded, "there's too much here I don't understand. Too much that Aloysious is not telling us."

"I think I understand. You have had more to worry about than the goat. What do you think Colonel Sornchai was telling you? Do you think he knows anything specific about what Aloysious has found? Has he learned of our marketing efforts? Or is he just fishing?"

"Sornchai's fishing all right, but he knows where the fish are. I don't know how much he knows. Some of the things he said make absolutely no sense to me. Where the hell does Hong Kong come into the equation? During our whole conversation, Sornchai was more interested in the 'bad elements' up North than in rumors of a new find of antiques."

"Is he somehow tying the two together?"

"I don't know, Jean Lee. The only connection I can see in what he said is that some of his 'bad elements' are probably the bad guys chasing Aloysious."

Jean Lee thought about it. "You may have something there. Sornchai's 'bad elements', whether chasing Aloysious or not, are the source of rumors about a huge new find of Khmer antiques. If they are the people chasing Aloysious, they may have learned something about the lost city. And now they are talking about it."

"What's the Hong Kong connection? I don't see any link to Hong Kong in anything we're doing."

"I can't answer that, Harry. I don't know."

"Well, maybe the Hong Kong connection is just a herring Sornchai is using for bait." Harry was getting a little weary of sitting. He stood up for a moment and tried to stretch out his arms. He immediately regretted it. "Uh, that hurt," he said. "You know, Sornchai really seems to see the art world as a troubled place, a place of strange and violent creatures."

"It does seem to be getting violent – from what you've told me about the goings-on up North."

"And strange?"

Jean Lee shrugged. "Not more so than the rest of the world. But, you know, Harry, this trip confirmed what I have known for a long time: Buyers of art, particularly antique art, can all be explained by two factors. They differ only in how much of each they possess."

"That sounds like pretty heady stuff, Doctor. I'm not sure I'm ready for the great unifying theory of the arts and antiquities market."

"Hear me out, Harry. I'm sure you'll agree." Jean Lee held up two fingers. "Every buyer of art can be explained by two factors, two human qualities that affect what he buys and how he buys it. And that includes you and me, Harry. The first quality is taste. The second is confidence. For example, some buyers of art possess a great amount of confidence, but they have absolutely no taste. They know exactly what they want. They buy quickly. Because they have no taste, what they buy is almost invariably bad. They are the worst of the buyers. It is difficult for an honest art dealer like myself and like you, Harry, to deal with them. You can tell them nothing. They already know everything."

"I know that kind well," Harry agreed.

"The second type," Jean Lee went on. "The second type has all taste and no confidence. They know what they want, but they have no confidence to buy – if left to themselves. They never accept the wisdom of their own good taste. Never trust their own choices. These buyers are easier to deal with. They can be guided to good things by a good dealer. But the dealer must be good. He must have taste to equal theirs. At least at first. Once these buyers come to trust a dealer, he will make all their choices. They will not buy a thing, unless he blesses it."

"Hmmm," was all Harry said.

"The third type," Jean Lee continued, "has neither confidence nor taste. In the hands of a clever but unscrupulous dealer, they are putty. A clever dealer can direct them to buy anything, good or bad."

"What about your average honest dealer with good taste – like the two of us?" Harry asked. "How does the honest dealer deal with this third type?"

"The honest dealer can deal with type three, but it is frustrating. They will know when he has sold them something good, and never accept that they have paid a fair price. To them, no dealer is ever honest."

"What about the ones that have both qualities, confidence and taste?"

"A contradiction in terms, Harry. An impossibility. The two qualities cancel each other out. I have never seen a buyer with an equal measure of both good taste and confidence. Why this does not happen is a mystery of art. It is the art world's equivalent of a square circle."

Harry laughed. "I know you're right, Jean Lee, and you've helped put things back in perspective for me. I almost feel like I can deal with Aloysious again. I think it's about time I get going."

"It's getting late, Harry. Why not stay here, tonight? God knows, in the morning you're going to feel sore."

"Thanks, I appreciate the offer. Trouble is that Aloysious and company won't know where I am. Aloysious will expect to get hold of me through the Sweet-T Hotel if he needs me. And God knows he may. Look, you and I have more to talk about, but not tonight. Tomorrow, I've got to set up another shipment with Sato. Maybe we can get together tomorrow. In any case, I'll see you before I head back up North. Do you mind if I get your clothes back to you then?"

"Harry, take what you want, and don't worry about getting it back to me. Just take care of yourself, and be careful. Don't go chasing after more goats."

Jean Lee accompanied him down to the lobby. Harry got a good look at himself in the mirror in the elevator. He looked considerably better than he did going up, but his face still looked like he had walked into a door. The scratch that ran from his chin, over his nose, and up to his hairline was thin, but the flesh around it was already starting to puff up. He would look great in the morning.

With a final wave to Jean Lee, he turned and stumbled off into the night. When he reached Silom Road, he turned away from the Patpong area, several blocks away. It was dark along here, but he thought his chances of getting a reasonable taxi fare were a lot better here than where the bright lights and tourists were. Traffic was light now. The evening rush hours was long past, and the end of the day, marked by the closing of the bars, was still hours off.

A number of cars passed Harry, and finally one pulled alongside. He turned toward it, but instead of a taxicab he found a big black Mercedes. The driver got out and opened the back door. As Harry stooped to get in, he heard a now familiar voice.

"Ha-Lee. Good to see you."

Harry sat down next to the old man. Sato took a hard look at him under the overhead light. "What have you been doing?" he asked.

"Sato-san, please don't ask. If I tried to explain, you would not believe me. It was just a little accident."

"Did this happen to you upcountry?"

"No. It happened to me after I got back to Bangkok."

Sato looked relieved. "I am happy it did not happen up North. I understand there have been problems."

Harry nodded. "There were problems. How did you know?"

Sato did not answer. Instead he asked, "Do you think Aloysious is working too aggressively? Do you think the situation is dangerous?"

"Yes, Aloysious is working too aggressively, but that's the way he works. It's his natural state. Is it dangerous? I don't know what the right answer to that is. We had a problem. I don't think it's over. So maybe the answer is yes, it is dangerous. But that's not the thing that concerns me. What concerns me is that something is going on that I know nothing about. Right now, you know more about what's going on than I do. How did you know where to find me tonight?"

Sato patted Harry's knee and smiled. "Ha-Lee," he said, "do not concern yourself about the small things. I have to know many things. I have ways to keep informed. I know you and Aloysious had a problem on the river, and that this was not the first problem with these people. I know the police are still very interested in Aloysious and his activities. The police know you are in Bangkok now and they will want to talk with you."

"They already have," Harry said, and went on to tell Sato about his talk with Colonel Sornchai. Sato listened intently. When Harry finished, Sato asked, "Was it Sornchai's position that the discovery of Khmer antiques and the counterfeits were somehow related?"

"That's exactly what I asked him. He said he didn't think so, but he wasn't sure."

Sato only nodded. It seemed he had no other questions, and Harry asked. "What do you make of what Sornchai said about Hong Kong? That Hong Kong is the source of the rumors about the Khmer cache? Does that mean anything to you?"

Sato did not answer immediately. "Yes," he finally said. After a moment he added, "But, like the injury to your face, don't ask me to explain. If I told you, you would not understand."

A faint smile passed Harry's lips. He shrugged his shoulders. "We may as well talk business. Aloysious and I brought a good many pieces downriver. He'll be hauling as much as he can down to Chiang Mai. We would like to get it to your warehouse as soon as we can. Then we want to sort the stuff and ship out the pieces we have already sold. Incidentally, my friend Jean Lee is back from Europe." Harry went on to tell Sato the details he remembered from Jean Lee's account.

At the end of it, Sato said, "You have had some interesting days. Now we will take you wherever you wish."

Harry told the driver where the Sweet-T was located, and asked to be dropped a block away. The reputation he maintained there as a carefree knockabout and occasional dealer in knickknacks would never survive a grand arrival in Sato's Mercedes.

When they reached the place where he wanted to be dropped, Sato had the final word. "Ha-Lee, you must be very careful. Here and upcountry. Tonight you must rest. Tomorrow we can work. I have something for you. There!" Sato pointed out the side window of the car to where a small figure stood in the shadows. Harry got out and walked over.

"Little Mouse! Where did you come from?" She pointed to a second black Mercedes that was pulling away from the curb behind Sato's car. "I came in that car. Sato-san said I would stay with you tonight."

"That was very thoughtful of him. Come on. Let's see if the bridal suite is available."

Harry never learned if the Sweet-T had a bridal suite. As he did with any customer who appeared with no possessions but a pretty girl, the room clerk winked and passed Harry a key to one of the Sweet-T's standard deluxe rooms. The standard deluxe room differed from the standard room by having a mirror where the headboard should be. There was also a long mirror on the wall alongside the bed, and another mirror on the ceiling. Little Mouse pointed at each mirror in turn and giggled. He shrugged and got undressed.

The hot bath relaxed Harry completely. It drained the last tiny molecules of strength and energy from his body. Closing his eyelids seemed to require effort beyond his ability. Which was just as well perhaps, because the only parts of him that could still move were his eyeballs. They still worked as a team, moving together quickly from the mirror overhead to the mirror on the wall. Then back again to the ceiling. Focusing on a muscle in Little Mouse's back as seen from above. Then moving quickly for a side view of the same area of rounded flesh and smooth skin. Then a quick glimpse of breast or buttock from above, and then to a more lingering look at the gentle curves from the side. It gave Harry a whole new perspective on things.

Little Mouse was bent over him, kneading a muscle in his shoulder. "I hope I do not hurt you, Harry." She stopped and closely examined his face. She used a fingertip to trace lightly the thin red line that ran from his chin to his forehead.

"This an interesting wound," she said, "if unsightly." When Harry did not respond, she added, "I hope her fingernail was clean."

"It was not a fingernail!"

"It was a long fingernail. The fingernail of a woman who does not need to work. A woman kept by a rich man."

"It was not a fingernail," he repeated. "It was a hoof."

"Shhh," Little Mouse said. "It does not matter to me, Khun Harry. I care only if her fingernail was clean. I know you are not a rich man."

He leaned forward on his elbows. "Now just what is that supposed to mean?"

Little Mouse pushed him back down. "It means that it is not a woman you keep who did this to you."

"Why do you insist it was a woman who scratched my face?"

Little Mouse looked at him with the certainty of all her 18 years. "Who else would want to do that? Who else would care?"

He chuckled and lay back again. "Nobody understands me," he said to himself.

"Was she beautiful?"

"Yes," he said in defeat. "She was beautiful."

Little Mouse moved to the end of the bed and started massaging his foot. She was using a lot of pressure. "Hey," he said, "take it easy there. You don't know your own strength."

"Ouch," he said a minute later when Little Mouse hit a nerve that made him feel like his big toe fell off. He got up on his elbows again. "Okay," he said, "what's the problem? What have I done? Are you pouting?"

"I am very sad," Little Mouse replied.

"Because I said the woman was beautiful? There wasn't even a woman. It was a goat that did this."

"But she was more beautiful than I am." Little Mouse looked at her hand. "I cannot have beautiful long fingernails. I must work." She turned her eyes to Harry. They looked very sad. "I am not your woman, Khun Harry, but I still like you. I would not scratch you like that, even if I wanted to."

"Come here, Little Mouse," he said as gently as he could. He patted the bed alongside him. "Come sit here." When she sat down on the bed next to him, he put his hand on her shoulder and then traced the contour of her back. "And why would you want to scratch me?"

"Because you do not want me."

"Does tiredness count?" he asked. But Little Mouse obviously did not understand that, or did not want to. "Look," he said, "I do want you. I thought I was tired, but I'm starting to feel like I'm not. Besides, it was a goat. I swear."

But the crisis had passed. Little Mouse had already noted the subtle change in his anatomy that indicated his growing interest in her. She slowly pulled away the towel that was draped over Harry's middle, and giggled.

28

The day started out promising. Harry woke refreshed and ravenously hungry. He looked in the mirror to see if the swelling around the scratch on his face was as bad as he expected. It was. The color was something to behold. Even that did not discourage him. He headed for breakfast after telling Little Mouse he would see her in the coffee shop. She did not look particularly eager to get out of bed, but said she would see him as soon as she dressed. Then she stuck her head back under the covers.

He grabbed a newspaper and settled down to enjoy his coffee, and then ordered fried eggs and all the fixings. He ate quickly as things were put in front of him. He was completely engrossed in his newspaper when his concentration wavered and his eyes were drawn to a young woman standing in the entrance to the coffee shop. He knew nothing about women's clothes, but the dress looked both casual and elegant. It was the kind of dress that he associated with spring and sidewalk cafes in Paris, not morning coffee in the Sweet-T Coffee Shop in Bangkok.

The young lady was elegant as the dress she wore. Her long hair framed an attractive face that was partially hidden by large glasses with tinted lenses. When she moved, every eye in the coffee shop moved with her. As she got closer to where he sat, he could not help but admire the confidence in her step. She was cool, but there was a sensuous grace in her walk. It was only when she stopped across the table from him that he looked again at her face and realized that he knew her.

"Little Mouse!" He stared in dumb silence while a waiter rushed up to pull back her chair. Little Mouse sat down. With a nice smile, she asked the waiter for coffee. The waiter became all smiles and bows, and Harry had never seen faster service in the Sweet-T Coffee Shop.

When her coffee was poured, she took off her glasses. This time when she smiled at him, he saw again the Little Mouse he knew and in fact had just spent the night with.

"I am sorry I took so long, Khun Harry," she said. A look of concern appeared in her eyes. "Oh, your face looks terrible!"

"You...you look very nice this morning," he said. "I like your dress."

"Thank you," she responded, looking pleased by the compliment. "Sato-san said that if I stay with you, I must be very beautiful. I am glad you like the dress."

"I like your dress very much. Where did you get it?"

"Yuko-san helped me pick it out."

"Yuko-san. Is she your friend?"

"Oh, no. Yuko-san is my teacher. She works for Black Lion Enterprises, Sato-san's company. She knows everything about clothes. She teaches me about make-up and how to walk. She taught me how to order things in expensive restaurants. And how to behave there. Mostly she teaches me how to look nice."

"Well, she certainly succeeded. You are not the little massage girl I met last night. My God, you even have fingernails."

She put down her coffee cup and gave Harry her hand so that he could better admire her nails. "Do you like them?" she asked. "They are not very long. Yuko-san says fingernails should not be more than a certain length. I hope you like them, Harry. They may not be as beautiful as the one that did that."

Harry touched his face. "You are more beautiful than the one that did that. I guarantee it." He studied her face. "You know," he said, "you look more...more mature. I can't believe you are the same little girl I spent the night with."

"The same," she said and put her hand on top of his. She looked happy.

"Little Mouse," he said with affection.

"Salika."

"Salika?" he repeated quizzically.

"Salika is my proper name. Little Mouse is my nickname. I think when I am dressed up and we are together you should call me by my proper name."

He laughed. "When we are together and there is someone to hear, I will call you Salika. When there is no one to hear, you will be 'Mouse'."

"That is okay," she said, "But if you call me Mouse and someone hears...." She held out a hand to show her fingernails and smiled a sweet smile at him.

"Okay. Now, let's talk about today. Today you will stay with me. Right? I have many things to do, but we can do most of them together. I also have to book a flight to Chiang Mai. I will have to leave tonight or tomorrow."

"You go tomorrow, Harry. Don't worry about a flight. It will be taken care of. Tonight we can stay together."

"You'll take care of my flight?"

"Sato-san said whatever you need will be taken care of. If you tell me the time you want to go to Chiang Mai, I will take care of it."

"In that case, I'll buy you lunch. In an expensive restaurant. Wherever you want. Deal?"

"A good deal!" she said. "But you must take me where I want." She gave the waiter a glance. He was at her side like a shot, the check for her coffee and Harry's breakfast on a silver tray. Harry always got the bill handed to him. Like magic, a 500-baht note appeared in Little Mouse's hand. With the slightest gesture she let the waiter know that the change – at least half of what she put down – was his. The waiter bowed and smiled all the way as he saw them out to the lobby.

"Now, let's see if I can find a cab," Harry said once they were outside. She put her hand out to hold him back and sent a regal look down the driveway. An engine started and in a moment a car was alongside. The driver hopped out and opened the rear door.

"Please come, Harry," Little Mouse said. He dutifully climbed in behind her. "Sato-san knows you do not like the black Mercedes. He sent this smaller car. It will be ours today." She had her tinted glasses back on. She sat with one smooth leg crossed over the other, looking like a real lady. He chuckled. "You know, I could really get to like this. Let's go buy me some new clothes. Maybe we can find you a trinket or two. Then we can go to lunch."

Harry found that having a car and driver, and Little Mouse, was a great advantage. She directed the driver to a shopping center where he was able to find everything he needed. She also gave him excellent advice about colors and fit and prices. He bought clothes to replace what the goat destroyed and what he left behind up North. At one point he remembered the bag he had left with Tong, and felt the slightest twinge of guilt.

"Harry, you do not look happy. Does your face hurt?"

He could never hide anything. Women always were quick to know when he was thinking about some other woman. Being with Little Mouse had driven away thoughts about his face and a lot of other things. He was having a good time. He was more relaxed than he had been since this whole lost city business started. The entire day felt like days he had known many years ago, a Bangkok R&R from Vietnam with all care left behind as long as the R&R lasted.

They passed a window full of gold jewelry. Most of it was heavy and encrusted with big semiprecious stones. There were also smaller, graceful pieces. "Come on, Mouse. Let's go take a look."

Little Mouse tried on some bracelets and found one she seemed to particularly like. "Like that one?" he asked.

"I like it, Harry, but I do not want you to buy it for me."

"Because I am not a rich man?"

"Because I do not want you to give me something just because I want it.

Now is not the right time." She was already starting out the door.

He shrugged. "Hey, wait for me," he called after her. To the clerk he said, "I'll be back. Put it aside."

Lunch was Big Macs at McDonald's. Harry offered to take her to any restaurant she chose, and she chose McDonald's. He had tried to entice her by suggesting one of the best restaurants in town, not really expecting that she knew the name.

"But I often go to there," she said, "and no one ever takes me for a hamburger." He did not ask who took her to one of Bangkok's most expensive restaurants. He could figure that out by himself. So they dined on Big Macs and french fries and enjoyed it.

After lunch, he suggested that she drop him at Jean Lee's shop, while she went off to book his flight to Chiang Mai and to do anything else she needed to do. The car dropped him in front of Jean Lee's shop. Harry waited only until the car was out of sight, then he grabbed a taxi and went back to the store where he and Little Mouse had looked at the bracelets. The clerk remembered him. The transaction took only a minute. When he arrived back at Jean Lee's shop, Jean Lee met him just inside the door.

"Harry, what are you doing?" Jean Lee asked. "I saw you get of a car here a half hour ago. Then you disappeared. Are police colonels chasing you again?"

"Had to run an errand. The car will be coming back for me in about 20 minutes. I thought we better sort out what we still need to do. I'm off to Chiang Mai in the morning. If you could show me the photos of the pieces we need to send to your clients in Europe, I can get that shipment under-way as soon as I get up North. Oh, I'll send the car over to your place tonight with the clothes I borrowed."

"I'm disappointed," Jean Lee said. "I thought we would have dinner together this evening."

"Sorry. Something came up."

"Yes, I noticed. She's attractive. Well, never mind, we can have dinner another time. If that thing on your face gets any worse looking, you may not have many more opportunities with young ladies. I will get you the photos of the pieces that need to be delivered. Have you any more news from up North? Or from the police?"

"Not a word. Which is good. Aloysious won't get in contact unless something serious happens. I have seen Sato. He'll be ready to move whenever I give the word. To be frank, I haven't really thought much about the whole thing since last night. Did you come to any conclusions after I left?"

"Only that your friend Colonel Sornchai knows something is going on. Something that he connects you and Aloysious to. I think he is also telling you to be careful up North. And that, I think, is a very good idea. The chaps on the river seem to be quite serious about whatever it is they have taken offense over."

Jean Lee went off to get the photos. When he came back, Harry asked, "Do you know anything about flying trees?"

"You mean flying goats, Harry." Jean Lee corrected.

"No, I mean flying trees. Look, I don't want to make the water murkier than it already is, but do you know if the Karen have any beliefs about flying trees? Or maybe tree spirits that fly around the hills up North?"

"The Karen, eh?" Jean Lee thought about it. "No," he said finally, "I don't know of any flying tree beliefs the Karen might have. I'm sure there's an interesting story that goes with this."

"There is, Jean Lee, but I think I better save it for another time."

The car appeared at some point while Harry and Jean Lee were talking, and waited patiently at the curb. When Harry was satisfied he had done what he could, he told Jean Lee he would be in touch and hurried out to the car. He realized he was looking forward to seeing Little Mouse. He was not disappointed. She had changed clothes and was wearing a light dress that showed a lot of her back and shoulders and closely followed the contours of her body. She looked happy to see him too.

"You know, Mouse, I think maybe we should go back to the hotel for a while."

She looked at him with wide-eyed mock surprise. "Are you tired, Harry? Perhaps the Bangkok sun is too hot for an old man."

"Well...ah, if you would rather go somewhere else...."

"Oh, no, Harry. I think going back to the hotel is a good idea," Little Mouse said. Then she winked at him.

By the time they reached the Sweet-T, he was quite ready for bed. He stopped at the desk for the room key. The clerk handed it him, then asked him to wait just a moment. After stirring things around in a drawer, the clerk found an envelope and handed it to Harry. He split it down the side. Inside was a fax from "The Director, The Happy Dragon Gallery."

"Dear Mr. Harry," the fax said. "Urgent you call Mr. Karlo now. Any time. Immediately. His phone number attached. He is not happy. Christmas sales are good. Uncle Noah shipment arrived and he has enough stock. After Christmas will need new stock. Pigs will sell good in January. Find penguin that walks. Annabelle has new work as Santa. She works hard. Best regard. Miss Lotus, Dir."

Thoughts of the Happy Dragon and an unhappy Karlo cooled Harry's ardor. He looked down at his watch that had not worked since the goat hit him. "Shit. What time is it, Mouse?"

"Almost 3:30," she said. He calculated time zones. Even if his calculations were screwed up, it was the middle of Karlo's night for all purposes.

"Go upstairs, Mouse. I have to call the States."

"Don't be long," she said as she started for the elevator.

Harry was much longer than he wanted to be. It can be difficult to make an overseas call from Bangkok, particularly if your telephone belongs to a hotel that is not in the best graces of the local telephone authority. He watched the hotel operator dial Karlo's number time after time and never complete the connection. The operator eventually turned to him and said, "There seems to be a problem with the overseas line, sir. If you want to wait in your room, I can connect the call there when I get through."

Harry agreed to wait upstairs. He found it very frustrating to know that some unspecific thing was wrong and not know more than that. He got to the door to find he had no key. He knocked. Little Mouse opened the door. She was still wearing the dress that he found sexy. The door closed behind them, and here he was, alone with this girl, who was familiar and yet a stranger – a new discovery from whom he had not been able to take his eyes all day. The thought that he was about to have his way with her drained all patience from him. He reached for her.

"Wait, Harry. Wait," she said. "I have something for you." She went to get a small package from the table in the corner of the room. "Close your eyes," she said. He felt her fingers on his face. "Now, open your eyes, Harry."

He opened his eyes, but nothing happened. The lights in the room seemed to have gone out. Then he realized she had put glasses on him, dark glasses. In the mirror on the sidewall he saw himself. The glasses were huge. They covered most of the upper part of his face.

"Ah, very good, Harry," she said, standing off and studying his face.

"I can't wear these. They're too big."

"They cover your face. You will not be so ugly."

It was like a blow to his chest. Then he realized she was laughing. She took the glasses from him and threw them aside. He felt her lips on his face, and then her tongue. Then she bit him. "Ouch," he said. As he pulled away, she was still laughing. "Time for your bath, Khun Harry," she said and pulled her dress over her head.

He was staring at their reflection in the ceiling mirror. His face was not pleasant looking. Maybe he should have worn the glasses. She was asleep, lying on her side and curled up against him. She looked young and soft, and completely defenseless. It was hard to believe this was the sophisticated looking lady he had seen in the coffee shop that morning. In the last hours he had experienced a range of emotion that surprised him. At the moment he was content. The day had brought all it promised, and more.

* * * * *

The telephone alongside the bed rang. Little Mouse stirred and he reached over to take the receiver quickly before it woke her.

"Your call to the United States, sir." This was followed by a long screech that turned into a blast of static. Then there was nothing but a faint crackle and a voice somewhere far away saying, "Hello, hello. For God's sakes, man, it's the middle of the night."

"Karlo. Harry Ross here. I had a message to call you immediately."

"Ross! Ross, where are you? I need to speak to you immediately. When can we meet?"

"Karlo, I'm still in Thailand. I don't expect to get back to the States for weeks. Can it hold?"

There was a long silence. "No. No, it cannot hold. Look, Ross, I don't like to discuss business on the telephone. Let's just say that several of the items that I received from you do not appear to be satisfactory."

"Karlo, I'm not sure I follow you. The items you received....You mean the pieces you took from me at the hotel about ten days ago. Right? I don't follow you. How are they not satisfactory?"

"They are not as represented." When Harry did not respond immediately, Karlo went on. "Look, Ross, I'll be blunt. At least two of the pieces may not be of the period they are supposed to be. Our Southeast Asian curator has grave doubts...." There was a blast of static and the connection seemed lost. He could still hear Karlo faintly in the background, but could only make out an occasional word. He heard "...thirteenth century...." The line cleared again.

"Karlo. I don't know if you can hear me now?"

"I hear you, Ross."

"I didn't catch everything you said, but I did hear you say 13th century. We may have misjudged the age of something a bit. If we have, we'll make an adjustment. What's a few hundred years among friends?"

"That's not funny, Ross. I don't think you understood me. I said 20th-century copy of a 13th-century piece. Twentieth century, Ross. It was made yesterday! Ross, are you there? Ross?" There was another blast of static on the line. Harry did not wait to see if the connection had broken. He quietly replaced the receiver on its cradle.

It was the end of a perfect day.

29

Made yesterday! Made yesterday! Made yesterday!"
Harry woke with the phrase like a drumbeat in his head. Little Mouse stirred and asked sleepily if he was all right. The dawn's gray light was forcing an entrance through an opening in the drapes.

"What time is my flight, Mouse?"

"I don't want you to go," she said and edged closer to him in the bed.

"Come on. We have to get going. What time is my flight?" She moved closer still. Her head was on his chest.

"Your flight is when you want, Harry."

"What do you mean my flight is when I want? You did book my flight, didn't you?"

"Don't worry so much. The plane will go when you want." Her hands were moving slowly over him, pinching and rubbing. It was starting to make an impression on him.

"Okay, Okay! We'll do it your way. Do we have time for breakfast?"

"We have time for whatever you want."

"Oh...." was all he could say. A small soft tongue was moving down his chest. His interest in airline schedules died quietly.

Their car and driver was waiting when Harry finally made it to the desk to check out. It was nearly noon. He really did not care. He was too relaxed to care. It did not matter what flight he caught. He would see Aloysious soon enough.

On the way to the airport, Little Mouse was lost in her own thoughts. This gave Harry time to think about what he would do when he did see Aloysious. There were a lot of questions to ask.

It did not make much impression on him when the car pulled off on a service road just before they reached the domestic terminal. They parked at a small door on the side of the terminal. An alert-looking young Thai in a suit came out, bowed in their direction, and stood by while the driver unloaded Harry's bag from the trunk. The young man started off with the bag, and Harry and Little Mouse followed behind.

They found themselves in an empty lounge. The young man told him it would be five minutes until their flight, and offered to bring drinks or coffee. Harry declined for both of them and then looked around. There was no sign of other passengers. He assumed he was flying first class. "I'm going to have to meet your travel agent," he said to Little Mouse.

The young man appeared and asked that they follow him down a short corridor. An ornately carved wooden door led to the blacktop apron outside. A gleaming white and gold aircraft stood there, an executive jet that made Buzz Dorkin's Learjet look like a runabout.

"Gee," Harry said, admiringly. "Look at that. A Gulfstream." It took him another moment to realize that this was the aircraft they were walking to. Painted on yhe tail was a small black Singh, the mythical Thai lion, rampant on a gold shield. At the foot of the stairway Harry turned to Little Mouse. "Sato sent this?" he asked rhetorically. She simply arched her eyebrows.

The aircraft's interior was designed to accommodate six or eight executives luxuriously where twice their number could have easily traveled in comfort.

"Over here, Harry." She led him to a soft leather lounge in the center of the aircraft. "This is my favorite seat." She waited for him to sit and then pushed her shoulder close into him.

"They will bring us drinks or lunch," she said. "Or leave us alone if we want." With the last sentence she squeezed his arm, a small but wicked smile on her face.

"Don't tempt me," he said and with a laugh pulled back from her. "I wouldn't be able to stand up, let alone get off at Chiang Mai." The aircraft was starting to roll out to the runway. A quick look around confirmed that he and Little Mouse were to be the only passengers. "You've been on this airplane before?" he asked.

She nodded as she pressed a button on the armrest. "This airplane is used to take people from Thailand to Tokyo. Or from Tokyo to Thailand. Sato-san thought you would like to ride in it."

A young woman in a bronze-colored kimono appeared. She bowed low and offered them hot towels. She asked if they would like lunch, which could be served right after takeoff.

"Why not?" Harry said. "It sounds like a good time to have lunch."

With a small discreet movement that the stewardess didn't see, Little Mouse stuck an elbow in his ribs.

After the stewardess walked off with tiny steps, Harry put his hand on Little Mouse's bare knee and moved it a few inches up her thigh. "Don't misunderstand me," he said. "I don't put food before you, Mouse, but it's only an hour flight."

She leaned over and gently put her face next to his. She looked into his eyes and moved her face even closer. With sharp little teeth, she bit his lip. "Shit," he said and pulled away. There was no blood. She looked at him with innocence written all over her face.

Lunch came right after takeoff, the freshest sushi he had eaten in years. They both ate with obvious appetite and too quickly to talk much. With just a little left on her plate, she said, "I cannot stay with you in Chiang Mai. Sato-san said I must go back to Bangkok. He said you will be too busy to have time for me."

He grunted and sipped at his green tea. He was expecting that, but he was still more than a little disappointed.

He took a long sideways look at his companion of the last couple of days, dealing with the final bit of raw shrimp, and doing so with considerable grace. She was wearing the makeup and the clothes of her sophisticated self. Against the soft leather of the lounge she looked cool and competent. There was no question that she was an attractive and desirable woman. And she was very nice to be with. It was not often he felt like that in the middle of the day about the women he slept with.

"Why don't you come with me? I'll talk to Sato about it."

She moved a napkin lightly over her mouth. "No. I must go back. It is what Sato-san wants."

"What Sato wants? What about what I want?" he asked with the slightest trace of chagrin in his voice.

She reached over, and quietly squeezed his hand. "Sato-san said that I must give you some telephone numbers." She reached for a little purse and pulled out an envelope. "Inside are two numbers where you can always reach me," she said. "Sato-san said to call these numbers if you need help from him. You should not try to call him. Sato-san said it is better if you and I talk. He said you will understand. He said you should call me only when it is important."

"So that's what Sato wants us to do." He took the envelope from her.

"Yes, that is what Sato-san wants. But I want you to call me when you want to." She said quietly, and looked down at the dishes in front of her.

Harry looked at the numbers and then stuck the envelope in his pocket. Lunch was cleared and the aircraft started its descent into Chiang Mai. From another pocket he took the small leather case that contained the gold bracelet he had bought yesterday. Little Mouse's face lit up when she saw it.

"Is it the right time for this?" he asked.

"Oh, yes, Harry," she said, sliding the bracelet over her wrist. "After eating is always a good time." She held her hand out to admire the bracelet, and then moved her arm so he could look at it. Then she turned toward him, bowed her head, and joined both hands before her face in a *wai*. "Thank you, Khun Harry," she said. "I like it very much." She pressed her head against his shoulder. She looked happy.

Once they were on the ground their separation came quickly. When the aircraft came to a full stop near the terminal, they walked to the aircraft's door. Little Mouse stopped. "I must stay here," she said. "A car will take you wherever you want to go in Chiang Mai."

He wanted to make some final gesture, but the stewardess was right behind, and the ground crew was coming up the stairs. "I'll call you" was all he could think to say. He started down the stairs with an empty feeling that grew even worse when he turned at the bottom and did not see Little Mouse at the door.

A dark blue Toyota took him into Chiang Mai to his usual hotel. He told the driver he would not need him and carried his own bag inside. As soon as he had checked into his room he telephoned the Pachyderm Tours office.

The pleasant old Thai gentleman answered, or at least Harry assumed it was. The response Harry got on the third ring was a brusque "yes?"

"Pachyderm Tours?"

"Yes."

"This is Harry Ross. I would like to speak with Ting or Tong."

There was no sign of recognition, only, "Someone will call. Your number, please?"

He gave the hotel phone number and his room number. He sat by the phone for a time, but got bored when nothing happened. Finally he went down to the verandah that overlooked the hotel's small swimming pool. The call came finally with the second gin and tonic he ordered to console himself for his loss of Little Mouse. It was Tong – he thought. Their conversation was so brief that he would not have sworn to it. "I'll be there in an hour," she said and hung up.

Harry was still sitting on the verandah when Tong walked in. He was not sure what to expect after their brief conversation, but she looked pleased enough to see him. Her eyes grew wide when she noticed the red line that bisected his face. All the Tiger Balm that had been applied to it had some effect, but some of the puffiness remained and the color was still a mean-looking red.

"My God, what happened?" She covered her mouth with both hands.

"Oh, it's nothing, Tong." He used the most casual tone in his repertoire. "A small accident. But you look good. When I spoke on the phone with you I was afraid something was wrong. Is everything all right?"

"Yes. Everything is fine." She could not seem to take her eyes from the center of his face. "But I think we should go now. You will stay with us tonight. If there is anything you need, you must bring it. I have the bag with your clothes."

Harry got his shaving gear and told the desk he would keep his room. Outside he found Tong waiting, not in the Pachyderm Tours Land Rover as he expected, but in an old white Mercedes. He recognized it as the car he had seen in her father's compound.

"We are going to my father's house," she said when he got in. "Ting and Aloysious are both staying there. Wit is there, too." As she slowly shifted through the gears she added, "Aloysious does not want us to drive the Land Rover into Chiang Mai. I had to bring my father's car." Harry let her go on. "Aloysious is not very happy. He seems very worried. I think he will be happy that you are back. I am happy you came back, Harry."

Harry patted her jeans-clad knee, gently, very conscious that she was not Little Mouse. He felt affection for Tong, although it was an emotion he had never completely trusted. Now, at least, he understood his feelings a little better than he had before. The few days with Little Mouse had given him some perspective on his emotions. He snapped back to reality.

"Wit's staying with you, too?" he asked.

"Yes, Wit is there. Some of my father's friends, too. Aloysious is worried that something will happen."

"What is he concerned about?"

"I don't know. He will not say."

"Were you able to bring all the statues down from Wit's camp on the river?"

"Yes. Ting and I made two trips for just the statues. Then we went back one more time and brought more statues and Aloysious and Wit. We hid Wit's boat in the brush." Tong put her hand up to her face to hide a giggle.

"What's funny, Tong?" Harry asked.

"There must have been elephants up there. They made a mess. Aloysious wanted to hide Wit's boat under the elephant mess. Wit was not happy."

"Yeah, well, I guess Wit just doesn't understand the finer points of camouflage."

Harry recognized Tong's family compound as they approached it. The steel gate swung open, and Tong drove in without slowing down much until she was through the door. Inside the compound a half dozen men stood around or sat at a wooden table near the garage. They were older men and tough looking. "Friends of my father," Tong explained.

"Hey, Mister Harry," a familiar voice said in English. Wit walked out of the garage, wiping his hands on a rag. He came up to shake hands. He took a good look at Harry's face and pursed his lips. "Oh, very bad," he said in Thai. "I hope she was beautiful, Khun Harry."

"See you later, Wit," Harry said and trotted toward the house to catch up with Tong. Inside, she led him up the stairs to the third floor where he had stayed with Aloysious before. Without knocking, Tong pushed through the door and into the large bedroom. Ting was sitting in a chair, while behind her Aloysious was poking around in the refrigerator.

Ting stood up. "Harry! How nice...," and then her mouth seemed to stop working. Aloysious stopped what he was doing to look back over his shoulder. "Heard you pounding up the steps. So happy you could join us, Harry. Hope you enjoyed your R&R." He got to his feet with two beers in his hands, and squinted at Harry's face.

"Oh my! You did have a good R&R." He turned to Ting and Tong. "Ladies, why don't you see to dinner. I have to brief Harry on a few things."

Aloysious waited until they were gone. Then he leaned close in to Harry and took another look. "They must be putting on some interesting shows at the Exorcist these days," he said.

"Yeah," Harry said. "Goats are big now."

"Goats? I haven't seen that one. By the look of you, the show is a real humdinger."

"You want to see what the tourists look like after the show."

"Yeah, I'll bet. But your R&R war stories will have to wait. Can you run a load of our stone and bronze over to Sato's warehouse tonight?"

"Sure. It's set with Sato. We can do it any time. Can I have dinner first? And maybe you could tell me where things stand."

"The ladies are making dinner now. We want to wait until after dark anyway. The main thing is to get moving as soon as we can. I'm really starting to feel like we're running out of time."

"You know, I'm starting to believe you. I ran into this cop down in Bangkok...."

"What cop? What's his name?"

"Sornchai, Colonel Sornchai. C.I.D."

"Yeah, yeah. I know him. What did he want?"

"A number of things. You for one. He had some interesting things to say. He told me about rings that counterfeit antiques. Which, incidentally, are made up of people who aren't very nice. He talked about a big new cache of Khmer antiques some place up here in Northern Thailand. He talked about rumors going around. Mostly, he made me think. One thing he made me think is that you and I have a lot to talk about, Aloysious."

Aloysious nodded. "There are always rumors," he said. "But right now there are more important things. I'm really concerned that those farts on the river are still looking for us. I'm the one they're after. That's why I want to get everything finished and then get out of here. I don't want anyone else to get hurt. Here, let me get you another beer."

Aloysious pulled two more beers from the refrigerator. After taking a long drink from his, Aloysious continued. "I guess you know Wit is here. We also brought some other heavies in. Thai army guys. Retired guys who know Ting-Tong's father. I told them we needed help. I want them to guard the compound so nobody here gets hurt. Once I'm out of here, I don't think there will be any problems. Come on, Harry. Drink up your beer, and let's go eat.

"Wait," Harry said. "One thing. Colonel Sornchai talked about a gang of bad guys who run a counterfeit antiques operation. These guys are pissed off about something. From the way he talked about them I got the feeling he was talking about the guys who are chasing you. Are they? Are these the guys after you?"

Aloysious had the door open. "Come on, Harry. Dinner will get cold. We can talk about that later."

"No, goddamn it. We talk about it now."

"Oh, shit!" Aloysious banged the door shut and came back into the room. He sat down on the bed and sighed. "Okay, what do you want to know?"

"Just that. Are those the guys chasing you? If they are, why?"

"Okay. I'll tell you, but then we go to dinner. Ting-Tong will be pissed if the food gets cold. So, I'll tell you, but we'll talk details later. Okay?"

"Okay. So tell me."

"Tell you what, Harry?" Raising his hands to ward off a not so imaginary blow, Aloysious went on. "Yes. The answer to your question is yes. The guys chasing me, the guys who abducted me and dumped my beautiful goddamn car in that stinking canal in Bangkok, the guys who accosted us in Chiang Rai, shot at us, and chased us up the goddamn river are one and the same. A rotten bunch of son-of-a-bitching counterfeit antique crooks! There! That's the answer to your question, Harry. Now, let's go eat." Aloysious started for the door again.

"Wait, wait. Tell me the rest. Why are they after you? What did you do to them?"

"Oh, come on, Harry. What did I do to them? I pissed them off. What do you think I did to them? I got them really mad. That's why they're chasing me."

"How did you piss them off?"

"Harry, let's go eat. I'm hungry. Look, it's a long story. We can't sit here and talk about it now. The food will get cold and everybody here will be pissed off at me. If I promise to tell you the whole story, tonight, after you make the delivery to Sato, can we go eat?"

"Okay. But I better get the whole story tonight."

"Cross my heart. Now let's eat." Harry sighed and followed Aloysious out the door. "I hope you're ready for a long night, Aloysious. When we finish talking about some of your dubious acquaintances, we're going to have to talk about Karlo."

Aloysious stopped in the middle of the stairs. "Karlo?" he said. "Oh shit."

30

I don't see any problem," Aloysious said, finishing his military-style briefing. "You drive to the warehouse. Unload. Get right back here. Like I said, I think it's best if I don't go with you. I'm easier to spot than all three of you together. Besides, it's me they're after," he concluded. "Ting-Tong, you guys suit up. Harry, you come with me." They walked out to the garage. "I hate to send you and Ting-Tong to do all the work. I don't see any reason why you would run into trouble. I'll be standing by here. You can call me from the warehouse or wherever if you do have a problem. Come on, take a look at the Land Rover."

Wit was bent over the engine when they stepped into the garage. "Hey, Wit," Aloysious said, "Step back and let Harry look at this thing. It's all loaded up and ready to go."

The Land Rover looked different. The Pachyderm Tours elephant on the doors was gone. The camouflage paint job was now dark green, more or less. "What did you guys do?" Harry asked. "Paint it with a broom?"

"Wit's the master painter," Aloysious said. "Look up here. We changed the license plates, too."

"Well, you've done all you can," Harry commented after walking around the vehicle. "It doesn't look like the same vehicle."

"That's the idea."

Ting and Tong walked into the garage together. They had obeyed Aloysious's order to "suit up." Both were wearing jeans and dark blue work shirts, apparently the duty uniform for the evening. Harry waited for Aloysious to order him to change his own light-colored shirt for something he thought more fitting.

"Okay, I guess you guys are set," Aloysious said. "Tong, you drive. You're most familiar with the roads. Harry, you ride shotgun in back. Keep your eyes open. Get rid of that stuff quick, and come straight back here. Tell the guy at the warehouse we have two more loads that we'll try to deliver tomorrow. I'll be sitting by the phone if you need me."

Harry climbed in back. There was a huge pile of bronze and stone statues and nothing else. "Wait a minute," he said. "Where the hell are the seats?"

"What do you need seats for?" Aloysious asked. "You're not going far. Wit, throw Harry one of those blankets." As Wit passed a blanket through the window, Aloysious said, "Bunch it up and sit on it. It's only a 20-minute ride."

"Wonderful" was all Harry could say. He took the blanket.

Tong pulled the Land Rover out of the garage and then wheeled it slowly through the gate to the road outside. The weight of the bronze and stone seemed to have flattened the springs. Each bump jarred through the frame like a brass knuckle punch. Harry hunkered over, sitting on air, keeping his weight off the statues with his arms. They were already aching. He should have known better than to let Aloysious casually get him into something like this without checking it himself.

As Tong turned the corner onto the main road, the Land Rover's headlights briefly passed over two pickup trucks parked side by side on the shoulder. There was nothing unusual about this, except that Harry thought he saw a couple of heads inside turn to follow the Land Rover's progress. Again, there was nothing particularly unusual about that. It was only because of Aloysious's concern that he noticed it at all. Harry looked back as they drove on, but he saw nothing else.

He was exhausted by the time they reached Sato's warehouse. He had finally given up using his arms as shock absorbers, and had sat down on a stone divinity. It was not as bad as he expected, but it was still not good.

Tong pulled the Land Rover up to the closed gate. On the other side of the fence, a man in black coveralls approached and carefully looked them over. Harry slid open a rear window and stuck his head out.

"It's me, Mister Harry. I think you're expecting me."

"Oh. Mister Harry. I did not know it was you." It was the same young Thai as the last time. He trotted over to the gate and swung it open. Tong drove into the compound. They waited until the guard rolled open the door to the warehouse.

"Do you have a phone I can use?" Harry asked. The guard pointed to a desk in the far corner. Harry said, "Help the girls start unloading. I'll be there to help you as soon as I make a quick call."

Aloysious picked up on the first ring. "We're unloading now," Harry told him. "No problems. But somebody should check the corner where the road from the compound meets the main road. There were two pickups parked side-by-side next to the bus stop. Probably nothing, but we better make sure. I'll call you before we leave here." Aloysious answered with a word. "Roger."

With the guard's help, the unloading went quickly. Statues were laid out in a single line on the warehouse floor. "We have two more loads tomorrow," Harry told the guard, "and we'll sort it all out then."

Harry made his call to Aloysious. "We checked the corner," Aloysious said. "It's all clear. Come on home."

The ride back was a lot more comfortable, and faster. Harry knelt on the floor just behind the front seats. He tried to peer beyond the headlights into dark places ahead that could hide an ambush. He swiveled around regularly to check their rear. There was nothing. There was little traffic. The land on either side of the road was mostly undeveloped. There were few buildings and almost no light. When they neared the corner where Harry had seen the two pickups, he leaned forward.

"Tong," he said, "be careful on the turn. If anything doesn't look right, floor it." Later, he could have kicked himself for not driving on the way back. But Tong was a good driver, and he would have felt silly telling her he wanted to drive.

As they approached the turn, Harry looked for the area where the two pickup trucks had been parked. The Land Rover's headlights picked up the sign for the bus stop, and then the small sheltered bench. Beyond was a wide shoulder. Harry got a glimpse of tire tracks pressed into the dirt on the shoulder before the beam of the Land Rover's headlights swung across the road as Tong started her turn.

The rest was a blur. Later, Harry recalled turning back to look over Tong's shoulder and the dimly lit dashboard. In front of them the twin beams of their headlights swept across trees and then centered again on the road. Suddenly there were lights where there should be none, blinding them through the windshield. A cry of surprise came from Tong as she instinctively twisted the wheel toward safety. From Ting came only a small "Oh." It was the last sound Harry remembered. A tree raced toward them in the Land Rover's windshield.

"Harry...Harry...Harry...." Somebody called to him in the darkness far away. He didn't want to answer. He was tired. It was too late.

"Come on, Harry. Here's some nice brandy for you. Open your mouth." Something burned. Then he was drowning. Down deep and drowning, and trying to push up. He fought toward a light far away. There was burning again, and he started to choke. He coughed hard and tried to sit up to keep from choking. Somebody held him down.

"Take it easy, Harry. If you're awake, you can have a beer."

"What the hell happened?" Harry asked. His voice had cracks in it. "Christ, stop shining that flashlight in my eyes."

"Harry," Aloysious was almost gentle. "Come on. Get yourself together." Then he asked, "Where are the girls?"

"The girls?" Harry tried to sit up again. "What do you mean? They're up front. Christ, they're all right, aren't they? What the hell's going on?"

"Harry, Harry, try to remember what happened. Do you remember what happened to the girls?" Aloysious's voice was very calm.

Harry twisted around frantically, trying to take in the scene. He could see the Land Rover a few feet away. Its nose rested against a tree. Its doors were flung open and one headlight pointed skyward at an odd angle, illuminating the leaves overhead. There was other light, a lot of it. It came from flashlights and headlights of cars parked some distance off. A small crowd of spectators stood in small groups at the edges of light. Most were strangers. Poking around the Land Rover were others, the older men Harry had seen at the house earlier that night. Kneeling on the ground next to him was Aloysious. There was a look of concern on his face.

"Aloysious, what the hell happened? Where are the girls? What's going on?"

"You don't remember, huh? Poor fucker. I guess we better get you back to the house." Harry put his head back and closed his eyes. He felt hands touch him and start to lift him.

He knew nothing of the ride back to the compound or how he was carried up to the big bedroom on the third floor. Gradually he became aware of being in a dimly lit room and of Aloysious sprawled on the bed on the other side of the room. He was thirsty and when he tried to get up, Aloysious heard him.

"How you feeling?" Aloysious asked.

"Like a bad hangover. My mouth feels like birds have been shitting in it. My head hurts. My body aches. Other than that, I feel great."

"Want a beer?"

"No. No, thanks. Not right now. Did you try to drown me with brandy? I can't believe what my mouth feels like."

Aloysious came over and stood next to the bed. He looked closely at Harry's face. "You do look like shit," he said. "Do you remember anything at all about what happened?"

Harry closed his eyes. "I remember we started into the turn. Something came at us. Tong tried to get out of the way. I guess we hit a tree. That's all. How bad was it?"

"Not bad. You guys weren't going very fast. Tong bumped the tree, bent the bumper and left fender a bit. No real damage."

"Then what happened? Where are Ting and Tong? Are they all right? I must have been dreaming. I thought you were looking for them and you couldn't find them. They are all right, aren't they?"

"I...don't think they got hurt in the crash. The windshield wasn't cracked. There was no blood up front."

"What the hell are you talking about, Aloysious? What do you mean you don't think they got hurt in the crash? Haven't you seen them? Goddamn! You really don't know where they are. Do you?"

"No, I don't know where Ting-Tong are." Aloysious said it very calmly. "I have a good idea about what happened to them. I was hoping you would remember something that might help. You don't remember much because you bumped your head. Twice. The doctor looked at you. You have a small bump up here." Aloysious touched the top of his own head just above his forehead. "You probably dented the roof of the Land Rover with that. Then the doctor found you had a second bump, a big one here." Aloysious touched the back of his head, down low near the base of the skull. "He said he couldn't figure how you could have done that to yourself. Figured somebody did it for you. Clobbered you while you were down."

"What do you mean? Somebody hit me? What the hell are you talking about?"

"In simple terms, Harry, you hit your head on the roof when the Land Rover bumped the tree and you knocked yourself silly. While you were still in la-la land, a good Samaritan opened the back door and sapped you in back of the head. He wanted to make sure you got a good night's sleep."

"Somebody hit me?"

"Yeah, somebody hit you. An old lady walking over to the bus stop saw the Land Rover turning. She saw two trucks parked on the side of the road pointing the wrong way. While Tong was turning, the trucks suddenly switched on their headlights. Full bright. Must have startled the shit out of Tong. The old lady saw the Land Rover veer to the other side of the road and slide into the tree. She counted five guys come out of the two trucks and run over to the Land Rover. She thought they were helping. Then she saw them get back in the trucks and drive off. When she looked into the Land Rover all she saw was you."

"What about Ting and Tong?"

"They're gone, Harry. Disappeared. The goons in the trucks hauled them off."

Harry tried to get up. The room started to rotate around him. "Oh, shit," he said. He dropped back to the bed.

Aloysious leaned closer. "Look, Harry, I feel like shit too. But we can't give ourselves the luxury of wringing our hands and blaming ourselves for what happened. That can come later if it has to. First we have to do everything we can do to fix what happened. Don't try to sit up. Stay down and listen. I'm going to need you tomorrow whether your head hurts or not. I know who did it, and we have a good chance of finding them."

Harry forced himself to sit up on the bed, his back to the wall. "I need something to drink. No beer, for God's sake! Some water and then some coffee. I won't be any use to anybody lying on my ass."

"Now that's the spirit, Harry. Just hang on." Aloysious went to the door and shouted something down the stairs. "You'll have all the water and coffee you need in a minute," he said when he came back into the room.

"Thanks," Harry said. "Now, tell me what you think. You said they kidnapped the girls. What kind of chances do Ting and Tong have with those goons?"

"I think they have a good chance if we can get to them quickly. I don't think they'll hurt Ting-Tong. Not right away. Those goons had a chance to hurt you good. All they did was to put you to sleep. I think they were surprised when they were able to grab the girls without a fight. Suddenly they had them, but they didn't know what to do with them. It will take them a while to look at their options and decide what to do. Hopefully that will buy us a couple of days. After that it gets hairy. Then it will be very dangerous for Ting and Tong. We have to get them back before that."

"How do we even know where to start looking?" Harry asked. "I can't believe we'll ever find them."

"We'll find them. Look, Harry, the guys we're after are tribals. Where the hell can a bunch of tribal guys with two pickup trucks hide a couple of women while they try to figure out what to do with them? They can't drive all over the countryside. They have to go to ground. The sooner the better. So where do tribal guys go to ground. They go to a tribal village where they are accepted. I know these guys, Harry, and there are three, maybe four villages within driving distance where they could hole up."

"Four villages. Wonderful. How the hell do we find the right one?"

"Wit and a couple of the guys are doing some preliminary reconnaissance now. Come morning, you and I will join them. By nightfall tomorrow we'll know where they are. Trust me."

"Okay, say we locate them. After we locate them, how do we get them back without really getting somebody hurt?"

"I can't answer that for you now, Harry. We'll just have to wait and see. And hope."

31

Y ou can't expect me to get on that thing!"
"Why, Harry? Are you still dizzy?"
"No, I haven't puked once in the last hour. That's not the point. I
haven't ridden a motorbike in 15, 20 years...."
"Look, I told you. If we want to get up in the hills where we need to go,
we have to use bikes. You'll do okay. You were a good rider once. You
never forget how to ride."

Harry reluctantly threw his leg over the tank and sat down on the leather saddle. It was a pretty machine, a bright red 250cc Honda. Small, but it
would do the job. Another time he would have enjoyed this. Today he was
not looking forward to it. He had already had one bout of dizziness this
morning. He figured that was due as much to his lack of sleep as it was to
the knot on the back of his head. Aloysious had rolled him out at first
light. He could handle that, but he had thrown up twice in the early
morning hours before he got up, and that concerned him more.

Harry familiarized himself with the motorbike, while Aloysious and Wit
sipped coffee and studied a map. "Harry, come look at this," Aloysious
called. "I want to show you what we're going to do." Harry dropped the
kickstand on the motorbike and walked over.

"Here." Aloysious used a finger to circle an area in the right quadrant of
the map. "Right here, Harry. Four villages. They could be in any one of
them. We'll check all four. We won't ride into them. We'll get as close we
can and look them over. With luck we'll find Ting-Tong real quick."

"And then what?"

The question still bothered Aloysious, but he tried not to show it.
"Depends on what we find. Wit has a helmet for you. We'll all wear them.
They'll hide our faces."

Wit handed Harry the helmet and looked at him with real concern. In
Thai, he asked, "How's it going?"

"Fine," Harry replied in Thai, "fine." He felt he should say something more to reassure Wit, but he didn't know what he could say. He thought he must look a real mess. The long scratch on his face had nearly healed, but being tossed around in the Land Rover had opened it again and the skin around it was puffy. His eyes were swollen from lack of sleep, and, overall, his face probably looked like he would not make the first mile.

Aloysious was helmeted and astride his bike. "Mount up!" he yelled and then watched while Harry and Wit fumbled with starters and clutches. Aloysious's mount was the biggest of the three, but still small for his size. It looked like a toy gripped between his legs. Wit's machine was the smallest, the one Wit felt confident he could handle. "Before I drive only boats," he told Harry while they were looking at the machines. "Now I am member of motorcycle gang."

With a small crowd to see them off, the three rode boldly out of the compound and down the street. Wit weaved unsteadily. Harry weaved too, as he tried to get accustomed to the machine. Only Aloysious rode like he was in control. Harry was glad for the helmet and pretended not to notice the stares they got as they made their way through the city and out toward the hills.

As the miles passed, Harry's confidence in his rusty motorcycling skills grew. Wit seemed more confident, too. His machine weaved less, and going into turns he assumed a racing crouch. He laid his machine daringly low on some of the curves. It was a good thing that Wit's engine was a small one. Aloysious rode at the rear, lost in thought and content to follow in Wit's lead.

It was early and the air was fresh. Where trees blocked the sun, or where they passed through the shadow of a hill, the air felt almost cold. Over the low burble of his engine Harry could hear the high-pitched chirps of birds. They were up in the hills now, and sometimes as they came out of trees they could see deep into a valley below. There were no houses and few signs of man. Only occasionally did they pass someone else using the road. Sometimes it was a vehicle. Usually it was someone on foot.

They topped the crest of a hill. Before them lay a vista of a dozen rolling green hills that rose high above mist-filled valleys. The scene was so unexpected that Harry released his grip on the throttle and was nearly bowled over as Aloysious rocketed by, engine screaming in low gear. His arm was raised high in the air. "Follow me!"

Where the ride had been enjoyable before, it was like a competition now. On his bigger machine Aloysious probably did not realize how fast he was going. To stay with him, Harry passed Wit in the first hundred meters. There was no birdsong now, just engine noise and a queasy feeling in his stomach. For a moment Harry's vision closed in on him. He rushed through a tunnel toward a distant light. He eased back on the throttle until Wit caught up with him.

A mile ahead Aloysious was stopped at a junction where the road they were following forked to the left. A narrow track turned right. Harry wiped the sweat under his helmet while Wit conferred with Aloysious. The map came out. Aloysious waved at the track and Wit pointed down the road. They debated. Harry found a canteen that Wit had strapped to the machine. The water was bitter but cool. His head cleared a bit.

Aloysious folded the map and set off down the dirt track. Harry dropped behind Wit for a long ride through the trees. They reached a clearing and Aloysious stopped. "Do you see it?" he asked when Harry came up. "There," he pointed, "near the top of the hill."

Harry stared at the hill for a time before he made out the thatched roofs of a tribal village among the trees. It was like a camouflage pattern. "We'll get a better look up ahead," Aloysious said and started again down the track.

They stopped again where an outcrop of rocks hung over the valley and gave them a good view of the village. Aloysious pulled binoculars from a bag on his machine and studied the village and the valley below it.

From where they stood, the village was a good distance off. Even without the glasses Harry could see signs of life. Wisps of smoke rose over the roofs, and he had glimpses of movement, though he could not say if a person or animal caused it. "Take a look," Aloysious said and handed him the binoculars.

With the binoculars, the village came to life. A group of women walked, carrying baskets of what probably was washing. A pig scurried down the main street. A chicken fluttered in the air above the dog that harassed it. There seemed to be few men and only two or three small children. "What do you think?" Aloysious asked.

"Looks normal. Not a lot of men, but it's the wrong time of day."

"Let's get closer. We can follow the trail down through the valley. We can leave the machines there and walk. You look like shit, Harry. Are you up to it?"

"I'll live. Let's go."

It was a slow ride down the hill. The valley was narrow and they crossed it quickly. They left their machines in a small clearing and started up the track to the village.

"We're not going to surprise anybody," Harry said. "I'm sure everybody up there heard us coming across the valley."

"That's all right," Aloysious said. "I don't think this is the place. But we might as well look."

The track soon narrowed down to where only one person could pass. It was furrowed in places where streams of water had coursed down in the rainy season. They had to step carefully, and it was getting steeper as they walked. Harry felt the blood pounding in his head.

Aloysious stopped. He held up his hand. "Listen," he said. Harry heard it. Laughter and little high-pitched shouts. A large rock and a dozen smaller ones came tumbling down the trail. Following immediately behind was the cause of the landslide – eight or ten laughing tribal kids.

"Hey, Mister! Give me one baht! You have bon-bon?" The biggest one was the leader. He was out in front. He was probably 12, but could have passed for eight. He stopped in front of Aloysious and boldly looked him over. Behind him, his gang of assorted sizes and ages formed a semicircle across the trail. "Hey, Mister!" the smallest one shouted as loud as he could. "Hey Mister!" they all shouted. They laughed together and attempted a second chorus, but it disintegrated into giggles and shrieks.

Aloysious looked down at the leader. In basic Thai Aloysious explained that he was looking for a friend. A big man with a beard who had been trekking in the area.

The 12-year old turned to his gang and asked if any of them knew of the big man with a beard. One by one they shook their heads. The leader turned back to Aloysious. No, he said, there had been no big man with a beard in the village. There had been no visitor to the village since a Thai health official had visited them some weeks ago.

"Well," Aloysious said, turning to Harry, "I hope you brought your wallet. Give our little friends a token of our appreciation."

Aloysious stood back while Harry distributed a handful of coins. As he finished, one of the smaller ones came over and reached for his hand. Aloysious already had a child at the end of each arm pulling him up the hill. Aloysious laughed and pretended they were moving him along. The 12-year old stepped up to Harry. "You come with us to our village," he said. "Everyone will be happy to see you. The women will make food."

"Definitely not the place we're looking for, Harry." Aloysious was grinning. "Come up with a good excuse to get us out of here." He looked almost like he was having a good time.

The ride back up the hill was tedious. Back on top Aloysious and Wit debated the map again while Harry just sat, trying to will himself to feel better.

"Harry," Aloysious called, "the next place is about ten kilometers from here. We follow this same road. It won't take more than a half hour to get to where we can look it over. Then we can eat. What do you think? Can you make it?"

"Let's do it," Harry said.

The road looked like the road they had traveled before, and the trail they took could have been the one they had just ridden back on. To Harry it was all starting to blur together into leafy, green backdrops that moved past him.

In a short while they were looking over a village on another hill. Aloysious used the binoculars first. Then he handed them to Harry. It was a lot like the first village, but noticeably bigger. There was a building that might have been a school. Near it, a half dozen children chased each other around in a game Harry did not recognize. It was richer than the last village, too. Several black and white pigs strolled casually in the rough streets, while a black and white mound in a pen behind a house was a sign of pig siesta.

"What do you think?" Harry heard Aloysious ask.

"Like the other one. Normal. The kind of activity you expect this time of day."

"Did you see the guys having lunch?"

Harry had seen them. In the shadow of a house, three men having a private feast. As he watched, a woman came out with another dish. As it was passed around, Harry started to feel hungry. It was a good sign.

They moved off the trail to a clearing where Wit made a fire. Soon there were familiar smells. "Spaghetti?" Harry asked. "And Spam!" Wit replied. "But, for you, Mr. Harry, there is fried rice. I will warm it. It is better when you are ill." Harry was starting to feel good.

"Beer, Harry?" Aloysious had a can with what looked like frost on it.

"No, thanks. I see Wit has some coffee on. How far to our next stop?"

"About 25 kilometers. It will take us a while." Aloysious opened the map and pointed to the place near a small river. "It's here, on the hill above the stream. There's a road that leads right in. It's not shown on the map, but I've been up there. We'll get a look at it from here," Aloysious put his finger on a spot close to the village. "If it looks promising, we'll leave the bikes there and walk in. I have a feeling about this one. I don't want them to hear us moving up on them."

Harry studied the map. "Can we get a good look at them from the spot you have picked out?"

"Good enough. We'll be looking right down on them."

It was mid-afternoon before they got to the vantage point Aloysious had chosen. They were well above the village and had a good view of it. Harry could see it was smaller than the other two villages they had looked at, and probably a lot poorer than either. This village had a crude, make-shift look about it. The houses did not seem to be well maintained. The roofs were not thatch, but rusted tin. There was nothing to indicate that comfort existed in the village in any form. No sign of telephone or electrical wires leading in. No antennas for TV or shortwave radio. Aloysious handed him the binoculars.

"What do you think?" Aloysious asked.

"Not my kind of town," Harry replied. With the binoculars at his eyes, he scanned the village more closely. "It's very quiet," he said, finally. "Maybe it's siesta time. Ah, there's an old man, sitting in the shade. At least he's not asleep." Harry swept past the town and down the hill to where it met the river. "That's a bigger stream than I thought. Are there any boats on it?"

"The village doesn't have boats. Sometimes visitors bring them. Look back at the town. See any kids?"

Harry swept over the village again, carefully. "Not a one. But it's afternoon and the sun is hot. They could be napping."

"You'd see them near the houses in the shade. Look in the shade. They're hard to see there. Even if some are sleeping, there's always a small one somewhere, crawling around with the animals."

Harry kept looking. "No kids," he said finally.

"That's what I thought," Aloysious said. "Now, look toward the front end of the village, where the road comes in. What do you see?"

"Just the old man I saw before. Wait. That's no old man. I see two others now. They're not sleeping either. Just sitting in the shadows, watching the road."

"That's what I saw," Aloysious said. "Harry, I'm pretty sure this is it. Kids are sometimes hard to see, but I don't see any. If there's hanky-panky going on over there, they would get the kids out of the way. You saw what happened at the first village. It happens every time. The kids love visitors and would give away the game in the first two minutes."

"You may be right. What do we do if you are?"

"I don't know yet. Let's see if we can get closer to the river. I want to see what's happening there. Let me see that map, Wit."

They had left the motorbikes on the far side of the hill, where sound would not carry to the village. The walk over to their vantage point had been a long one, and Harry was not looking forward to crawling up and down the hills. Wit and Aloysious bent over the map again, speaking quietly. When he finally joined them, Wit was the one to explain.

"There is a trail down to the valley," Wit said, "but if you just want to look down at the river, you can walk on the ridge, here." He pointed at the map. "From there you can see down to the river."

"Sounds good," Aloysious said with a shrug. "What do I know?"

It was not a bad walk. When they reached the place Wit had showed them on the map, they had a clear view of the river and the little sand beach that served the village. Aloysious studied the scene with the binoculars.

"Look at that," Aloysious said. "Two boats. Everything else is very quiet. Not one person to be seen. Nobody washing clothes. No kids playing by the boats....Oh, my...wait a minute. Somebody just moved there. A guy in the shadows. Scratching his ass. Now he lit a cigarette. I'd say he's on river watch duty."

Aloysious took the binoculars from his eyes. "Harry, I may not be a hundred percent certain. But I'll go as high as 96 percent."

They stayed there for another hour, and nothing down by the river seemed to be alive. Every ten minutes or so Harry swept the area with the binoculars, but there was nothing new. Finally, he spotted movement on the trail.

"One guy going down the trail to the river," he alerted Aloysious.

"Let me have those glasses. Ha! They're having a little chat. Now the first guy is heading up the trail. The other guy took his place in the shade." He turned to Harry with a smirk. "Ninety-seven percent! Let's get back to Wit. We're going to have to move fast. We can talk as we walk. I think I know how to do it now."

Aloysious took off at a dog trot that Harry found difficult to maintain. "Maybe we can't be a hundred percent sure, but we have to move fast," Aloysious said.

"Even if the girls are in the village, how are we going to locate them?" Harry asked. His breath was coming hard.

"We could spend days here. Ultimately we might spot a pattern in the village that would tell us. But we don't have that kind of time. And it doesn't matter. That cop you met in Bangkok, the fake art guy, Sornchai. Do you have a telephone number for him?"

"Yeah, I have his card in my wallet."

"Good. I want you to get to a telephone fast and call him. I'll tell you what to say when we get to the bikes. You're going to have to go almost all the way back to town. Wit will go with you. You may as well stay in town tonight. You'll never get back in here in the dark. Be back here at first light tomorrow. Whatever happens, you have to be back then."

They reached Wit and stayed long enough for Aloysious to look the town over one more time. As they started walking back over their hill to the motorbikes, Aloysious told Harry what he wanted him to tell Sornchai. Harry listened, but when Aloysious finished he just shook his head.

"It's crazy," Harry told him. "The guy met me once. He's a professional cop. He's not going to stick his neck out on the basis of one telephone call."

"You just tell him what I said. He wants something bad enough. He'll do what we ask."

"Even if he does, that solves only part of the problem. We still won't have the girls."

"I'll solve the rest of the problem tonight. I'm going to poke around the ass-end of that village, and see what I can see. By morning I'll know exactly what to do."

"Look, I know you're convinced Sornchai is going to help us. But what if he doesn't? Or what if I can't reach him tonight?"

Aloysious looked over with a grin. "If you don't get ahold of Sornchai, old buddy, it's the charge of the Light Brigade. You, me, and Wit right up the middle. Hey diddle, diddle."

"Christ, I hope your military plans are better than your poetry."

32

It was an hour when one would not expect even the most diligent of police officials to be at his desk, but Colonel Sornchai of the Thai Criminal Investigation Department answered his phone on the first ring.

"Sornchai speaking," he said in Thai.

"Colonel Sornchai. Harry Ross here. How you doing? I'm surprised to find you in this time of day."

"It's the paper, Harry. There is always paper to shuffle. What can I do for you?"

"Colonel, when we met, you said to give you a call if I ever came across something interesting. Well, by one of those little coincidences of life, I came across something I think you will find very interesting."

"Wonderful. Tell me about it."

"I'll want something from you."

"If it's good, Harry, you can have what you want."

"It's good. I can tell you where you can find the art counterfeiters you told me about."

"You have names?" Sornchai was definitely interested.

"I have names, Colonel. Better than that, I can tell you where you can find them if you move fast."

"It sounds good, Harry. What do you want from me?"

"What I want from you is a police sweep of a hill tribe village. The sweep must start tomorrow at precisely 12 noon. Precisely."

"You're joking, Harry....Aren't you?"

"I'm not joking, Colonel. It has to be a proper sweep. At least three official vehicles and 12 uniformed officers. More if you can arrange it. They will need authority to go into the village and to search the houses."

"And what are they searching for?"

"It doesn't matter. Whatever makes it easy for you to get the warrants or the authority you need. The important thing is that the sweep team must arrive at the entrance to the village precisely at noon. Once they get into the village they must carry out a house-to-house search for at least an hour."

"And if I do this, I'll have the art counterfeiters?"

"You'll have them, Colonel. I'll give you names of six that are in the village now. If you move into the village at noon precisely, you'll have them. Can you set this up, Colonel?"

"Wait. You say six are in a hill tribe village. That's not the whole organization. Those six are just some of the thugs. The strong-arm boys. I need the ones at the top, the bosses."

"You'll have those too – if you hit the village at noon tomorrow. If your raid goes off on time, I'll give you the names of the bosses when it's over."

"Harry, let me make sure I have this right. A police team is to enter the village precisely at noon. It is to conduct a search of the houses. If we do this, I will have six art counterfeiters in the village. Later you will give me the names of their bosses. Do I have it right?"

"You have it right, Colonel. Can you do it?"

"What guarantees do I have?"

"If I don't make good on what I say, you have my ass next time I pass through your airport. Can you do the raid?"

"I can do it, Harry. I'll be in Chiang Mai in the morning. I will lead the team to the village myself."

"Thank you, Colonel Sornchai."

"Don't thank me yet. There's one other thing. If you happen to run into your good friend Aloysious, tell him to contact me immediately. There is now a warrant for his arrest. The team I will lead to the village tomorrow was formed two days ago to hunt him down."

"Christ! What's the charge?"

"There are various charges. Fraud is the primary one. Murder the most serious. In between are theft, general mayhem, and adultery. Anyway, you tell him it's best if he talks to me before the upcountry team catches up with him. Now, what did you say is the name of that village you want us to sweep at noon tomorrow?"

By the time he finished with Sornchai, Harry's head throbbed. He realized how keyed up he had been during the call, and now that he could relax he felt exhausted. He had played it the way Aloysious wanted. At the same time he did not fully understand what he had asked Sornchai to do, and was not sure that he could deliver everything he had promised. Aloysious had seen him off with no further explanations about what he was to tell Sornchai. Only a pat on the back and a cheerful "Trust me."

As Harry replaced Sornchai's card in his wallet, he came across another card with two telephone numbers. On impulse, he dialed the first.

"Yes?" The voice sounded sleepy.

"Mouse? Is that you?"

"Harry!" The voice sounded alert now. "It is me. I was waiting for you to call."

"You sound good, Mouse. Listen, I have just a minute. We're having some problems up here. I want you to tell the boss something. Tell him that Sornchai is after Alo-wichit, and it looks serious. Tell him I think we will have more problems with the guys we met on the river. Tell him that if I don't call you in two days, he should send somebody to look for us."

Harry finished and waited for a comment from Little Mouse that expressed her concern. Instead she said, "I have the message, Harry, and I will tell the boss the following...." She repeated word for word what he had told her. She finished by saying, "Is there anything else you want the boss to know? Do you want me to give him your location?" Harry answered "No" to both questions.

There was a moment's pause. He could visualize Little Mouse seal an envelope and pass it to a waiting messenger in a black uniform.

"Now," she said, turning her attention back to him, "tell me how much you miss me, Harry."

"How do I miss you? Let me see. I miss your fine long legs. I miss the feel of the smooth skin on your thigh. I miss the reflection of your rump in the mirror on the ceiling."

"What about my eyes, Harry? There will not always be a mirror on the ceiling."

"There won't? What a waste. Mouse, I do miss you. On the ceiling and in the flesh. That doesn't sound right, either. I have to go now, Mouse. Talk to you in a couple of days. I'll be thinking about you."

Next morning Harry and Wit were back in the hills as the sun was rising. They had spent the night in an inn on the road that led into the hills. Harry slept well and woke feeling almost normal. His head was still sore, but the dizziness and nausea that had troubled him yesterday seemed to have gone.

Aloysious was waiting where they had left him. He grabbed at the jug of coffee Wit brought him, and then poked through a bag of groceries. Once these preliminaries were out of the way, Aloysious stared at Harry and pulled his eyebrows back inquisitively when Harry caught his stare.

"It's done," Harry said. "Sornchai will be there at noon. At least that's what he said."

"He'll be there. I know Sornchai. He's good. Come over here a minute. I want to show you something. Wit, make us some sandwiches from that stuff you brought."

Harry followed Aloysious to where they could look down on the village. The village was awake, but barely, it seemed. Thin wisps of smoke rose from cooking fires, and a few women were moving around. But that was almost all. There were no men to be seen. Or almost none.

Harry looked to where he had seen the watchers yesterday. One sat by the side of a house near the entrance to the village. Another stood nearby. Once a man came out of a house briefly. He looked around, hitched up his sarong, and went back inside. There were no children to be seen at all.

Aloysious handed Harry the binoculars. "Take a look over at the far side of the village. The third house from the back. Just beyond it is a group of banana trees. Look a little beyond the banana trees."

Once he focused on the area, Harry saw them right away. "Pickup trucks. Two pickup trucks. I'll be damned."

"Think those are the ones?"

"I don't know. They all look alike after a while. Maybe."

"It struck me when I saw them," Aloysious said. "They're not parked there. Nobody parks trucks by wedging them in a grove of banana trees. They're hidden. Not hidden well, but they tried. Anyway, I wanted you to see that. It's another sign that we have the right place."

"The names you gave me," Harry asked, "the names for Colonel Sorn-chai. Are they the ones in the village? Or are you making that up?"

"I gave you the names of guys that I thought would be involved in something like this. I was right about three of them. I'm not certain about the others. After you and Wit took off yesterday, I got in close to the village. I watched the changing of the guard down at the river. I recognized both of those guys. Their names were on the list. The third one I spotted through the glasses, walking through the village. I think there's another one I named. The guy standing near the entrance to the village. I think he's name four on your list, but I'm not certain."

"You know these guys pretty well," Harry commented. It came out as a statement of fact.

"Yeah, I know 'em. I know them all." Aloysious stared out over the valley, looking at where clouds of mist drifted slowly over hills far off in the distance. "You're wondering how I know them, Harry. You really want to ask me that. But you won't."

Aloysious turned to face him. "I know you well, Harry," he said. "You're a nice guy. Too nice sometimes. You don't want to put me on the spot. I appreciate that. But I'm going to tell you anyway."

"The guys over there," Aloysious continued. "Those thugs and dozens of their friends are people I worked with once. Very closely. The first ones I got to know were the smart ones. Five or six small-time hustlers. They worked alone mostly. The one thing they had in common was fake art. They all dealt in it in some way. They bought from the guys who had talent to cut stone and cast bronze, and sold to tourists with bad eyes. It was pretty hand-to-mouth for most of them."

"Anyway, I saw an opportunity, so I showed them how to organize. I taught them how to read the market and how to hone their marketing skills. Eventually they did pretty well. They divided into three or four different groups and organized the individual craftsmen in villages. Their production went up, and they were more attuned to the market. For a while it all went pretty well. They did all right. So did I."

Aloysious seemed to run out of steam. He sighed heavily and stared down into the village. Harry knew he would talk again when he was ready. He got up quietly and got two beers from Wit. He returned and handed one to Aloysious. After a while, when nothing happened, Harry broke the silence.

"So what happened?"

Aloysious took a pull from the beer. "What happened? Progress happened. The hustlers I trained honed their marketing skills to a razor's edge. They figured out what the market wanted and they provided it. Sales went up. Production went up. There was only one problem. They went after the wrong market. They discovered that tourists are blind. That they can't see worth a shit when it comes to spending money. Show a tourist a real bargain, add a hint of illegality, and they'll buy it every time."

"So they started producing these tourist bargains. Turning it out by the ton. My God, what shit. Each piece looked like it had a tag: `I am a poor fake reproduction of a bad work of art'. Not that there ever was an original of some of the shit they produced. Harry, you wouldn't believe how bad that shit was." Aloysious was still trying to talk when he took his next pull from the beer. He started to choke and cough.

Harry waited until Aloysious was back to breathing normally again. "And then you went your own way?" he asked.

"Of course I went my own way. That was not the market I wanted to serve. I wanted to make nice pieces. Copies of old masterpieces. Copies that were so true to the original that the guys in the ninth century could not have pointed to the difference between their work and mine."

"You started your own operation?" Harry said, feigning only a moderate interest.

"It was a great operation, Harry. You wouldn't have believed it. I found craftsmen. Guys with real pride in their work. They were eager to get up in the morning and get back to their carving. They worked so hard that the birth rate in those villages nosedived. But the work they turned out was beautiful."

"You were serving a different market than your friends who were working the tourist market," Harry noted. "What got them all pissed off?"

"I got too good, Harry. I got too big. I had the best craftsmen and the most craftsmen. I got too organized. At the peak, I had 18 villages working for me. I guess they started seeing me as a threat." He turned to Harry. "Can you imagine that? I was the threat? I was the guy who showed them how to do it."

Aloysious was sitting on the ground now, staring at the empty beer that he held on to with both hands. He looked abused.

"That's quite a story, Aloysious. I'm almost sorry those guys drove you out of business."

Aloysious looked up at him, defiance written across his face. "They didn't drive me out of business. They tried, but I did what I wanted to do. We finished every piece I wanted. When I had what I wanted, I closed down my operation." Aloysious shrugged. "But they're still after me. Now it's just revenge. That's the part that pisses me off."

"Does that mean I get the names of their biggies, their bosses, to pass to Colonel Sornchai? If I don't, he's going to have my ass."

"Sornchai will get his names. The guys he really wants are in Chiang Mai. Three guys who are the financiers and who deal directly with local antique dealers and big-buck tourists. They're the same guys who sent yonder thugs after us. They piss me off."

"Oh, bye the bye," Harry said casually, "Sornchai said you should call him. There's a warrant out for you. The police unit that Sornchai is sending to sweep the village is the same one looking for you."

"Shit!" Aloysious said and flung the beer bottle in a high arc into the trees. "Warrant! What kind of warrant?"

"Sornchai said the charges include fraud, murder, theft, adultery, and general mayhem."

Aloysious looked absolutely flustered. "I didn't commit adultery," he said. After more thought, he added, "Not that I know of."

33

Okay, okay, listen up. I want everybody to understand what's happening today." Aloysious's morning briefing had started. In their absence he had constructed a mock-up of the village and its environs, using sticks and stones and lines drawn in the dirt. Wit winked at Harry. The response was immediate.

"Hey, you! Wit! You have a problem? Maybe a joke you want to share with us? Save it for later. I want you to listen up now."

"This here is the village." Aloysious waved the stick over the five-foot square area that contained his mock-up. "Over here is the river." He pointed to one end with his stick. "And here is where the road enters the village." He pointed to the other end. "That's where Colonel Sornchai and the police will appear – at 12 noon precisely. Right, Harry?"

"Right, Chief."

"Now," Aloysious continued, "before I go further and tell you what we're going to do this morning, maybe somebody can tell me what's going to happen when Sornchai arrives at the gates of the village. Harry, do you want to comment?"

"As a matter of fact, I was hoping you would tell us what will happen. What do you expect Sornchai to do? I told him to enter the village with his cops and search it," Harry answered.

"Right. And that's what he's supposed to do. But that has no bearing on the action that will affect us. Now, don't look funny at me, Harry. Sornchai is playing a key role. I've been through a half dozen police sweeps of villages. As a sweepee. The same thing happens every time. The police arrive. They knock on the front gate and ask to come in. Anybody in the village doing something he shouldn't, leaves by the back door. You see what I'm saying? Sornchai arrives at the village. The bad guys have one option – the back door. They grab Ting-Tong and vamoose."

Harry listened and the light came on. He knew Aloysious was right. If Aloysious had thought the rest of it through, it could work.

"What do you think so far? Harry, do you agree?" Harry nodded.

Aloysious continued. "Okay. When the cops arrive at the front, the bad guys head for the back door. The river. Right here." He pointed at thick wavy lines scratched in the ground. "I'm sure that's their escape route. There is no place else for them to go. The two boats there make it easy for them. I got close in last night. The boats look good, but Wit will have to confirm that later."

"The action plan." Aloysious outlined his words as he said them, stabbing at the air with his stick. "Phase One. We move down to the river. Wit creates a diversion and distracts the watchman down by the boats. When the guard looks the other way, I take him out. Disable him. Then we move to Phase Two. In Phase Two we prepare the ground for an ambush. Phase Three is the ambush of the bad guys running from Sornchai. Phase Four, we grab Ting-Tong and leave. How's that sound, Harry?"

"It sounds good. As far as it goes. How exactly do we ambush these guys? How do we get Ting and Tong back from them without anybody getting hurt?"

"I won't bore you with the details. You'll understand it all when we get down to the river. I'll show you there. Nobody gets hurt. At least none of us."

"Oh, there's also that unfortunate problem with Sornchai," Harry pointed out. "Your problem. Are you going to talk to him?"

"No, Harry, but that brings us to Phase Four, part two. In Phase Four, part two, we grab a boat and get the hell out of there. I don't want to meet Sornchai today."

Harry shook his head. "It's the perfect time for it. He'll have his counterfeiters and you'll be a hero."

"No, Harry. It's not as simple as that. Sornchai will not let me walk away afterwards. Anyway, we gotta get rolling. Make sure Wit understands about the diversion. He has to get the guard interested in the river so I can get behind him."

Before they started off down the hill, they stripped the motorbikes of anything they needed. If everything went well, they would not be coming back. Harry explained the problem of the guard to Wit, and Wit quickly got in the spirit of things. Wit thought about his assignment for a minute. Then he went to his motorbike, stripped a saddlebag from it, and slung it over his shoulder. "I go fishing, Mr. Harry," he said. "I catch big fish."

Aloysious got somber as time passed. The seriousness of what was happening finally seemed to be making an impression on him. Harry found him going through a canvas bag, taking things from it, and stuffing them in his pockets. "Harry," he said quietly, "Take this. You know how to use it." He handed Harry a 9-millimeter Browning pistol. The gun had been around. It was worn and shiny. Without a word Harry took it and stuck it in his pocket.

They moved down the hill to the river. A path ran along the bank, and the foliage there was thick enough so they could walk toward the boats without being seen. They were still out of sight of the boats when Aloysious called a halt.

"Wit," he whispered, "this is where you get into the river. Harry, do you think Wit knows how to handle this?"

"Yeah, he knows. Go get 'em, Wit."

Wit took off his shirt and laid it over a branch. He rolled up his trousers as far as he could. He pulled a rope from the saddlebag and carefully tied it to the bag. From a pocket he took a bright red handkerchief, rolled it into a band, and tied it around the top of his head. Then he mussed his hair so it stuck out in all directions. Finally, he let a peculiar smile slide over his face. He fixed it there and let his jaw droop open. He turned and looked at them with unfocused eyes. Harry wanted to applaud. Wit had achieved a look of simple, unmenacing madness.

Wit's eyes focused for just a moment. He snapped them a salute and stepped into the river. He bent to shove river mud into the saddlebag, then started wading down the river towing the bag behind him.

"Oh, boy, I have to see this," Aloysious said. "Come on, Harry."

They walked quickly but quietly to where they could see the boats and a man lying back against a tree near the water's edge. He was puffing on a cigarette and looked very relaxed. A splashing noise made him sit up straight. Harry and Aloysious simultaneously turned their heads to see Wit knee deep in the river pulling strenuously on his rope and fighting his way upriver. The guard was on his feet now. He flipped his cigarette to the side and started walking towards the water.

"Hey! Hey, you there!" he shouted at Wit. "Go back. This is a private place."

Intent on his struggle with the rope, Wit ignored him.

"Hey!" The guard tried again. "What do you have there? What are you doing?"

Wit moved closer to the guard, struggling hard with the rope. Water was splashing high in the air. It looked like whatever was on the end of the rope was big and fighting back.

The guard was really curious now. "What do you have there? Is it a fish?"

Wit turned to look over his shoulder at the guard. "Huh?" he grunted. His eyes seemed to roll around in his head.

The guard was getting excited. He was at the water's edge. "Is that a fish? Fish? Fish? Fish?" he repeated loudly. Wit's appearance was having its effect.

"Huh?" Wit grunted again, then said. "Fish, fish, fish." After a moment he added, "Shark."

"Shark?" the guard said, stepping back from the water.

"Unph," Wit grunted, and almost dropped the rope that seemed to give a great yank before he had it under control again. He stared at a spot about three feet over the guard's right shoulder as he spoke to him. "Shark," he confirmed. "River shark," he said, then added, "Delicious meat."

"Delicious, eh? Here, I want to see." The guard's curiosity had him in ankle-deep water, peering at where the tugging rope met the muddy water.

"Look at that," Aloysious whispered to Harry. "Old Wit's got him."

"Don't you think it's time you made your appearance?" Harry whispered in return.

"Yeah, yeah," Aloysious replied quietly and started off on tiptoe. Harry watched in amazement at how so big a man could move so stealthily. There was not a sound as Aloysious closed in behind the guard.

"Let me help with the rope," the guard said to Wit.

He was in the river in water up to his knees. He reached for the rope as Wit was pulled into still deeper water and fought back against the struggling "river shark" amidst loud splashes. "Don't let him get away!" the guard yelled as Aloysious came up behind him.

From where Harry stood, Aloysious seemed to tower over the guard, who was not a big man. He saw Aloysious bring both of his arms around the man. One arm encircled his middle. The other went over the guard's mouth, just as the man started to scream, convinced that the mate of the "river shark" had grabbed him. "Aarrgh..." was all he got out before Aloysious crushed the breath out of him.

"Good show, Wit," Aloysious said as pulled the limp body to the small sand beach where the two boats were moored. "Don't lose that rope. We're going to need it."

Harry helped tie the man up. They dragged him behind the bushes and laid him against a banana tree. The man was conscious now and breathing easily over the gag in his mouth. Just to make sure they were on the same frequency, Aloysious pulled an automatic pistol from his waistband. He touched his own mouth and shook his head. Then he smiled and patted the pistol. The guard's head nodded up and down. He understood fine.

Aloysious looked up the trail toward the village, and then at his watch. "Okay," he said. "They can't see us here, and they can't hear us. We have about 20 minutes before Colonel Sornchai arrives. Come up here, Harry, I want to show you what we're going to do."

Harry followed Aloysious about 30 feet up the trail in the direction of the village. Here the trail rose steeply for ten feet or so. It was not a sheer drop, but anybody walking along here would have to move very carefully.

"We're going to ambush them at the top, right where the trail drops." Aloysious pointed up to a tree at the side of the trail. "I have more rope. We'll fix it on that tree and run it across the trail. The old trip-wire gag, Harry. Cover it with leaves and they'll never see it. They'll be running.

When we put them down, they'll spill all the way down to the bottom of the hill. That's where we grab them. You and me. Wit will be on the trip wire."

"How many do you expect will come down the trail?"

Aloysious shrugged. "Four. Maybe five."

"And they'll have the girls with them?"

"Guarantee it. That's the only thing they have going for them. They won't give up Ting-Tong." Aloysious looked at his watch again. "We better get set up. It's almost time."

They worked quickly, and everything was set with time to spare. Aloysious told Wit what he wanted him to do, and Harry explained it to Wit again in Thai. There was still a little time. They walked over to look at the boats. Wit had selected the better of the two. It was ready to go. The other one Wit had disabled. Nobody would be able to follow them down the river. At least not in that boat.

Off in the distance they heard a faint "blap." A car horn. Then "blap, blap, blap" again. Then silence.

"That's a bad guy signal," Aloysious said, looking at his watch. "Sornchai got here early. It's only five to. Let's get ready. Wit, you get up there and hold that rope. Try to get them all. But remember, Ting-Tong will be with them. Try not to knock them down."

Wit went up to crouch under his tree. Harry took a last look around and joined Aloysious where he crouched in the bushes near the bottom of the trail.

"Harry, you better check your gun."

Harry pulled out the pistol and chambered a round. Just in case. From where he was sitting he could see Wit's head. Just then Wit turned, saw him, and gave a little wave. After that there was nothing, no sound but insects buzzing for what seemed like a long time. Sweat started to run down Harry's nose.

Wit heard them first. Harry saw Wit's face turn toward him. Wit made a couple of small jerky movements with his chin, pointing up the trail to the village. Then Harry heard them too. Grunts and heavy breathing. The rustle of leaves crushed underfoot and twigs breaking. Then running sounds. It all went quickly after that.

Harry saw them all at once. There were five of them at least. And Ting and Tong. They were so close together. Running in a group, with Ting and Tong at the center. Wit saw the problem right away. Harry saw Wit look his way, questioning. There was no time. Wit made his own decision then. He yanked hard on the rope.

Ass over teakettle. One big, big ball of elbows, knees, and stunned-looking faces rolled down that hill. The funny part was that it was all like a silent movie. The only sound Harry heard was an "umph" once or twice as wind was forcibly expelled from somebody's lungs.

The ball of people exploded at the bottom of the trail in a tangle of arms and legs and squirming bodies. Ting was the first one up. She found herself at the outside of the tangle, but moved back into the center and started kicking one of the men in the ribs. Harry noticed only then that her hands were bound. Not to be outdone, Tong was beating the man next to her with a stick she must have found on the trail. Aloysious had beat Harry to the scene. He stood there with pistol drawn, snarling, "Okay, goddamn it. Don't nobody move. Stay on the ground or I'll blow your goddamn head off." He watched for a moment, then, "Okay, Ting-Tong. That's enough. Come over here. We got things to do."

"But that man...," Ting yelled and pointed at the man she had been kicking. "He touched me. Here," she said touching her breast. She went over and kicked him one more time.

Tong ran over to Harry. She threw her arms around his neck and clung to him. "Harry! I knew you would come. It was so terrible! They made us eat bad things. I think it was dog meat."

"Oh, my God," Harry couldn't help saying.

Aloysious was already working with Wit, tying up arms and legs where they found them. Somebody had a broken arm it seemed. He screamed when Aloysious grabbed him. "Shut up, or I'll break the other one too," Aloysious told him. The screaming stopped.

Harry decided his job was to keep the bad guys covered and to console Ting and Tong. Actually, the girls looked pretty good. Their clothes were a little wrinkled and dusty, but the roll down the hill probably accounted for that. For kidnap victims they looked reasonably well groomed.

Tong had let go of his neck, but she stayed next to him and kept her hand on his waist. Ting brushed the dust off her clothes, then stood back and watched Aloysious and Wit. When one of the men still on the ground reached a hand out, maybe just to balance himself, Ting put her boot down on it. Hard. It made Harry think that he never wanted to get these two mad at him.

When Aloysious finished, he stepped back to survey his work. "Let the rabble lie there. Make it easy for Sornchai. Hey, Wit, get that other guy, your fisherman friend. Dump him over here with the rest." He turned to Harry. "Well, I don't want to push our luck. Sornchai will come down this way sooner or later. We better get moving."

They walked to the boat and everybody but Harry climbed in. When everybody was set, Harry pushed the boat off the shore, and waded out alongside. He waited while Wit poked at fuel valves and pulled levers, and finally said he was ready. Harry walked the boat farther into the stream. When the water got too deep, he climbed over the side. Wit waited until Harry had picked a spot to sit next to Tong. Then he gunned the engine and turned the boat downstream.

Behind them the little sand beach looked quiet and peaceful – until one noticed the squirming, groaning mound of men tied to one another, with no hope of escape from the police, who even now were moving carefully down the trail toward them.

34

Out on the river and away from the beach, Harry felt an overwhelming sense of relief. Out here, skimming across the smooth surface of the river, it was like nothing had happened. They could have been on their way to a picnic. In the bow, Ting and Tong lay back, eyes closed, enjoying the wind washing through their hair. In the stern, one hand lightly on the tiller, Wit sat and squinted into the distance. A small, satisfied smile played over his face as he relived his brief role as actor and warrior. In the center of the boat, Aloysious sat, looking tired, but relaxed and pleased with himself.

The ordeal was over. Everything had worked out. They were done with tension, with concern, with morbid thoughts fed by overactive imaginations. They had all survived. Now, on their way to only Aloysious knew where, they were looking forward again to whatever came next.

Aloysious gestured to Harry. The two of them slid forward, away from the engine noise where they could talk easily with Ting and Tong.

"You two all right?" Aloysious asked. "Did those guys hurt you?"

"They were terrible people," Ting said, her nose wrinkling at the memory. "We had no clean water to wash. We could not brush our teeth. The food was bad."

"You said one of them touched you."

Tong could not wait to let Ting answer and spoke first. "Just once," Tong said. "He touched Ting just once. She kicked him on his knee. He shouted at her. Then Ting threw her dinner at him."

Ting shrugged. "I wasn't hungry anyway. We knew you would come for us, but we thought you would come yesterday."

"When you didn't come," Tong continued, "we weren't worried, but we were hungry. Did you bring food?"

"Not much," Aloysious said. "Here." He tossed a couple of cans. "A can of Spam, a can of tuna. Wit brought it for you."

Tong examined the cans and Ting waited expectantly for the can opener. Aloysious searched through his pockets.

247

"We put a lot of pepper on the food they gave us," Tong said. "A lot of small green peppers."

"Anything tastes good with enough peppers," Ting added.

"But not coffee," Tong giggled. "Ting put peppers in their coffee. They all coughed and spat."

Ting laughed at the memory, and then turned her attention to the can of tuna when Aloysious finally produced a pocketknife. "It has a can opener," he said as he tossed it to her.

Something was obviously bothering Aloysious. Harry noticed that he was checking his wristwatch every few minutes. In between he kept looking back over the stern. Finally, he slid closer to Harry. "Listen," he said, "I figure we have another ten minutes before the bloodhounds arrive. I have an idea. Are you up to getting a little wet?"

If Aloysious was bothering to ask, it was going to be more than a little wet. "How wet?" Harry asked.

"Oh, maybe ten minutes worth."

Harry hesitated. What were the options? "Why not?" he finally answered.

"Good," Aloysious said. He crawled down the center of the boat to the stern and squatted next to Wit. Harry watched him shout something in Wit's ear, but he was too far away to hear it over the engine noise. Wit's face took on a skeptical look. Aloysious pointed into the distance over their bow. Wit stood up and looked. Whatever Wit saw must have satisfied him. He sat down and nodded. Aloysious clapped Wit on the shoulder and crawled back up front. He squatted next to Harry.

"Colonel Sornchai is a good man," Aloysious said. "I've seen him operate. He won't do anything to screw up his agreement with you – until the hour you asked for is up. Then the cavalry comes charging in. Sornchai knows we have a boat. He'll figure we'll try to get as far downriver as we can. That's not what we're going to do."

Aloysious punctuated his last sentence with a wink. As if the wink signaled it, the pitch of the engine changed as Wit throttled back and turned the boat toward the shore.

Ahead of them, the river branched into two channels. The main channel was narrow and water moved through it swiftly. The other channel opened wide and spread out to become a long shallow pool. Here the river moved slowly before rejoining the main channel a hundred meters farther on. Wit turned the boat into the second channel and cut the engine. The boat drifted slowly until it was almost stationary.

"Looks good, Wit," Aloysious finally broke the silence. "I even see fish down there." Aloysious turned back to them. "I hope everybody remembered their swimsuits. We're all going to take a swim."

Ting and Tong exchanged some rapid Thai. Harry caught the jist of it: Aloysious was being foolish again and was best ignored. Wit stood up and started to wrestle with several fishnets that had been stowed near the stern. Harry watched Wit spread the nets and drape one over each side of the boat. Finished with that, Wit turned to a wooden locker in the bottom of the boat and pulled from it a conical straw rice farmer's hat. Harry glanced back at Aloysious and saw that he had his shoes and socks off and was stripping off his shirt.

"Come on, Harry," he said. "Let's get in the water. Ladies, get your bathing suits on."

Tong turned at this and found Aloysious down to his boxer shorts. She poked Ting and pointed, and they both laughed. Above their laughter, Harry picked up a familiar sound in the distance.

"Chopper coming in," he said.

"Ladies," Aloysious said. "We have about one minute before the police get here. Get down to your scanties and get in the water. Or all your clothes will get wet."

With that Aloysious stepped out of the boat and into the water. Instead of splashing out of sight as Harry expected, he stood there, in water up to his waist. "Harry," he said, "if they're not in the water in five seconds, toss them overboard."

"Aloysious," Ting said plaintively, and looking perplexed, "why do we have to hide from the police? We were only victims."

The sound of the chopper was getting closer. "You were victims," Aloysious replied. "I am the criminal. Now get your asses in here, or we all go to jail."

In seconds Ting and Tong were stripped down to panties and bras. Wit shouted for them to throw their clothes to him. He stuck them in the locker. Harry stood transfixed, struck by the sight of these two young women whom he thought he knew so well and yet not at all. The skin of their young bodies set off by the white of their brief underclothes gleamed like gold. Suddenly they were not anyone he knew. He watched them move, enthralled. His sense of urgency left him, and he neglected to start unbuttoning his own clothes.

"Harry! Goddamn it! Get in here." There was no mistaking the urgency in Aloysious's voice.

The chopper sounded close, almost overhead. Harry wasted no more time. He stepped out of the boat, saying, "Oh, shit" as water rushed up his trousers. Standing in the water next to Aloysious, he looked across the boat to where Ting and Tong stood looking at him from the other side.

"Ting-Tong," Aloysious shouted, "get down in the water. Stay next to the boat. Wit will throw a net over your heads. Harry, get down. I'm going around to help the girls."

Harry crouched down, low, his face just above the surface of the water. Wit threw the net over him and he felt it sting his face as it splashed into the water and over his head and shoulders. The net was bunched up over him, but he had more than enough room to breathe and could see through it easily. It was unlikely that anyone looking at him from a few feet away could make out his face through the close mesh of the net.

The helicopter had been following the river, skimming low over the water. That was probably what saved them. The pilot was too low to be able to see them from a distance. For a moment it seemed the helicopter would continue to follow the main channel and pass them by. Then the pilot must have seen Wit and the boat. The helicopter's nose dipped as it turned abruptly toward them.

Over the boat the pilot hovered, then let the helicopter turn in a slow circle. Below him he saw a solitary fisherman, casting a net into the sluggish water. Two other nets hung over the side of the boat, drying out. What the pilot could not see were the four pairs of eyes that watched him anxiously through the nets. In the boat, Wit surreptitiously squinted at the chopper from under the wide brim of his hat.

The chopper circled a second time, coming lower still. The down blast from the rotors now turned the quiet surface of the water into a miniature maelstrom. The boat started to rock. Wit bore it for a full five seconds. Then he had enough. He turned his face to the sky. His hat slipped back and rolled to the bottom of the boat. Wit never noticed. For a moment Wit's eyes locked with the pilot's. He raised his fist and shook it at the sky. Behind the helicopter's canopy a man saluted and the helicopter started backing slowly away. A moment later, the helicopter spun on its axis and headed back to the main channel.

Harry pulled the net from his face and stood up. Aloysious popped up on the other side, and next to him Ting and then Tong.

"What do you think?" Harry asked.

"I think we're good," Aloysious answered. "They're looking for three men and two girls in a boat. Not an old fisherman. They'll chase the river all the way to Chiang Mai now."

"I am old fisherman," Wit said, "but I am good fisherman. You play in water. I catch lunch." Three sizable fish flopped about in a tangle of net he held over them.

"Hooray for Wit!" Ting shouted.

"We eat!" Tong cried.

They lunched on a small beach that was shielded from the sun by a tree that grew on the edge of the river. Harry's clothes were spread out on the sand to dry, while he lounged, not uncomfortably, in a sarong that Wit had pulled from the locker in the bottom of the boat. The sarong smelled of fish, but it was dry.

Aloysious sat back against the tree and studied his map. After a while he called for everyone to listen.

"We're not all that far from Chiang Mai," he said. "Another mile or so down the river is a sizable town. We can dump the boat there and find a vehicle."

"Where will we go?" Ting asked.

"You guys are going back to Tong's family."

"But where will you go, Aloysious? And Harry? And Wit?"

"I don't know," Aloysious said. "We have to wait to see how the wind's blowing. We have time. Harry's still drying out. We'll wait till sunset."

The sun was setting behind a distant hill when they finally pushed off from the beach. There was no dusk. The sky where the sun dipped below the horizon briefly turned a brilliant red. Then, like a spreading ink stain, deep purple overran the red and turned it all into black. They were in darkness.

"Harry, take over from Wit," Aloysious said. "You're used to running in the dark."

Wit did not argue. He moved aside and let Harry take the tiller. Within minutes Harry saw on the horizon a distant glow of light. When they got through the next bend in the river, the town itself was visible, outlined by dots of light from street lamps and houses. The river was wider here, and boats traveling on it were well lit. For once, navigating was a piece of cake.

Harry ran the boat ashore just short of the town. Beyond them was a well-lit area full of activity. Aloysious guessed it was an open-air restaurant next to a river ferry landing. Tong and Wit walked over to explore it while the rest of them waited in the darkness to see what they learned.

Tong was the first one back, her arms overloaded with cardboard buckets that contained a feast of spicy fish and rice. They wasted no time setting out paper plates and plastic chopsticks, and were well into their dinner when Wit finally joined them.

"Pull up a plate, Wit," Aloysious mumbled through a mouthful of fish. "Good eats."

Wit sat down next to Harry. He took a plate and some food, but he did not eat with his usual gusto.

"What did you find out, Wit?" Aloysious asked.

"It is not good," Wit said. He finished what he was chewing on, put down his chopsticks, and continued. "I heard the radio news from Chiang Mai. It said the police raided a village near Chiang Mai today. They captured six art counterfeiters. The ringleader escaped. He was a Westerner. The assistant ringleader was a Westerner, too. He also escaped. The police are looking for them in Chiang Mai. There are roadblocks. The police are checking everyone at the airport, at the train station, and on the buses. Not so good, huh?" Wit concluded.

"It may not be so bad," Aloysious said. "Did they give any names? Did they say anything about Ting-Tong?" he asked.

"No," Wit answered.

"Then it's not so bad," Aloysious said. "At least they're not looking for the girls. Or for you, Wit."

Wit grumbled something.

"What was that, Wit?"

"I think nobody knows my name," Wit said. There was disappointment in his voice. "On the radio it sounded like I was not there. I think nobody knows my name."

"Wit, don't worry," Aloysious said. "You hang around me a little longer and they'll know your name. I guarantee it. Hey, Assistant Ringleader," he shouted to Harry, "how do you feel about making the evening news?"

"Better than seeing my picture on the front page of the morning paper. Or does that happen tomorrow?"

"Look at it this way, Harry. It makes it easier for us," Aloysious said.

"Makes it easier!" Harry said. "Just how does it make it easier?"

"Now we know we can't go back to Chiang Mai. That means all we have to worry about is where we will go."

"Wonderful," Harry said, and then asked, "What are our choices?"

"Not many. Bangkok is out. They'll watch everything going that way. If we can't get to Bangkok, we can't get out of the country. Unless you want to swim the Mekong. Or walk into Burma. We'll work it out. We can always go back up the mountain. Wait for things to simmer down."

"How about you talking to Colonel Sornchai?" Harry asked. "Maybe we can work something out."

"The only thing Sornchai will work out is how much time we'll spend breaking rocks in Chiang Mai prison. But feel free, Harry. If you want to do that, go right ahead."

"Aloysious, what will happen?" Ting asked, putting her hand on his.

"What will happen is what I said. You and Tong will go and stay with Tong's family. The police won't bother you there. Harry and I will go up on the mountain. We'll wait until things calm down. Wit can come with us, too, if he wants."

"I don't know if I want to come," Wit said quietly to Harry in Thai.

Aloysious caught the Thai. "I heard that, Wit. You don't have to decide now. Think about it. While you think about it, why don't you see if you can get us a nice car. Maybe a nice roomy van."

Wit looked at Harry, uncertainty on his face.

"He wants you to steal a car," Harry told him in Thai. "A van with a lot of room. A nice one."

"Oh," Wit said. He got up and brushed himself off. "Does the color matter?" he asked sarcastically. Without waiting for an answer he started walking toward the lights.

"Get us some beer!" Aloysious shouted after him.

35

Wit showed up well after midnight, driving a weary red Datsun truck with an enclosed pickup body. "Enclosed" was stretching the point, but the Datsun did have a metal roof, and metal panels partially covered the sides. A worn wooden bench ran down each side of the pickup body. Aloysious got in and looked around. "Ouch," he said. "I have a goddamn splinter already. Hey, Wit, this is just like home."

"I could find no van," Wit said. Deliberately, Harry thought.

"We might as well get rolling," Aloysious said. "Ting-Tong, you get up front with Wit. Pile in back, Harry. Not much sleep for us tonight."

The ride into town was slow and bumpy. Wit stayed on the back roads, trying not to run into a police roadblock. They were still on the edge of the city when Aloysious banged on the driver's cabin. Wit quickly pulled off to the side of the road.

"Wit, the big hotel up ahead. Ting-Tong can get out here and walk over." Aloysious hopped out of the truck and walked around to open the door for Ting and Tong. "Well, guys, this is where you get off," he said. "Go into the lobby and call your Dad, Tong. He can come and get you."

"Can't we go with you?" Ting asked plaintively. Ting and Tong both looked at Aloysious with moist eyes. "You need us to help," Ting said emphatically. "Who will carry beer up the mountain? Wit can cook Spam and spaghetti, but who will cook other things?"

Aloysious put an arm around each of them. "Not this time," he said. "You can help us best by going to Tong's place and staying out of trouble." Ting's head hung low. One of her hands came up to wipe her eyes.

Harry could hear Ting sniffling. Goodbyes always affected him. He turned and walked to the rear of the truck. Tong was right behind him. "Harry, I'm very sad, too," she said, "Ting will be concerned about Aloysious. And I will be concerned about you. And Wit."

"Nothing to worry about," Harry said in what he hoped was a reassuring tone.

"In the truck Wit said that Aloysious made some people lose a lot of money, and that they will come after you. Wit said that if they don't get you, the police will."

Wonderful, Harry thought. He took Tong by the shoulders. "Hey, you don't have to worry about us. Aloysious knows his way around. So do I. And don't worry about Wit. He does pretty good for himself."

"When will we see you again?"

"Not long. We'll be back before you know it."

"I hope so." She looked around to see if Ting and Aloysious were still talking. She put her head closer to Harry and in a confidential tone said, "I wrote to Miss Bupha and asked her about old Western men. Do you remember Miss Bupha?"

"Yeah," Harry chuckled. "The lovelorn lady."

"Yes." Tong continued, "She wrote that in old Western men their fires burn low. And maybe not too hot. But Miss Bupha said that if you meet an older Western man, especially an American, you should try to hold him. She said their fires may not glow hotly, but usually they are foolish in love. They are loyal and sometimes rich." As she finished, she put her arms around him and squeezed. "I will miss you," she said.

"I'm not rich, Tong," Harry said. She did not seem to hear.

"Let's break this up now." Aloysious was alongside. "Come on. Tong, you had enough time with Harry. Say goodbye to Wit. We have to get rolling."

Tong broke away from Harry very slowly, holding on to his hand as she moved back. She gave him a last sad smile and turned away. Ting came to Harry to say her goodbye. She looked distraught. He hardly heard what she said. He was almost glad when he heard Aloysious's call from inside the truck. "Let's roll!"

Wit gunned the engine. The last sight Harry had of Ting and Tong were two sad little figures standing alongside the road in the dark, waving goodbye. He and Aloysious watched from the back of the truck until there was nothing, but the faint red glow of the tail light.

The wind blowing through the back of the truck was cold. Through the back window of the driver's cab Harry could see Wit, snug and comfortable, one hand tapping the steering wheel, keeping time with the music on the radio. After watching for a while, Harry said to Aloysious, "Hey, why don't you get up front with Wit?"

"Fuck it" was Aloysious's answer. Harry waited for a while, half hoping Aloysious would say, "Why don't you go up front, Harry?" but he never did. Fuck it, Harry thought.

Harry experimented, twisting around in different positions. Eventually he found that if he leaned forward, with his body slightly to the left, the wind went around him. Then he could also have a conversation with Aloysious in almost normal tones. That was important. His mind had ranged over events of the recent past and kept sticking on a couple of things that did not add up. He was not sure he could get Aloysious focused on them.

"Hey, Aloysious!" he finally said. "I told you Karlo called me, remember? Karlo said that several of the items I sold him were not satisfactory. He said that at least one was – and I quote – 'made yesterday'."

It was too dark for him to see what expression Aloysious wore on his face. When there was no response at all, he asked, "Did you hear me? Are you awake?"

"Yeah, I'm awake. I heard you."

"What do you think? Did a piece from your fake art project get mixed in with our stuff from the city?"

There was still no response from Aloysious. Harry tried again. "You know, if I could visualize a way that you could get some of the big stone and bronze statues up the mountain, I'd be concerned. If I could think of a scheme big enough, I could see you right in the middle of it. But I don't see how you could do it. Or why. The piece I gave to Karlo was a small one. A small piece could be carried up the mountain easily enough. But I can't see why. There's so much real stuff up there, why bother?"

Harry waited again, patiently. The only sound was the wind whistling through the back of the truck. Finally, Aloysious spoke. He sounded weary.

"Harry, I don't know what Karlo's problem is. Personally, I think he's full of shit. Elephant shit. I don't see how he got anything but what we brought down off the mountain."

"Was there some kind of mistake? Did one of your reproductions accidentally get mixed in with the ones we brought down off the mountain?"

Silence again. Aloysious seemed lost in thought. Finally he leaned in closer to Harry. "Just think about that, Harry," he said. "How would something like that happen? You were there when we winched that stuff down off the mountain. You loaded it on the boat yourself. You were in the Land Rover when it went down to Chiang Mai. You unloaded it at Sato's warehouse. I was up on the mountain during that time."

Aloysious waved his hands in the air. "If somebody stuck a phony piece in the shipment, where did it happen? In Sato's warehouse? On Sato's ship? Frankly, I doubt it, Harry. A guy like Sato doesn't play petty games when there's a lot of money involved. And his underlings wouldn't dare. Frankly, I think Karlo is bullshitting you. If you can see how a fake was added to the shipment, you tell me. Think about it, Harry."

Harry stared back into the blackness for a long time and thought about it. He kept coming back to the same place. A switch was made after he unloaded the first shipment at the warehouse. Or the fake pieces came right off the mountain. Neither possibility made a lot of sense. Why would anybody bother with copies if there was so much of the real stuff in the shipment? Why bother making a switch if you could just grab a real piece that wouldn't be missed?

Maybe I'm making too much of this, Harry thought. Aloysious was probably right. Karlo made a mistake and called a good piece bad. Or Karlo was up to something else. A hidden agenda. Harry shifted that around in his mind for a while. In the end he decided there was little possibility that Karlo would involve himself in a scam. Karlo simply did not have the balls for it.

Harry sighed. He had no answers. He was not even sure there was a problem. Well, what the hell, it had been a long day that had turned into an even longer night.

The sky had been brightening for a while, and soon there was enough light to see into the rice fields that lined the road. There was nothing they recognized. Harry had no idea where they were.

They passed a sign announcing a town ahead, and almost immediately drove down its main and only street. The new day had already started here. People were walking along the road and a few were on bicycles. Lights still on in the shops could be seen through open doors. When they reached the far side of the village, Aloysious banged on the cab. "Hey, Wit," he yelled. "Stop up there by the trees."

Wit pulled up alongside a grove of small trees. Aloysious hopped out and walked stiffly around to Wit's window. Harry dropped off the back of the truck, stretched, and then walked up to join Aloysious.

"...And get something sweet," Aloysious said to Wit. "Candy, cough drops or something." When he noticed Harry alongside, he turned to ask, "Do you want anything special? I told Wit to go back to the village to buy some food and stuff. We may be a long time up on the mountain."

"Coffee," Harry said weakly. "Just some strong hot coffee."

"Wit, see if you can get a local paper." Aloysious beat the side of the cab with his fist as Wit pulled out. "Get back as soon as you can," he yelled after him.

"How much farther do we have to go?" Harry asked.

"Not far, I think. Christ, we've been on the road all night. I didn't think Thailand was that big."

"What do we do when we get to the mountain?"

"We wait. We wait until everybody else gets bored and goes home."

"When will that be?"

"When the game is over. When the fat lady sings. I should have told Wit to get a new pack of cards. There are only 44 cards left in the pack on the boat."

Aloysious looked around for a place to sit, turning circles like a dog. He finally picked a spot and dropped down on it. "Harry," he said, "I wish I could tell you how long we're going to be on the mountain. If it's too long and we start going bat shit, maybe we can work a deal. But I doubt it.

Sornchai really wants my ass. He won't deal with me. Maybe he'll talk with you."

Harry stood looking off into the rice fields. The air smelled sweet. Insects were starting to buzz. It was going to be a hot day. He picked a place near Aloysious and dropped down. They sat and waited gloomily for Wit to return.

36

I can't believe you did this, Aloysious," Harry said disgustedly. "Why would anyone cover a boat under a pile of elephant shit?" He shook his head. Somewhere under all that dung was Wit's boat, where Aloysious had hidden it ten days ago.

"Nobody bothered it, did they?"

"You're right about that. Maybe we shouldn't bother it either. It smells like it died."

"Come on, Harry, be a sport. See if you can get Wit to come over here. If we work together we can have this thing in the water in 20 minutes."

"Wit's pissed off," Harry said, but walked off to find him.

With the three of them working together it was not too bad. The elephant dung – and there was a lot of it – had dried out for the most part. It was the flies that were bad. Wit cut branches that they used to fork the dung and other debris off the boat. When most of it was cleared, they pushed the boat into the small inlet, and walked it the short distance to the river. It was hot work and the water felt good.

Wit was pleased to have the boat back in the water and personally took charge of washing it down. Harry and Aloysious stood back and then walked to the bank where they watched as water splashed and flew through the air. After a half hour of a heavy cleaning, Wit pronounced the boat ready. As Harry climbed aboard, he turned to Aloysious. "This thing still stinks."

"Quiet, Harry. I didn't know Wit was so sensitive." Looking a little sheepish, Aloysious climbed in. "Boat looks good, Wit," he added casually. There was no comment from Wit.

The boat may have smelled bad, but it was familiar. Wit opened the throttle wide. Spray whipped back over their faces. As their speed increased, a plume of white water rose high behind them, a rooster tail over their stern. They skimmed over the water and Harry relaxed. For the first time in days he felt lighthearted. He could almost convince himself that Ting and Tong would be waiting on the beach at the mountain with lunch.

The spell of a carefree afternoon ride held until they approached the area of the little hill where Aloysious had been fired on and where the chase had started on their last trip upriver. That seemed long ago.

Harry glanced at Aloysious and saw that he was alert, too. Harry carefully looked over the hill from where they had been watched the last time, and then let his eyes slowly follow the line of the riverbank, trying to identify the spot where the boat had come from – the boat that almost rammed them and then chased them upriver.

As Harry shifted his gaze toward the back of the boat, Wit caught his eye. Wit pointed at something far off their stern. Harry saw nothing at first. Then he made it out – a dark speck with a crest of white above. Another long-tail boat like theirs, far behind. Harry leaned toward Aloysious.

"Boat behind us," he said.

Aloysious turned to the stern and watched for a while. "Wit, slow down. Let him get closer."

Wit throttled the engine back, almost to an idle. Harry squinted, and the speck seemed to grow bigger and bigger. Suddenly the white tail seemed to contract, and then disappeared completely. Harry could still see the dark spot that was the boat. Behind him he heard Aloysious say, "He's slowing down. Now he stopped. Wit, start moving again."

Wit cranked up the engine. They seemed to leap ahead. As they watched, they could see the rooster tail of the boat behind rise again into the air.

"Fucker's following us," Aloysious said.

Wit started to change speed. One minute they were at full speed. The next they were at a crawl. They drifted for a time. They watched as the boat behind mimicked their actions, speeding up when they did, then cutting speed and drifting. The distance between the two boats never varied.

"Look at the bright side," Aloysious said. "At least it's not like he's trying to catch us and shoot us."

"What?" Wit asked Harry, not catching all of Aloysious's English. Harry translated into Thai. Wit nodded. "Oh," he said. He failed to see any humor in the remark.

"What do you think?" Harry asked Aloysious.

Aloysious wrinkled his brow. He held up three fingers. "We have this many options. We lie dead in the water and hope he gets bored and goes away. We turn around and chase him off the river. We carry on to the mountain like nothing happened. What do you think?"

"It may be futile, but I'd like to give option two a try."

"Okay. Option two it is. Wit, turn us around and let's go get him." When Wit had the boat turned around, Aloysious stood up and shouted, "Charge!" Hands cupped over his mouth, he did his imitation of a bugle cavalry charge.

"Sounds like elephant," Wit said.

As they came up to speed, the boat in the distance started to move too, its white rooster tail rising high as it accelerated. The pilot of the boat, too far away to see them any better than they saw him, did not immediately realize they had changed course and were now heading back downriver toward him. For a few moments the two boats raced toward each other at full speed.

Harry laughed. "I wonder how long it will take him to figure it out."

Aloysious smiled smugly. He had a pistol in his hand now, and looked toward the sky. "Just another minute, God. Just let him keep coming a little more." Then, "Oh shit! There he goes now."

The two boats were closer to each other, close enough to make out that the boat following them had only the pilot in it. As they watched, the boat slewed around clumsily as the pilot suddenly realized what was happening. The rooster tail behind him collapsed as he chopped the throttle to turn around. A moment later the tail rose again as the pilot used every bit of speed the boat had to get away from them.

Wit got right behind, chasing him at full speed down the river. In minutes it was obvious they were not gaining. Aloysious tapped Harry's knee to get his attention. He shook his head. "No good. We'll never catch him. He'll lead us into something we don't want."

Aloysious turned to Wit and with his finger made a circling motion in the air. Wit nodded. He cut speed and turned the boat around.

Only minutes after they were heading back upriver, Harry saw the boat in the distance shadowing them again. He caught Aloysious looking at him. Aloysious shrugged. He held up three fingers. It was going to be option three, motor on up to the mountain like nothing happened. There was no other option.

When Wit throttled back to a comfortable cruising speed, Harry watched the other boat for a while. He asked Aloysious, "Who do you think? Cop or bad guy?"

Aloysious shrugged. "A cop. I hope. For once I hope it's a cop."

The boat continued to keep a respectful distance behind them. When they reached the mountain, just off the beach Aloysious stood up in the boat. "Let's hit the beach fast and get the boat out of sight. He's far enough back. He may not spot us.

As the bow scraped on the beach, Harry and Aloysious jumped into the river, pulled the boat up between the huge rocks and quickly covered it with shrubs. Then the three of them got into the bushes behind the beach and waited.

It did not take long. They heard the low burble of an engine moving a boat with just enough speed to overcome the current. A few moments later the boat slowly rounded the far bend and moved toward them. It stood well off the beach, closer to the far bank. They could see the pilot looking their way, scrutinizing their beach. Without warning, the boat suddenly whirled around and, with the throttle wide open, roared back downriver.

"Shit," Aloysious yelled after it. He picked up a rock and threw it as far as he could. It fell into the river with a plop far short of where the boat had been. Aloysious threw his hands to heaven. "Why" he asked. "Why?"

"What happened?" Harry asked. "What spooked him?"

"Nothing spooked him. He knew we were here. He knew we were coming here. Shit! Just what we need! That was no cop, Harry. The son of a bitch! We're going to see more of him. And all his goddamn friends."

"I don't follow you."

"It was a bad guy, Harry. They know where we are now. He was just confirming it."

"This may sound stupid, but should we worry about it? I mean once we're up on the mountain, we're in pretty good shape. Aren't we?"

"Let me put it this way, Harry. A cop we wouldn't have to worry about. But it wasn't a cop. Some of those guys used to be my colleagues. They'll figure out things that the cops wouldn't think of in a million years."

"Your colleagues in the art reproduction trade? Are you suggesting they know something I don't know?"

"I'm not suggesting anything, Harry. Let me just say that I see problems ahead. Not big problems. The bottom line is we're in good shape. If push comes to shove, we have nothing to worry about. Trust me."

Harry threw his hands up to the sky and implored, "Why?" There was no answer.

Farther up the beach, Wit paced back and forth, throwing uneasy looks at the mountain. When he saw Harry looking his way, he waved for him to come over.

"What's up, Wit?" Harry asked in Thai.

Wit looked over his shoulder, as if afraid something were watching. He leaned close to Harry and said softly, "This place. This is it. Isn't it?" He took a step back, but kept his eyes on Harry's face, waiting for an answer.

"Ah...what place, Wit?" Harry asked, and felt a little foolish when he realized he had whispered.

Wit threw his hands to the sky. It must be catching, Harry thought.

"This place," Wit said. With arms extended he turned slowly around to include the whole area from the mountain back to the river. "This place. This is the place the Karen spoke of. The place of the trees that fly!"

Oh, shit, Harry thought. He felt a shiver run down his spine. To Wit he said only, "Oh, that." Trying to be reassuring, he added, "I've been up here before, Wit. I've never seen any flying trees. Maybe the Karen were talking about some place farther up the river."

Wit looked at him closely. A grin slid over his face. "You were here before? Maybe you were lucky."

"What the hell's going on?" It was Aloysious, and his question was rhetorical. He had a bulging backpack in each hand and one on his back. "Here. Everybody gets one," he said, handing one to Harry and one to Wit. "They're loaded and ready to go. We got to get moving."

Without further ado, the three of them started walking along the riverbank, Aloysious in the lead. Wit paused and looked back toward his boat. Aloysious caught him at it.

"Don't worry about the boat, Wit. When this is over we'll buy you a new one."

Harry and Wit trailed behind Aloysious, but moved closer when he turned into the brush and started forcing his way through the heavy foliage. The going was as rough as Harry remembered, but having Wit there was a real advantage. He and Aloysious worked well together to open a path they could easily move through, then close up again behind them.

It was not long before they broke through the final tangle of vines and dropped onto the dry streambed. They rested there a while under the green canopy. Wit looked around, full of curiosity, but more relaxed than he had been out near the river. He probably felt something of what Harry had felt when he first came here, a feeling of security, a sense of being well hidden in this green tunnel. Safe from anything that might ever come looking for him.

Hours later, when the three of them walked doubled over to stay below a leafy roof that seemed to get lower with each small stumbling step, Harry felt less romantic about the tunnel. They were near the end of it, he hoped. They had to be. Minutes later Aloysious poked out through the canopy into what Harry remembered as the "garden of black rocks." Out of the streambed, they rested for only a few minutes, then started up the slope toward the rock face.

As they walked, Wit kept one eye on the mountain and the other on the old gnarled trees that stood like guardians along their route upward. The steep rock face, just ahead, now dominated the entire scene. As they approached, Aloysious could not resist pointing out its features to Wit. "Hey, Wit. Up there. See the cave? Looks like a big open mouth, doesn't it? See the bones? Must be some real wild spirits up there."

Wit looked, but said nothing. As they turned and started walking along the rock face, he suddenly turned, joined his hands in front of his face in a *wai* and bowed, paying his respects to whatever spirits dwelled in the cave. Probably wise, Harry thought.

They reached the crack in the cliff face, and dropped through it into the passage that Harry remembered as the "Holland Tunnel." They came out of the darkness of the cave onto the lush grass of the small valley where the stone steps started up the hill.

Harry could feel excitement welling up in him. He walked faster and soon was well out in front of Aloysious and Wit. He tripped over one of the stone steps in the grass, but this time stayed on his feet. He was eager to see the great stone serpents, the Nagas that guarded the entrance to the hill. His eyes quickly picked out the two huge mounds despite the layers of vegetation that camouflaged them. He walked under the arching neck of the great stone serpent. Standing there, he savored a moment that made worthwhile all the hardships and worries of the last few weeks.

Wit walked up and stood nearby, looking around. He touched the mound under which the Naga rested, then squinted up at the great serpent head. Harry, still riding the high of his own excitement, asked, "What do you think of all this, Wit?"

"Oh, very nice."

"Know what it is?"

"Yes," Wit answered, "a Naga."

Wit's manner was so casual that Harry had to say, "You don't seem surprised."

"Oh, no," Wit said. "Nagas are very interesting. We see them all the time."

"You do?" Harry asked in astonishment.

"Oh, yes," Wit answered, and went on with a burst of enthusiasm. "Maybe one week ago. Before I met you and Alo-wichit. In Chiang Mai I went to a movie. They had Nagas like this. Maybe bigger. It was in the old time. The Nagas were clean. No trees were growing on them. There were witches...and real snakes as big as this Naga. Oh, and there was much fighting. Maybe the fighting was not as good as you and Alo-wichit do."

"But these are real Nagas, Wit."

Wit was no more impressed to hear that. "Yes, real Nagas," he said. "Very nice." His eyes followed the undulations of the Naga's body up the hill. "There's Alo-wichit. I think we have to hurry to catch him."

Wit started off after Aloysious. Harry shrugged and stood by the Naga for a while longer. The lack of enthusiasm shown by Wit and Aloysious could not dampen his own. He went up the hill slowly, taking his time to savor glimpses of ancient structures half-hidden among the trees. When he finally reached the top he was quickly plucked back to the present.

"Hey, Mr. Harry. Alo-wichit wants you to have a cold beer." Wit was sitting on the top step.

That will taste good, Harry thought as he reached for the beer, and then almost dropped it. The can was ice cold. "How the hell did Alo-wichit keep the beer so cold?"

Wit looked at him and shrugged. "I don't know. He must have got it from his pack."

Harry walked with Wit past the line of stone lions that guarded the grand entranceway to the city. Inside the wall, Wit turned and walked across the courtyard away from the main temple.

"Where's Alo-wichit?" Harry asked.

"In the library. He says it is a library. But it is only an old stone building."

They got to the library, a small, elegant building set on a raised base and decorated with elaborately carved stone panels. A small cooking fire was burning in front of the stairs leading to the entrance. On one of the stairs halfway up was a styrofoam cooler. Harry recognized it as one Ting and Tong had lugged up the mountain. Aloysious came through the doorway, wearing a sarong over his trousers and looking very domestic.

"Welcome," Aloysious said with a deep bow, "Welcome to the abode of Aloysious the Conqueror, the Finder of Lost Cities, the King of the Hill."

"Thanks for the beer, mighty one. How do you keep the beer so cold?"

"A secret learned in the mysterious precincts of the Orient. More cold ones await you. I don't know about the rest of the meal. Wit's in charge of that."

"Spaghetti!" Wit cried.

"Spaghetti, bullshit," Aloysious said. "There's steaks in the cooler."

Wit asked Harry in Thai, "Steak? Did he say steak?" Without waiting for an answer, Wit started up the steps and opened the cooler. "Yes," he answered his own question. "He said steak."

The steaks turned out to be first rate and not aged buffalo as Wit feared. Harry did not bother asking where Aloysious got the steaks. He knew whatever answer he got would tell him no more than he knew now.

After the meal Aloysious went into the library, to nap he said. Harry decided to use what was left of the daylight to explore the main temple complex. Wit wandered off to look at stone carvings, although he seemed as little taken with the vast complex on top of the mountain as he had been with the Nagas at the bottom. He had explained his views to Harry and Aloysious as they all ate.

"Oh, yes," Wit had said, reaching for more potato chips, "I have seen many films with places like this. Usually there are also women in beautiful dresses. And dancing girls who throw flowers. Here I have seen none of that. When we go back to Chiang Mai, I will take you to a proper film. One that has a place like this. But better."

Harry reflected on this as he walked down a long outer gallery in the main temple. On the wall alongside him, cut into the stone, were battle scenes that easily could have come from one of Wit's epic movies. He ran his fingers over the stone face of a warrior. It was surprisingly rough. He smiled. Wit, he thought, next you'll have me talking to myself.

But Wit's words stayed with him. They touched a sore spot, an irrational fear that had started when he first set his eyes on the city, that he would blink his eyes and it would all be gone. All that would remain would be a memory with less substance than one of Wit's films.

"Harry! Mr. Harry! Where are you?"

It was Wit's voice, carried on the wind from somewhere far away. Harry made his way out of the gallery and trotted in the direction of the sound. Outside the main temple he heard Wit again.

"Mr. Harry! Where are you?"

"Over here, Wit!" he cried and started off again. He could see Wit ahead, standing by a building on the far side of the compound. Wit saw him and waved. "Over here, Mr. Harry. Come over here."

Harry was winded by the time he got to the building. Wit had already moved on well beyond the building to where a gradual down slope led toward the edge of the mountain. He stopped when he saw Harry and waited for him to catch up.

"Hurry, Mr. Harry. I want you to see." Wit pointed down the hill.

When Harry reached Wit, they walked together to the edge of the mountain. They were both breathing hard. Wit stopped by a large upright rock and pointed over the side of the mountain.

Harry lodged himself against the rock and peered down to the river far below. He saw the beach, but his eyes just skimmed over it. What drew him was a small helicopter buzzing above the beach like an angry insect.

The helicopter hovered, then dipped down toward the beach. Suddenly, as if it glimpsed the shadow of the flyswatter, it whirled away in a steep climb. It hovered some distance off, making up its mind, then dove for the beach again.

Shifting his eyes to the beach, Harry quickly spotted the source of its agitation. Pulled up on the beach were three long-tail boats. Another boat drifted slowly a few meters off shore. From where Harry stood, the boats looked like toys. All seemed to be empty. He scanned the brush near the beach and soon had a count of seven men and three more probables. As he continued to watch, he saw two tiny puffs of smoke rise from the brush where most of the men were gathered. The helicopter went into a steep climb. Taking ground fire, he thought.

With as much control as he could muster, he said to Wit, "You better try to find Aloysious. I'll stay here and keep my eye on things."

37

ow many did you count?" Aloysious stood by the rock and peered down at the river. The helicopter had veered off and abruptly departed the area just before Aloysious got there. There was no sign now of the men crouching in the brush. The only evidence that anything had occurred was three boats pulled up on the beach. The fourth rested on a sand bar where it had been carried by the current.

"About ten. Seven I was sure of," Harry answered.

"Four boats. Probably more like 20 of them down there. I'm surprised they let the boats just sit there. Probably send somebody back to guard them once they figure out what they're going to do. Could you tell if the chopper was police or military?"

"Police. Couldn't see the markings from here, but the paint job was white. All military birds are camouflage."

Aloysious leaned far out over the edge of the cliff. Harry grabbed for Aloysious's belt and braced himself against the rock. "Christ, you don't want to join them down there," he said.

Aloysious ignored him and kept looking. "I don't see a soul down there. Not one. The chopper must have scared them off." He pulled himself back from the edge. "Now the fun begins," he said.

"What do you figure they're doing down there?" Harry asked.

"Oh, they should be on their way up here."

"Will they find the way up?"

"Probably. Maybe not today. There's not enough daylight left. But sooner or later they will. They know we're up here. They'll figure if we got up here, they can. They'll find the way."

"You sure are casual about all this."

"I had a premonition, Harry. I knew this was all too good to last. Come on over here. We need to talk about what we're going to do."

They walked over to the base of one of the huge trees that grew here on top of the mountain and sat down.

267

"Not much daylight left," Aloysious said, "but maybe enough to do a couple of things. Harry, I think you should stay here. Somebody should keep track of what happens on the beach. We won't see much activity down there tonight. But we need to know what the Army has when it gets here."

"The Army? You're expecting the Thai Army?"

"Yeah, the Army will be here." Aloysious smiled when he saw that Harry seemed surprised. "Well, think about it," he said. "There are 20 or more bad guys down there. They're running through the trees, shooting at helicopters. Up here on the mountain are the master criminals – you, me, and Wit. Who else has the firepower to flush all the crooks out of the brush and to get us off the mountain? It will take a major operation. And more resources than the police have. It has to be the Army. God, I hope that if they use loudspeakers to flush us out they remember Wit's name."

"What are you going to do while I'm up here waiting for the Army?"

"Wit and I are going to take a walk down the hill. I want to take a look at the 'Holland Tunnel'. I want to see if there's a way to block it before the bad guys pour in."

"You need dynamite to do that," Harry said.

Aloysious said nothing, but he winked at Harry as he got to his feet. "Keep your eyes open, Harry. I don't think much will happen tonight. Come over to the library at sunset. I'll keep a cold beer on for you."

Harry moved back to where he could watch the beach. He found a place to sit near the big rock. He could see the river easily and if he craned his neck out just a bit, he could see the beach. Nothing moved. He wondered if the guys who came in the boats had brought anything to eat.

The light started to fade as the sun dropped slowly behind the mountain. The beach itself was in deep shadow, and Harry could no longer see anything down there. There seemed little point in staying hare now, but it was comfortable. There was a cool breeze and it felt good. He stayed there longer than he had reason to. Nothing would happen on the river tonight. At least nothing he could see from here. It was time to get that beer.

It was a bright night, but in the shadows of the trees he walked slowly, careful where he stepped. Approaching the library, he saw Aloysious and Wit coming from the opposite direction, each walking behind the bright beam of a flashlight. When they reached him, they were both breathing hard. In a stray beam from one of their lights he glimpsed their faces, streaked with sweat. They walked together to the library, and when they reached it, Aloysious dropped down on the bottom step. He sat for a while, holding his head in both hands.

"Wit, get us a beer," he asked wearily.

"Wit, stay there," Harry said. "I'll get it." Harry climbed the stairs to where he could reach the cooler. It was filled with water, and the cans were warm.

"Sorry," he said as he handed a beer to Aloysious, and another to Wit. "No ice left."

Aloysious took the can. "Like piss," he said. "Another long day." He tipped the can back.

"How did it go down there?" Harry asked.

Aloysious answered with a shrug. He took another pull at the beer. "Not too good. We'll know for sure in the morning. Anything happen on the river?"

"Not a thing."

"I'm bushed," Aloysious said. "We better rack out early tonight. There will be lots happening in the morning. We have to be ready."

Wit made spaghetti. Afterwards, Aloysious hauled sleeping bags out of the library where he had them cached, and they picked places to sleep around the cooking fire. Harry sprawled out on his sleeping bag and was starting to doze when something cold touched his arm. Startled, he sat up.

"Here. I saved you a cold one." Aloysious handed him an ice-cold can of beer.

"Where in the hell did you get that?" Harry asked.

"Don't ask, Harry. Just enjoy it."

Harry did. Then he fell into a sound but not dreamless sleep. In his dream he walked down the stone staircase following the great undulating Naga bodies down the mountain. At the bottom, he glimpsed a girl, standing just under the Naga's neck, coyly watching him. "Mouse," he said, and started toward her. He was close enough to touch her when the Naga's huge head erupted in an explosion that blew it into a thousand pieces.

KAPLOOOOOOW!

Harry bolted up. His ears were ringing. "Mouse," he said. It came out like a whimper. He looked around, almost frantic. The light was gray. Dawn was just starting to break. Wit and Aloysious were nowhere to be seen. The fire looked like it had gone out long ago. The explosion was no dream. His ears still rang from it.

Harry got to his feet. He had no idea where the sound had come from. Take your time, he said to himself. Think it through. He could see two possibilities. The river or the Naga stairs. Either the Army had arrived and was engaging the bad guys, or the bad guys had arrived and were engaging Aloysious. Good Christ! He started off at a fast jog for the overlook from where he could look down on the river. After 50 meters, he changed his mind and turned toward the Naga staircase. The dream must mean something.

He reached the top of the staircase in record time and started loping down the steps. He stopped suddenly, halfway down the first set of steps, when he spotted Wit. Wit was on the staircase, some distance farther down. He seemed to be coming up, but walking backwards.

As Wit got closer to him, Harry found it difficult to believe what he was seeing. Wit was walking up the stairs backwards. In his arms he held a large spool of wire that slowly unwound as he climbed the steps. Wit's shirt hung from his back in tatters. His hair was matted and covered with a layer of fine white dust. When he turned to Harry, his face was as white as his hair.

"Hallo, Mr. Harry," he said. "We wake you up, huh?"

"Wit! What the hell happened? What are you doing? Where's Aloysious?"

"I am unrolling this wire. Aloysious is down by the Naga. He is plugging the wire into the dynamite."

"What are you guys doing?" Harry asked incredulously. Even as he asked the question he turned to see a white figure moving up the staircase like an apparition. "Good Christ!" he said. Behind him Wit laughed. "Alo-wichit needs a bath," Wit said.

If Wit looked bad, Aloysious looked ten times worse. He was completely covered with the fine white dust. When he got closer, Harry could see his shirt was completely gone and his bare chest and back were snow white. When he reached Harry, Aloysious pointed up the stairs to Wit and laughed. "Look at Wit, Harry. It's bat shit. He's covered with it."

"Christ," Harry said. "You both look like you've been swimming in it. What the hell have you been up to?"

Through the layer of white dust on his face, Aloysious suddenly looked serious. "It didn't work the way I hoped. I wanted to knock down the rock where we climb into the 'Holland Tunnel'. But the rock face is too thin there. I was afraid I would just blow a big hole in it and make it easy for the bad guys to get in. I set some charges farther back. Thought I could collapse a part of the tunnel and close it down. Looks like all I did was to blow the batshit off the walls."

"That explosion was you? Where the hell did you get the dynamite?"

"Not dynamite. It was C-4. It's a lot more effective. Come on, walk me to the top, Harry. Wit's almost there. I have to get up there to rig the detonator."

Aloysious went on talking as they walked up the stairs together. "The Army should be getting here soon. You ought to get over to where you can see the beach. Hey, Wit! Is everything set up there?"

"Everything is ready, Alo-wichit."

"Good. Harry, I'll join you as soon as I finish here. I need to get cleaned up. Try to get a count of anybody on the beach."

Harry felt some of the excitement that Aloysious was generating. He started off quickly for the overlook. He trotted past the main temple and crossed the far side of the city at a half run. He was breathing hard when he reached the overlook. His concern was that he would get there too late and miss something down on the river.

It was quiet down there. Too quiet. The boats were gone. All four of them, including the one he had last seen grounded on the sand bar in the middle of the river. Harry scanned the brush behind the beach. There was nothing.

He was ready to conclude that they had all gone when he remembered Wit's boat. He looked for the two big rocks where they had hidden it on the bank. He found the rocks easily enough, but he could not quite make out the boat under the foliage they had piled on top of it. Then he realized it was a problem of scale. He was trying to see something smaller than what he was looking at. The space between the rocks was filled with more foliage than he and Wit had put there. Once he thought of it that way, he could just make out where there were three, and possibly four boats hidden in that space now.

The helicopter was there before he heard it. It appeared suddenly, banking over the bend in the river. Then it dipped low and buzzed over the beach. It was a bigger machine than the one that flew over the beach yesterday. It was also a lot harder to see it when it dipped down among the trees. It was painted in the drab camouflage colors of the Thai Army.

The machine made a second low pass over the beach that seemed to satisfy the crew that the beach was empty. The helicopter moved out over the middle of the river, where it hovered for a time. Then the machine started to rise, higher and higher in an almost vertical climb that brought it level with the top of the mountain. Harry looked into the cabin at the two faces looking at him. The helicopter slowly turned its nose toward him. Harry dropped behind the rock as the machine started toward him. It climbed higher as it came. When it passed over, it was high above him. The canopies of the huge trees on top of the mountain made it unlikely that the machine would get any closer.

"I see the Army's here."

It was Aloysious. With all the noise the chopper made, Harry never noticed him come up. Aloysious was wearing a fresh shirt. He looked cleaner, but Harry could still see traces of the fine white dust in the creases of his face.

"What's happening on the beach?" Aloysious asked.

"Not much," Harry answered, and told him where the boats were hidden.

Aloysious turned to stare down at the river. After a while he said, "Well, there they are. I told you so."

Harry looked down. Two other helicopters hovered low, just off the beach. Behind them, coming through the bend in the river was a convoy of small black rubber boats, each with at least a half dozen men in camouflage uniforms.

As the boats approached the beach, the first helicopter suddenly reappeared in the airspace high over the river, facing Harry and Aloysious, its nose pointed at them ominously. Harry was sure a machine gun was pointed at his chest.

Aloysious ignored the helicopter and hung over the edge watching the action below. "Christ, there must be over a hundred troops hitting the beach. That's more than we can handle." He turned around to look at Harry. "Look at the bright side. The bad guys will get to us before the Army does. Those guys we can do something about. Let's get back to Wit. He'll need some help before long."

As they started back Harry asked, "What about the choppers?"

"Don't worry about the choppers. There's not a square meter up here that doesn't have a tree branch hanging over it. Choppers can't land unless somebody cuts a landing zone. Harry glanced up at the vast canopy of overlapping trees that hung over them. Aloysious was right. They had nothing to worry about from that quarter.

They found Wit squatting at the top of the Naga staircase, looking intently toward the bottom.

"Anything happening, Wit?" Aloysious asked.

"I thought I heard a noise."

All three of them looked down. After a while they were sure there was nothing moving down there. Aloysious looked at his wristwatch. "It's only an hour since dawn. Nobody should be here for another two hours, at least. Anybody interested in breakfast?"

"I'm not hungry," Harry said. "I could use something to drink."

"I'll get you something," Aloysious said. "I have to go over to the library to get some stuff. Be right back."

Harry sat down at the top of the Naga staircase near Wit. Even now he was not too concerned. It was unreal to him. He had trouble convincing himself that anybody could get up the mountain and that in a little while they could be fighting for their lives. At the same time he was still not certain who was after them, or why. And now the Thai Army was marching on their position. Sweet Jesus, what was he doing in the middle of all this?

Near him, Wit was working industriously at something. Harry looked closer. Wit was stuffing tan putty into a small but obviously ancient bronze vessel. Nice piece, Harry thought, viewing it with a dealer's eye. Then it struck him. "Wit, what are you doing?" he asked, afraid of the answer he might get.

"Making a grenade. I fill it with this. Alo-wichit calls it See-for. We will roll it down the hill. There are more pots over there if you want to help."

Harry walked over to a small pile of bronze vessels stacked under a tree. Nearby, a wooden box was full of the small blocks of tan putty. Harry examined several of the vessels. They weren't masterpieces, but he would have prized any one of them. He looked up to see Aloysious walking up, a sack over his shoulder like the Santa Claus of the antiques world.

Aloysious dropped the bag with a metallic clatter. He reached into it and pulled out beer. "Here, Harry, ice cold."

It wasn't yet seven in the morning, but Harry took the beer. With his toe he prodded the bag Aloysious had dropped. "More pots?" he asked, trying to control his voice.

"Yeah, good ones. Got a couple in there small enough to toss like a baseball."

Harry could not hold it back. "I can't believe you're going to use antique bronze vessels to make grenades."

"We got a lot of them," Aloysious answered.

Harry felt weak. He sat down. "Look, before the shit starts, could you at least tell me who we're going to fight? And why?"

"Before I get into that, Harry, let me tell you guys what's going to happen here this morning. Wit, come on over here." They waited for Wit to walk over so Aloysious could begin his formal briefing.

"Wit, grab a beer. Harry, need another one? Okay, listen up. The enemy will come down the 'Holland Tunnel' in an hour or so. We have some charges at the bottom of the hill. We won't stop them there. All we want to do is scare them. Buy some time. After we blow the charges and roll some grenades down on them, we'll get out of here. We'll pull back to the bathing pool, and from there into the caves. Harry, you know the caves. Wit was in them last night. Once we get down in the caves, we seal up and sit tight. The Army will be in right behind the bad guys. The Army should clean them up real quick. Then – with a little luck – everybody will leave. We'll be home free. Any questions?"

Harry had one. "You're saying they're going to fight each other? And we stay off to the side and stay out of it. But aren't both these bunches looking for us, too? What if the Army doesn't finish quickly and go home?"

"They would still have to find us. They won't. Harry, don't sweat it. We can hold out here as long as we have to."

Wit raised his hand.

"Yeah, Wit," Aloysious asked. "What's your question?"

"I have no question, Alo-wichit. I heard shouting. I think the enemy is here."

Harry had a physical reaction to the news. Little animals started to fight in his stomach. The bones in his legs melted away. "Oh, shit," Aloysious said, and started to run for the staircase. Harry was right behind him without realizing he had moved.

Aloysious picked up the little black box with wires hanging from it. "Where are they, Wit?" he yelled.

"They are still by the tunnel, I think. I can't see them now."

Aloysious turned to Harry. "Can you be the forward observer?" he asked. "See if you can move down the hill a bit. Get down to where you can see the Nagas and see me from the same place. I need you to signal when they get to the Nagas. Pump your arm up and down three times when they get to the Nagas."

Without thinking about it, Harry started down the hill. He stayed clear of the staircase and walked on the ground, alongside the curvy balustrades that was the body of one of the Nagas. When he could see both of the big mounds that were the two great serpent heads, he looked back to assure that he was still in sight of Aloysious. Then he went down farther.

Finally he was sure he was where he could not miss seeing anyone start up the hill. Aloysious was far off, but still in sight. He waved. Aloysious waved back. As he crouched there waiting, it struck Harry that he should have asked where the charges were placed. It was too late now. He hoped he was well back from the blast zone.

The tunnel amplified any sound that came from it. Harry suddenly heard a babel of distant voices, but none distinctly. He kept low and watched. He could see beyond the Nagas, and watched for the first sight of the enemy.

One appeared. Then another. Then three more. They carried rifles and moved warily. They all looked tough, but wore no common uniform. Some had dressed for the jungle in tiger-striped camouflage. Others wore jeans and bright shirts. As they moved ahead, one looked up and saw the Naga head. He stared at it in astonishment. Then he called quietly to the others. They all started walking toward the Naga.

To Harry it seemed as good a shot as he would get. He raised his arm in the air, and pumped it up and down three times. The Naga head exploded into a thousand pieces.

KAPLOOOOOW.

Pieces of stone and tree rained down around him, none bigger than a pencil point. Nothing of any size struck him. He was covered in dust and shredded bits of leaves. Harry poked his head up, expecting to see a scene of great slaughter. The first thing that struck him about the scene was what was missing from – the Naga's great head was gone! Even as he looked on, small human heads popped up out of the grass. He did not even try to count heads. He was sure that the greatest and perhaps the only real damage that the explosives had caused was to the Naga. He turned and started back up the hill, keeping down as low as he could.

At the top, Aloysious waited, smug with success. "How did it look?" he asked eagerly.

"You pulverized it, goddamn it! You blew it into powder! How much of that stuff did you use?"

"How many did we get?"

"You may have scared a couple to death, but there wasn't a piece of stone big enough to kill a mosquito."

Aloysious looked stunned.

Wit came over to Harry and handed him a can of cool beer. As Harry drank from it to wash the dust out of his throat, he felt his anger rising in his chest. By the time he finished drinking, he was outraged. He put the beer down. Carefully.

"Aloysious," he said in measured tones, "I can't believe you did that. That Naga was there for a thousand years. It was almost perfect. And you blew it to shit! You fucking pulverized it! I can't believe that."

"I'm sorry, Harry. I must have overloaded the charge."

Before Harry could say more, Wit called. "Alo-wichit. They're coming up the steps."

"I'm coming, Wit," Aloysious said. He paused long enough to say, "We'll talk about it later. Come on, let's roll some ancient bronzes down the hill. You'll feel better for it."

Harry could not bring himself to roll any antique bronze vessels down the hill, but he did watch. Aloysious heaved the vessels as far out as he could, and they bounced and rolled farther down the hill before exploding ineffectually a good distance from their intended targets. While they seemed not to hurt anyone, the explosions did clear the hill of the enemy. Amid great commotion they all ran for the shelter of the tunnel after watching the first few pots explode.

It was all so unreal that Harry did not feel guilty about watching valuable old pots bursting in the air and scattering bronze shrapnel over a magnificent thousand-year old stone staircase. Once he even caught himself yelling "Good one!" when an old tripod vase bounced all the way to the bottom before blowing into smithereens. They could mourn the antiquities tomorrow – if they survived today.

"Let's get out of here," Aloysious said after he flung the last bronze high over the staircase. "There's nothing more we can do here."

The three of them turned and ran for the bathing pool and the entrance to the caverns.

38

Come into my parlor." Aloysious walked ahead of them through the caves and led them into a chamber filled with light from the outside. "Remember this, Harry? It's where we winched the stuff down to the beach. I've furnished it since you were here last." Aloysious said this with evident pride. Facing the opening in the cave, like a living room picture window, were a table and two benches. Looking closer at the arrangement, Harry saw that the tabletop was a long and ornately carved wooden panel. In a previous life it had probably been a temple door. It looked heavy and was set on the backs of two bronze elephants. The benches along its side were also old wood panels, probably shutters from the same ancient structure where the door had hung.

There were a couple of other "arrangements." A pair of stone Singhs with flattened backs that once had served as bases for a column or pillar were now end tables. Other creatures of stone or bronze that stood around the cavern seemed intended as seats.

"I did all this while you were screwing around in the States, Harry," Aloysious said. "It's not much, but it's home. Make yourself comfortable. Let me get you a couple of beers."

Aloysious left the room, and Harry joined Wit at the cave opening. The winch was still there, but it had been pulled back from the edge. Far below them was the river. There was a lot of activity down there now. They watched it until Aloysious reappeared. He carried a large round tray with three beer cans on it.

Aloysious set the beers on the table and passed the tray to Harry. It was a beautiful old thing, pure silver, and tarnished glossy black with age. A hunting scene was delicately etched into the center. Around the edge, in high relief and exquisitely detailed, ware the 12 animals of the horoscope.

"Isn't that nice?" Aloysious asked. "That's one I'm keeping for myself. I'll have to polish it up."

"Absolutely beautiful," Harry said. "It would be almost a shame to polish it. The patina is like black lacquer." As he put the tray down on the table, he reached for his beer. It was ice cold again. He turned to Aloysi-ous."I can't understand how you get the beer so cold."

"This is a cave, Harry."

Harry took a long slow pull at the can. When he finished he said, "It is cool in here, but not that cold. You must have a freezer hidden away."

Aloysious, enroute to the cave opening, mumbled something that Harry didn't catch.

Standing near the cave's mouth, but with his back to it, Aloysious pointed to a small area just inside that was lined with rocks. "This is where we'll cook. We'll have to be careful so they don't spot us in here. If the Army figures out where we are, we'll have a real problem." Aloysious turned to look down over the beach. Harry and Wit walked over to join him.

The riverbank looked like a military beachhead. An armada of rubber boats was pulled up on the beach. Others scurried back and forth on the river. A helicopter had landed farther up on the riverbank. Two others hovered protectively out over the river. Crates of supplies had been piled on the beach, and several boats were still being unloaded. Half a dozen tents were up, and a dozen radio antennas stuck high in the air.

"God Almighty," Aloysious said. "It looks like Normandy on D-Day. To think we are responsible for all of that."

He went to the table and picked up a beer. Eventually Harry and Wit joined him there. The three of them sat at the table and morosely drank their beer. The hardest part would be sitting there under the ground, while around them things would be going on that they could only guess at.

"What do you think is happening up on top?" Harry asked, pointing up with his beer can. All three of them looked up at the cave ceiling.

Aloysious shrugged. "They should be all over the place by now. Probably wondering where we are."

"How about the Army? When do you think the Army will get up on top?"

Aloysious wrinkled his brow. "Days. I think it will take them days. Unless the bad guys left a big trail behind them when they came up the mountain. The Army won't find it easy. Ultimately, if they can't get in any other way, I guess they would probably drop some guys in to cut a landing zone for the choppers. That would be chancy. Even with an LZ, the chop-pers could come under heavy fire getting in. With all those stone buildings up there, it will be hard as hell to root the bad guys out."

"How are we going to know when the coast is clear? So we can get out of here."

"Oh, we'll know. We can probably tell by what happens on the beach."

"The way the Army is building up supplies and equipment on the beach, I'd say they're planning to be here a while. They may never leave if they don't find us."

"I hope you're not right, Harry. We'll just have to wait and see."

A shadow passed over the room. Aloysious stood up. "Chopper just went by the window. Listen! Do you hear shooting?"

"Heard it. Must be somebody right over on top of us. Near the edge of the mountain. Shooting at the chopper."

That brief excitement had to last them for a couple of hours. The day dragged on. Aloysious came and went, leaving the room for long periods of time. Sometimes he came back with a small figure or a decorative wooden panel from an old shrine to show Harry. One memorable time he returned with their lunch, a piping hot antique pot full of steaming beef Bourguignon. It was savory stew with great looking potatoes. As they dug in, Harry caught Aloysious's eye, and put on his puzzled look.

"Freeze-dried combat rations." Aloysious said. "Courtesy of Pachyderm Tours, the gourmet tour company."

"Where the hell did you cook it? You weren't over by the rocks."

"Chemical fire in a can. All it takes is a boil. Don't worry about it, Harry. Just eat it. Want a beer? How about some red wine? I got a couple of bottles of French stuff squirreled away."

"Sure," Harry said, "why not? You have any French bread?"

"Sorry, Harry, fresh out of French bread."

Wit was eating the stew with the gusto he usually reserved for spaghetti with a nice Spam sauce. Aloysious poured the wine. It was good.

After their meal, Aloysious gave Harry a couple of novels to help kill the time. They were murder mysteries set in quaint little villages in the English countryside. Harry had long been convinced these villages were the most dangerous places on earth.

Time passed slowly, and Harry found it hard to concentrate on reading. Eventually he amused himself by wandering through the caves with a flashlight, looking at the incredible horde of art objects the caves contained. Here and there he saw pieces he remembered from his last visit. But the overwhelming number were things he had not seen.

Out of boredom Wit soon joined him. Wit said little, just looked on, quietly for the most part, but sometimes he identified a deity or one of the strange and fabulous beasts that had probably served as guardians in the temples. As Harry examined one of these more closely, Wit wandered off. A little while later he came back. "Mr. Harry," he said, "come with me."

Harry followed Wit to the center of the big chamber they were in. "Listen," Wit said.

They were both quiet. Harry heard something. It was muffled, and seemed to come from far away. Kling, kling, kling. Kling, kling, kling.

"What is it?" Wit asked. "Are they digging?"

"I don't know. Get Aloysious."

Wit was back in moments, Aloysious in tow. "What's going on?" Aloysious asked, rubbing sleep out of his eyes. "What's up?"

"Listen," Harry said.

They were all still. There was nothing. "What..." Aloysious started.

"Quiet," Harry said again. "There it goes." Kling, kling, kling.

"Oh, shit," Aloysious said immediately.

"What is it?"

"It's a chisel. Somebody cutting stone with a chisel. They're trying to get through the roof!"

It was Harry's turn. "Oh, shit," he said.

Aloysious stood still, head tilted back and grimly stared at the ceiling. After a while he said, "I need to find out more. You guys go back to the parlor. I need to poke around some.

"Let me come with you."

"Not this time, Harry. I need to think. Go back to the parlor. Take Wit with you. I'll see you there."

"Come on, Wit. We're not wanted here."

They went back to the chamber that was the living quarters. They looked down on the beach. The activity seemed to have increased. There were more people on the beach. As they watched, another helicopter landed, and several men got out.

"Sure is getting crowded out there," Harry said to Wit. There was no answer. Wit was gone. Harry shrugged and walked to the table. He sat down and picked up one of the novels. He tried reading, but after a few minutes gave up. Just then Wit walked in.

"What have you been up to, Wit? Seen Aloysious?"

"I think Alo-wichit went outside."

"He went out? Damn fool." Harry got to his feet and headed for the direction of the pool, where they had entered the caves.

"Alo-wichit did not go this way," Wit called after him.

Harry stopped in his tracks. "You said he went out."

"Yes, Alo-wichit went out. But not that way. He went over here."

Harry followed Wit into another chamber. They walked to the far wall where it was marked by a huge fissure.

"Alo-wichit went in there," Wit said. He added, "I don't like this place," summing up his feelings about the caves in general.

"I'd sooner be someplace else too, Wit," Harry said as he examined the fissure. It was big enough to walk through with no problem. At first look, it seemed to extend right through the floor. Looking closer, he saw that it was only a long step down. He shone his light straight ahead. Although it looked as if the fissure ended about six feet inside the rock face, it now appeared to him that it simply took a sharp turn to the left.

Harry stepped into the fissure. After three steps he knew he was right. The wall right ahead was not the end of the trail. It turned sharply to his left. He followed the turn and walked into a narrow shaft that led up. On the wall farthest from him was a ladder, fixed into the wall.

He looked at the ladder closely. He struck it lightly with the flashlight. From the sound of it, it was metal. He followed the ladder up with his light. At the top a square plate of some kind was fixed in the ceiling.

Harry started up the ladder. Near the top he reached up to touch the plate. He shoved. It was heavy, but it gave easily. The sunlight almost blinded him.

He wasted no time. He shoved the plate aside and scrambled to the top of the ladder and into the sunlight. He crouched low on a stone floor next to the opening he had just crawled through. The plate he had pushed out of the way looked like stone on the top, but it had a metal base. He looked around. He was in a structure of some kind. Sunlight streamed through open windows. He started to get to his feet to see better.

"Keep your head down, Harry. They'll blow it off." Aloysious was near, and his voice was not as loud as usual. Harry turned to look behind him. Aloysious was in the shadow near one of the windows. He waved one hand at the floor. "Stay down, Harry. You don't want them to see you." On his hands and knees Harry crawled over to him.

"If you want to see them, stick your head up slowly," Aloysious said when Harry reached him. "Stay near the corner of the window."

Harry moved close to the stone wall and brought his head up very slowly. Out in the courtyard, not 100 meters away, were a dozen men standing in a rough circle and staring intently down into a hole. After watching for a while and seeing nothing change, Harry ducked back down.

"I guess that's where they're digging. Where the hell are we?"

"We're in the library. Right where we camped last night. They're too interested in other things right now, but keep your eye on that door just in case. I want to look some more." Aloysious stuck his head back up.

Harry looked at the open doorway. They were a good distance above the courtyard. Sitting in the shadows inside the building, they would not be easily seen by a casual passerby, but their position was vulnerable. He hoped Aloysious would hurry.

"Shit. Look at that!" Aloysious said.

Instinctively, Harry stuck his head into the window to look. The men who had been standing around the hole were running now. Wildly. In all directions.

KAPLOOOOW!

The hole erupted, puking a great gush of black smoke and pulverized earth into the air. Some of the running men were knocked off their feet. Several others kept running, but faster, as if hurried along by the blast. Dust, dirt, and clumps of ground rained down on them.

"Harry," Aloysious said. And again, "Harry!" Harry finally heard and looked at him. "Get down there. Quick!" Aloysious pointed to where Harry came through the floor. "See if they cut through the roof of the cave."

Harry clambered down the ladder. For a moment he couldn't see. He groped in his pocket for the flashlight and flicked it on. When he reached the bottom, he called for Wit. There was no response. He flashed the light around. Everywhere its beam picked up heavy dust. The air was full of it.

He went to the big chamber where they had heard the digging, half expecting to find daylight streaming in. There was nothing. He turned off his light. It was pitch black.

He flicked on the light again, and beamed it toward the ceiling in the center of the cave. There was at least one large jagged crack, but nothing that seemed ready to come down.

"Wow," Harry said aloud to himself. "Wow. Wow. Wow," the cave repeated back to him. As he listened, he realized he was breathing hard. He wanted to get back to Aloysious, but he needed to catch his breath first. "Wit!" he shouted. "Wit, Wit, Wit," the cave repeated. And then...

"Mr. Harry! Mr. Harry! Where are you?"

"Over here, Wit. Where they were digging."

The beam of his flashlight preceded Wit through the entrance to the chamber. "Mr. Harry, what happened? It sounded like dynamite."

"It was dynamite, Wit. Up above. Let's get out of this place." They headed for the room with the fissure. Aloysious was at the bottom of the ladder.

"How's it look down here?" Aloysious asked.

"They didn't get through, but there's a crack in the ceiling."

"Let's go sit in the parlor," Aloysious said. "Everything is secure here. I need a beer."

Wit pulled some lukewarm beers from the styrofoam cooler. They sat at the table, holding their beer cans, waiting for Aloysious to say something.

Finally, Aloysious spoke. "Thank God for a lack of talent," he said. "The boneheads up there set a pretty big charge, but they didn't tamp it down with anything. The explosion wasn't directed into the ground. It just blew up in the air." Aloysious took a pull of his beer. "We're goddamn lucky."

"Do those guys have more explosives?" Harry asked.

"I don't know. I didn't see any, but they wouldn't drag all they had over to where they were using it." Aloysious stared down at the top of the table, saying nothing for a long time. When he finally raised his head, he looked at Harry and sighed.

"Shit," he said. "We may have a real problem, Harry. If those guys have more C-4, sooner or later they're going to get it right. All they need is one good one. In fact, it doesn't even have to be a good one. A half-assed one could blow the roof in. Then they'll have us like fish in a barrel."

"If the Army gets here in time...."

"I don't know if the Army is going to be much help to us. Once they grab those guys, there will be some frantic plea-bargaining going on. Then the Army will dig for us."

Aloysious started to his feet. He got halfway, and sat back down. He looked at Harry and then at Wit. "Harry," he said, "Wit. One thing I want you guys to know. We do have a fallback. If everything goes to shit, we're out of here. We're not going to be caught down here like trapped rats. But we can't use our final option until that's all we have. You understand what I mean? Wit? Harry, you better translate for Wit."

Wit had not looked pleased since they made their move underground. When Harry finished his translation, Wit shrugged and said fine. Then he added, "Wouldn't it be good to go now, while there is still time?"

"Better translate it again, Harry," Aloysious said and started to his feet again.

"Wait a minute," Harry said. "Wit has a good point. And there's another thing that bothers me. That ladder that leads up to the library. The damn thing is made of steel!"

"Steel, Harry? Steel? Did you look at it closely? Maybe it's bronze. Or some kind of alloy."

"Aloysious, don't bullshit me. That thing is steel. Even if it weren't, I've never heard of a ladder in an old Khmer structure, bronze or steel."

"Shit, Harry, don't we have more important things to worry about?"

As if to emphasize the point, a sound came to them faintly from far away. Kling, kling, kling. Kling, kling, kling.

"Oh, shit," said Aloysious. "Here we go again. Come on Harry. Let's go."

They headed right for the ladder. On the way up Aloysious said, "I gotta see if they're setting another charge. If they are, it may be all over for us."

Harry was right behind Aloysious. Aloysious lifted the panel in the ceiling and daylight flooded in. "Watch your head up there," Aloysious said, and pulled himself through the opening.

Harry peeked through the window at the hole. Only three men were there now, and none was looking into the hole. In fact, they had their backs to the hole. All three were crouched down low, rifles at the ready. They were looking up, up into the trees.

"Over there," Harry heard Aloysious say. His voice was a whisper. "Do you see it? Do you see the crate? They have more C-4."

Harry saw the crate. When he turned back, he saw Aloysious looking back over his shoulder, watching something through the window at the back of the library. Aloysious put his head down and on hands and knees crawled to the back window. "Harry, come look at this," he said a moment later.

Harry crawled to the window. He could see the peaked top of another building. Beyond it, visible every few seconds when it was not obscured by the tree canopies, was a helicopter. It was moving slowly, and below it, having already penetrated the tops of the trees, was a man rappelling down a rope that hung from the belly of the helicopter.

"The first guy's down already," Aloysious said. "If those two stay alive, they'll cut an LZ and the choppers will come in. I think it's time for us to get out of here."

Harry turned and was ready to start back when he heard the sound of someone coming up the stone steps to the library. A hat appeared at the entrance, then a fat soft-looking face. The man stooped and peered in. "Who's there?" he asked in Thai, squinting into the shadows where he could not quite make them out.

"Quick, you fool," Harry ad-libbed in his best Thai, "Run to the temple. Reinforcements are needed there immediately." Without a word, the man turned and was gone. They heard his footsteps moving rapidly across the courtyard. Aloysious sat with his back against the wall, the pistol in his hand pointed at the entrance. "I don't know who's luckier," he said, "him or us." Behind them was a rapid burst of gunfire. A helicopter whirred by overhead. There was another burst of gunfire, longer this time.

"Choppers firing through the trees. Covering fire for the guys they just put down." Aloysious peered through the window toward the hole. "Scared the pee out of them. They're running somewhere. Come on, Harry, let's get out of here. The Army just bought us time. We gotta use it."

At the bottom of the ladder Aloysious said, "Find Wit. Make sure he stays with you. Take him to the parlor."

"Where are you going?"

"I'm going to review our final option. See you later."

Harry found Wit in the parlor, sitting on a stone elephant where he could watch the river.

"Oh, Mr. Harry," Wit said when he saw him, "there are a lot of Army people, many helicopters, big operation." Wit whistled. "Very expensive. I hope Alo-wichit has a good plan to get us out of here."

"Don't sweat it, Wit. Alo-wichit always has some kind of scheme in his back pocket."

"Will we leave soon?"

Harry was thinking about what to say when Aloysious walked in, carrying the old silver tray. "Taking longer than I thought. Some tidbits for you guys. Eat the ice cream before it melts." Aloysious set the tray on the table.

On the tray was a dish of thinly sliced ham and another of smoked salmon. A third dish held crackers, and the fourth contained capers, onions, and other condiments. In the center stood two parfait glasses filled with chocolate ice cream, Aloysious's favorite.

"Don't tell me that's freeze-dried," Harry said, but Aloysious was already gone. Harry threw his hands in the air. "Life has never made a lot of sense to me, Wit," he said, but Wit had started on the ice cream and was not paying any attention.

After they finished the ice cream, salmon, and ham, Harry felt guilty because it was all good and Aloysious had not had any. It was well over an hour since they had last seen him.

"Wit, stay here. I'm going to see if Aloysious needs any help."

Harry was concerned that Aloysious might have gone up the ladder again. When he reached the ladder he was undecided, but finally he went up. Very carefully he pushed aside the plate that covered the floor of the library. He stuck his head out slowly and looked around. There was no one in the building.

He stayed there a while, listening. He could hear gunfire, the occasional pop of a rifle, and once a long burst from an automatic weapon. He raised himself up so that he could see the hole through the window. No one was near the hole. He dropped back down.

In the cave he wandered aimlessly through the rooms, throwing his light on treasures stacked like cordwood. He sat down in the lap of a bronze deity and turned off his light. It was incredibly dark and quiet. He let himself relax. After a while he felt as if he was floating to the ceiling. The darkness was absolute. The silence was absolute, except for a small sound from faraway that he recognized as Aloysious's voice. He concentrated on the voice and started to make out words.

"Seaweed, Seaweed. Lobster, Lobster. Seaweed, Seaweed. Lobster, Lobster."

It was like a prayer. The same words repeated over and over. Finally, it got the best of him. He got off the comfortable bronze lap. He turned his light on and went in the direction of Aloysious's voice, which, like a mantra, repeated over and over, "Seaweed, Seaweed. Lobster, Lobster."

39

Harry found the door by following a faint glow of light that came from the darkest corner of the cavern. There he found a small natural alcove that extended beyond the cavern's main chamber. The door was set into a wall of the alcove. It had a rough finish and was of a dull brown-black color that blended into the rock. The door would have been all but impossible to see but for the small pool of light that seeped past the front edge of the door where it had been left open just a tiny crack.

He put his hand on the door. It was metal and heavy, like something that hung on the front of a bank vault. He curled his fingers around the edge and gave it a good yank. The door swung open smoothly. It was much easier than he expected, and never made a sound.

"Oh, Harry. Come on in."

A single step took Harry from darkness into a room bathed in blinding white light. He felt he had stepped into a big white enamel medicine cabinet. Everything was orderly and sterile looking. Whoever designed it loved spotlights and the color white.

At a white metal desk, overloaded with an impressive array of electronic equipment, sat Aloysious. Lining the walls on either side of him were equipment racks crammed with esoteric-looking instruments, and rows of computer monitors and TV screens. A low hum of smoothly running machinery was in the air.

"Make yourself comfortable, Harry. There's more ice cream back there." Aloysious pointed at the door at the far end of the room. "There's beer, too. Help yourself."

A sharp crackle of static from the equipment in from of him grabbed Aloysious's attention. "Excuse me a minute, Harry." Aloysious bent toward the microphone on the desk before him.

"Seaweed. Seaweed. This is Lobster. Lobster. Seaweed. Seaweed. Lobster. Lobster."

Despite the rush of emotion that seemed about to overwhelm him, Harry could not suppress a smile. "That must be the dumbest call sign I ever heard."

"I didn't pick it," Aloysious shot back, defensively. He turned back to the microphone, repeating it again. "Seaweed, Seaweed. This is Lobster, Lobster. Do you read me? Over." There was no response, nothing, not even the crackle of static.

"Nobody home?" Harry asked.

"No, and I don't understand it. This has always worked before. Somebody should be listening on this frequency." Aloysious went back to his chanting.

Harry walked around the room, looking at the equipment in the racks. He turned a switch below one screen and was rewarded with a Thai soap opera. At the end of a short passage flanked by equipment racks was the door that Aloysious had pointed to. Harry opened it.

Just as he suspected, right inside the door stood a huge, upright freezer. There was a refrigerator next to it, a microwave oven nearby, and what looked like a dishwasher. There were cases and cases of beer, and other cases of what seemed mostly to be Scotch and cognac. The room was lined with rows of shelves heavy with boxes and cans of food. Most of the labels were Japanese. Harry was trying to decipher some labels when a shout from Aloysious brought him back to reality.

"Get us a couple of beers. There's a stereo in there if you want to turn on some music."

Harry took the beers and some potato chips, and walked back into the radio room. The incongruity of the scene astounded him. There sat Aloysious, in a chrome and black leather executive chair in this improbable high-tech cell that had been set in the caverns below an ancient city. At that moment Aloysious was as close to a mad scientist in a movie as Harry ever wanted to get.

"Tell me, Doctor Frankenstein," Harry said, handing him a cold beer. "Is this where we create our ancient arts? Or is this simply the Pachyderm Tours Remote Command Center?"

Aloysious swivelled around to face him. "You must have expected this. You must have figured most of it out, Harry." Aloysious gestured at the ceiling. "It looks like it's all over now. They're not going to give up until they find us down here. You may as well know all of it."

"I probably haven't figured out as much as you think I have," said Harry with more than a little modesty. He realized now that he had no idea of what was going on, but he knew that displaying his ignorance would not induce Aloysious to say any more. He would have to bluff it out.

"I knew you had a freezer down here, somewhere," Harry said, holding up the one straw he had managed to grasp. He scraped together all the

confidence he could muster and put it into his voice. "That meant a gener-
ator," he went on, stating the obvious. "From there on, it was extrapola-
tion." Harry punctuated this last sentence with a modest shrug. Aloysious
just nodded. Then Harry made a calculated guess. "Did Sato buy off on all
of this?" He put the stress on "all."

"Oh, shit, no!" Aloysious said with a snort. "Sato liked the idea. At least
he liked it at first. My original scheme was a hell of a lot simpler than all of
this." Aloysious waved a hand at the equipment racks. "God, we sure went
a long way past that."

"What did you originally propose to Sato?" Harry asked.

"Only that I wanted to make antiques. Good antiques. When I first had
the idea and started looking for markets, a Japanese guy I know put me on
to Sato. Sato doesn't like to do small-scale, one-of-a-kind stuff. But I told
him my scheme anyway. He got caught up with the idea of selling expensive fakes to collectors. He figured a serious collector who couldn't tell a
fake piece from a real one deserved to get suckered. Sato was willing to
support my original scheme if I could work it on a large scale. I told him
that was okay by me. But then some of Sato's friends in Tokyo got involved. When that happened, we really started thinking big."

"Those guys up above, the ones trying to dig us out of here. Why are
they so pissed off?"

"Well, some of them were part of my original fake antique cooperative.
I mean, when all this got started, we had a modest operation. We were
going to do a few pieces, do them really well, and sell them at good prices.
I scaled that up for Sato. Then Sato's Tokyo friends got involved, and we
really went big scale. I had to find more workers, more artists, more everything. Everybody worked their ass off. Everybody got paid well. Everybody
was happy. Then we started to hear rumors about how much money the
Japanese were going to make off this operation."

Harry recalled Colonel Sornchai talking about rumors, something that
Harry did not understand at the time. "What rumors?" he asked. "Something that got started after Jean Lee and I started marketing the stuff
abroad?"

"No, no," Aloysious said wearily. It was before that. It was when the
Japanese managers from Tokyo started dealing with the Hong Kong Chinese.

"The Hong Kong Chinese? The Chinese are involved?"

"Sato thought it was premature. He didn't want to deal with the Chinese until after you and Jean Lee did your thing. In retrospect, he was
right. The Tokyo bosses overrode him. The young guys from Tokyo – the
managers – they wanted to sell the whole goddamn thing to the Chinese.
Right from the start. Sate said, wait. But the whole thing started turning
into a billion-dollar deal. That was all the young Japanese guys could think
about. One goddamn billion dollars. Imagine that in yen, Harry. I can't

even count that high."

"Wait," Harry pleaded. "Wait. You're losing me. I don't understand how the Chinese were going to buy everything. Let me backtrack a bit. Make sure I have it right. When you got started, your cooperative produced good fake antiques. Then you hauled those antiques up here...."

Aloysious interrupted. "No, no, Harry. Maybe some were hauled up here. But most of them were made here. Right on site."

"Really!" Harry shook his head as if to clear it. He thought about this for a moment, then started again. "So...you salted the caves here with fake antiques. That would explain some of the pieces Karlo got. And I guess some of what is here in the caves right now is fake. Am I right so far?"

"Yeah, more or less. The smaller pieces you and Jean Lee showed to your customers were mostly fakes. There were supposed to be more real pieces in that group. I had them lined up here when we were loading them. You accidentally switched them around when you loaded the boat."

"What about the big pieces, the ones we took pictures of and showed to customers?"

"Oh, those were all fakes, Harry."

Harry had a vision of Karlo doing terrible things to him. Another picture flashed by. Buzz Dorkin's big silver airplane at 12 o'clock high started a steep dive toward him. "Christ! You mean...." His mouth was dry. The words would not come.

"Harry, you gotta understand," Aloysious said impatiently, leaning toward him. "This is all fake. Everything you see up here is fake. That neat silver tray I showed you this morning. One of Sato's chemists worked out the patina on that. We can make any silver piece you have look just like that. A thousand years of patina in five minutes."

"Everything is fake," Harry said feebly. "And the Japanese were going to sell it in Hong Kong for a billion dollars."

"Well, the price included the city too. You have to factor that in."

"The city!" Harry said. "The city! The Japanese were going to sell an ancient Khmer city to the Chinese?"

"Actually, I think it was some kind of ultra long-term lease," Aloysious said, wrinkling his brow. "Black Lion Enterprises owns leases on land all over this part of Thailand."

"Jesus Christ, Aloysious. You were the one who discovered this city. That's something for the history books. And you let the Japanese exploit you like that?"

Aloysious stared at him quietly for a moment, looking puzzled. Then he brought his fist down hard on the top of the desk and started to laugh. He tried to say something to Harry, but his body shook so hard he could not get it out. When his laughter finally subsided, Aloysious pulled a handkerchief out of his pocket and wiped his face.

"Harry," he said. "Son of a bitch! Now I know what pissed you off so bad when I blew up the Naga. You thought it was real! You think this place is real. An honest-to-god ancient thousand-year-old Khmer city. Harry, you better sit down."

Harry didn't sit down. His body no longer felt capable of movement. He stood and stared at Aloysious, absolutely speechless. He was starting to see where this was leading and hoped he was wrong.

"We built this city, Harry," Aloysious said proudly. "Me, my stonecutters, and a couple of hundred Japanese. We worked on top of this bloody mountain for almost two years."

"The city's not real?" Harry asked, his mind trying to grasp the enormity of what Aloysious was saying. "I can't believe that," he said and looked dumbly around for something to sit down on. Aloysious pushed a chair toward him with his foot.

"It's no more real than all those statues down here," Aloysious said. "So why not sell it to the Hong Kong Chinese?"

"Look, Harry," Aloysious continued when Harry did not answer. "You have to understand my original scheme and how it evolved. My idea was just to make some nice antiques. When Sato became my partner, all that changed was that we produced more pieces than I originally planned. But that was it. Period. The quality stayed the same. Now – and this is important, Harry – it's a clever twist. I knew that if we started selling fake antiques on a large scale, the market would react. Where the hell was all this stuff coming from? Any collector, any good art dealer would spot a big new flow of stuff and ask that question. My solution was...well, Sato said it was absolutely brilliant. My idea was to create a small archeological find. A cache of old stuff somebody found up in the hills. Maybe even a small stone temple to go with it. Did you hear that, Harry? I said a 'small' temple. When the guys in Tokyo got hold of it, they turned my modest temple scheme into a whole goddamn city."

"Jesus. You guys built a whole city," was all Harry could say.

"Yeah, we built a city, Harry. You should have seen it. We had hundreds of people up here. My guys did most of the stonework. We choppered them in. They lived here for months at a time. They weren't supposed to know where they were, and I don't think most of them ever figured it out. Until now. We even made a lot of these caves, quarrying stone to build the city. Sato's friends brought in a lot of guys from Tokyo. Engineers and even some fancy Japanese stonecutters. Most of the Japanese were what they called 'specialists'. They were technicians who knew how to make things look old."

Aloysious sighed heavily. "And we had Japanese guys with the suits. Managers. Bean counters. Art gave way to high finance. Just making and selling antiques wasn't good enough for them. As time went on, I think what they wanted from all this was a kind of 'Antiquity Land', a real ancient city that would be a major tourist attraction. Down on the river they had plans for hotels. Even a massage parlor. They were going to run boat tours on the river. The money they made from all that would be supplemented by the antique 'gallery' in the caverns. And boutiques. They were going to put boutiques down here. A food court, too, I think. And, of course, there would have been major international sell-offs of the stone carvings and bronzes that were 'found' here in the caves. Anyway, I thought that was all pretty neat."

Harry sat and listened, his eyes wide with astonishment. He waited for more. It came. Aloysious went on. "After our work up here was well under way, somebody finally figured out that the Thai government is too serious about its antiquities to let something like this go on. The Thais sure weren't going to let somebody "find" an ancient city and blatantly exploit it. Shit, I could have told the Japanese that. But they never asked me."

"So then they decided to sell it to the Hong Kong Chinese," Harry said.

"Yeah. Yeah, it had to go. The Japanese were suddenly like a fire sale. Dump everything or lose a lot of money. And I mean a lot of money, Harry. They looked around to see who had enough money to buy a city lock, stock and barrel. There aren't many people in the world with that much money who want to buy an old city. Even if it was real. They found these Chinese guys up in Hong Kong. They must have told them a good story. Or maybe the Hong Kong guys were brash enough to think they could run a tourist operation here where the Japanese could not." Aloysious ended his last sentence with a shrug.

Harry felt sick, but he could not let it go now. Aloysious was not always so talkative. If he could not get to the bottom of it now he would never know. "Where did I fit into all this?" he asked. "If everything was being sold to the Chinese, why did I start to sell the stuff in the States? And Jean Lee in Europe?"

"Credibility. We needed credibility. I had you factored in from the beginning, Harry. Under my original scheme you and Jean Lee were our sales force, marketing our product in America and Europe. When the scheme evolved, you two became even more important to the Tokyo guys. They weren't interested in selling individual pieces just for the sake of selling them. To them, the real pay-off – the big money – would come from selling the city. To do that, they needed somebody to stir up the art world. They needed real sales in the world market. It didn't matter how discreet you guys were. Word had to get around the world art market that a huge new cache had been found somewhere in Thailand, and that you guys were selling from it. The Tokyo guys helped get the word out through big-time dealers in Japan and a few in Hong Kong. Once the 'new find' in Thailand was accepted as real, the city's credibility with the Hong Kong Chinese was established."

"Incredible," Harry mumbled.

"Isn't it!" Aloysious said. "I won't take credit for the whole thing – I really can't. But the original scheme was mine."

Harry sat at the table, a shaken man. "So here we sit," he said so quietly that Aloysious had to lean closer to hear. "Under a faux city. In caves filled with phony antiques. Above us some disgruntled stonecutters are trying to dig us out. With dynamite. Because they got cut out of the company profit-sharing plan."

Not dynamite, Harry," Aloysious corrected. "It's C-4 they're trying to dig us out with. "It's left over from our building project. C-4 is a hell of a lot more effective than dynamite. Anyway, they're not all stonecutters. Some are just competitors who think I cut them out of something lucrative when I signed up with the Japanese. A lot of those guys just don't like the Japanese, you know. They think the Japanese are devious. Maybe with good reason."

Aloysious swiveled around in his chair to face the radio again. "But you reminded me. I got to get us out of here."

40

S eaweed, Seaweed," Aloysious repeated into the microphone. "This is Lobster, Lobster. Do you read me? Over." Aloysious continued the incantation through many repetitions until his voice grew hoarse. The only response was silence. Finally he turned back to Harry.

"Christ, Harry. I'm getting worried. I've been trying to raise Black Lion. They're supposed to have somebody on this frequency whenever I'm up here on the mountain. But I'm not raising anybody."

"Maybe they don't know you're up here. Besides, what can Black Lion do for us now?"

"They'll get us out of here. Sato has a very efficient bunch in Bangkok. They're not like the Tokyo guys."

"If Sato's so goddamned efficient, how the hell did everybody get into this mess?"

"I told you, Sato gave up control of the scheme. He said to hell with it, once the Tokyo guys expanded it to build the city. The Tokyo guys ran it. Sato was keeping his eye on it as a favor to somebody. He was helping out where he could."

Harry mulled this over. "You're saying Sato pulled back from it when it got too big. But you stayed on."

Aloysious shrugged. "I needed the money, Harry. I was already in this thing pretty deep by then. What the hell else was I going to do?" He turned back to the radio.

"Seaweed, Seaweed. This is Lobster, Lobster. Do you read me? Lobster, Lobster. Please, are you there?" Aloysious turned to Harry. "The Tokyo guys set up the radio link. They picked the call signs. You know how the Japanese love seafood."

"Too bad we don't have a telephone," Harry said sarcastically. "Might be more efficient."

Aloysious snapped his fingers. "That reminds me," he said. "Did you meet that neat little trick that Sato has? Did she talk to you before you left Bangkok last week?"

295

"Neat little trick? I know all kinds of neat little tricks. Which one?"

"You must have met her. Nice little girl. Young. The one Sato sometimes has playing at being a massage girl."

"Mouse?" Harry blurted out. "You mean Little Mouse?"

"Yeah, that's the one. You did meet her! Did she give you a way to contact her?"

"She gave me some phone numbers."

"Did you call her?"

"I called her a few days ago. The night before we went into the village to get Ting and Tong."

"What did you tell her?"

"For Christ's sake, Aloysious..."

"Come on, Harry. I'm not trying to pry. Did you tell her you would call her again? Or what?"

"I think I told her I would try to call her in a couple of days. In fact, I told her that if she didn't hear from me, she should have Sato come looking for us."

"Couple of days, huh? Harry, you're a genius!" Aloysious swiveled back to the radio. "Let me try something else," he said and twirled some knobs. He started to chant again, a little differently this time.

"Yellow Fin, Yellow Fin. This is Lobster. Do you read me? Yellow Fin, come in please. Puh-leees come in."

The response was almost instantaneous and as clear as if the speaker had stuck his head in the door. In lightly Japanese-accented English, Yellow Fin responded. "Lobster, this is Yellow Fin. I read you loud and clear. How do you read me? Over."

"You are loud and clear, Yellow Fin. Lobster is at Coral Reef. Our position here is deteriorating rapidly. Lobster and two fish need to evacuate as soon as possible. Request Yellow Fin execute Option Four. Repeat. Execute Option Four. As soon as possible. Do you read me? Over."

"This is Yellow Fin. I read Lobster and two fish need to evacuate. Yellow Fin will execute Option Four. Yellow Fin is ten minutes from Coral Reef. Repeat ten minutes. Yellow Fin will contact you one minute from your position. Do you copy? Over."

"I got you, Yellow Fin. Lobster will stand by for next contact in nine minutes. Lobster out." Aloysious put the microphone down. "We're on our way, Harry. Yellow Fin is Sato's chopper. Sato must have sent him up into this area when you didn't call your girlfriend back."

"Sounds great," Harry said. "But where the hell is he going to pick us up?"

"Up on top. We worked out an evacuation plan a long time ago. I insisted on it. Let's find Wit and get going. Take along anything you need. We won't be seeing this place again. First, give me a minute to get my shit together."

Aloysious hurried into the back room. He was back in less than a minute, carrying two small bags in one hand and a portable radio transmitter in the other. "My escape kit," he explained. "Now let's get out of here."

They moved quickly through the caves to the cavern Aloysious called the parlor. Wit was stretched out on a sleeping bag, sound asleep. "Come on, Wit," Aloysious prodded him with his foot. "Time to go home."

With Wit wide awake, they headed through the caverns for the steel ladder. At the bottom, Aloysious held them back for a moment. "Let me go up and look." Aloysious climbed up the ladder carefully and pushed the steel plate aside. He poked his head up into the daylight and kept it there for what seemed a long time. Finally, he pulled himself back inside and looked down at them. "Coast is clear," he said. "Come on up."

"We're lucky," Aloysious said when they joined him crouching on the library floor. "Everybody seems to be over at the main temple complex. Harry, give me those bags."

From one of the bags Aloysious pulled what looked like a miniature ladder. The "ladder" proved to be blocks of explosive tied between two long pieces of rope. Aloysious put it aside and picked up the radio. "Yellow Fin, Yellow Fin. This is Lobster. Do you read me over?" There was only silence.

"He's not ready yet," Aloysious said. "Okay, guys, listen up. Yellow Fin will bring the chopper into the area from the other side of the mountain. He will be opposite the river and down low. That's part of Option Four. Worst Case. The way he's coming in, the Army choppers won't see him until it's too late. What we need to do is cut a Landing Zone. This is what will do it."

Aloysious held up the explosive "ladder." "I'll wrap this around that big tree over there," he said and pointed to one of the huge trees that grew near the side of the library. "The tree will topple away from the library. The space it leaves will be big enough for Yellow Fin to land. Any questions?"

Harry had one. "What if the tree doesn't go down the way you want?"

"It will. We tested it when we set up this plan. Now, let me try Yellow Fin again."

"Yellow Fin, Yellow Fin. Lobster, Lobster. Do you read me?"

"Lobster, this is Yellow Fin. I am standing by. Orbiting one minute from Coral Reef. Please advise when you are ready. Over."

"Yellow Fin. Stand by. I will advise when we are ready. Over." Aloysious turned to Harry. "It's time to wrap this around the tree. It will take me a minute to get it right. You and Wit keep watch. Give me covering fire if I need it." Aloysious pushed his pistol toward Wit. Harry had his own pistol ready. He cocked it. Aloysious crouched low and headed down the library steps.

Harry looked out over what he could see of the city from the window. There was no one to be seen. The sound of sporadic gunfire came from the direction of the temple complex. It had died down to an occasional unenthusiastic pop. He looked to where Aloysious was working on the tree. The rope ladder of explosives was stretched around the trunk, but Aloysious seemed to be having trouble tying it down. Finally, it looked secured. Aloysious looked up at the sky. He turned back to the ropes and tugged them back and forth until he had the "ladder" just where he wanted it. He turned toward Harry.

"I left the radio up there." His voice was a loud raspy whisper. "Tell Yellow Fin we're ready. Tell him to start his run."

Harry picked up the radio and pressed the transmit button. "Yellow Fin. This is Lobster. We are ready. Please start your run. Do you read me? Over."

There was a long silence. Then, finally: "Lobster, this is Yellow Fin. Did you transmit? I have transmission that does not sound like Lobster."

This was no time to argue. Harry pressed down hard on the button. "Yellow Fin, this is Big Fish. Repeat, Big Fish. Lobster One is preparing LZ. Start your goddamn run! Now! Over."

"Big Fish. This is Yellow Fin. Starting run...now!"

Aloysious was down on his knees, impatiently watching Harry. When he saw Harry stick his thumb in the air, Aloysious turned his full attention to the face of his wristwatch. His right hand grasped a plastic cigarette lighter.

After what seemed like a long time, he touched the lighter to the fuse. When he saw it smoking, he flipped the lighter over his shoulder, lurched to his feet, and started running for the library.

"Get down!" he yelled. "Short fuse!" He cleared the last step and sprawled full length on the floor next to Harry and Wit.

BLOOOOOM!

Harry went deaf. Almost. He could still hear Aloysious. "Come on! Come on!" Aloysious sounded far away. There was a clear space now where the tree had been. Beyond the space was a tangle of tree limbs and leaves where the huge canopy had crashed to the ground. Aloysious stood at the top of the steps, waving his arm and yelling. "Come on, come on! Goddamn it!" Like Harry, Wit stared dumbly out the window to where the tree had stood seconds ago. Harry grabbed Wit's sleeve and pulled. "Come on, Wit. We gotta move!"

They were halfway down the stairs when the helicopter came in. It did not land, but settled down slowly, until it was three feet above the ground. There it hovered.

Aloysious was at the chopper's open door first. He threw his bags aboard, then turned back to wave them to hurry. Harry reached the door, but stopped to wait for Wit. He grabbed one side of Wit's shirt and trousers and Aloysious the other. They heaved.

Then it was Harry's turn. His hands scrabbled inside the door, trying for a grip on the floor he could use to lever himself up. Someone grabbed an arm and pulled. He popped into the chopper at the feet of a tough-looking old Japanese. One of Sato's NCOs on the River Kwai campaign, Harry thought. Then Aloysious was on the floor next to him, and he felt the chopper start to lift.

Harry watched through the open door as the chopper skimmed just over the tops of the trees. The mountain edge fell away from them suddenly, and they were high over the river. Harry felt himself float toward the ceiling when the chopper dropped down the cliff face as it dove for the river. Inches above the water, the chopper's nose lifted and they leveled off. Their speed never dropped as they roared along the riverbed, well below the tops of the trees.

It took Harry a few minutes to orient himself. The chopper was heading upstream. The next moment the chopper turned south, away from the river, skimming over the trees.

Aloysious never left the open door. He stood there, hands clinging to the door frame, his head and shoulders out in the wind. Suddenly he pulled himself back inside and started looking around wildly, until he spotted Harry. He shouted something at Harry, and pointed out the door. Harry could not hear over the wind and engine noise. He half crawled across the metal floor to get to Aloysious.

"The mountain!" Aloysious shouted in his ear. "The mountain!" Aloysious pointed out the door. Harry saw it, off in the distance now, but still black and ominous. He looked at Aloysious and nodded his head.

"It's still there!" Aloysious shouted. Harry nodded again, but not really understanding.

"It's still there!" Aloysious shouted again. This time Harry shrugged his shoulders. Aloysious cupped his hands over Harry's ear and shouted.

"In the movies the mountain always explodes! At the end! When the heroes escape!"

Harry nodded. He understood. He got close to Aloysious's ear and shouted back.

"You did your best, Aloysious! You did your best!"

41

The inside of the chopper was all noise and vibration. They were still down low, skimming over rolling hills. Harry watched Aloysious try to communicate with the crew chief through the noise, waving his hands in the old man's face to give emphasis to his shouts. The man watched quietly until Aloysious exhausted himself. Then he handed Aloysious a headset that combined earphones and a mike in a single unit. The crew chief tapped the unit he wore on his own head and gestured for Aloysious to put it on. He handed another set to Harry.

Harry experienced a brief moment of silence and peace as he slipped the earphones on and they momentarily blocked out the noise of the wind and the engine. Reluctantly he adjusted them and the silence was replaced by the sound of Aloysious shouting.

"....Can't go there. They'll he waiting for us. Sato has to get us out of the country." The shouting stopped when Aloysious noticed Harry looking at him. Aloysious tapped his headset. He pointed at Harry and raised his eyebrows quizzically.

"I hear you, Aloysious," Harry said into his mike. "Loud and clear. What's happening?"

"Shit's happening! The pilot – Yellow Fin – he's taking us to Chiang Mai. I told him we can't go to Chiang Mai. Chiang Mai is the first place they'll look for us."

Another voice cut in. Harry recognized the precise accent of Yellow Fin. "Mr. Sato asked that...," he started to say.

"Sato has to get us the hell out of the country!" Aloysious's shout drowned out Yellow Fin's voice.

"Wait a minute. Hold on," Harry found himself shouting back into the mike. "What are our options? Do we have any? Where can we go? Yellow Fin, what did Sato-san say?"

"My orders are to take you to Sato-san in Chiang Mai. We will go directly to his country residence."

"And where the hell do we go from there?" Aloysious's voice again.

"Has anyone thought of that?" He turned to Harry. "Listen, Harry, it's time to look out for ourselves. You and me are the ones who will get the chop for what's happening back there on the mountain. The only real chance we have is to head for the border now."

"Hang on a minute, Aloysious," Harry said into his mike. "Burma's the closest border, and I sure as hell don't want to go to Burma. Let's look at what we're doing before we do it. Yellow Fin, what does Sato have planned for us once we get to Chiang Mai?"

"I do not know, sir."

"See" was all Aloysious said, as he sat staring morosely at the metal floor.

"It may not be all that bad," Harry said into his mike while looking at Aloysious. "Sato must have a pretty good idea of where things stand. He doesn't strike me like a man without a contingency plan. I don't have any problem waiting to talk with Sato before we decide what to do."

"That's your problem, Harry. You trust people. Shit, I had all kinds of contingency plans. I never expected things to get this bad. Christ, Harry, if I'm not prepared, who is? We can't count on anybody now. The shit has hit the fan. Instinct tells me to hunker down. Down real low. We got to get out of the breeze until somebody turns off the fan. Or until we can short it out." The last phrase came with a small grin. It was the first time Harry had seen anything like a smile on Aloysious's face in what seemed like a long time.

Wit had been sitting quietly next to Harry, his head stuck in the window intent on what was passing below. Harry had all but forgotten him until now. He suddenly became very agitated and tried to get Harry's attention. When he succeeded, Wit pointed out the window into the distance.

Harry moved closer to the window, but he could not see what it was that Wit was pointing at. They were higher now, perhaps 500 feet above the terrain. The green tree-covered mountains were far behind them. Directly below were small brown hills.

Wit was getting more excited. He stood up to get a better look out the window. Harry looked again into the distance off to their left. This time he saw it easily. A line of dark gray on a ridge. About twenty elephants marching single file on a track paralleling their own course.

"Karen," Wit shouted. "Karen people."

The shout alerted Aloysious, who stuck his head in the window. He spotted the elephants immediately and reacted quickly. "Yellow Fin!" he shouted into his microphone. "Go over those guys. Get down lower."

The helicopter's nose dipped gently as Yellow Fin leaned it into a wide turn. In a moment they were on course to intercept the line of elephants. Before they crossed over the elephants, Yellow Fin banked the helicopter again and eased back on the throttle. They moved slowly, parallel to the elephants, but stayed a respectable distance off from them. Harry could see men seated on the elephants watching them. As they ambled along, the elephants swung their heads in the direction of the helicopter, as if trying to get a better look.

"Karen all right," Aloysious said. "I think I recognize a couple of those guys. Yellow Fin, try to land in front of them. I need to talk them."

Yellow Fin let the chopper move some distance ahead of the elephants before starting down. As they dropped, Harry heard Yellow Fin in the headphones.

"We must keep our distance. The beasts may not understand our intention," Yellow Fin explained.

Harry waited for a burst of sarcasm from Aloysious, but none came. The land where the helicopter settled was flat. Even before the engine shut down, Aloysious was fumbling at the door. The old crew chief used a Tokyo subway technique to elbow his way around Aloysious to open the door. Through the doorway Harry could see some of the elephants, bunched together and looking back at him with great curiosity.

"Wit! I need you. Come with me," Aloysious shouted as he flung himself out the door.

By the time Harry got himself untangled from the wires of his headset and made it out the door, Aloysious and Wit were halfway to the elephants. He trotted after them and caught up just as Aloysious shouted out a welcome.

"I am sure happy to see you guys," Aloysious called to the Karen. "Elephants and all," he added.

A dozen elephants stood around Aloysious in a ragged semi-circle. Other elephants lumbered up behind in no particular hurry. Aloysious looked over his shoulder. "Hey, Wit. Tell these guys to get down and rest a while. Harry, see if Yellow Fin is carrying any coffee or tea. And anything to eat. Anything at all."

Harry turned back toward the chopper. The old Japanese crew chief was talking with a much younger man who was dressed in a sport shirt and slacks. He looked more like a college kid than a pilot. When Harry reached him, the young man extended his hand.

"Yellow Fin," the young man said, introducing himself. "Ando is my usual name. My friends call me Andy. You are Ha-Lee san."

"Yeah, I'm Harry. Look, Yellow Fin...Andy, do you have any coffee, tea – maybe some biscuits? It's tea time for the elephants."

"Yes, I think we can manage," the pilot replied. He turned to the crew chief and said something in rapid Japanese. The old man bowed and quickly climbed back into the helicopter. The pilot turned back to Harry. "Perhaps we should join your friend. Sato-san said that Alo-wichit will have his own ideas about how to proceed. Yellow Fin gestured toward the setting sun. "It is best not to stay here too long."

The Karen had dismounted. In various ways they were now taking advantage of the unscheduled pit stop. Off to one side Aloysious, Wit, and one of the Karen were sitting together, deep in a conversation that was a mixture of Karen, English, and Thai. Aloysious's voice was loudest, as he went on in fast, heavily accented Thai.

"...Well, I don't really give a shit where it is. Just so I can get some beer. Tell him that, Wit. Tell him that's all I need. And I won't take no for an answer." Wit looked a little dazed as he turned to address the Karen sitting next to him in his own language.

Aloysious started to his feet as he saw Harry approach. "Harry, help me find some twigs and stuff to get a fire going. We gotta get the tea moving. Yellow Fin, you're in charge of getting all the fixings together. Come on, Harry." Aloysious led Harry to an area behind the elephants, keeping well away from the animals as they walked past. "Stay alert for elephant shit," Aloysious cautioned.

When they were well away from everyone, Aloysious stopped. He looked over his shoulder to assure himself that no one was nearby. "I don't want Yellow Fin or the other Japanese guy to hear us," he said in his most confidential tone. "The Karen are on their way into Burma. They know places in there where nobody's ever been. If we get up there nobody will ever find us. Wit's talking to them, trying to cut us a good deal."

As he said this, Aloysious watched Harry's face very closely. When he finished, he paused for a long moment. Then he added, "That's if you want to come, Harry."

It was Harry's turn to hesitate. He tried to find the right way to put it. Finally he said, "You don't make it easy, Aloysious. In one way I'm ready to go with you. But I think this is one that I'll pass up. Maybe I'll regret it, but I just can't imagine living up in the hills of northern Burma – stuck there without knowing when we'd be able to get out again. There's nothing up there, Aloysious."

"It wouldn't be for long. Just until the Thais forget why they're mad."

"Aloysious, some of them are never going to forget. I really appreciate the offer, but I'll take my chances here. There's still Sato. I wouldn't discount what he might be able to do...."

"Maybe you're right, Harry. For you, it might be best to stay here. Nobody is as pissed off at you as they are at me. Just tell them I made you do it."

There was nothing more to say. They turned and started walking back to the others, picking up an occasional stick as they went. After a while Aloysious said, "I don't think anybody will bother Ting-Tong. Keep your eye on them if you can. Those two know how to take care of themselves, but stay in touch with them just in case. Once I'm settled, I'll find a way to let them know where I am." He stopped then and reached for Harry's arm.

"You never believed me, did you? When I told you there was a lost city." Harry took a step back and swatted at him with a long stick he had picked up. Aloysious jumped out of range, still quick on his feet for his size.

"But it was fun. Wasn't it, Harry?"

Harry laughed. "It was fun. It was a great lost city. I wouldn't have missed it for anything."

By the time they got back, the crew chief had a fire going and had already served tea and biscuits to the Karen. He gestured for Harry and Aloysious to sit, and then brought them steaming cups of tea. Harry noticed that Wit was sitting by himself, very quietly, staring into his teacup.

"Hey, Wit, what did the guy say?" Aloysious asked.

Wit looked uneasy. He glanced at Harry and then spoke into his teacup in rapid Thai. "They don't want to take him. They think he will frighten the elephants. There is no beer in the mountains where they are going. They do not think he will like it there. They did not hear him speak of money."

"What did he say?" Aloysious asked.

"There's no beer up there," Harry told him.

"Tell him we'll make beer up there. We'll build a brewery. Export it to Thailand. Everybody will make a million dollars."

Wit picked up a few of these English words. A million dollars," he repeated in Thai. "Who gets a million dollars?" he asked Harry.

"Everybody," Harry replied in Thai, "if Aloysious builds his brewery."

"Really? Then I will tell them," Wit said. Before Harry realized what was happening, Wit stood up and in a very formal way addressed the Karen loudly in their own language. He spoke for some time. Some of his comments were punctuated by shouts from the Karen, and once by a loud cheer.

"Wit," Harry tried several times to interrupt. "I don't think ...." But Wit was not to be interrupted.

When he finally finished, Wit turned to Harry. He was smiling as he said, "Now they will agree." He looked toward Aloysious, but went on in Thai, saying to Harry, "You tell Alo-wichit. They say for one million dollars each, Alo-wichit can go with them into Burma. To make beer for export."

"Oh, shit, Wit...." Harry shook his head.

"What he say?" Aloysious asked.

"Wit fixed it up for you. The Karen will let you go into Burma with them for a million dollars a head. And a brewery."

"That's fine," Aloysious said, expansively. "Promise them anything. I don't care. All I need is a ride across the border. I have friends there who will sort things out. Tell Wit to tell them what they want to hear."

Harry shrugged. "Okay, but they will be mad as hell when they get there."

"That's a long way off, Harry. You worry too much. Just tell them."

"Okay." He turned to Wit. "Wit, tell the Karen they get a million dollars each and a brewery."

Wit shouted something in Karen. This brought a loud cheer from several of the younger Karen. The older Karen looked incredulous as they started talking among themselves. The Karen leader walked over and saluted Aloysious. The two then shook hands. Finally all the Karen stood and saluted.

"You going too, Wit?" Harry asked.

"No, sir, Mister Harry. I want to go home." He looked over the hills. "Maybe I can walk."

Harry slapped him on the shoulder. "Don't worry Wit, we'll get you there."

Yellow Fin had been standing some distance off, watching. He walked over and asked, "What is going on?"

"I think you are going to lose a passenger."

"Ah, so," Yellow Fin said. There was a small smile on his face. "Mister Alo-wichit goes to Burma. Sato-san thought that might be the case."

"Did you know those elephants were out here, Andy?" Harry asked Yellow Fin.

"I know very little about anything, Ha-Lee. I am only a pilot. But I know we must leave soon. There will not be enough daylight to reach Chiang Mai."

The farewells were over quickly. Aloysious shook hands with Wit. The two spoke quietly for a moment. Wit was smiling as he turned away.

Aloysious turned to Harry. "Give me a couple of months to get set up before you visit. Give Ting-Tong my best. I'll be seeing you." They shook hands.

Harry was turning back toward the helicopter when he remembered something. He stopped. "Aloysious," he said. "One last thing. What were the trees that fly?"

"Oh, that," Aloysious snorted. "That's an easy one. We had to make the city look like it had been there forever. We hauled all those Banyan trees and all kinds of other weeds up there. We flew most of it in with choppers. It was something to see, a full-grown tree dangling from a chain under a chopper. Sometimes it's misty up there in the mornings. I guess what the Karen saw was the tree while the chopper was in the mist above. That's how legends are made."

Harry shook his head and smiled. "Thanks for the lost city," he said and turned back to the helicopter.

Yellow Fin took the helicopter off the ground at a shallow angle so as not to frighten the elephants. When they reached 1,000 feet, Yellow Fin turned back in a wide arc. Below, the elephants had already formed in a line that pointed in the direction of the Burma border. Harry's eyes swept over the line of elephants but without seeing Aloysious. He looked back to the head of the line. There, on the largest of the elephants, on the swaying chair on the elephant's back, stood Aloysious. His arms were raised over his head. Harry could not hear him, but he was sure Aloysious was venting his best vintage Tarzan yell at the hills.

Sitting next to Harry, Wit was craning his neck to keep the elephants in sight as long as he could. When they were finally out of sight, Wit looked over and saw Harry watching him. He pointed out the window.

"He is a little crazy. Alo-wichit. He is a little crazy. There is no beer where they are taking him."

"Alo-wichit is a little crazy," Harry said. "At the least. But you know, Wit, I wouldn't be surprised if six months from now everybody in Bangkok is drinking Alowichit Beer from the Burma hills."

Wit considered this for a moment. Then he nodded. "Yes, that is possible. Very possible."

42

The sun set before they reached Chiang Mai and darkness settled over the land below. Yellow Fin kept the chopper low and well away from the edge of the city. They crossed a river that wandered through the darkening rice fields like a lazy black snake, and followed it for a while. Wit could not hide his eagerness to get back to earth and on his own. When they came to a bend in the river that Wit recognized, Yellow Fin set the chopper down. When the door opened, Wit wasted no time getting out. From the darkness outside he shouted back at the helicopter.

"Khun Harry. I go now. Good luck to you."

Peering out through the open doorway, Harry could just make out a hand waving in the darkness. "Take care, Wit," he shouted back. There was more he wanted to say, but it would have been drowned out by the roar of the engine as Yellow Fin hauled the chopper back into the air. "I'll be seeing you, Wit," Harry said quietly. He said it to himself; there was no one else to hear.

Directly below there was nothing now but black shadows rushing by. Yellow Fin skirted the southern edge of the city and then headed north, keeping the lights of Chiang Mai off to their left. They flew in a straight line for a time until the lights of the city drifted well behind them. Yellow Fin turned suddenly and flew back toward the lights for a minute or two. Then he descended deeper into the black shadows below them.

There were no lights that Harry could see. The cabin was dark and the helicopter was showing no running lights. It seemed they must be down among the trees, down where no radar would find them. Dark shapes slid by the window, and Harry hoped there was no tree taller than its neighbors, that no power lines stretched across their path.

With no warning, Yellow Fin dropped them like a block of iron into a deep black hole. Harry lifted off the edge of his seat and he felt like they were falling into a well. Then there was light everywhere, and the helicopter touched down lightly on a smooth grass pad. Outside the windows it was bright as day.

The light lasted just an instant, then it was darker than before. Harry's retinas trapped an image: Three stocky figures in white coveralls running in a half crouch toward the chopper. And a fourth figure – small and graceful – just at the edge of the grass.

Little Mouse was at the door when it opened. "We expected you earlier," she said and looked closely at Harry's face. "You look very tired and hungry. Come."

She took his hand and led him through the darkness down a winding path to a Thai house. He recognized it as the one he had stayed in when he visited Sato's compound before.

In the cool bedroom he stood alongside the bed and let Little Mouse strip off his clothes. He could still feel the vibrations of the chopper in his body. When Little Mouse went into the bathroom, he sat down on the bed. In seconds he was flat on his back. He did not even not try to stop himself from drifting away. He was completely at peace, then Little Mouse was there again, shaking him awake.

"Harry! Harry! You cannot sleep now. You must take a bath and get dressed. Sato-san waits for you."

"Oh, Mouse.... Can't we see him tomorrow?" But Harry let himself be pulled from the bed and docilely followed Little Mouse to the bath.

The hot water and Little Mouse's kneading hands revived him. Bathed and dressed in fresh clothes, he was ready for anything. He looked at his reflection in the mirror, where a tanned, healthy face stared back at him with an expression of bemused curiosity. He saluted the image. Somewhere behind him Little Mouse giggled. He gave her a jaunty wave and set off for Sato's house.

"Ha-Lee san. Welcome back."

Sato waited at the top of the teak staircase, looking delighted to see him. "I hope you do not mind a late dinner with an old man," he said, examining his face. "You do not look as tired as I expected, Ha-Lee."

"I've had some long days, Sato-san. It's good to see you."

Harry paused at the edge of the verandah and looked out over the small lake. A flash of silver came from where a fish broke the surface.

Sato looked out to the lake. "Much has happened since we last watched the carp," he said. "But come now, let us go inside."

They sat at the low table and waited for drinks to be put in front of them. Then Sato asked, "What did you think of our city, Harry?"

Harry smiled, but he was silent for a moment. He was not quite sure what to say. Sitting here with Sato, the city was a thousand years away. And yet he had left there just a few hours ago. Finally he said, "I don't know how to express my feelings about the city. It's still too fresh in my mind. In a few words, Sato-san...the city was absolutely magnificent. You guys did a hell of a job."

"Yes. Thank you." Sato smiled broadly and inclined his head in appreciation of the compliment. "I think we did do a good job," he added.

"Maybe as good as the ancient Khmer could do. You saw the hand of the Khmer in the construction of the city, didn't you, Ha-Lee?"

"You're right, Sato-san," Harry admitted. "I did not see the hand of Japanese craftsmen, either in the city or in the artifacts we found in the caverns below. It was an excellent job. An excellent job of fakery. I will always be disappointed that the city was not what I thought it to be. At the same time, it was so well done that I'm almost sorry you didn't get away with it."

"A pity," Sato said. "I agree with all you say. Our major fault was that we allowed the whole project to become too magnificent. On a smaller scale, we might have succeeded."

"On a smaller scale we might not have fought a war over it."

Sato smiled, a small smile this time. He looked almost embarrassed. "That was unfortunate," he said. "Unfortunate, but inevitable, perhaps. One could blame the young ones for what happened – our young men from Tokyo. They had no sense of proportion. No experience. In Alowichit's idea they sensed an opportunity for great profit."

Sato paused after saying this and stared silently at the drink on the table in front of him. He raised his eyes again to meet Harry's. "And still," he continued, "with all my years, with all my experience, I did not foresee what could happen. I did foresee problems. Problems that I thought the young ones would learn from. But I did not foresee a problem as big as it became. I can blame only myself."

Sato took a sip of his drink. With a small gesture he started the first course on its way to the table. "Come, Harry, let us eat. You can tell me what happened these last few days."

As they ate, Harry told him the whole story from the kidnapping of Ting and Tong, to Aloysious's fateful decision to return to the mountain, and of the pursuit that eventually evolved into a military operation. Harry couldn't keep himself from telling Sato how the city looked to him when he first saw it, when he believed it was real. And how he felt afterwards, when he learned that nothing on the mountain was what it seemed to be. Sato listened, making no comment, but nodding occasionally to show he understood.

At the end, Sato said, "An interesting story, Ha-Lee, and in many ways a sad one. Everything that occurred was the consequence of ideas I did not agree with when I first heard them. But ideas that I did nothing to stop." He sighed deeply. "It was a beautiful city," he said, and then fell into silence.

They sat quietly for a while, each with his own thoughts. Sato had spoken of consequences, and there were indeed consequences that concerned Harry greatly. Certain questions loomed over him as ominously as the mountain itself. "Sato-san," he finally asked, "what happens now? Who gets the city? How much trouble are we all in?"

Sato's eyes met his. "It is too early to say. The city is an important resource." Sato paused for a moment, as if preoccupied with something, then continued. "The city will be important. Someday it will have a use. But Tokyo will have no role in the city's destiny, nor will Black Lion."

"Where does that leave you, Sato-san?"

"I have friends here – or perhaps I should say there are people who owe me favors. In the end, the way will be made smooth."

There was a long silence again, while Sato sipped from his teacup. Harry fidgeted during this pause, and finally had to reach over and pour some cognac in his glass to keep from showing his impatience.

But Sato noticed Harry's discomfort. "Ha-Lee san," he said, "I am sorry. I see you are worried for yourself." Sato put down his teacup and continued, all business now. "First, let me say that it is well that Alo-wichit chose to cross the border. His problems in this country were too big and involve too many people. I could not have done much for him.

"As for you, Ha-Lee san," Sato went on, "some of your actions had the appearance of being wrong – from a legal point of view. Most of what you did is of no real consequence. Your major problem is that you sold art forgeries on the world market – counterfeit artifacts that appear to have originated in Thailand. The Thai authorities are most unhappy about that."

"Oh, for God's sake...," Harry started.

Sato raised his hand for silence. "I am simply telling you the major problem. Your major problem. The problem I had to involve myself in."

"I'm sorry, Sato-san," Harry said, regretting the outburst.

Sato sipped at his tea before starting again. His face was stern now. "Earlier this evening I met with Colonel Sornchai. The Colonel was not happy with what happened – on the mountain or before. There was only one thing you did that pleased him – you left some people behind for him in the village where the kidnapped girls were held. To Colonel Sornchai that showed your good faith.

"I'm glad we did something right," Harry mumbled.

"You must hear me out, Ha-Lee," Sato said. "The Colonel's concern – and the concern of his superiors – was that the international art market would resound with the screams of your clients to whom you sold fakes and counterfeits."

"Goddamn it, Sato. If there are any complaints, they are made to me, and not to what you call the international art market."

"And if your clients do complain, Ha-Lee, what will you tell them? What will you say?" Sato waited for a moment, but nothing came from

Harry but a frown.

"So," Sato went on, "there is no answer. No answer you could give. But I had an answer for Colonel Sornchai. I assured him that the philosophy of Black Lion Enterprises is that a perceived wrong will be made right. While Black Lion was involved in your actions in only the smallest way, I assured Sornchai that Black Lion would make a full refund where a complaint was voiced. A justified complaint. So, if you have unhappy clients, and their money is returned, they will have no bad feelings. And if there are no bad feelings among your clients, or your friend Jean Lee's, Colonel Sornchai has no problem with you, Ha-Lee."

The ominous cloud that hung over Harry just a moment ago popped like a bubble. "That means I have no problem?" Harry said. "Christ, I was visualizing the end of my business...the end of my life as I have lived it for years. But what about Thailand? Can I come and go here as I want?"

Sato sighed and looked down into his teacup. "I think you should leave soon, Ha-Lee. Tomorrow, if possible. You should stay away for a time, until some of the others forget. A year, perhaps even two. After that...." Sato shifted his eyes into the distance. "I see no reason why you cannot come and go as you please."

Harry thought about this. "I hate to have to stay away from here for two years. On the other hand, I expected I would have to sneak out of here and never come back. I owe you my thanks, Sato-san."

"You owe me nothing. I did what I had to. It is only good business. I regret that your efforts and mine were not successful. Perhaps, in the future....But now is not the time for that. I have some excellent cognac."

Little Mouse was waiting for Harry when he finally made it to the top of the stairs. He stood there and looked at her. God, he thought, he should be more careful when he drank with that old snake. The old man had all but drowned him in cognac.

"Mouse," he said finally, after staring at her for a full minute. "You look great. Both of you. I brought you some cognac." He handed her a large balloon glass filled to the top with the last of Sato's excellent cognac.

Little Mouse took the glass and put it aside. Then she reached for his hand. "Come, Harry," she said and led him inside.

"Let me sit down on the bed for a minute," he said, and he did. He watched her, until she briefly took her eyes off him, then he sprawled out on his back on the bed. Little Mouse said nothing, but unbuttoned his shirt and pulled it over his arms. She examined his chest closely and then his stomach.

"What's the matter?" he asked when his curiosity got the best of him.

"I had to see if you were with that woman again. The one with the long fingernails."

He looked at her, uncertain for a moment. Then he chuckled. "There were no women where I was. Far as I remember, anyway." He moved his hand around to his neck and rubbed it hard. "I felt young just a little while ago. Now I feel like some of Sato's age rubbed off on me."

"You are very tired. And you had a lot to drink." When she moved her arms forward to rub his shoulders he saw she was wearing the gold bracelet he had given her on the airplane. "Do you still like it?" he asked.

"Yes. I like it very much. I wear it every day." She touched the bracelet gently. "When you were not here," she told him, "I look at it and think of you."

"Mouse," he said, and propped himself up on his elbows. "I have to leave tomorrow. I will not come back for a long time. Up on the mountain, I did a lot of thinking...."

While he thought of just how to say it, she asked, "How long will you be gone?"

"A long time. A year. Maybe more."

"A year," she repeated. She looked concerned now.

"Look, Mouse...." He put his hand under her chin and gently raised her head. "What I'm trying to say is that I really like being with you. If you think you would miss me too.... Look, it's no big deal. You can come with me, Mouse."

Her eyes brightened. "Is that what Sato-san said?" she asked quickly.

"No. No, that's not what Sato said. But he will if I ask him to."

Her reaction was not what he expected. She pulled away from him, sat up straight on the bed and said, rather sternly, "You must not ask him. Sato-san will think I am not happy here." She saw something in him collapse. It was her turn to touch his face. "What is wrong, Harry?" she asked, a softness like velvet in her voice. "Now you look sad."

"Of course I'm sad. I thought you would go with me."

"I cannot. This is my place. This is my work. You can understand, Harry."

"No, I cannot understand. I thought that you would want to come with me."

"If I want to, I cannot. But I will be here when you return. I will wait for you."

Harry lay back on the bed and pulled the pillow over his eyes.

"Don't hide from me, Harry," Little Mouse said.

"You're another illusion," he groaned. "You're like the city – a dream." His voice was distant, muffled by the pillow that he had dragged completely over his head.

"Harry!" she said. "You are being like a little child. I am not a dream." She tried to wrest the pillow from him. Suddenly she found herself holding the pillow, while Harry held her captive in his arms. She tried to twist away, but he held her tight.

"I know you're not a dream, Mouse," he said, pinching her gently. "I know just how real you are. I'm sorry you won't come with me. Somehow I didn't think you would. But I'll expect you to be here when I get back. Now, let's see. We have about six more hours together. Enough for a massage. And maybe for some other things."

Little Mouse smiled up at him. Her eyes sparkled. She looked happy. "I am glad you understand, Harry," she said.

She pulled herself even closer to him. "We will meet again, Harry. Tonight I will make you remember me always. I will show you how women made love in ancient times, in a city on a mountain. I will show you things, Harry, secret things, that were cut like pictures into the stone...."

Harry listened to the sound of Little Mouse's voice and felt totally at ease. He was there. He had found it. He was about to enter his own lost city – with a most knowledgeable guide.

Epilogue

I t was the morning of a bright day in the following year. Only Little
Mouse remained as a vivid reality in Harry's mind. The lost city and
all that happened there were something in a dream. The cold winds of
winter were also a dim memory. Spring had come early and now was
almost gone. Each day was warmer than the one before; soon it would be
hot and muggy.

Business at the Happy Dragon was a little slow as it always was this
time of year. At Uncle Noah's Wonder World Imports Incorporated, business was moving more briskly. Harry spent much time in the basement
these days, packing ceramic pigs and wooden elephants into boxes for his
distant clients.

On that particular day, Uncle Noah had an order for a dozen prancing
horses that no one else had ordered for a long time. Harry walked into the
far corner of the basement where these wooden horses pranced across a
shelf. He brushed the dust from them, and when he picked one up, something fell soundlessly to the floor. He stepped back to let light fall on it,
and saw it was a small piece of cloth, wrapped like a tiny bundle. He
picked it up and started to open it. But then he had second thoughts and
carried the bundle upstairs.

"Lotus," he called at the top of the stairs. When the she came, he asked,
"What is this? Did you drop it downstairs?" With a glance the young
woman could tell it was not anything that belonged to her. "Has anyone
else been down there?" he asked.

"No one but you and I," she said. "Except...except for Miss Annabelle.
But that was months ago."

"Could it be hers?" Harry asked, looking down at the little bundle that
rested in his open hand.

"It could be," Lotus said. Then she laughed and added, "Maybe she left
it for you...I mean for Uncle Noah. She thought Uncle Noah was very
handsome."

Harry was even more reluctant to open it now. Lotus waited for him to do something, so finally he said, "Well, if it's anything, we'll keep it for her." And he opened it.

"What the hell is this?" he asked. The question was rhetorical.

The cloth wrapping of the little bundle lay like a ribbon across his open hand. On top of it now was a shiny black object, a tiny animal carved of black stone. It was beautifully carved, exquisitely detailed. Harry knew what it was as soon as he saw it, long before Miss Lotus said it.

"It's a Singh," Lotus said, "a beautiful black lion."

Harry stared at it. "My God," he mumbled. "Lotus," he asked, "when did Miss Annabelle leave here?"

"It was just before Christmas," Lotus answered. "In fact, it was a day or two before you got back from Bangkok. Remember, I showed you where she sat when she was Santa Claus for the children."

"Did she say where she was going?"

"No," Lotus answered. "One morning she was gone. It's too bad. She had many talents."

Harry sighed. "Yeah, too bad," he said. "She had no English, but you said her Japanese was pretty good?"

"Her Japanese was excellent," Lotus said, and then went up front to attend to a customer.

Harry looked down at the black lion. He would probably never know. Or maybe one day he would meet Miss Annabelle in Bangkok. She was probably there now, monitoring a computer screen. He was suddenly overwhelmed with homesickness. For Little Mouse, for Bangkok, for the lost city, even for Sato and Aloysious. For a little while he had had it all. He shuddered when he thought of how it all ended. Up front he heard the telephone ring. Without thinking, he shouted to Lotus, "Miss Lotus, if that's a call from Bangkok, tell them I'm on my way."